Penn

Olive Township Book One

Copyright © 2025 by Jennifer Millikin
All rights reserved.

This book or any portion thereof
may not be reproduced or used in any manner whatsoever
without the express written permission of the publisher except for the
use of brief quotations in a book review. This book is a work of fiction.
Names, characters, and incidents are products of the author's
imagination or are used fictitiously. Any resemblance to actual events,
or locales, or persons, living or dead, is entirely coincidental.
JNM, LLC

ISBN: 979-8-9909048-3-5
www.jennifermillikinwrites.com
Cover by Okay Creations
Editing by Emerald Edits
Proofreading by Sisters Get Lit.erary

*For those who believe in true love,
and those who are skeptical, too.*

Author's Note

Dear Reader,

The Olive Township series was inspired by the 1987 film The Princess Bride. Some of my fondest early childhood memories include sitting with my aunt and watching this movie. Legend has it I often quoted this film in public, including a certain scene involving a dagger. Without a doubt, this film contributed to my love of romance and story.

Whether you've seen the movie or you haven't, this series is still for you. It's my contemporary take on a beloved classic, full of adventure and love, comedy and romance. If you adore The Princess Bride as I do, you'll pick up on the small nods here and there. Either way, you'll read a series crafted with love, expressly written for the purpose of bringing a smile to your face and warmth to your heart.

Xoxo,
Jen

Chapter 1

Olive Township

I've outlived so many of the inhabitants I've loved.

Trailblazers and pioneers, land grabbers and cowboys. I was nothing, until they made me something. Big dreams accompanied them, along with grit and determination. Together we rose, piece by piece. Even today, we grow.

They named me Olive Township, a nod to the fruit tree growing in the arid Sonoran Desert. From a few came many, until it was an orchard. The people came, they built their homes and grew their families. There have been struggles and triumphs, feast and famine. Through it, I've loved them all. I've celebrated their birth, and grieved their passing.

I never claimed to be magical, but there is something about me. Something special. The residents feel it, even if they can't define it. Is it in the searing summer heat, the way the sun permeates the skin and curls into the marrow of the bones? Perhaps it's in the majestic Saguaro, the way it chooses the month of May to show off hundreds of the white waxy blossoms it hides all year long. Maybe it's in the survival despite an inhospitable environment, the way residents have learned to work around the dust and summer heat, the frigid winter nights and spindly flora. It's as though the terrain tests a person, and if they prove their mettle, they're in for life.

What the desert lacks in hospitality, she makes up for in beauty. The landscape produces a special person, one who is tough and bold. All that said, the inhabitants of Olive Township are fallible. They make mistakes. They demonstrate their knowledge, their courage, their idiocy. There have been a few bad apples along the way.

Oh, how I have loved them. Some have moved on, and I haven't wished them back. Others leave, and I long for them.

For one, in particular.

Chapter 2

Penn

I wouldn't say I'm hiding, but it would be hard to make the argument I am not at least *hiding out*.

Summerhill Olive Mill, by way of Summerhill Road, is the perfect place to lie low while I wait for the relentless sun to loosen its grip on Olive Township. Lucky me, a road winds around the town and north to the turn off for the mill, saving me from having to drive through town.

Inevitably, I will make that drive, and probably soon. But I'll avoid it if I can, and right now, that is within my control.

I'd planned to arrive in the town in which I was born, and spent the first thirteen years of my life terrorizing, under the cover of darkness. I wanted one night to ease back into this place, to give myself some breathing room. My plan was derailed by the fact I made damn good time from San Diego. With only a few eighteen wheelers to slow my progression, my truck tires ate up Interstate 8.

The dust storm in the distance spurred me to step on the gas, as did the lead foot I adopt when I'm anxious. I stopped once at a famous hole-in-the-wall in southern Phoenix for the largest size they sell of prickly pear lemonade, and a second time on the Salt River reservation for fry bread drizzled with wildflower honey and dusted with powdered sugar.

The sugar induced coma was worth it, not to mention the reprieve it gave me from having my nerves being the only thing making me queasy.

Olive Township and I, well, we have a storied history. Some of it pretty, some of it ugly, and some of it I'd rather forget.

The single glimmer of relief for my apprehension comes from my best friend, Hugo De la Vega. He's the only person who knows I'm returning, but not even he knows why I left. Now that my mother is gone, there is nobody but me who knows the truth, and I wish I could take a Magic Eraser to that memory.

It's only been a few months since I last saw Hugo face-to-face, when he came to San Diego for my mom's funeral. He won't mind me crashing his place at the olive mill for the next hour while I wait for the sun to set. Once that happens, I'll mosey on back to Hugo's rental property in town, one of those cookie-cutter stucco homes where there's an HOA and your neighbor is too close.

I roll my window down and prop my forearm on the frame, taking a deep, clarifying breath as I climb slightly in elevation. Slim Jim, my two-year-old Belgian Malinois, pokes his nose out of my window from his place in the back seat.

He sniffs frantically, catching new smells. He's a K9 defense trained dog who washed out of the program because he won't bite to the corners of his mouth. I was lucky enough (or unlucky, depending on how I look at it) to be available when he needed a home. We've only been together five months, but I already love him.

Beside my head, Slim Jim continues his sniffing, acquainting himself with the place that will be our home for the next five or six weeks.

As much as I hate to admit it, I missed Olive Township. The gently sloping hills, the olive grove stretching as far as the eye can see. It's a gorgeous little corner of the Sonoran Desert, but there's something else about it, something a little extra. Almost...*magical*.

I could kick my own ass for saying that, sounding like a tourist who has just exited the world famous Sagewood Wellness Spa in town, but something about being gone for so long puts this place in a different perspective.

Or maybe it's me who has changed. Hell, I know that to be true. I'm not even a fraction of the person I was the last time I called this place home. Thirteen-year-old me and twenty-eight-year-old me are nothing alike. On the inside, and most definitely on the outside.

The worn metal sign announcing the Summerhill Olive Mill with its olive branch logo appears a quarter mile away. I take the turnoff, steering my truck with motions that are second nature. I didn't have my driver's license when I lived here before, but I'd rode passenger enough to know each shift and bump, the way the road rises higher on the right a moment after the turn. And, just like I knew it would, my body shifts left to accommodate the rise.

I feel oddly comforted knowing that although almost everything else has changed, this hasn't. The constancy grounds me a bit, puts me back in a feeling of control. I'll be ok. I've got this. I can tango with Olive Township, and come out the other side.

Buildings appear on the horizon. One, maybe two stories, white-sided buildings with the modern farmhouse look, as if that famous interior design couple had their way with the place. The olive mill restaurant sits behind these buildings, and set back a quarter mile behind a copse of trees, is Hugo's home.

Hugo has kept me in the loop over the years, telling me about the updates his family had been doing at the mill. What I'm seeing now is far greater than I imagined. It looks cozy as hell, and I'd very much like to lay out on one of those porch swings the size of a bed.

Considering the number of cars filling the medium-sized parking lot Hugo had poured last fall in front of the Summerhill store, I'll have to live out my porch swing fantasy another time.

The corners of my mouth turn down. I avoided town, only to find most of the town is here. Must be some kind of event. Hugo mentioned he made the decision, along with his sister and his mother, to expand on the offerings of the already bustling olive mill. He called it agro-tourism. Olive oil tastings, cooking classes led by his

Penn

sister, and hosting events. Hugo mentioned they're considering splurging on some kind of locally built fancy wedding arch so they can begin offering weddings.

Since I'm steering clear of everybody, that would include any and all gatherings, though I admit, I am just a little curious. I'd like to see what Hugo and his family have accomplished, but it'll have to be another time because there is no way in hell I want to run into people on my first night back. I'm almost positive they won't know it's me, especially once I introduce myself as Peter.

There will be no using my real name while I'm here. The very last thing I want or need is Daisy St. James finding out I'm back, even if only temporarily. I'm not here to disrupt her peace, or the life she's built for herself. Just like all those years ago, the most thoughtful gift I can give Daisy is to be absent from her life. Back then it was for her own good, and it's much the same now. Who am I to show up and throw a wrench in whatever it is she's doing? Then again, maybe it would mean nothing to her to see me again. Maybe she'd say *Penn, oh my gosh, how are you?* and offer me a friendly, incredulous hug and we'd make small talk that would fizzle out, leaving us checking our watches and making excuses to scurry away. But probably not.

Daisy and I might have been kids, but we were something exceptional and outrageous. Lungs beginning their first deep breath. Possibility a hair's breadth from discovery. We had *potential* with *certainty*.

Selfishly, I want to hunt her down and force myself into her orbit. Catch her eye and the rise of her chest as she gasps. It could just as easily be from horror as relief, and the thought pulls me from nostalgia and puts me squarely back where I belong.

Fuck, but it hurts.

Necessary though, so I press on, driving around back of a different building and slowing to a stop. I could leave, but then I risk drawing more attention to myself by going back the way I came, and since there is no other exit, I'll hide away back here and wait for the sun to set.

It's fine. Concealment is my modus operandi for the next month anyway. After that, I'll point my truck west, hopefully with a bank account newly padded with cash, and leave Olive Township in the dust.

For a second time.

Chapter 3

Penn

My seat belt is off, window down and playing a word game on my phone with my foot propped up on the dash, when I see her.

Legs for days in a dress that hits just above her knees. Blonde hair, curled and long and sweeping the middle of her back. She clutches a champagne bottle by the neck as she scurries across the grass, checking behind her as she darts.

Is there anywhere to really go from here? The olive orchards begin, and then stretch on and on. Beyond this grassy lawn, there is nothing to do. Nowhere to go.

She throws another look over her shoulder, prompting me to peer in the same direction. What is it she's checking for? Is somebody coming after her? My hackles are up, but nothing comes of it. No wild animals, or wild people. There is nobody out here except her and the insistent hum of the air conditioning units. And me.

I should probably look away, give her a modicum of

privacy. I'll bet she thinks nobody's out here, and here I am sitting in my truck like a creep, watching her.

Yep, I should look away. It's just that, well, she's teetering around in those tall heels, each one sinking halfway into the soft earth as she goes. She's probably going to twist an ankle.

She stumbles slightly, her forward progression halted by a spike that has sunk all the way into the dirt. She makes tiny fists at her sides and pumps them angrily, just once. With one knee bent to make up for the height difference from her sunken shoe, she tips her face up at the sky. I'll bet what she really wants to do right now is let out a scream, but judging by the quiet around me, the most expressive sound she's making is a groan. Speculation, of course, but the way her shoulders are bunched, she resembles a string pulled taut.

She's ok, right?

Is she pulled so taut that she might snap?

Fuck. I can't sit here and wait for her to lose it. I can't have that on my conscience. *Well, you see, I saw a distressed woman, but did not offer help.*

My mother may not be alive anymore, but something tells me she would come back from the dead and break a paddle on my ass the way she always threatened. Jokingly, I think, and back before the bad stuff started happening.

The woman bends to cup a hand around her heel, yanking at the trapped shoe. It comes away from the dirt without difficulty. She peels it off her foot, rears back, and fires it across the yard. She takes one more step, realizes she is now off-balance because of the other heel, and chucks that one, too. It lands near the second one, halfway between her and a set of Adirondack chairs.

Um, yeah. She's a brand of pissed I haven't seen in some time. And Lord only knows why. But here I am, tossing my phone in the passenger seat with a soft thud.

"Stay," I tell Slim Jim, who's been lying on his blanket in my back seat. I roll the windows down an inch and climb out, closing my door gently so I don't startle her. I walk closer, ignoring the reluctance spinning through me. I really shouldn't be doing this. So much for lying so low I was practically horizontal.

I slow as I approach. She's turned in such a way that I cannot see her full profile, but there's something familiar about the partial view. The graceful slope of the nose, the exquisite shape of the jaw. The closer I get, the more I make out her muttering.

"Of course," she sputters angrily, reaching the spot where her first shoe landed and swiping it from the ground. She snags the second shoe, saying, "This is what I get." She runs a finger over what is probably mud on the tall, pointy spike of her shoe.

I stop a handful of feet from her, careful not to crowd her. "Ma'am?" I say softly.

She whirls on me, shoe lifted. *Great*. She's making it into a weapon. I could disarm her in half a second, but I'd rather not have to. Her eyes flash up at me, surprised at my presence, but in those absolutely unbelievable toffee brown irises I see indignation.

That same feeling of familiarity washes over me, stronger this time.

"Do I look like a *ma'am?*" She scrunches her nose on the word, as if it tastes like black licorice.

My stomach lurches, dropping somewhere around my knees. My heart? I don't know what that bastard has going on in my chest, but it's not doing its job. The beats are erratic, sucker punching my breast bone.

Run. Get away from her.

Ok, wait. No. I'm not a runner. I do not flee. I'm a Navy SEAL. *The ability to control my emotions and my actions, regardless of circumstance, sets me apart from others.*

A single line in an otherwise long creed, but a promise I've issued to myself and others. Even if I now have to talk about being a SEAL in past tense, using words like *former*, it remains deep in the center of my bones.

I will not run. I will face tough shit head-on, and right now, Daisy St. James is tough shit.

God Almighty, this girl is stunning. A showstopper.

She snaps her fingers in front my face, because yes, I'm openly staring at her. "Hello?"

I nearly groan in relief.

That sass, coming from that mouth, is tattooed on my heart. I could be blindfolded and wearing noise-canceling headphones, but still feel its tenor in my chest.

Daisy! My heart bellows and trips, misbehaving and beating against my sternum like a coked out squirrel. It takes every ounce of everything I have in me not to blurt out something astoundingly stupid, namely *It's me, Penn*.

She was always beautiful, even running around with me when we were kids. Daisy St. James never met an awkward phase like us other mere mortals. But now? This? I have to assume other women secretly hate her, because she's a one hundred on a scale of one to ten. Cheeks flushed, mouth pink like a rose and budded like one, too.

Daisy! Her name balances on the tip of my tongue. I came to town with the intention to hide my identity, accomplish what I came here for, then get the hell out of Dodge. But running into Daisy on day one, hour one must mean something, right? The exceptions and caveats and excuses trip through me, accompanied by the sting of adrenaline. What if I—

Dumb. Ass. Listen to me, talking foolish.

The only person who is supposed to know I'm here is Hugo. And there are good reasons for that. Reasons I can't forget just because fate pulled a cunty little move and made Daisy the first person I saw upon my return to Olive Township.

Setting aside the pain from having just died a little inside, I clasp my hands behind my back, rocking on my heels. "My apologies, *miss*."

Daisy takes me in for a long moment, and a heat steals up my neck. Does she recognize me? Feel an inexplicable but immediate connection?

Do I want her to? My ego screams yes, but the

rational part of my brain bitchslaps my ego, putting it in check.

It would be nice though, if that were to happen. If Daisy knew it was me, said my name, identified me as that boy who left town fifteen years ago, I wouldn't have to lie, wouldn't even get the chance to. I can't deny there is a part of me that wishes she would, saving me from going down a road I know is fraught with peril, but feels like my only choice.

Of all the emotion swimming in Daisy's beautiful brown eyes, none of them consist of recognition.

She squares her shoulders, pulling herself up as if there is a string inside her leading out through the top of her head, and someone has plucked at it. The indignation in her expression recedes, replaced with careful patience.

Um. What? That's...bizarre. And off-putting, if I'm being honest. And not AT ALL how I remember her.

The carnation pink sequined dress she wears catches rays of the darkening sunshine. She curls a strand of hair behind one ear, revealing a small gold hoop studded with diamonds.

Heels hooked on two fingers from the same hand, she says in this detached and nauseatingly polite tone, "Please excuse my outburst. Events, such as these"—she pauses to motion smoothly behind her, I'm assuming to whatever it is people are gathered for—"can be very emotional, and sometimes get the better of people. You caught me in a rare low moment."

Honestly, I'm proud to be reining in my upper lip

muscle that is fighting to curl. Why is Daisy talking like this? Who the hell cares if she has an outburst?

Two totally different emotions are at war inside me. Part of me is in shock. Daisy is standing in front of me in this very moment. *It's her! It's really her!* Another part of me is confounded that this is the same girl I once knew. A smaller part of me is angry this woman is standing in front of me explaining and apologizing for having typical human emotions. Who made her feel like she needs to do that?

"You don't have to worry about me," I tell her, slipping my hands in my back pocket and rocking up onto the balls of my feet. "I'm an old friend of Hugo's. You can take that rare low moment you're having and sink into it a little deeper if you want. Kick, cry, scream, curse the world. Won't bother me."

She lets out a little breath, her shoulders lowering an inch. She nods, the tip of her tongue slipping out to dab at the center of her top lip like she's considering. I'm doing some considering myself, and it mostly consists of trying to reconcile this woman with the girl who would regularly stand up for me in the classroom when math didn't make sense to me. It's not the prim and proper behavior that's rankling me. More like the way she swallows down how she feels. I'm not saying we have to give in to every emotion we have, but is it a good idea to bury them?

"Well, friend of Hugo," she turns, walking in the direction she was going before her shoes slid into the earth. She's a few inches shorter now, thanks to the loss of those shoes.

I follow after her. It's clear that's what she expects of me. Daisy St. James was used to being watched, and followed. It appears she still is. She reaches the end of the small yard, stopping just before the beginning of the grove, where two Adirondack chairs have been placed on the far side of an electric fire pit. She settles into one, her pink dress inching up her smooth thighs, and looks up at me.

Butterscotch sunlight glances off the bottle of champagne as she offers it out to me. "Join me?"

I absolutely, totally, and unequivocally should not agree.

"Yes," I hear myself say, beating back that mouthy asshole inside me who is bitching about how far off course I already am when I've only just arrived.

I'll have this one drink with Daisy, this one time, because denying myself feels unimaginable. I'll sit, if only for a few moments, basking in Daisy's inherent warmth, taking the opportunity I can't quite believe has been tossed in my lap. After this, I will double down on my resolve to accomplish what I came here to do, and then leave without a backwards glance.

Chapter 4

Daisy

I CANNOT SHAKE THE FEELING I ALREADY KNOW THE man standing in front of me.

He claims he's a friend of Hugo's, but there's something about him that puts me at ease immediately. And that never happens to me. I can't think of the last time I felt at ease in my own skin. I love it here in Olive Township, this little hamlet I grew up in, but the sad truth is that the inhabitants of Olive Township don't really love me. They love an idea of me. An image. A mirage. If I let just one of them get close enough, everything they think they knew about me would disappear. So when I come across somebody who looks at me like I'm crazy for apologizing for something most people wouldn't label an outburst, and then in the next breath tells me to feel free to have whatever response I feel like having, I can't help but feel uneasy about the feeling of ease.

A mindfuck, I believe it's called. Not to mention the guy is physically attractive in a distracting way. Buttery blond hair slipping over his forehead, unruly and stubborn. Blue-gray eyes the color of the sky before a summer monsoon rolls in. A scar, maybe two or three inches long, grips the left side of his face, from forehead to the top of his ear. It doesn't look too new, but it doesn't look old either. However he got it, it must have been painful.

It's almost enough to distract from the rest of him, except *who am I kidding no it's not*. The way that faded black T-shirt hugs those biceps is enough to kick a girl's salivary glands into hyperdrive. And those thighs. I mean, really. Is it necessary to be that muscular? Even the black canvas cargo pants, made more for utility than fashion, don't detract from the delightful muscle tone beneath.

Get yourself together, Daisy. You're engaged.

I clear my throat, remembering my manners. "You haven't told me your name," I say. His fingers brush mine just a touch too slowly as he takes the half-full bottle of champagne from my grasp. A ripple of gooseflesh rises on my arms, and there's something else, too, a pinch low in my belly. Too low to be my belly, if I'm being honest with myself.

I'm pathetic. Imagine being so starved for a man's touch that the brush of fingertips could elicit such a response from me. I have got to get myself together.

He sinks down in the Adirondack chair beside mine, stretching one long leg out while the other stays bent.

Bottle lifted to his mouth, lips poised a quarter inch from the rim, he replies, "Nor have you told me your name." He takes a drink, his gaze remaining on mine. It's only a drink from a bottle, but his lips are in the same place mine were a moment ago, and something about that feels intimate.

"I guess I forgot." A lie. More like I assumed he already knew who I was. An uncomfortable feeling flips through me. I don't like that about myself, how I assume someone knows me. The truth is, outside of this small town, I am simply just another girl. Maybe that's why I returned after college. Out there, I'm a nobody. Here, in this town that raised me but doesn't know me, I'm somebody.

Shifting the champagne bottle to his left hand, he offers his right. "Peter."

It's not at all the name I expected him to say. He looks too *loose cannon* to have a straight-laced name. There's some kind of ink on his left forearm, but it's almost too dark now to make out the details and I'm not bold enough to ask to see.

"You don't look like a Peter." My hand slides into his waiting palm.

"No?" He squeezes, not afraid to grip me tightly. Almost roughly. There's something about it that I love. Something I'm thirsty for. "What do I look like?"

My hand stays captured in his as he awaits my response. "I don't know." I shrug, squinting and making a show of looking over his face, but I stop quickly because he's too handsome. "Gage," I answer, deciding on the first ultra-manly name that comes to mind.

"Hah," he laughs once, loudly. "Gage," he repeats, quieter, shaking his head. "Out with it, princess. Give up that name of yours."

"Daisy St. James," I say, practically purring because I'm way too damned proud to have made him laugh. It doesn't look like something he does often.

I drop his hand and replace it demurely in my lap, waiting for him to tease me for adding my last name to the introduction, or maybe offering his so we're even.

But he doesn't. Instead, he shifts forward, extending the bottle to me.

"Champagne?" he asks when I take it, but the question is more *why is this your drink of choice?*

"It's a celebration," I explain, nodding back at the event room.

He doesn't say anything, just stares at me intensely. His lower lip is fuller than his top, giving him a perpetual pout. It's boyish, and somehow endearing, on this man who otherwise oozes masculinity.

Finally, he asks, "What are you celebrating?"

"An engagement."

He nods, just once, but doesn't ask a follow up question. There's no reason for me to keep talking, except that his apparent disinterest spurs my desire to speak.

"It's for me."

The lack of excitement in my tone should be embarrassing. It should be something I cover up, replace with forced elation. I should, but I don't, because this man makes me feel like I don't have to. Like I don't need to.

His eyebrows lift, eyes widening, silently asking a question.

"The party," I add. "It's to celebrate my engagement." My left hand dangles in the air between us, an ostentatious diamond ring parked on my finger. If it were broad daylight, the rock would sparkle like the surface of the ocean at midday.

The muscles in his jaw flex. He works a palm over the popped muscles, rubbing at them. "Congratulations." Any warmth in his voice before is gone now. He almost sounds defeated, but of course such a thing is not possible. My ability to read emotions is way, way off tonight. Maybe it's the champagne. Maybe it's me.

In the distance, someone yells my name. A man's voice. My jaw clenches, the corners of my mouth climbing, a conditioned response from all the automatic smiles I plaster on my face.

I don't turn to the sound, but Peter does, his eyes tracking, looking for the source.

"That's Duke," I explain. "My fiancé."

Peter rises up from his chair like a red hot poker was pressed to his backside. He whirls to face me.

Ok. Wow. Maybe I'm not so bad at reading emotions tonight. His face looks not only defeated, but stricken.

"What did you say?" he asks tightly.

"My fi—"

"Never mind," he snaps.

The guy is clearly upset, but there is no way it could be directed at me. Something else has his panties in a cherry-stem-in-the-mouth level knot. Belatedly it occurs to me this guy might've been lying to me. What if Hugo doesn't know him? What if this guy isn't who he says he is? Could he be an intruder? At an olive mill? Who does that? Is an olive thief a thing?

My imagination snowballs.

Dammit. There I go, being too trusting. This guy is going to shank me and hide me in the olives. Which would actually be pretty tough to do because olive trees don't exactly have enough surface area for hiding something. Which means he'd have to cut me up.

Oh shit. I should make a run for it. Except, I don't, because not only have I decided this guy won't actually make me into a kebab, but also, my curiosity about him is insatiable at this point.

He's Hugo's friend, but who is he really? Why does he feel familiar?

I'm dying to get a read on him, but it's impossible because his back is facing me. I watch his shoulders lift, then slowly lower like he's taking a deep breath before he turns around.

The sun sinks fully below the horizon, leaving the sky bruised in deep cantaloupe and aubergine. He turns his head, back lit by the color, his face in partial shadow. "It was nice meeting you, Daisy St. James. I think I'll be on my way now."

Irritation spreads through me. I don't understand what just happened, but my head is spinning, and there is a part of me that wants to keep him here just a little bit longer. I don't understand that part of myself, but I give in to her.

"What?" I challenge his retreating form. "Let me guess, you've been jilted? Left at the altar? Cheated on by your fiancée? And now you want to get the hell out of here before you get on your high horse and tell me you don't believe in the institution of marriage. Are you saving me from your negative opinion?"

Halfway through my barrage of questions he turned, and now he stares back at me. His arms cross in front of him, biceps popping. His tone is so even, so practiced. "I didn't say that."

"You don't have to." I take a drink from the bottle. "Your body language says it for you."

He moves forward quickly, long legs eating up the space in three strides. A gasp steals up my throat when he leans down, eyes on mine as he swipes the bottle from me. He overturns it, what's left of the bottle splashing to the ground.

A sound slips from my lips, something between a gasp and a disbelieving grunt. "What the hell?" I watch him closely, unsure of what he might do next.

Instead of standing, he holds some of his weight on the armrest of my chair, leaning closer until his face is a foot away from mine. He could put both his hands on the armrest, caging me in, but he doesn't. His eyes are intense, and he smells of cedar and citrus. So unlike Duke, who wears a ridiculously expensive cologne made by one of the oldest perfumers in London.

Peter levels me with a heavy gaze, eyebrows pinching in the center, eyes squinting with whatever he is about to say. "You don't know me, Daisy St. James, so don't go assuming you can read my body language."

His voice is deep, his chide curling into me, leaving me with the childlike embarrassment that follows an admonishment. He pushes off the chair and strides away. Indignation darts through me.

Oh, I am definitely going after him. I am going to tell him just where he can take his admonishment. If only I were wearing sensible shoes that wouldn't stab the ground, I would... *What am I even talking about?* I'll do nothing of the sort. I'll swallow my anger and say not a word. I've already snapped at him once, and quite nearly a second time, saying precisely what I was thinking in the moment without caring what he thought. Something about this man, and my reaction to him, unsettles me.

"There are universal messages received through body language, you know," I yell after him. "Frowns are sad. Smiles are happy."

He doesn't turn around, not even to argue with me. This annoys me, because I know what I just said is flat out wrong. Frowns can mean a hell of a lot more than sadness. The same is true for smiles. How many times have I smiled, but felt everything except happy?

I watch Peter cross the yard, his walk confident, his strides long. He arrives at his truck, hopping in, and a dog leans into the front seat and nuzzles his face.

The guy is too handsome for mere words, and he has a dog. Why am I jealous of whoever dates him next?

Without a glance my way he starts the engine and spins the wheel. A moment after he's gone from sight, my fiancé rounds the building and spots me sitting in the near-dark.

"What are you doing?" Duke yells, waving me toward him. "Come on."

Penn

Sighing, I pick up the almost empty bottle and wince as I roughly bump my ankle against the chair, hitting the exact spot where an ugly bruise colors my leg. I'd been careless with a pry bar a few days ago, losing my grip on it when I tried to wedge it behind my kitchen cabinets. I suppose that's what I get for attempting to remodel with zero personal experience. And without knowledge. And also, without a plan.

Ignoring the dull throb, I slip my heels on, choosing to walk the perimeter of the yard where the ground is harder packed.

Duke takes the bottle from me when I reach him, tossing it into the first trash can we see. He frowns at me, his hair perfectly coiffed. This man never, and I mean *never,* has a hair out of place. "I almost made a speech without you in attendance. That would've been embarrassing."

"Seriously," I mutter, brushing my hands through my hair and swiping under my eyes in case any makeup has accumulated there.

Duke halts outside the door to the event room. Turning to face me, he chucks my chin. "Big smiles, future Mrs. Hampton."

He waits patiently, watching me, and I spread my lips wide, revealing my pearly whites. A blankness settles over me, maybe it's the same way an actress feels when they occupy a role. I'm stepping into this version of myself, slipping her back on.

I'm an old friend of Hugo's. You can take that rare low

moment you're having and sink into it a little deeper if you want.

The opposite of what I'm doing now. I'm Daisy St. James soon-to-be Hampton, and my moments are nothing but high. I'm gracious and grateful, and I smile.

The stab of restlessness I've been squashing? It doesn't exist.

Appeased, he takes my hand, pulls open the door, and leads me into a room filled with people thrilled to be celebrating our impending nuptials.

Duke's dad stands at the bar, drink raised while he says something to my dad. My dad catches my eye, smiles and waves. Duke's dad glances over at us, shows no indication he's clocked who we are, and turns back to my dad. It's not surprising. Glenn Hampton is the kind of man who pretends you don't exist until he needs something from you. Duke's mom sits at a table with two of her friends, hawkish and quiet. There's a reason why Duke's two younger sisters never moved back home after they left for college.

My mom holds court at a table filled with loving, chatty, and slightly inebriated women. It seems as though most of Olive Township has shown up, though that's wrong. Our small town has grown steadily over the years, bursting at the seams with newcomers. Those in attendance tonight are part of the old guard, the people who have lived here for decades, or generations.

They have all gathered to take part in the festivities, culminating in the wedding of a St. James to a Hampton.

It's been a long time coming, and everyone is counting on it.

Chapter 5

Penn

I'VE BEEN BACK IN TOWN FEWER THAN TWENTY-FOUR hours and this is the third wedding invitation I've been subjected to. *For the same damn wedding.*

I force my gaze from the offensive paper, though it does little to quell the indignation rising up inside me. Why am I here? Why did I return? I could've hired a company to clean out my mother's home after her passing. I could've begged Hugo to do the job for me. At this moment, I'm deeply regretting my decision-making ability.

Had I thought I could sail into town, deal with the house, and move on like it was nothing? Yes, I did. Was that naïve, foolish, and downright idiotic? Apparently. Not only did I run into Daisy immediately, but here I am staring down her wedding invitation.

Mr. & Mrs. St. James request the honor of your company...

Ugh. Un-fucking-believable.

Penn

The worst part about it is that Daisy probably should marry Duke. The joining of the St. James and Hampton families has been in the works for decades. Their ancestors founded Olive Township approximately one hundred and sixteen years ago. Arizona, the state in which Olive Township resides, entered into statehood four years after. Royalty marries royalty, right?

The entirety of Olive Township appears to be in support of the union, including Sammich, the sandwich shop in which I'm currently standing, attempting to hide my disdain at the blown up wedding invitation pinned to the corkboard behind the counter. It's so large it outshines the all-caps casting call for the lead role in the upcoming town play. My petulant groan stays inside, but only barely. Is this sycophant level of celebration necessary?

"Two Monte Cristos, please," I say to the woman behind the register when she returns from delivering sandwiches to a table. "And two iced teas." I'm meeting Hugo at my old place, and I've promised to bring lunch.

She rings me up, and my traitorous eyes stray to the stupid pale pink invitation plastered just beyond her head. I must be a masochist. Or, perhaps I'm trying to stay in this angry state so I can keep my guard up, my armor unyielding, in an effort to get through what I came here to do.

"First time in Sammich?" she asks as I hand over two twenties.

I catch the *No* on its way out of my mouth and swallow it down. "Sure is," I lie. The truth is, I came here with my mom when I was a kid, and I've been dreaming about a Monte Cristo from Sammich far longer than I care to admit.

"Just passing through?" she asks, pressing my change into my palm. "Or having yourself a long weekend at the spa?"

Something tells me I don't fit the profile of people who typically visit Sagewood. Instead of pointing that out, I say, "I was hired to come here and look into a home that was kept in a family but left behind a long time ago." This is the sanitized version I dreamed up on my long drive from San Diego.

Everyone in this town knows everybody's business, but none more than Margaret, the owner and operator of this place. She is the eyes and ears of this town, and I'm not interested in supplying her with gossip about me.

But Margaret cannot be stopped. She is a 5'2", faux redheaded Jack Russell Terrier on my heels. She leans forward, eyes squinting and shrewd, propping her fleshy forearm on the counter. "You look familiar. Do I know you?"

I shake my head slowly. "I don't believe so." That's not a lie. She doesn't *know* me. At all. If I gave her my real name, she would most definitely remember me, though.

I nod toward the white paper bag the chef has placed in the open window between the kitchen and the rest of the place. "I better get going. My dog is waiting in my truck."

Margaret offers me a friendly smile as she hands the bag my way. "Finally nice enough outside that we can start taking our dogs on car rides."

Penn

I dip my chin in thanks and leave the store. Slim Jim stares me down from the passenger seat. My guess is that he's been mean-mugging passersby from his perch, delivering a menacing stink eye. He's doing what I wish I could do, but basic politeness dictates I choose otherwise. Dogs don't give a fuck, and I envy that.

Slim Jim watches me climb in my truck, sniffing voraciously at the bag of food. "That is not for you," I tell him, handing over one of his treats. He takes it and turns his back on me. I tell myself it's so he can stare out the window, but the truth is, he gets his feelings hurt. How I wound up with an emotionally sensitive dog, I'll never know.

Halfway through the short drive to my childhood home, Slim Jim turns my way, leaning over the center console to lick my face once. It's like he's saying, *I forgive you*. Not that I asked for forgiveness, or needed it. Like the sad sack I am, I accept the affection, trying not to think about what a deficit I'm in. Plenty of women like the idea of being with a SEAL, but few can handle the demands of a job we are all but married to. Few can handle me, either, and the fact I'm no good at relationships.

Slim Jim is all I have, but honestly, the guy is pretty damn good. I'm lucky to have him.

Scratching behind his ears, I stare out the windshield and fight against the gut-punch feeling left by the wedding invitations that assaulted my eyes. *Thrice.* "She's marrying him, Slim Jim. My Daisy is marrying one of the worst people I've ever met."

Dread hangs heavy in my stomach as I roll down Lickety-Split Lane. The last time I was on this street was the day I packed up my mother's car, with a little help from her. The vehicle had a new front bumper and hood, and engine parts that sounded complicated, repairs courtesy of Daisy's dad following the car accident.

An accident that had injured Daisy, but not me. Physically, anyhow. Plenty of pain accompanies the knowledge that I was at fault for hurting my best friend.

Some days I wish I could take it all back. Other days, I know some of it had to happen. My feelings about that time in my life are convoluted. Similar to the way I feel about my childhood home. Is that why my mom never sold it? Never attempted to deal with it at all? Alone it sat at the end of the lane, a relic, a story, a slowly crumbling structure. Was she keeping it for me, hoping I'd return to Olive Township? Did she want me to? Why?

I have questions, but no answers. Her will said only that the home belonged to me now. No instructions, no letter of explanation. I was with her before she died, and even then she said not a word.

It's confusing and frustrating, the same way I feel about the bits of excitement bubbling up around the dread in my stomach as I draw closer to my old home.

"There it is," I breathe the words, the old structure

coming into view. It's smaller than I remember, but so was I when I lived here.

The paint is peeling, the windows clouded. A bird's nest clings to the chimney.

My chest constricts, but I push past it.

Hugo waits in front of the house. He leans his backside against his fancy ass cherry-red Audi R8, a car he loves with a fervor that should be reserved for a woman. His right foot crosses over his left ankle, and his hands shove into the pockets of his jeans. I can't resist rolling my window down and giving him a little shit.

"Posing for the cover of GQ?" I ask from the open truck window as I roll slowly past.

He responds with a middle finger. "Hello, *Peter*."

Hugo hates my decision to come back here and use a different name. I call it *identity management*. He calls it *a flat out lie and you're a shithead for it*.

I understand where he's coming from, but he hasn't been where I've been, or done what I've done. He doesn't know I'm protecting Daisy from learning the truth about why I left.

Slim Jim and I come to a stop and pile out. He trots to a tree and lifts a leg.

Hugo pushes off his car, walking up to my truck in the short driveway. I'm surprised he didn't immediately turn around and buff out any fingerprints he may have left behind on his precious car.

"Hey, asshole," I greet him, missile-launching the paper-wrapped Monte Cristo at Hugo's chest. He catches it like a football, which is funny because it's Ambrose,

Hugo's other best friend, who's in the NFL. Never in a million years would I tell Hugo this, but I brag about him every chance I get. Not many people can say their long-time best friend earned a gold medal fencing in the Olympics. He's retired now, but he'll take on brand deals he feels are right for him. For the most part, he spends his time running Summerhill.

I open my tailgate and prop my ass on the end, one foot planted on the ground and the other dangling. "Thanks for giving me a heads-up that Daisy is marrying the equivalent of a wet paper towel."

"Nice to see you, too," Hugo grumbles, hopping up beside me.

It's been three months since Hugo came to San Diego for my mom's funeral, and less than one month since I got the harebrained idea to come back here and deal with the house in person.

Hugo removes the sandwich from the wrapper and takes a large bite. "If I told you she was marrying Duke, you never would've come back here."

"Correct, because torture isn't on the list of hobbies I enjoy."

Hugo munches thoughtfully. "Please explain the wet paper towel comment."

I stare up at my old house. Memories, both good and bad, burst from the peeling wooden windowsills. "A wet paper towel is an item that cannot fulfill its intended purpose."

Hugo nods slowly. "And Duke's intended purpose is..."

Penn

I chew angrily, my back teeth mashing together. "It sure as hell isn't marrying Daisy St. James."

Hugo wipes grease from his hands with a napkin. "I'm guessing"—his hands lift in the air near his chest, one palm facing out and the other still grasping a napkin—"and this might be a long shot, that you still have a thing for Daisy."

Absolutely not. I may have loved Daisy with an insane, beyond reason fire when I was a kid, but that was when I didn't know shit about shit. Before I grew up, became a man, survived hell week, boarded an aircraft carrier and flew in a helicopter over a totally different desert than the one I grew up in. "Hugo, not wanting Daisy to marry shit-for-brains Duke Hampton is about basic human decency. It has nothing to do with whether or not I have a thing for her. Which I don't."

He delivers a nice, long, level gaze, then finally says, "Sure."

"Let me put it this way. Somebody's pant leg gets stuck on a railroad tie, and there's a train not far off. The rules of basic human decency state that you help them."

He blinks hard, once. "In this analogy, Duke is the train and Daisy is the innocent civilian stuck to the tracks?"

"Precisely."

"She should take off her pants."

My gaze sharpens. "What?"

"You said her pants were stuck. If she took them off, she wouldn't be in them anymore, therefore she wouldn't be stuck to the tracks. Problem solved."

Using the pad of my thumb, I wipe sauce from the corner of my mouth. "Say another word about Daisy without pants on, and I will take that pretty face of yours and give you a scar that matches mine."

Hugo grins, eyeing the jagged scar that cuts down the left side of my face. "Yeah, you definitely don't have a thing for Daisy. Not at all."

I point at his sandwich. "You're lucky I gave that to you. I contemplated throwing it out the window on my drive here."

"You would never." He drinks from his iced tea until there's nothing left, and then he continues so it makes obnoxious sucking sounds. My frown deepens, and he smiles around his straw. He is enjoying my foul mood a little too much. "I'm the only free help you have."

"Dick," I mutter, but he's right.

"Asshole," he corrects cheerfully, delivering a half-gentle smack to my chest. "Get it right."

His joke, at long last, coaxes a smile from me. My first since I saw Daisy last night.

"Anybody recognize you?" Hugo asks, pointing down at the last bite of his sandwich to let me know he's asking about my stop for our lunch.

"Margaret is perceptive, but even she can't see into the future." I look nothing like the boy I was the day I scurried from this town, my head hung down in shame. *Scrawny* was an accurate description for my body at the time, with all four limbs being a little too long for the rest of me. My clothing never fit, but that was from lack of money, not lack of choice. My mother gave me haircuts in the kitchen until she decided to stop participating in what it took to be a mother, and I began to use clippers on myself. The haircuts were bad at first, but I developed my skill, and eventually I didn't look too terrible.

Hugo studies my face, and the uneven flesh, a bit too close for comfort. "The scar isn't that bad anymore."

I push off the edge of the tailgate, landing on my feet with a bounce. "It's not great."

"You're like a modified Harry Potter."

"But without the powers."

Hugo scratches the back of his neck. "How about your body?"

That's a different story. Keloid scar tissue has formed on my chest and over my ribs on my left side, bumpy and lumpy and unsightly as hell.

I reach for his trash, balling it up and adding it to the bag that held our food. "I need laser treatments."

"So," Hugo hops down, watching me toss our trash in my back seat and call Slim Jim over from his very important job of sniffing everything in the vicinity, "they're going to sear your ass?"

"Not my ass." I throw him a look and start for the front door of the place I once called home. "Just my chest." And my ribs. And part of my stomach. "Some fancy ass laser thing. I don't know. My doctor back home suggested it."

Hugo slaps my back as we walk over the dead-grass front yard, and as we do, I begin to realize something that should have struck me the moment I pulled into the driveway. Why aren't there mile high weeds around this place? Plants, bushes, spindly Palo Verde trees, cacti growing wherever it damn well pleases? This front yard should resemble a walk through the middle of nowhere, but it almost looks as if it has been kept up.

I pause at the foot of the likely rotten porch steps and glance at my best friend. "Have you been coming here, Hugo? Maintaining the landscape?"

He shakes his head, but my question spurs him to look around. "It's..." His head swivels, taking in the unnatural tidiness. "Not what it should be."

"Not by a long shot."

Who has been here? It had to have been more than one big cleanup, because there's no evidence of anything being uprooted, of disturbed earth. Has somebody been maintaining this place?

"If not you, then *who*?"

Hugo says the last word with me, the same question hovering in his eyes. "I can ask around town, see what I dig up?"

I'm already telling him *no* with the shake of my head. "I don't want to stir up curiosity. Better to let sleeping dogs lie."

Using the toe of my boot, I give the first front porch step a tentative push. The wood does not crumble, so I test it using the full weight of my foot.

"Solid," Hugo comments, stepping up and lending his entire six foot frame to my testing. "Looks like you managed to avoid termites." He does the same to the next two steps, and I wince each time as I wait for him to fall through.

"You coming?" he asks, from the porch landing.

We could be nine years old again, Hugo's black, expressive eyebrows cinching as he tells me he doesn't have all day to play because he needs to train. Even then, Hugo took fencing seriously.

Slim Jim leaps from the ground onto the landing in one graceful arc.

"Your dog is an acrobat," Hugo mutters as he hurries up to walk in front of Slim Jim, just in case any of the wood is rotten.

"You don't have to tell me that," I reply, following my dog and my best friend. "Should have seen him counter surf after I made beef tacos a couple weeks ago. Damn stealthy about it, too." If it hadn't been for the *tap, tap, tap* of the glass leftover container hitting the countertop, I wouldn't have realized what he was doing.

Hugo stops at the front door. "You know that's bad for them, right? Not only can they eat food that's harmful to them, but they could touch something hot or sharp."

I roll my eyes to the porch overhang, taking note of a giant wasp nest in the corner. "Thank you, Uncle Hugo. You've saved me from almost tying a dinner napkin around Slim Jim's neck and making space for him at my table."

Hugo slaps my back as I fit my old key into the lock. "Someone has to look out for you."

Pretending like his comment doesn't remind me of exactly how alone I am in this world, I shove open the door and stare down my past. "After you." I extend an arm. "If there are any furious raccoons in there, they'll scratch you up instead of me."

"Nice. Then we'll match." He elbows me out of the way and stomps inside.

Hugo has never, not for a single second, allowed me to feel bad for myself. Not when he came and saw me in the hospital on base in San Diego. Not when I stopped returning his calls and he showed up without notice, threatening to kick my ass if I didn't shape up. There definitely won't be any naval gazing allowed now, either.

I understand why. I might have been in a terrible accident that resulted in a handful of surgeries and some massive scarring, but I'm alive. That's more than he can say about his father.

I think I'll tone it down.

Following Hugo into the old home is like being reintroduced to my childhood, albeit with an inch of dust and what is almost definitely mouse droppings. Through the west-facing windows, sunshine bulldozes its way through layers of dust and dirt, relentless and undeterred. The filtered natural light gives the place an eerie quality, leaving parts of it dark and other places dully highlighted.

"I forgot about this wallpaper," Hugo muses, moving to the far wall of the small living room. With one finger he swipes over the royal blue background, the gold flourishes stretching out like fingers, and the tigers in position to pounce. *Why the tigers,* I'd asked my mom when she finished papering the wall. I was seven. Maybe eight. *Because,* she'd replied, running her warm palms over my shoulders, *tigers are majestic and bold, and they are self-*

sufficient. It took me a long time to figure out my mother saw such qualities as something to aspire to. She wanted to be self-sufficient, to not let her heartbreak over my dad's departure pull her into the depths. Neither of us could have known that one day, in the not too distant future, it would. And it would be the beginning of the end.

"Yeah," I answer Hugo as he wipes his hand on his jeans. "My mom liked weird shit."

A stab of guilt assails me. I don't mean to sound crass or reductive, but I can't wax poetic on the subject of eclectic wallpaper right now. There are too many feelings, too much emotion to wade through, and what I'd really like to do is set them all on fire.

I knew it was going to be a lot coming in here, coming back to Olive Township at all, but I wasn't expecting to feel quite this affected. Nor was I expecting to see Daisy right away, to talk to her, to watch her tuck away a part of herself, to watch her lips form the words that knocked me over even as I stood tall.

That's Duke. My fiancé.

I wanted to snatch the words out of the air, crush them in my palm. Instead, I snapped. Practically stormed off. She must have thought *Peter* was a few bricks shy of a load. Maybe I frightened her. It would be for the best, maybe encourage her to stay away from me if she sees me again.

Daisy is an engaged woman, and I am here for a short time to offload a house that should've been dealt with a long time ago. I'm not here to make friends or rekindle foes. No reminiscing, no *I remember when*, no nothing.

That's it. That's all.

Thunk.

In unison, Hugo's and my head whip toward the sound. Slim Jim bounds to the window, and we follow. A dove lies on the porch floor, unmoving.

Shoulder to shoulder, we stare out the window. "I think that's a bad omen."

"Maybe if it were a raven," Hugo argues. "But doves are, you know, sweet and shit."

"Sweet and shit," I mimic.

The dove blinks, spending half a second in the space between stunned and reality, and begins flapping its wings manically. It rights itself, hopping around before giving its wings a try. It takes off, flying low and unsteadily across the unexpectedly short dead grass.

Hugo turns away from the window, walking into the kitchen and cursing about something he finds there.

I spend another moment gazing out at the yard, mentally sifting through who would keep the yard from disrepair. Someone who only had access to the front yard, which is everybody. Someone who cared, which narrows it down. And someone with the fortitude, loyalty, or just plain stubbornness to keep coming back to a thankless job and zero recognition.

As much as I would like to write this off as an anomaly, or something of little consequence, the truth is, this mystery is going to keep me up at night.

Chapter 6
Daisy

"This one is a dark chocolate cake with a Cabernet curd, fresh raspberries, and vanilla buttercream." Kathleen, the general manager of Sweet Nothings, places the bone china plates on the table in front of us, alongside fresh forks. The chocolate frosting glistens, the overhead light reflecting off the edible gold sprayed on the cake.

It's wedding cake tasting day, and Kathleen has made the drive out to St. James farm. I helped her carry box after box into the small kitchen at Spot Of Tea (affectionately shortened to Spot), the adorable little tea room on the property. My parents built the tea room before I was born, and my mother has operated it since. Spot was officially my first job in high school, but I helped out long before that, organizing the tea offerings and eliminating water spots from the china. When I became an employee and got my food handler's license, I began assembling the finger sandwiches and quiches, arranging them artfully on tiered serving stands.

Spot has always been one of my favorite places in the world, a home within a home. A fancy trunk bedecked in gold metal and filled with fascinators sits in the corner beside an ornate gilt full-length mirror. There's a French feel to the space, though the tea service is English proper. The walls are covered in a cream textured wallpaper, with a gallery wall displaying photos of female royals. Duchess Kate, Princess Diana on her wedding day *and* post-divorce, and of course, Queen Elizabeth. Notably missing from the wall is Camilla, who my mother refuses to include, or acknowledge her new title of Queen Consort. When asked to explain the snub, my mother will only say *my memory is long*.

The view from the cozy dining area is one of my favorites on the property. A long window opens up to the largest section of pasture, where rare white and multicolored thoroughbreds spend their days. It's almost magical, and a big contributor to my young, and naïve, love for fairy tales. Well, that and my mother's insistence that I had true love waiting for me in the future. It was as if she'd said, *follow the yellow brick road, and there you'll find it*.

I believed her at the time, but now I know true love is as real as a pot of gold at the end of a rainbow. My mom meant well, but it was a parcel of lies wrapped in the silkiest of ribbons.

She's happy today, energized, the shadows under her eyes slightly less than usual. I'd give almost anything to go back in time, spend a Sunday with her preparing pot roast, mulch her flower bed, work alongside her in Spot. What used to feel like a chore would now be a gift. Just more collateral damage of the late cancer diagnosis.

It's important to find the good in every moment with her, even when it hurts. Today, she isn't wincing from pain. Her hair, held back from her face in matching mother of pearl barrettes, is curled at the ends. She wears more makeup than usual, trying to cover the pale of her skin. In her eyes is a twinkle makeup could never deliver. That is courtesy of our current activity.

My mother delicately deposits a forkful of our third sample of wedding cake in her mouth. "Mmm." The groan is borderline indecent.

Vivienne, my best friend and maid of honor, takes a bite, dark eyes squinting in ponder while she chews. "It's delicious," she concedes, "but I think the first cake is more your style."

The glass and wood door to the tea room opens, the bells hanging from the door handle tinkling. Duke steps in, smile charming and swagger on point. Warm affection surges over me. Duke has been my friend for so long, and he has always been good to me.

My mother claps her hands, eyes wide like this man has hung the moon. According to her, he has. "Duke!"

He strides over, all long legs and arms swinging in perfect cadence. Butterscotch hair flipped and styled just right. He stops beside my mother, bending to kiss her cheek.

She pats his cheek affectionately in return. "We're sampling wedding cakes."

"I see that." His deep timbre floats over us, his cologne fighting with the smell of sugar for top scent. "Where are all the customers? I've never seen this place so empty."

"Brenda closed the place for cake tasting," Kathleen explains, glancing at my mother, who confirms it with a nod.

"Aren't you going to say hello to your bride-to-be?" Vivienne eyes Duke, one of her perfect and expressive De la Vega eyebrows lifted.

"Of course," Duke says smoothly. "But greeting the woman responsible for giving life to the love of my life is of equal importance."

Vivienne, to her credit, manages to stop herself from making the finger in the mouth gagging motion. Vivienne's been down on love, and the institution of marriage, since her husband decided the attached life was no longer for him. She insists she's fine, that she got the best parts of him already. Everly is five, and Knox is three.

Three sets of expectant eyes on us now, Duke bends to brush a kiss to the space beside my ear. I let a small smile curve my lips, just like a woman in love would.

Duke turns his attention back to my mother. I don't blame him for choosing to engage her instead of Vivienne. They have never been one another's biggest fans. Vivienne is too brash for Duke, and he is too reserved for her. "Do you have a favorite flavor so far?"

"This one," she says, pointing with her fork at the slice before her.

Duke snags my fork from where it's perched on my plate, smoothly spearing a bite of my slice for himself. "Delicious," he says, replacing my fork. His hand moves to my shoulder, where he gives me the slightest squeeze.

"Ok," Kathleen trills, pivoting to lift a tray of water from the counter. She places crystal goblets in front of each of us. "Drink some water, ladies. Cleanse that palate for the next cake."

I opt for the flute of champagne, bubbles bursting crisply. My mother, the dutiful rule follower, drinks her water. Like me, Vivienne reaches for her flute.

"Duke, let me get a fourth place setting prepared for you," Kathleen says, already starting to rearrange the table to create more room. "Daisy said you weren't going to be able to make it today."

"My meeting wrapped up early," Duke explains, "and I had a little time before my next one starts, so I thought I'd drive out. Please, though, don't go to any trouble for me. I'll steal a bite from my bride-to-be, and trust her to choose the best wedding cake flavor."

Kathleen and my mother practically swoon at Duke's charm. Vivienne, with that best friend instinct, rakes her eyes over my face.

I turn away, standing up quickly from my chair. My knee hits the underside of the table hard enough to rattle the cutlery on the china. "Sit down, babe." I coax Duke onto my seat. "I'll sit on your lap."

Duke settles into my vacated chair, and I perch across his thighs, draping one arm over his shoulders.

My mother appears positively enthralled at this

public display of affection. She is the heart-eye emoji, come to life.

"This," Kathleen says grandiosely, placing our plates in front of us. "This is my personal favorite. A delicate almond cake with strawberry rhubarb jam in a lemon curd buttercream."

Mouth full and eyelashes fluttering, Vivi groans indecently. "I could bathe in this."

"Superb," I declare. "Sign me up."

"Daisy," my mother admonishes softly. "Don't you want to at least think about something fancier, like the chocolate? What about the second cake, with the Grand Marnier frosting?"

"Sure, Mom," I acquiesce easily. "Chocolate with Grand Marnier it is." What do I care? At the end of the day, this wedding is for her.

Vivienne's gaze drills into me. She's been suspicious of me and Duke since the beginning, when we made a show of announcing we were dating, and not long after, marrying. The town didn't mind the brisk pace of our relationship, but Vivi took notice. Apparently, living life as a single mom of two and being an acclaimed chef has not used up all her brain cells. She can still assault me with her razor sharp attention, and her eagle eyes.

Guilt gnaws at me. Every moment I spend with Vivi a war rages in my head. I want to tell her the truth about it all, but I can't.

I change course in an attempt to throw off the lady version of Sherlock sitting across from me. "They were all beyond delicious, and I would be perfectly happy to have any one of them at my"—I glance quickly down at Duke, whose face is only inches from mine—"*our* wedding."

"I just can't believe it," Kathleen bursts in, gushing. "A St. James and a Hampton union, at long last. Something my grandmother said might never happen. Your families were at odds for the longest time." She grabs herself a flute, filling it with champagne and taking a long sip. "I would do some bad things if I could see the look on some of your ancestors' faces."

My gaze cuts down to Duke, where I find his eyes on mine already. We share a knowing smile. Both us were raised on the tales of our families intermingled and often opposing motivations over the years. "Great-Grandpa Byron is rolling over in his grave."

Duke shakes his head affectionately, a smile on his face. "I can't believe my great-grandfather Quentin challenged him to a duel."

I laugh and chuck him on the chin. "All because Byron convinced Quentin that his father had buried coffee cans of money on Hampton land."

"If Quentin was gullible enough to believe him," Vivienne chimes in, "I'd say he deserved the blisters and broken back from digging up his backyard." Vivienne's family, though not town founders, have been here almost as long. One could argue the De la Vegas are the real reason behind putting Olive Township on the map. Without their locally famous Summerhill Olive Mill, I don't know if there'd be enough tourists visiting our small town to warrant all the other shops and attractions that followed. The Sagewood Wellness Spa definitely wouldn't exist, or the small physical therapy practice I operate that's connected to the spa.

"He probably did deserve it," Duke admits. "He was a mean son of a bitch." He glances at my mother. "Pardon my language."

She smiles like Duke is Sir Galahad's more handsome, more gallant brother. And you know, he might be. The guy is great. Amazing, even. He has his flaws like anyone else, but somehow even his flaws aren't that *flawy*. Can he be domineering? Sure, but his motivations are pure of heart. Duke believes he's responsible for the general happiness of everyone around him, and that sometimes results in some unpleasant personality characteristics. But overall, Duke is a genuinely good man, the embodiment of every mother's dream for her daughter.

He pats my knee. "I should probably get going. My next call starts in half an hour."

It's a twenty-minute drive to his family's downtown office. Duke is there most days, and travels to other states a few times a month. His family owns an ever-growing chain of boutique hotels, and Duke is set to take over soon so his dad can step back from the day-to-day running of the family empire.

I hop off Duke's lap. He says goodbye, dropping yet another kiss on my mother's cheek. He angles me away from the table, dipping his head, lips hovering for a beat beside mine. From behind him, it would appear we're kissing.

He leaves with all the confidence and swagger he walked in with, and Kathleen pretends to fan herself.

Penn

Her champagne flute is almost empty. I guess now that we've chosen a wedding cake, her job is finished for the day. "You are one lucky lady," she says to me.

I drop back into my chair. "Don't I know it." Once again I avoid my best friend's gaze, choosing instead to pick up my champagne and finish it.

"Did you know"—Kathleen leans in conspiratorially, her lips loosened by the bubbly—"that Margaret told me a man came into Sammich today?"

"Breaking news," Vivienne interjects, mimicking the grave tone of a news reporter.

Kathleen pointedly ignores her. "She said he had a scar running from his temple to the bottom of his ear, and he looked like something sculpted by da Vinci."

I sit up in my seat. How many men are running around Olive Township with scarred faces and impeccable physiques?

Those corded forearms.

That tiny vertical indentation in the center of his lower lip.

Don't even get me started on those muscled thighs.

Is it hot in here? It is. It must be. It most certainly isn't me getting hot and bothered.

I tuck my hands under my legs to keep from fanning my face. Daring a peek across the table at Vivienne, she catches my gaze and rolls her eyes. She's still on the comment made by the two older women at our table. She has no idea that my enthusiastic libido has taken over my thoughts. That thirsty bitch is shouting from her place below my navel, reminding me how long it's been since I've had *relations*.

This is what I get for hanging out with my mother and her friend, not that there was a chance I'd use anybody but Sweet Nothings to bake my wedding cake. If there's one thing I've learned by spending time with the early sixties crowd, it's that they are horny. Vivienne's aunt, who lives with her mother, has a collection of dark romance novels. *The smuttier, the better.* Her words.

I share a knowing look with Vivienne, who has been on the receiving end of her aunt's bawdy humor one too many times.

Playing at being offhand, I ask, "Did Margaret get a read on the guy?"

Not because I care to know if it was the stranger from my engagement party. Simply because I'm curious. I could pull out my phone and call Hugo, getting an answer in less than a minute, but that feels like the wrong approach. I'm not trying to stir up gossip. Not that Hugo would gossip about me, but he might mention it to Vivienne, and there's almost nothing worth tipping off the human equivalent of a bloodhound.

"I'm sure she did," my mom says, tapping her bare nail on the table. "Margaret's so good at acting like she's making conversation, when what she's really doing is filing away everything you say and don't say in that mental Rolodex of hers."

Vivienne and I mouth *Rolodex* and laugh.

"I happen to know she did." Kathleen's head bobs enthusiastically. "He told her he was hired to come to town and clean out that old abandoned house on Lickety-Split."

What? My heart beats hard in my chest as I swallow my surprise. Abandoned for years, that house used to be home to someone very important to me. Someone I've never been able to shake. A towheaded boy, shaggy and scrawny and mine.

A boy I promised myself I'd forget.

Last night, Peter conveniently forgot to tell me about his mission here. Not that I asked. Did I? I don't remember clearly. I'd grown weary of smiling, of responding to *congratulations* with a warm *thank-you. It'll get easier over time,* Duke had whispered in my ear. *Go get some air.* I went outside, far from anybody who might glance outside the beautifully decorated room and see me. And then... Peter. I still can't shake the familiarity, the way even the tips of my fingers thought they recognized him when they brushed against his hand.

I replayed it over and over through the end of the night. While I clasped hands and exchanged cheek kisses with my happy guests, I thought of Peter. Scurrying away as soon as he heard the word *engagement*.

"Lickety-Split, huh?" my mother says, her thoughts going to the same place as mine. *Penn Bellamy.*

Worry sinks into the wrinkles around her eyes. She knows. She remembers the love I had for the boy who lived there.

"Well, the old Bellamy place had to be dealt with some time." Mom sits back in her chair, and I'm grateful she's taking the conversation away from my personal history. "Might as well be a looker. Do you think he'll wear tight jeans?"

"Mom!" Playfully, I tap her upper arm.

"What?" she challenges. "I'm not dead yet."

The wind leaves my sails. Judging by the stricken expressions on Vivienne and Kathleen, everyone else's sails are hanging limply as well.

Mom shrugs. "Just a little bit of maudlin humor."

I force a laugh. Because if I don't laugh, I'll cry.

My mother has stage four uterine cancer. With her options exhausted, she has resigned herself to her fate. The pain medicine she's on keeps her comfortable, and our job is to make her happy. My dad does his best for her, but she hates him fussing over her, and he still has the farm to run anyway. The tasks and responsibilities keep him busy, not to mention the extra hours he's putting in at Spot.

She has an in-home caregiver now, *the very best money can buy*, according to Duke.

He would know, because he's the one footing the bill. It's hard to say what possessed him to offer me such an arrangement. Was it the fact our families have been intertwined for decades, trading status as friend and foe? Or was it me, and the fact Duke and I have never been at odds with one another? Maybe it was how we grew up laughing at the ancient antics in our families' past, never feeling like we had to carry a revenge torch. Duke and I always had an easy friendship, born from understanding what it's like to grow up in a locally famous family, shouldering the inherent pressure that comes with an infamous last name.

On the outside, Duke and I together make perfect sense.

But the truth I will never utter to a soul is that we are not marrying for love.

Duke will pay for my mother's end of life care for however long we are blessed with her presence, but the real gift is giving her the opportunity to watch her only child walk down the aisle in the wedding dress she once wore. In return, I will provide Duke with a wife of status (gag me) to mollify Duke's despotic father.

There you have it.

The real reason I am marrying Duke Hampton.

And the flavor of the cake I eat during the charade?

I really don't care.

Chapter 7

Daisy

What I am doing is very, very stupid, I'll admit. But you know how sometimes something is really dumb and you do it anyway because you just can't help yourself? You need an answer, even if you don't dare to hope you'll receive one definitively. Even a hint, the tiniest morsel, would be enough to subsist on.

After helping my mother into her house, where her in-home nurse, Bonnie, awaited her, I loaded Kathleen's car with everything she'd brought out to the St. James farm. Vivi left to go start food prep for dinner service at Dama Oliva, the upscale but still attainable restaurant she owns in town.

With my dad busy caring for the horses, and my mother napping, I decided it wouldn't hurt to swing by Lickety-Split.

That's how I got to where I am now, winding through town in the opposite direction of the home I live in by myself, slipping past the recently-built neighborhood of houses with their trimmed yards and HOAs. Leaving behind Pour Me with its neon sign lit and the words *dive bar* scrawled underneath. I pass the Rowdy Mermaid hair salon, and Lunker, the bait and tackle shop with the secret entrance for the moody underground speakeasy, King's Ransom. Locals are under strict orders to never, ever share the location of that door, not even if the tourist offers sexual favors in exchange. Oddly specific rule, but it exists because things got *drunk and disorderly* a couple years ago at Pour Me when some tourists tried to convince Crazy Cliff the information was worth a blowie. Personally, I think if someone wanted to get into a secret speakeasy enough to contemplate performing that act on a fifty-something man who refuses to wear matching shoes and gave himself the nickname he now goes by, she should've been given directions. Sans blowie.

I leave the most populated part of town, and with it goes my grasp on the present. I am firmly in the past, sitting in the passenger seat of my father's brand-new Lincoln and bumping over the road to Penn's house while he tells me to be nothing more than friends with a boy like Penn. *Sympathy is important, but don't mistake it for attraction.*

I was twelve, flat-chested and certain boys were mostly disgusting. Except for Penn. He was the exception to every rule, though I couldn't have articulated why. I knew I liked the way he laughed, and how he'd scrunch one eye and look up when he was thinking, but was that enough to set him apart from all others? It must have been something else, something undefinable.

I readily told my dad *Ok*, because I couldn't fathom being attracted to any boy. Not in the way I knew he was talking about. Penn climbed in the back seat when my dad pulled up and honked. Polite and talkative, he held up his end of the conversation about Arizona's newest sports franchise, the Diamondbacks. I cared for baseball almost as much as I cared for the idea of wrestling a rattlesnake, but I was happy to sit there listening to their back-and-forth. Penn was going to spend the day at our thoroughbred farm, helping my dad and his employees. It was a trial run, to see if he'd be a good fit and able to work for the farm all summer. I was just happy to get to see Penn all day, until my dad crushed my spirit by informing me that I was to leave him alone while he was working.

I was crafty though, and when Penn went to work for my dad that summer I came up with ways to see him. Mostly they involved me needing help with something, like repairing the tire swing, or setting up a raised garden bed. My favorite was asking him to help me reach a pitcher on a high shelf. He knew what I was doing. He always knew, and that was sort of the fun in it. My dad caught on, telling me to knock it off. So I got craftier, making sure to call Penn in from his work when my dad was too busy to notice. Penn, smirking the whole time, would wait for me to make my request, then respond with the same three words: *Anything for you.*

If I heard that phrase tomorrow, I'd drop dead. Well, maybe not *dead*. But I'd hit the deck for sure.

Memories envelop me as I turn onto Lickety-Split. I didn't spend much time at that house with Penn, at least

Penn

not after his mom went downhill. He preferred anywhere else to his home, and I knew it was because he didn't want me to see what his home life was like. He had me and our friendship, and then he had the other half of his reality, and he kept us on parallel paths.

The day he moved away, I cried the kind of ugly cry my mother called *unseemly*. Penn and I hadn't seen each other in weeks by that point, because I'd been told not to see him after the accident. I'd agreed because my father was irate, and I believed the faster I went along with the consequence of my choices, the quicker he'd be to take back the ban on my friendship with Penn. But the call came that day, and Penn had said *My mom and I are moving away. I'm sorry. For everything.* He hung up, and ugly sobs wracked my body. My mother said *I hope you cry like that for me when I die* and I carried that with me until the day she announced her cancer was too far along to fight. That damn sentence moved like ticker tape through my mind, and soon after, Duke and I devised our plan.

I grip the steering wheel tighter, clearing my throat and straightening my shoulders. Even if that busybody Margaret got it all wrong and somehow it really is Penn come back to handle his mother's house, I would be just fine with that. I would shake his hand, maybe offer the slightest, friendly embrace, and that would be that. My heart wound has healed and scarred. Is there anything stronger than scars? Scars know. Scars have been there. Visible scars are like messages to others, and emotional scars are messages to ourselves. Like little pieces of information, they inform us. *Stay away from that person, avoid that situation, keep them at arm's length, guard your heart.*

And Penn? He left a long, jagged scar over the top of my heart, and the message it left is tattooed on my soul.

Is my breath quickening as I approach the Bellamy house, knowing somebody is in town with the specific purpose of handling affairs that concern Penn? Someone who probably knows him? Maybe. Do my knuckles turn white on the wheel until the joint aches? Possibly.

Creeping up to the Bellamy house with a belly full of cake and not nearly enough champagne was not on my agenda for today. But, here we are.

The truck parked out front catches my eye. It's a newer model, shiny black. And I recognize it. My eyes squint at the car parked beside it.

"Hugo," I whisper into my air-conditioned cabin. At least this confirms Peter really does know Hugo. I was not in danger of being made into confetti.

A waving hand catches my attention. Hugo, rounding the house and walking until he stops beside the porch steps. I slow but don't stop, delivering my best impression of a nonchalant wave. A man strides from the home, glaring at my car. Peter.

But...wow. Ok. He looks mad. Or maybe it's just unhappy. Either way, he scowls in my direction.

He strides to Hugo, those well-honed arms crossing as he settles into place. He's not in all black today. He wears a gray T-shirt, and light colored jeans. I know it's not Penn, but still, my heart hammers my breastbone, doing its best impression of a toddler banging on a drum.

Penn

It's the house, playing tricks on me. Making me get creative and envision the man Penn may have grown to be.

For the briefest of seconds, I consider stopping and saying hello, but given the scowl that may have taken up permanent residence on Peter's face, I'll pass.

I tap the gas pedal, picking up speed and leaving the two men in the rearview. I don't know what I was expecting to find, what answers I wanted, or even what questions I had. I only wanted to see for myself what Margaret was telling people about.

For years I held back from trying to find him online, or ask Hugo if they were still in touch. I guess hearing that one mention of him from Margaret really tapped a nerve.

But I know better. Peter being hired to handle the abandoned Bellamy house changes nothing. Penn left without a trace, leaving not even a breadcrumb trail to follow. The smartest thing I can do for myself now is remember that if someone wants to be found, they'll make a way.

Penn must not want to be found, because he's not who returned.

Chapter 8

Penn

"Well, that didn't take long." Hugo shakes his head. He peels off his dirty shirt, reaching into his car for a clean tee.

He has row upon row of ab muscles, his arms nearly as well-defined as mine. The sport of fencing might not call to mind buff specimens, but Hugo has a gym at Summerhill. The Olympics are in his rearview now, but exercise has remained a part of his daily routine.

"Alright, alright," I say, delivering my best Matthew McConaughey impression as Hugo stretches his hands above his head, bare muscles flexing. "How much is my ticket to Thunder Down Under?"

"First show is free." Hugo threads his arms through his clean shirt. "Next show is even better, and I charge."

I look down at my own dirty shirt. We worked for two hours, making lists and picking through dusty detritus. Unlike him, I do not have a fresh T-shirt to change into.

Penn

I'm sure people at the grocery store I'm stopping by on the way back to his rental won't be afraid to look askance at my filthy shirt.

"What didn't take long?" I ask, moving past the joke and referring back to his comment from before his strip show.

Hugo twists the top off a water bottle flavored with lemon-lime electrolytes. "Olive Township rumor mill."

"Margaret," I say matter-of-factly.

"Yep." Hugo stares in the direction of Daisy's long-gone car. "You feel like telling me why Daisy drove up to your old house?"

I scratch my jaw with the edge of my thumbnail. That was my first question, too, as soon as I got over the shock of seeing her in her car. Shrugging, I answer, "She must've been one of Margaret's first recipients of fresh gossip and decided to come see for herself."

"It's possible. She was cake tasting with my sister today."

"What the actual fuck is cake tasting?"

"Tasting cake."

"Yes, thank you. But what else is it? Does it have a special meaning? Is this some new Olive Township tradition?"

Hugo eyes me warily, making it clear he doesn't want to say what he's about to say. He forges ahead. "*Wedding* cake tasting."

Ah. He left out a word. Because...*why?*

"Why didn't you just say that?" I whistle for Slim Jim,

and a few seconds later he comes bounding from the back of the house.

"Because you make the worst face when Daisy's name comes up. Like you smelled something disgusting, but also like your dog died."

I shake my head at him in a *what the fuck* way. He lifts his hands, proclaiming his innocence. "Don't shoot the messenger. Get a mirror. You'll see."

I open up the passenger door for Slim Jim, making a motion with my finger. He hops up and I close the door.

I turn back around to say *goodbye* and *thank you* to my best friend, but the apprehension in his eyes stops me. "Out with it, Hugo."

Hugo sighs, hands tucking into his pockets. It's obvious he's taking great care to keep his face devoid of emotion. "Are you sure you're making the right decision not telling Daisy? If she finds out you were here and didn't call her, she's—"

"Doesn't matter, because I'll already be gone." Just because I ran into her last night doesn't mean anything. It was a chance encounter, and nothing more. I'll be more careful from now on. Olive Township might be a small town, but it's not *that* small.

"Thanks for thinking about the rest of us. We have to live with her."

"She's about as ferocious as a doe." At least, that's the impression I'm getting. The old Daisy St. James has been smothered.

Hugo snorts. "Given the right motivation, even cool

tempered, sweet as honey Daisy will grow claws. Especially"—he slams a stiff pointer finger to my chest—"where it concerns you."

I scoff, batting away his finger. "You're above appealing to my ego, De la Vega."

"You've never believed in how much Daisy cared about you. Always wrote it off, called it something else."

I'm getting tired of this conversation. Of insisting Daisy doesn't care about me. Mostly because it *hurts*.

"Hugo, has Daisy ever asked about me?"

He knows I have him there. From his own mouth he once told me she stopped years ago.

But the way he's eyeing me now, almost like he pities me, is not what I was expecting from him. It gives me the feeling of being intruded upon, and I turn away slightly, angling my body toward that fucking house that brought me back here.

Stupid, dilapidated house. Except for the front yard. Quite the conundrum.

"Not in a long time," Hugo admits.

I double down on my scoff, this time adding a derisive sound in my throat. "No matter what you think is true from before, let me remind you that Daisy is engaged—"

"—to a wet paper towel."

I smirk. "Exactly. And she does not give two shits about little old me."

"Sure, yeah." Hugo claps my back and walks backward to his car. "If that were true, there'd be no reason to keep your presence a secret."

I open my mouth to argue, but I have nothing to say. He's wrong. I don't know how, but he is. I just need a few more minutes to figure it out.

Hugo smiles smugly, wearing his conversational win like a beauty queen's sash. "Forgot to mention, trash pickup day is Thursday, and you can't keep the empty can on the curb longer than twenty-four hours or the HOA will fine you."

"Ask me if I care." I used to fight real bad guys, and now an HOA is going to tell me what I can do with my trash can? No fucking way.

He ignores me, driving off with a parting wave, and in lieu of returning his wave I offer a friendly middle finger.

I didn't tell him I ran into Daisy last night, because I got the feeling she didn't want anybody to know where she was. Maybe it was the panic in her eyes, maybe it was the way she kept looking over her shoulder, but she looked like a woman who wanted to *go*. Somewhere. Anywhere.

Daisy's body screams to the front of my mind. She is all woman now. Filled out, and gorgeous. Honestly, I don't know how anybody in this town gets anything done with her walking around.

If I end up in her presence again, which I won't, it's possible I'll pass out. I hope Hugo is there to catch me because people die from that shit.

Up close or from a distance, Daisy is a sight to behold. A beautiful woman God created just to test my mettle. If I can withstand a life where Daisy is not mine, I can withstand anything.

Penn

Something about the way she looked when she drove by earlier is bothering me. That expression on her face, framed perfectly by her car window, really threw me. Why did she look wounded?

The question torments me while I swing by the grocery store and pick up a few items. Am I making a mistake by not telling Daisy I'm here? By concealing my identity, like I did earlier with Margaret at the sandwich shop? Like I did last night, with Daisy?

For the briefest moment I allow myself to get carried away with an alternate reality, one where I tell Daisy it's me. She throws her arms around me, chucking Duke's engagement ring out into a desert filled with prickly pear. Daisy and I live happily ever after, and Duke disappears into a puff of smoke.

But then I catch my reflection in a door on my way down the freezer aisle, and the fantasy disintegrates. That scar running down the side of my face, raised and waiting to one day turn flesh-colored. The pink skin needs time, I'm told, but that's not the worst part. What's hidden from view on my body is worse. I've been put through hell, mentally and physically. I am a former Navy SEAL with scars, both visible and invisible.

I'm an idiot for allowing myself to dream of a happy ending with Daisy. There won't be one now, and it was never an option before. I did not return to Olive Township to introduce difficulty into Daisy's life. From now on, I'll treat this like a mission. I'm here to gather information, execute on what I find, and extract myself.

In civilian terms, *do what I need to do and get the fuck out.*

THE UNIVERSE HAS JOKES.

Why else, on my way to the rental property from the grocery store, would I be sitting at a streetlight watching Daisy and Duke take their seats on the outdoor patio at a corner restaurant? The corner table, naturally. I'm sure Duke asked for it, so everybody could see him. Always showing off, always posturing, *preening*.

Fucking peacock.

The light turns green and I switch the brake for the gas pedal. Just to be a real dick, I lean on the pedal a little heavier than necessary, gunning the engine. Daisy glances over, gaze landing directly on me through the windshield. Recognition lights in her eyes. Surprise races through me for the shortest second until I remember she's not really recognizing me, or at least not who I really am.

The moment passes and then they are gone, growing smaller and smaller in my rearview. My resolve strengthens, growing and stretching. I will leave Daisy alone.

When I get home, a glance at my phone tells me I have a message from my old squad leader, Plato.

> Don't forget you promised to continue your physical therapy while you're gone.

Penn

> Did I promise that?

Literally. You literally said the words.

> Was I under the influence?

Get your ass to PT while you're there.
That's an order.

Chapter 9

Daisy

"New patient today," Isla says, brown bob partially covering one cheek as she sticks her head in my small office. Her neon yellow nails grip the doorframe. Isla has been my office manager/assistant/work companion for approximately eight months. A single forty-four year old mother of two teenagers, Isla is flighty and scattered, but there's something about her I find incredibly endearing. "Name is—" she straightens, glancing down at the office iPad. "Bravo."

I breathe a short, disbelieving laugh into the half-full coffee cup poised at my lips. "Bravo?"

Isla shrugs. "That's what he said when he called yesterday. I'm not sure if it's his last name, or his first name. That's all he said."

"Sounds fake. Did you collect his insurance info?"

"He said he was self-pay." She taps a nail on the top edge of the tablet. "I think it sounds cool. With that name, you almost have to become a spy, or an actor on Broadway, or someone who jumps out of airplanes."

I lean back in my ergonomic and also astronomically expensive desk chair. "You have a great imagination."

Isla steps into the small space and flicks a finger on the Alice Cooper bobblehead on the end of my desk, making it dance. A gag gift from Vivi six years ago, this bobblehead is a reminder of a carefree time in our lives, when we sang *School's Out* at the close of every school year.

Isla gives Alice's head a follow-up flick and asks, "Should we put my great imagination to the test and dream up what somebody named Bravo might look like?"

I shake my head firmly. "If we were sitting in King's Ransom or Pour Me having a cocktail, I'd say yes. But since we're *at work*"—I deliver a pointed look—"it would be very unprofessional to talk about a client that way."

Isla sighs dramatically. "You're right. Damn it."

"Maybe you should spend a weekend in Phoenix." I turn back to my computer screen. "Far more fish in the sea. Or, desert."

"I don't know," she drawls, "Hugo De la Vega is looking mighty good these days. I would let him do questionable things in my presence. With or without that fencing outfit on."

My cheeks puff out as I pretend to barf. "Please, Isla. That man is basically a brother to me. His sister is my best friend."

"Good thing I'm not saddled with either of those afflictions." She looks at me pointedly. "And good thing you snatched up one of the last eligible bachelors in this one-horse town."

My eyebrows pinch in confusion for what can't be more than a nanosecond, but Isla catches it. "Duke," she says, with a *what the hell is wrong with you* undertone.

I roll my eyes to make up for my faux pas. "Obviously. I'm just a little slow today. Didn't sleep well last night."

Isla's eyebrows pop and flex. "Duke kept you up until all hours of the night delivering mind-blowing orgasms?"

I stare at her long and hard, no expression save for the grim line of my mouth. Isla has a lengthy history prodding relentlessly for juicy details about my sex life. She never seems to tire, or become discouraged by my total refusal. At this point, I think she sees my sewn lips as a challenge.

She grins. "Bravo will be here in an hour. Like it or not, I will spend the next sixty minutes giving him a total makeover in my mind. By the time my brain is finished with him, he'll be a tall, tan, rippling stick of man candy."

I open my mouth to chide her *again* for sexualizing my patient, but she's already disappeared back the way she came, and she forgot to leave the iPad with the new client information for me to look over.

Briefly I consider texting Hugo and requesting his new-to-town friend's last name. But then he'll ask why I want to know, and it'll go from there, and I don't want to start a conversation that ends with me explaining why I was hiding out when I should've been at my engagement party. Also, I don't like the feeling of knowing things about people before they've shared them with me, especially when I have no reason to dig.

This Bravo guy is probably somebody's cantankerous old grandpa.

I don't have time to think about it, because my next client, a sweet seventy-two-year-old woman recovering from hip surgery, has just walked in the door. If I'm lucky, I'll have five minutes between clients to scarf down a muffin I grabbed from Sweet Nothings on my way to work this morning.

※ ❀ ※ ❀ ※

"Gird your loins," Isla mutters as she waltzes into the kitchenette on the other side of my office. It's just big enough for a small fridge, microwave, and bistro table. "Bravo has arrived."

I swallow down the last of my poppyseed muffin. "Why?" I whisper, alarmed. "Did Bravo behave badly?" I won't hesitate to eject someone if they display objective behavior toward my assistant.

"My loins are"—she positions her hands in front of her lower stomach and makes frantic motions—"doing this right now."

I relax. I don't have to bounce anybody from my office. Except Isla herself if she doesn't take an ice bath, stat. "Isla, that saying doesn't mean what you think it means. And for the love, stop talking about a patient that way."

She makes a face like *oops* and drops theatrically into a chair. "I'm sorry, ok? Just wait until you start menopause."

I pull a confused face. "What does that have to do with anything?"

She gestures the length of her body. "Estrogen and progesterone dip, and testosterone starts flexing and strutting around. There's a horny teenager living inside me right now." She presses the iPad into my hands. "There's even a name for it. It's called the 'Sex surge.'"

"Ohh my."

"Yeah," she nods, pointing a neon nail my way. "Just you wait, youngin."

I'm not sure how to respond, but I manage a *sorry to hear about your issue* and dart away.

Isla has led Bravo into the consultation room. It's a small space, enough room for a 3x5 gunmetal gray desk and two white leather chairs. The largest wall is windowed, looking out on the main area and all the equipment. The wall opposite boasts framed inspirational quotes.

A little progress each day adds up to big results.

When you think about quitting, consider why you started.

A dream becomes reality through sweat, determination, and hard work.

A snake plant in the corner keeps the space from looking too aseptic, but beyond that, it's boring.

Penn

For the life of me, I cannot figure out why I *sorta kinda maybe* want this Bravo guy to be the Peter guy from my engagement party. It's not a stretch, is it? Olive Township is a small town, but it's ever-growing, constantly adding to its population. Tourists flock here from that viral travel article, calling our little hamlet a *Jewel in the desert*. Once they arrive, they see the author was right. They fall in love with our eclectic vibe, our white stucco store façades, our little honor system store *Inconceivable!* with its unmanned old-fashioned cash register for payment.

A few steps to the left, and Bravo comes into view. Even folded into a seat with his back to me, I recognize those broad shoulders, the gentle slope.

It's him.

My throat takes on the attributes of the dry, dusty desert outside as I propel myself forward, catching sight of myself briefly in a windowed reflection. I'm a mess.

I coax back flyaways, swipe at muffin crumbs on my chest.

Muffin! Poppy seeds, also known as *tiny hell raisers,* are probably lodged in my teeth.

I steer right, filling a paper cup of filtered water from the little machine in the corner and swishing. Then I take a deep breath to quell my nerves.

Oh-kay. Loins are girded. Shoulders are straight. This is my town, and my business. I've got this.

"Bravo," I say smoothly, sailing into the small room. "*Peter* Bravo."

His gaze snaps to mine. Surprise parks itself in those

turbulent irises, and is that a flicker of *horror*? Why? It's unexpected, shaking my confidence a smidge.

There's no way he had a look of horror. I'm misreading his emotions. The last words he said to me float through my mind. *You don't know me, Daisy St. James, so don't go assuming you can read my body language.*

Corralling my unease, I take the seat opposite him. "I didn't take you for a last name only kind of guy, but with a last name like Bravo, I see why you would go that route."

His hand, palm resting on the table top, flexes. "It's no St. James, but it'll do." His voice is deep, gruff, smoky, like he's recently spent time around a campfire.

The comment sparks confusion, and curiosity, in me. Does he already know what my last name means to this town? Perhaps Hugo filled him in.

Balanced on the tip of my tongue is the question of why he shot daggers my way in front of that house yesterday. On its heels is the question of why he left so abruptly two nights ago. It would be unprofessional of me to ask, and also, it doesn't matter. Because this guy, Peter Bravo, doesn't matter. I mean, I'm sure he does somewhere, to somebody. But not to me. Not in the long term.

In the short term, however, he is my client. At least, I'm assuming so. That's why he's here, right? Physical therapy. Clearly I should've completed at least one minute of due diligence before whipping in here. My eyes fall to the iPad, lying haphazardly on the table in front of me.

Penn

"So," I begin, adopting a detached, but friendly, tone. "What brings you to my office today?"

His eyes squint, regarding me with laser-like focus. He leans forward, hands clasped on the desk. Tattoos I could not make out two nights ago are on full display now.

A frog skeleton, wrapped in—

I swallow my gasp.

No way.

Daisies?

A coincidence. It must be. I mean, it definitely couldn't be anything but. We're perfect strangers. Or nearly, anyway.

Strangers who shared the same champagne bottle, a hell of a sunset, and some terse words on engagements. But strangers, nonetheless.

And now, very likely, my patient.

"What's wrong with you?"

His question snaps me from my thoughts. "What do you mean *what's wrong with me?*" I hear my tone, how affronted I sound. I have got to rein that in. What is it with me around this guy?

"You're making a face."

"I'm not making a face," I say, pleasant this time. I gesture vertically, the same length as my face. "This is just my face."

He points at me, one long, masculine finger held aloft between us. "Now it is, but it wasn't before."

I stare him down, trying to come up with any plausible excuse for why I made whatever face it was I was making. He stares right back, and I'm starting to think this guy's superhuman strength is stubbornness.

I sigh, forgetting myself yet again. "Are you going to let this go and allow me to do my job?"

"One hundred percent no."

I sigh once more, adding a deep grumble to it so he will know how absolutely aggrieved I am. He did tell me to feel whatever I wanted to feel around him.

"The answer is still no," he says. "It doesn't matter how many times you sigh."

"What if I sigh until I pass out?"

"That's not a thing." He crosses his arms, and it does something to his biceps and pectorals I'm trying very hard not to notice.

"Sure it is."

He smirks, and dammit if it isn't obnoxiously adorable. "Where did you get that little fact?"

"From the fact fairy," I say loftily.

It works. He breaks. He *laughs*.

Deep and rumbly, settling into my bones in a delicious way that brings with it discomfort. Because this man's laugh should not be delicious, or yummy, or any other food based adjective. It should be a zero. A nothing burger. A non-event.

"Anyway," I say forcefully, tapping the iPad screen. It comes to life, and I tap until I've reached the patient file labeled *Bravo*.

"You didn't give my assistant much to write about," I say, skimming the notes Isla entered. Aloud, I recite what it says. "Patient is nearing the end of progressive strengthening, and is ready to begin advanced rehabilitation." I stop, giving him the chance to add to it, to fill in details about how he was injured, and what exactly it is he's rehabilitating from, but he doesn't say anything. "Ahh. The stoic, military type."

He frowns. "Did the fact fairy also tell you I was in the military? Because I know I did not offer that information when I called to make this appointment."

I bite the inside of my lower lip to keep from laughing. "No. Your tattoo told on you."

He uncrosses his arms, holding his right arm out to appraise his inked forearm. "The flowers?" With the tip of one finger, he outlines a daisy. "This one right here? One of these basic, nondescript, typical flowers? The kind that are found anywhere?"

Does he want me to ask what kind of flowers those are? Because it really feels that way. But of course, I already know by sight the flower I'm named after. It feels like he knows I already know, but for some reason he wants me to ask. Which means I absolutely will not be asking, not only because I already know the answer, but also because I do not want to give him the satisfaction.

"One hundred percent no." It's my turn to smirk.

He drops his forearm on the table, poking at the frog skeleton. "I was a Navy SEAL."

There we go. A morsel. A little nugget of information from this otherwise tight-lipped man.

"Was?"

He nods. "I got a little too froggy."

A grin bends my lips. It's not a real grin, like I'm genuinely smiling, but more like *I understand.*

"Tell me more."

"A service-connected injury while on a mission. Our team was ambushed while we were setting up an explosive, and it detonated before we were clear of the area. I was luckier than some." He looks down. "Several broken ribs, and shrapnel. A little nerve damage." He makes a circular motion on the left side of his midsection.

I do my damndest not to show the distress sweeping through me. I can only begin to imagine the fear that accompanied his experience. "Surgery?"

He nods. "To repair the damaged nerves."

"In the torso?"

He nods again, and I add *Peripheral nerve surgery* to his notes.

"Thank you for your service," I say, to which he offers a small nod of his head. I ask more questions, mostly about timeline and what he remembers doing when he first started physical therapy. There are holes in his memory, which isn't uncommon for somebody who has undergone extensive treatment and physical therapy. It's hard to remember dates, times, names of exercises, especially when they consist of unfamiliar words.

"We can start with stretches for today while I put together a treatment plan. Does that work for you?"

"I guess so." Peter pushes back from the table. "I've started running again."

My brows knit. "Is that advisable?"

He shrugs. "Sometimes it hurts."

"Where?"

He points to his midsection.

"You might not be ready to run."

"I don't care," he says stubbornly. "I need to do something. And Slim Jim needs the exercise."

"Slim Jim? Like the highly processed, very salty meat stick from the gas station?"

"No."

My next thought, which is totally unacceptable, unprofessional, and impolite is *please tell me that's not your nickname for your dick.*

Wow. Isla is rubbing off on me.

I'll take the bait. "Who's Slim Jim?"

"My dog."

"Right," I nod, remembering the big animal I saw in his vehicle. "He was waiting for you in your truck."

It's the first mention of our interaction. Peter eyes me tentatively. "Man's best friend."

A pang of sadness seizes my heart. Peter has more to his story than appears at first glance, but then I suppose most of us do. From the outside, I look like the town's golden girl preparing to marry the town's golden boy.

It's so wrong, it's almost laughable.

"Let's start those stretches, if you're ok with that."

Peter follows me out to the large open space. "If you're going to insist on running"—I frown to let him know I'm not particularly happy with his choice—"let's at least get you properly stretched so we can reduce your pain, and help you avoid injuries elsewhere."

I take him through basic dynamic stretches to warm up the main muscle groups, doing them alongside him. "I like to run too, and I haven't stretched yet today."

"Do you run with somebody?" There's a gruffness to his voice.

"I usually run alone, in the early morning. I like getting out before the town is awake."

He looks askance at me, head tipping down slightly. "It's not safe for you to run by yourself."

"You're new in town, so you probably don't realize this, but Olive Township is safe. Low crime."

He follows me into the next position, a full-length stretch that requires Peter to follow me onto all fours. I demonstrate for him how to tuck his toes and lift his knees, coming into a full leg extension. He copies me, and from his almost upside down position, says, "Crime doesn't have a zip code, Daisy." He looks at me meaningfully, like he's determined to drive home his point.

Annoyance flares, especially because he's right. I feel safe here, but bad things have happened. It's been a long time, but Hugo and Vivi's dad was murdered right here in Olive Township, on a road just off the main part of town.

"Pedal your legs," I instruct.

Peter listens, but says, "Why doesn't that fiancé of yours run with you?"

Because he's a workaholic, and he's on calls early in the morning, up and working with people on the East Coast.

"He has a home gym he works out in before he starts his calls." I say it flippantly, like it's no bother. It really doesn't bother me, but it obviously makes Peter think poorly of Duke, and for some reason, that's what bothers me.

We straighten, and that's when I notice Peter working the side of his bottom lip with his teeth.

"What?" I challenge. "You have opinions about fiancés, and me running by myself?"

Peter doesn't say anything, but he looks like he wants to. I decide against prodding him to say whatever it is he's thinking, because I don't want to hear it. Nothing nice could possibly come from an expression like the one he wears.

And that tiny but persistent feeling of appreciation over Peter's protectiveness? I'll be ignoring that, as well. I absolutely do *not* like the way Peter seems irritated by the idea of me running alone. It doesn't make me feel cared for, AT ALL. Not in the least.

Peter has one shoulder lifted higher than the other, and it negates the point of stretching if he keeps one side locked up. Using a light touch, I reach out to adjust his positioning, but when my fingers touch him, he flinches as if I've burned him.

His repentant eyes find my curious, and I'll admit it, hurt gaze. "Sorry about that," he says, brusque.

"It's fine," I answer, plastering on a smile.

"Don't do that," he says quickly.

I blink, smile wavering. "Do what?"

"I'd rather see you scowl for real than smile for show."

Oh.

I clear my throat, because what else is there to do?

This man, *this stranger*, sees through me as if I'm made of something sheer. It's unnerving and confusing.

We move through the remainder of the appointment, and Peter keeps his eyes cast down as he focuses on his stretching. He says nothing. Absolutely nothing.

He has gone radio silent, but I am full of questions, all of which I will not ask.

Did Penn hire you?

How well do you know him?

Depending on his answers, more questions.

Has Penn ever mentioned me?

I want to know, and I don't want to know in equal measure. The answers will lead to more feelings, very likely not great ones, and I've done such a good job keeping myself numb towards Penn for years. I need to stay that way, even with the unexpected presence of this newcomer to town, to my life, to my job.

I carved Penn out of my heart, banishing that piece of him to the depths, and I made a life for myself. I'm marrying Duke in a little more than a month. Whether or not I love him feels irrelevant at this point.

I cannot look back. The past is where all that, including Penn, should stay.

Feeling reinvigorated by my determination, I continue our session by showing Peter specific stretches that will help warm up the smaller muscles. We finish with rolling out his fascia, which is also a low-key form of torture.

"I've done a lot of tough shit," he grunts, moving the backs of his thighs over the foam roller, "this ranks up there as being almost unbearable." He's grimacing, but almost everybody does. Me included.

"You can do hard things," I tell him, and he tosses me a look that plainly says *come the fuck on.*

"You should put that on your wall," he quips, thumbing back toward the small room where we had our consult.

"Maybe I will," I say, reaching under him and sliding the roller out from under his bent knees.

I reach out a hand, offering to help him up. His eyebrows tug in determination, and he chooses not to take the help, using momentum to roll up onto the balls of his feet and stand upright.

I look at him knowingly. "How much did that hurt your torso when you used your ab muscles for that maneuver?"

He drops the act, grimacing. "Like Chucky was in my stomach."

"That's what I thought." I work my hair back into the hair tie I had around my wrist. "Next session, I'll be ready for you. I'll know everything you've been working on, and I'll have a game plan. Arrive ready to work."

He gives me a playful and unofficial salute, and offers Isla a short wave on his way out the door.

"I hope you know how lucky you are," Isla says, fanning herself.

"He's an attractive man," I say in a carefree voice. "That's all. The world has plenty of them."

I hurry next-door to use the bathroom we share with the spa before my next client arrives. Peter's face, his hesitance to offer details about himself, and his readiness when it comes to teasing me, it all sits at the forefront of my mind.

Sure, he's an attractive man. But something tells me there is so much more to him.

Chapter 10

Penn

"You all set, buddy?"

Slim Jim sits on his haunches, staring at me with that intense gaze. It's 6:14 in the morning, but Slim Jim is ready for anything. Everything. He could scale a ten-foot block wall right now if I gave the command. He is fast like a bullet and just as deadly. An assassin on four legs. Unbelievable, this dog.

I finish my pre-run electrolyte water, then clip a leash to Slim Jim's utility vest. In large, white-stitched letters on either side of his vest, is the directive DO NOT PET. And still, invariably, some well-meaning and air-headed doofus will reach a hand out to him. Slim Jim's a good dog, and not dangerous to anyone who isn't a criminal or trying to inflict harm, but he's not up for snuggles. He's a work dog, and his favorite thing in the world is to have a job to do. Everything Slim Jim does is a fulfillment of everything he was made to do.

Unlike Paper Towel Duke.

Slim Jim and I slip out the side gate, and I spend a short minute looking over the chalk drawings on my driveway. Some neighborhood kids cornered me yesterday when I was getting out of my car, asking if they could use it to draw on. The smallest kid, smiley and gap-toothed, informed me he'd already filled up his driveway. I'd told them to have at it.

Slim Jim and I set off, his big paws hitting the sidewalk with soft thuds in a comforting cadence.

She's marrying Duke.

We come to a break in the road, turning right onto a road that will eventually lead to the main drag through town.

Slim Jim keeps perfectly in line with me, never falling behind and never attempting to lead.

What the hell does she see in the guy? Their families were always close, the moms in book club and serving on the Olive Township restoration society. The dads tolerated each other, from what I could tell. Duke has two siblings, but for the St. James family there is only Daisy. Duke and Daisy were friends because of their families' connection to one another.

When did Duke go from friend to fiancé?

The question gnaws at me, its barbs tearing at my insides as it races around my body. My trainers smack the pavement as I pick up speed. My heart batters my breast bone, my breath heating and tearing at my throat.

I had no idea she was going to be my physical therapist, or that she owned the practice. It was only all those years of being a SEAL, of learning how to conceal

Penn

surprise, that kept me in my seat when she walked in that tiny room. Her assistant, Isla, said not a word about the name of the person I was making an appointment with.

Fuck, but that was difficult. Being next to her, enveloped in her scent that is fist-bitingly luscious (plum, I'm almost positive, and maybe a little vanilla), and then she adjusted me and I thought I was going to come out of my skin. Her touch, electric and heady, overwhelmed me. Seeing her for my next appointments might end me. Survival is unlikely at this point.

Here lies the motherfucker who pretended not to be Penn Bellamy.

The thing is, I don't have to stay here. I could leave tomorrow. Today, for that matter.

I don't have to subject myself to this. Or Daisy, to me. To what it might do to her if she finds out I am not Peter Bravo, but Penn from her childhood.

Or you could be honest with her.

It's Hugo's voice in my ear. Hugo's advice from the second I called him and told him I would be returning to deal with the house.

What should I do about Daisy? I'd asked.

Tell her you're coming, he'd deadpanned.

For Hugo, honesty is paramount. Maybe it's all the sword fighting, all that upright posture and civility. Or maybe it's the fact his family is almost as influential as Daisy's and Duke's. Hugo has never been the poor kid in the ramshackle house with the catatonic mother. He's never been forced to make hard choices, the kind that hurt others at the expense of keeping yourself and your parent alive.

I pause on Olive Avenue, the main street running through the town. Shops line either side, two traffic lights placed equal distances on the long street. My gaze pulls to the far end, the second shop in on the left. The scene of the car accident. Fifteen years have passed, and still I hear the crunch of metal, the protesting screech of tires, glass breaking. Daisy's scream weaving through it all, and then, even worse, her silence.

I know I'm supposed to be kind to my younger self, but really, what the fuck was I thinking taking my mom's car when I was thirteen?

I take off at a faster pace, running hard all the way down the street, forcing myself to cross and run on the sidewalk I drove over as a kid.

Exhausted, I stop, hands on my knees as I gulp large lungfuls of air. I've been sprinting without meaning to. Slim Jim stares up at me, barely winded and waiting for whatever I say to do next. He's practically a machine, unlike me. Frail and fallible, even when I wish I weren't.

Though Slim Jim would go and go and never let on he has needs, I look around for water. A few stores down, an old man holds tight to a broom, sweeping the sidewalk with slow, fluid strokes.

Slim Jim and I head his direction. "Excuse me, sir?" I say as we approach. He pauses, bringing himself as upright as his slightly stooped posture allows.

Recognition fires through me. My mind had been so preoccupied while running that I hadn't realized where I was. *Sweet Nothings*. A bakery operated by Sal and Adela Kingman, a couple who, on more than one occasion, set aside day-old donuts and other sweets and charged me a single dollar for it all.

Did Sal and Adela know how their kindness affected me? How they were sometimes the reason I ate that day?

"What can I do for you, young man?" Sal's gnarled voice spans the two squares of sidewalk separating us.

Unsure of Sal's response to dogs, especially ones who look like Slim Jim, I choose to keep the polite distance. Assuming he's hard of hearing, I raise my voice and ask, "Are you open? I was hoping to buy a bottle of water for my dog."

Sal frowns. "I'm right here, boy. You don't need to yell."

I tuck back my laugh, in case he decides to take offense to that, too. "Yes, sir."

He waves a hand. "Give me a second." He turns, his well-worn jeans pulled up an inch too high, hugging his waist at an unnatural point. Behind Sal's fluffy white head of hair, nearly a half block away, a figure appears around the corner.

Long blonde hair swings back and forth with the cadence of her jog. Her arms pump, the motion fluid, as beautiful as any piece of music nearing its crescendo. It's not the brick red leggings and black sports bra, though I'm not complaining about the outfit wrapped like a second-skin on her body. It's just...*her*. She has never stopped being the most beautiful sight I've ever had the privilege of placing my eyes upon.

The moment Daisy clocks me is obvious. She falters, but only slightly. Her eyes narrow, a determined set to her perfectly arched eyebrows, and she closes the space between us.

Why did God make her this beautiful? Was it not enough that she is funny and playful and kind and all-around the best person I've ever met?

My heart lurches just looking at her, as if it's reaching for her. Wanting her.

Daisy stops on the sidewalk a few feet away, gaze switching from me to Slim Jim. Wariness peeks from her eyes, but I can see she's trying to hide it. Or ignore it.

For some reason, that makes me furious. Who turned her into this pod person? Empty, devoid of her fire?

Duke. This is his fault. If he didn't do it, he's still responsible because he's letting it exist. He's not encouraging her authenticity. That fucker.

"Hello," Daisy chirps, far too chipper for both the time of day and the way we left things yesterday. As much as I want to keep her at arm's length, I'm not interested in watching the hurt and confusion take over those pretty brown eyes every time my response is gruff.

"Good morning," I answer, making my voice friendly. Maybe too friendly, given the way Daisy's eyes have narrowed suspiciously.

"I didn't realize you have a bodyguard," Daisy says, nodding down at Slim Jim.

Slim Jim looks every bit the bodyguard with the way he's seated in front of my legs, expression serious.

"He's actually a goofball, but he hides it." With two fingers I scratch under his chin. There is no motion to show he enjoys it, only the maintaining of intense eye contact. "Right now he's coming off as a bit of a standoffish asshole."

"You, or the dog?" Daisy's eyes fly open, her hand covering her mouth with a dull *thwap*.

"There it is," I say, at the same time she says, "I'm sorry."

"For what?" I ask, at the same time she asks, "There's what?"

We fall quiet, waiting for the other to speak, and then we exchange quiet laughter.

"Ladies first." I wave my hand, motioning like the floor is hers.

Her head tips an inch, sunlight spilling over her honeyed tresses. "You said 'there it is.' What were you talking about?"

"Your fire."

"I don't have fire."

"Sure you do. I remember that very well from a couple nights ago."

Her pretty mouth twists. She doesn't believe me. Or, and this is more likely, she doesn't want to believe me. Doesn't want to entertain the possibility, because the outcome isn't one she'd like to face.

She looks so uncomfortable that I let it drop. "Were you apologizing for calling me a standoffish asshole?"

She eyes me for a solid two seconds, then I see it in her eyes. A spark.

"Actually, I was apologizing to your dog." Her cheekbones lift, her smile mischievous.

Something in my chest rejoices.

It's me, Penn.

How I wish I could shout the words.

I bend my ear to Slim Jim. "What's that?" I cock my head like I'm listening, then straighten. "He says he accepts your apology."

"How gracious of him. Now, I—"

Sal shuffles from the store. He's carrying a metal bowl and a bottle of water, a paper bag clutched in his opposite hand.

"Good morning, Daisy. Saw you out here, so I asked Adela to get your mother's order prepared."

Daisy sends a million dollar smile his way. What would I give to be on the receiving end of one of those?

My last almond Snickers bar?

All future ability to call Hugo rude names?

The option to block telemarketers?

The answer is obvious and immediate. *All three.*

"How's that wedding planning coming along?" Sal asks Daisy. Without waiting for an answer, he adds, "You sure looked beautiful at your engagement party."

Air streams tersely from my nose, earning me pinched eyebrows from Daisy before she turns back to Sal. "You're sweet. Nothing layers of makeup and plenty of hairspray can't accomplish."

Sal hands the bowl and water bottle out to me. I busy myself with filling the dish for Slim Jim, and Sal presses on about the wedding. "Kathleen says you went with the chocolate cake and the Grand Marnier frosting."

That gets my attention. Unless something has changed, chocolate is Daisy's least favorite cake flavor.

It shouldn't matter, but it does. It most definitely shouldn't matter *to me*, but it does.

It's cake. Who the fuck cares?

"Hmm?" Daisy says in response to Sal, her far-off tone taking my attention from Slim Jim and his water.

She's staring at me. At the scars on my rib cage, cascading down and across the right part of my stomach. Raised and mottled and lumpy.

Fucking ugly, and an even worse reminder of what I went through.

My pulse picks up, my mouth runs dry.

Daisy's wide eyes meet mine, her question floating right there on the surface.

An inexplicable anger slices through me. Daisy and I used to run around barefoot and see how long we could stand the heat of the pavement in the summer, daring the other to cave first. We ate ice cream cones as fast as possible, then moaned until the brain freeze wore off. Now I'm scarred in more ways than one, and Daisy's pretending like her feelings and preferences are something to suppress. How did we get from there to here?

Sal's gravelly voice continues on, repeating his comment about the cake Daisy chose, but it's background noise for me.

Retrieving my T-shirt from my pocket, I slip it over my head and thread my arms through. "Slim Jim and I are going to get going." I flip over the remaining water from the bowl into a nearby planter and hand it to the old man. "Thank you for the water, Sal."

I don't have a parting word for Daisy. I can't. I just *can't*.

Slim Jim and I take off. I feel Sal and Daisy's eyes on my back, so I peel off the main street at the first chance I get, lengthening my route back to the house where I'm staying.

Not that it matters. Nothing matters.

Daisy is marrying Duke.

Daisy has seen my scars.

It's me, Penn.

Chapter 11
Daisy

My eyes linger on the street for a moment after Peter disappears around the corner.

Those scars on his side, trailing off to his stomach, I've never seen scars like that before. And then the look in his eyes when he saw me see them, the way he shuttered. The guy is an emotional fortress, but he was standing here with us, early morning sun increasing its grasp on the street and stores, and for a brief moment he looked relaxed. Almost *playful*, gently chiding me about my internal fire.

"I don't remember telling him my name."

Tearing my gaze away from the empty street, I turn my attention to Sal. "I must have said it when you were still inside the store." I can't remember if I did, or didn't. Everything from the last ten minutes feels fuzzy around the edges. Rarely do I interact with anybody but Sal or Adela on my morning runs, when I stop here and get something for my mother. Her appetite has been slowly dwindling, but if I bring her something from Sweet Nothings, she'll eat it. Or pick at it, at least.

Sal leans on his broom, staring into the now-empty trail blazed by Peter, eyes screwed up in curiosity.

Gently, I touch his shoulder. He is frail under my hand, his shoulder smaller than it appears in his shirt. "Are you ok?"

My question finally gets Sal's attention. "Does that boy look familiar to you?" he asks.

Peter's face flashes to the front of my mind. The straight nose, rugged jawline covered in a swath of stubble that wasn't there yesterday. The way he immediately struck me as familiar, like my heart knew him, but my brain did not.

"Maybe he has one of those faces, you know?"

Sal grumbles, dissatisfied with what I've said. "Nah." He starts sweeping, and I take it as my cue to go. "There's something about him. He's dead inside, but only mostly."

Has Sal been spending time with Crazy Cliff?

It must've been a joke that I missed, so I smile and ask, "Mostly dead?"

Sal does not pause his sweeping efforts when he responds with, "Better to be mostly dead than all dead."

"True," I agree slowly. Ok, yeah. Sal's been getting into the wacky tobacky with Cliff. Adela sometimes bakes it into treats for my mom.

Lifting the paper bag, I say, "Thanks again for the chocolate croissant."

"Adela threw one in for you, too."

"Not the extra-special kind, I hope." I made that

mistake once, and I swear there were elephants dancing behind my closed eyes.

Sal guffaws. "No, no. The only high from these will be from sugar."

I search through the glass front window until I see Adela behind the register, and when she looks over, I give her a wave and blow her a kiss. She returns the sentiment, and I pivot to leave Sal to his work.

Mumbled words behind me pull me back around. "What was that?"

"You didn't say my name. To that boy. At least not in front of me, you didn't."

I nod at his insistence. "Have a nice day, Sal."

I start for my house, and the further I go, the more clarity I have. And here's the thing. I am positive I didn't say Sal's name to Peter.

There are other ways he could've known it.

But...

Call it women's intuition, call it a sixth sense, but something about Peter Bravo's story isn't adding up.

Chapter 12

Daisy

"Peter's an old friend," Hugo says, breathing heavily into the phone. He answered my call in the middle of rearranging tables at Dama Oliva, Vivi's restaurant in town, and informed me he would not be taking a break because *"My sister aka your best friend is a power hungry egomaniac who is also too poor to hire real help and she has forced me here against my will."*

The phone must've been on speaker, because Vivi's voice not so kindly reminded Hugo that she's providing him with dinner, and she expects him to sing for it.

"How old of a friend is he?" I prod Hugo, frowning at my phone screen as I switch it to speaker and lay it on my desk. I'm in between clients, and I thought I'd use the time to look a little deeper into Peter Bravo. I've been unable to think of little else since running into him at Sweet Nothings, the thoughts parading back and forth in my mind until the gentle pushing turned to shoving and I finally picked up the phone.

Penn

I don't know what I was expecting from Hugo, but it wasn't cryptic responses. Hugo is not the strong, silent type. In fact, he can be quite the chatterbox. So his reticence right now is sparking suspicion in me.

"Umm, I don't know. We go way back." Hugo grunts with exertion, the loud sound of something heavy sliding across the floor filters across our connection. "When did you meet him?"

"I took a walk at Summerhill the night of my engagement party, just to, uh, get a break from all the well wishes." I better watch what I say. This is supposed to be a fact-finding mission, not a tell-all about myself. "Peter was there, parked behind one of the other buildings."

"Peter was at Summerhill?"

"Yeah. You didn't know he was there? That's when I met him for the first time."

"There's been more than one time?"

"He came to see me for a physical therapy appointment yesterday, and my curiosity was piqued. So I called you."

"Hold up," Vivi instructs, her voice coming through louder than before. I picture her standing next to the phone, arms crossed as her brain shifts the puzzle pieces into place. "The tall drink of water the old ladies turned into horn dogs over is the same guy who came to a physical therapy appointment with you yesterday? But you already knew him from your engagement party?"

"Correct."

"And you know him?"

This question is not directed at me, but I answer for Hugo. "Apparently they go way back."

"You go way back? No you don't." Vivi has adopted her bossy sister tone. "I know all your friends."

On this, I am silent.

"I have friends besides Ambrose," Hugo says in that annoyed tone a brother reserves for his sister.

"Who?" Vivi challenges, in a voice that clearly says *No you do not*.

"You know I've traveled the world, right?" Hugo sounds like he is finished with his sister's sass. "I've made friends you've never heard of. I have a gold medal."

"Pfft." Vivi scoffs so vehemently, I hear it clearly through the phone. "I'll bet it's made out of chocolate and wrapped in gold foil."

"Bite it and find out."

Their sibling banter incites a hollow feeling in my stomach. I don't have siblings, and when my mother goes, it'll just be me and my dad. I'll have Vivi, of course, but it's not exactly the same.

And Duke.

Shit. Right. I really need to stop doing that. Note to self: the man is going to be my husband in about a month.

"De la Vega siblings," I bark, using a tone I've heard from my mother over the years. "Pay attention to the subject at hand."

"Right," Vivi responds.

"Sorry," Hugo adds, sounding like he's talking through his teeth. Either he's fed up with his sister, or he's moving something heavy. He must take me off speaker, because all of a sudden his voice is coming through the phone, loud and clear.

"I met him at a K9 dog show in San Diego. I went out there to meet with a guy I was hoping would coach me for the Olympics, and I wandered into a dog show. He was there with some of his SEAL buddies."

"And you struck up a conversation and became best friends forever?"

"I—" Hugo starts, but I cut in.

"Here's the thing, Hugo. Peter Bravo does not strike me as the kind of guy who makes friends with perfect strangers. He's standoffish. There is literally nothing about him that advertises he is open to small talk with somebody he doesn't know, let alone enough conversation to become the basis of a friendship."

Hugo sighs. "Daisy, what do you want me to say? You asked me a question and I answered it."

It's very unlike Hugo to sound this annoyed, this *exhausted* with me. We've known each other a very long time, and well enough that I know these questions shouldn't get a response like this from him. If Vivi and I belting Kelis' *Milkshake* at the top of our lungs while dancing around the kitchen table where Hugo did homework never prompted an eye roll or sigh, pretty much nothing else should. This, in and of itself, is an additional tally on the side of reasons I have to be suspicious.

"Hugo Alexander De la Vega," I say in a warning tone.

In the background, Vivi crows, "Your ass just got middle-named by the sweetest person in town."

Now I'm happy I decided not to FaceTime, because there's no way I'd be able to hide the smile my best friend's verbal antics have put on my face.

Hugo ignores his sister. "Daisy, I promise you, I met him there. He was with his friends."

The line goes quiet. I think Hugo is waiting for the natural follow-up question, and as much as it hurts to talk about the boy who left me without a backwards glance, I dig down deep, put on my big girl panties, and ask the question we both know I want to ask. The real question I've been dancing around. The name I've been dancing around, but not daring to speak, for years. Peter was hired to come here and handle the house. *By who?* Only one answer makes sense.

"Was Penn one of the friends he was with? I mean, that must be how you met Peter, right? Through Penn?" And then, the question that's plaguing me. "Did you see him?"

"Yes. To all your questions." Relief breaks through in Hugo's tone. Almost like he's been dying to tell me. "You should know that I'm sorry, ok?" Across the connection comes the sound of a door closing, then water gurgling. It's the fountain in front of Dama Oliva, the weird one Vivi bought secondhand.

"What are you sorry for? Not telling me?"

A long silence, and then, "I suppose."

"I'm not upset with you. It's not like we had an agreement where you were supposed to tell me if you saw him, or heard from him." It would've been nice though, to know Penn is doing well. "Is he happy?"

Penn

I think this whole time I've been worrying that he wouldn't grow up happy, that his mother's problems would irrevocably alter him.

"Happy?" Hugo repeats, voice lifting on the second syllable like he hadn't considered this before. "I'm not sure if I would say he's happy."

The possibility saddens me. We haven't talked in more than a decade, but I still want to see Penn win. He deserves it, after the childhood he had.

"Look, Daisy," Hugo starts, and it's almost as if I can see him doing that thing he does when he gets frustrated where he runs the side of his finger over his eyebrow. "Penn might be happy. I'm not sure. He doesn't say one way or the other. But you are, right? You're planning a wedding to someone you've been friends with your entire life. The whole town wants to be in your bridal party. The only time you'll make people happier than they are now is when you and Duke announce you're having a baby, should you decide to."

A baby. I can't even begin to think about a child. Not because I don't want children, because I actually do. Hugo's comment is making me realize Duke and I need to have a conversation ASAP.

"You're right," I tell Hugo. "Of course you are. Voice of reason, and all that." Hugo has always been level-headed and pragmatic.

"Everything will work out," Hugo reassures. "Peter will be here long enough to tie up loose ends on the Bellamy house, and then he'll be on his way back to San Diego."

And Penn. Back to San Diego *where Penn lives*.

"Oh, I almost forgot," Hugo adds. "I hired an event coordinator last week. She said to ask you about flowers. She said you haven't chosen any yet."

"Daisies," I answer automatically.

"Because of your name," Hugo responds, in a sure tone that is both a question and an answer.

Peter's tattoo flashes in my mind. "Yep," I lie.

We say goodbye and hang up.

So now I know where Penn lives, and his profession. Like a desert pack rat depositing treasure into its midden, I tuck away the details.

I will not obsess.

I will not obsess.

I will not obsess.

Can a person obsess about not obsessing?

Chapter 13

Penn

HUGO:

Tell. Her.

TELL.

HER.

Chapter 14

Penn

My second physical therapy appointment is today, and I'm fighting the anticipation that has me hastening my morning routine. It's a dangerous feeling, this anticipation, but it's there, growing and stretching and filling my chest.

Daisy. Again. Daisy everyday since I drove back to this place. I could laugh at the previous version of me, from just last week. The me who thought I wouldn't see her when I was here. The me who was positive I'd hide out, be careful, slipping from proverbial shadow to shadow.

I'm a fool, of course. A fool for putting myself through this, for basking in her glow while knowing she's engaged.

I don't have to go to physical therapy, even though I promised Plato. It can wait until I return to San Diego. Except if I take away these appointments, I take away the times I'm scheduled to see Daisy. And, since I pre-scheduled my next five appointments, wouldn't that be rude?

Raise a flag, at the very least? When we're there, our roles are fixed. I'm her patient. That's it.

Daisy, it's me, Penn.

Hugo is pushing hard for me to come clean. It's not that I don't want to, especially when I look in Daisy's eyes, into her open and honest expression. Nothing can change what made me leave Olive Township, which means nothing can change the way I need to protect Daisy from knowing the truth, even now. I need Daisy to think of me fondly when she parses her past. I can't stomach it any other way.

So here I am, doubling down on my resolve. I will scowl my way through my appointment to mask that I pine for her in a way that's absolutely inappropriate when she's someone else's fiancée. Even if that person is Duke The Twat.

Honor among thieves, and all. And it's fucking depressing.

"Hi," Daisy says brightly when I walk in. She's standing at the small front desk area, and instead of exercise clothes like she had on at our first appointment, she's in light blue fitted scrubs. From what I can tell, she was doing a whole lot of nothing when I walked in. No phone, no tablet, no papers shuffling. It's like she was waiting for me. And damn if that doesn't make my chest swell.

I should really slap myself. This is Daisy I'm talking about. She makes every person she talks to feel like they are the most important person, the center of the world. It's one of her many talents. I am not special.

"Hey," I respond, my tone unnecessarily gruff.

"Ooh," Daisy volleys, unperturbed. "Are you a grumpy pants today?"

"No." I try to adjust my tone, but it's only marginally improved. Gruff *adjacent,* at best.

"Careful," Daisy teases. "You're about to come off as downright cheery."

My mouth twitches into a smile, a gleam stealing into Daisy's incredibly beautiful brown eyes. "Are we here to put my tone under a microscope, or work through my physical issues?"

"Physical issues," Daisy chirps, walking back to a contraption that looks a lot like a torture device.

"What is that?" I ask, eyeing it with trepidation. No matter what it is, I'd still take it over the foam roller.

"It's to stretch you out before we start." Daisy lies down on the padded table, hooking one of the straps around her thigh and demonstrating a stretch. "It doesn't bite."

"What a relief."

Daisy hops off the table, and when she does, I notice a bandage wrapped around her palm. Nodding at it, I ask, "Did you hurt yourself smacking your fiancé upside the head?"

Daisy gives me a look like she can't believe what I just said. To be honest, I can't believe I said it either. I've got to be better about not word vomiting my thoughts.

"Close," she says, patting the table to let me know she wants me to get on. "I was using a pry bar and I cut my hand."

Penn

Without thinking, I reach for her hand, intent on examining it myself. At the last second I think better of it, turning the maneuver into an awkward way to hoist myself onto the table.

Clearing my throat to cover up my supreme dumbassery, I ask, "Why were you using a pry bar?"

"To pry something."

"Oh, really?"

She lifts her eyebrows twice, affirming.

"Let me try this again," I start, but Daisy presses on my shoulder with a fingertip, trying to coax me down. I press back against her, refusing to lie down. "*What* were you prying that required the use of a pry bar?"

"My bathroom sink. Cabinet. Vanity *thing*. I don't know exactly what it's called."

She pokes at me again. Again I press back. She audibly sighs at me.

"Did you just weaponize a sigh?"

Daisy puts her hands on her hips. "I don't know why we're having this conversation. I hurt myself. People do it all the time, in varying degrees of severity. Have you never given yourself a paper cut, Peter Bravo?"

"Never," I respond solemnly.

She laughs. "Right, right. You just get yourself in a situation that requires you to need physical therapy."

"Paper cuts are for amateurs."

Instead of poking me, Daisy places her palm on my shoulder. It's warm, and comforting, and when she flexes her fingers, gripping me, I melt. Like a human popsicle, I dissolve into her touch, allowing her to gently guide me down. In a honeyed voice, she says, "Tell me what happened to you when you were serving. You said a little bit about it at our last appointment, but I'd like to know more. Why are you in physical therapy?"

I gave her the short version of my injury story before, but she's seen my scars, and she's curious. I get it.

She stands over me, an angel, so beautiful it hurts. I thought of her that day, when taking a breath felt like being stabbed, when my skin screamed with the sharp sting of lacerations, and the back of my head throbbed in reverberation.

"It was a maritime operation. The mission was to intercept arms smugglers who had also taken an American contractor hostage." I've talked about this so many times, recounted the events to military provided therapists, that it's no longer upsetting. It's become a recitation of events.

"I take it everything did not go as planned?" She threads the strap around my thigh.

"I'm not at liberty to give details."

Her brown eyes meet mine briefly before flitting away.

I have the urge to tell her as much as I can. For her to know me. "There was an explosion on the ship. We were supposed to be all-clear from the vessel before detonation, but it didn't work out that way." I point to the jagged line on my face, the scars hidden beneath the fabric of my shirt. The memories of that day aren't foggy, but it all happened quickly, and it's hard to focus on some aspects. "There was hand-to-hand combat, the broken ribs I already told you about. And then the explosion. I was concussed from the blow. Ended up in the water."

Daisy, who has been nodding along with my vague report, finally gives in and looks horrified. "The water? As in, the ocean?"

"Maritime, Daisy."

"I know you said that, but it didn't fully sink in. No pun intended." She smiles despite her dismay. "I can't believe you were a part of all that. I was here in this small town, doing whatever it was I was doing that day—"

"Night," I correct, though it was probably daytime for her.

"Night," she echoes, shocked. "You were in the ocean at night with broken ribs, concussed, and lacerated."

And I thought of you.

I saw her in my mind's eye, but it was thirteen-year-old Daisy. The way she looked the last time I saw her. I never looked her up on social media, not for lack of wanting to. Once, in a group photo posted by Hugo on his professional page, there was Daisy in the background. I clung to that image too, as I did my best to tread water in the dark sea, on a night shot through with stars. I told myself Daisy would be waiting for me on dry land. She'd be on base, or in the hospital, or in my living room. Though I knew it impossible, I clung to the falsehood. Daisy, and the lie I told myself, saved my life.

I was located and pulled to safety, and then the shock wore off and the pain took over. And now I'm here, in front of Daisy, breathing the same air. I know how I got here, but also, *how did I get here?*

"Paper cuts are most definitely for amateurs," Daisy says, bending my knee and crossing it over the opposite thigh.

I tap her wrist with a finger. "Tell me how you hurt yourself with a pry bar."

"I'm remodeling my master bathroom," she says reluctantly. "The sink is basically superglued to the wall, and I had to pry it off. I guess I pried a little too enthusiastically, and"—she lifts her bandaged hand—"this happened."

"Pry bars aren't known for cutting people. Bludgeoning, sure, but not slicing like a knife."

"Leave it to me," she shrugs, releasing my leg. She slips the strap around my opposite thigh, rounding the table to stand on the other side. "It slipped and there was enough force that when it grazed my palm, it cut me. It's not deep, but it's a tender area." She sighs, and this time it's not directed my way. "It'll make it harder for me to keep going on the remodel."

"So, a remodel, huh?" I ask as she guides me into another stretch.

"Yes." She quirks an eyebrow at me. "Why do you sound dubious?"

"Seems like a lot to take on. Wedding planning, remodeling"—I gesture around us—"running a business."

"I like to be busy." A defensive edge sharpens her tone.

"I'm not criticizing you," I say, gentling my voice. I'm dying to ask her if she still helps out on her parents farm, and at her mother's tea house.

"It wouldn't matter if you were," she says, chin lifting. "I know what I'm doing."

"Right." I point to her bandaged hand. "Looks like it."

She growls at me. Literally. Daisy fucking *growls*. It takes everything I have not to smile, pumping my fist in the air celebrating Daisy's authentic response. It's not that I want to celebrate her unhappiness, but her willingness to show me her genuine emotions elicits a feeling of pride in me. *That's right, it's me who she feels comfortable being herself with.*

"Anyway," she says, being less than gentle as she puts me in my next stretch.

My groin protests. "Daisy, I don't know if my body should—"

"You're fine, Sailor," she snaps.

Everything inside me seizes. Sweet Mother Of Dragons, did she just call me Sailor? And did I like it?

My body warms. Tingles. Blood pumping. Muscles swelling with the desire to be used. Oh yeah. I liked it. Probably too much.

She finishes torturing me, releasing my leg and stepping back while I sit up. She has me help her roll out yoga mats, and I eye them skeptically. "Yoga?"

"Core strength," she responds. "You need to work on it. I watched you run down the street the other day and noticed you hunch in, like you're protecting yourself. We're also going to work on upper back strength to help pull you up and correct your form."

"Whatever you say, boss." I ease off the table, stepping onto the top of the yoga mat to match Daisy's positioning.

I look down at her, waiting for instruction, and find her already looking at me. Seriousness overtakes her face, and she gazes at me in a way that makes me want to squirm. "What?"

Her head moves back and forth slowly, only a few inches in each direction. "It's stupid, but sometimes you seem familiar to me."

Rubbing the back of my neck with my hand, I mutter, "I wouldn't call it stupid." Remorse tears at me, hot and angry. I feel its chant, along with Hugo's, in stereo. *Tell her, tell her.* If I thought it was best for Daisy, I'd tell her who I really am in a heartbeat. But Penn is a ghost to Olive Township, and resurrecting him will bring nothing but strife.

Daisy's quiet for the rest of our time together, leading me through exercises with detached professionalism. At one point, Isla interrupts to tell Daisy she needs to leave, that the school principal has called her about an issue in class with one of her kids. Daisy wishes her the best in dealing with the situation and offers to let Isla have the next day off if she needs.

At the end of our session I hover near the front desk, unsure if I should say anything else, or let it go. Letting it go is probably best, considering I'm nothing to her. A patient, but nothing beyond that. To her, I'm temporary.

"I'm sorry," Daisy says, catching me off guard.

"For what?" I ask.

"I hope you don't think I was being rude. I have a lot on my mind, and, well..." she fidgets with a gold link bracelet. "Something you said triggered me. But that's not your fault—

"What did I say?" I interrupt.

"—or your problem," she finishes.

But here's the thing. If something has upset Daisy, it is my problem. It shouldn't be, but damn if it doesn't make me want to wear myself out finding a solution.

Daisy shakes her head. "You made me think, that's all."

"I apologize profusely for making you think."

She bats at my arm, a playful blow. "Very funny."

I persist. "What did I make you think about?"

"Something I don't particularly want to give my attention to." She picks up a stack of papers from the desk, straightening them into a neat pile. She taps her iPad, then her phone. Notifications glow on her phone's screen.

"Daisy?"

"Hmm?" She glances up.

"Tomorrow I'm spending the morning at the Bellamy house." Cue an internal wince at referring to my childhood home in such a detached term. "There's going to be a lot for me to throw out, but I'm sure I'll still have space in the back of my truck if there's anything you'd like me to haul away from your remodel for you."

Daisy bites the side of her lower lip. "Actually, that would be great. I wasn't sure how I was going to get stuff to the landfill."

Fucking Duke. Worthless.

On the ledge of the front desk sits a tray of Daisy's business cards, alongside a sleeve of marketing material listing services found at the Sagewood Wellness Spa next door. Plucking out a business card, I turn it over, my eyes searching the desk for a pen. Daisy seems to understand what I'm doing and hands one over.

"There," I say, drawing out the word as I attempt to make my handwriting neat and legible. "My number." Using one finger, I slide the card across the wooden desk top. "You let me know what works for you tomorrow."

Daisy nods. "Ok. Thank you."

I take a step back, hands going into my pockets. "Have a nice day, Daisy."

"You as well, Peter."

Something slices through me at the sound of that name. Guilt, perhaps? The feeling intensifies, growing teeth.

Jealousy.

What a dope.

I'm jealous of my alternate identity.

It's my name I want on her lips.

Chapter 15

Daisy

> Hi, it's me.

Who?

> Daisy St. James

Doesn't ring a bell.

> Sorry, wrong number.

Daisy, I'm kidding.

> <angry emoji> I hope fire ants attack your big toe.

Arizona doesn't have fire ants.

> Fine. I hope a scorpion stings you.

Now that's just mean.

> I take it back.

> Don't take it back. Stick to your guns. Say what you mean, and mean what you say.

> I should remain steadfast in my insults. Got it for next time. As for today… Are you still able to come by and help me? It's ok if you can't, or you've changed your mind.

> Did I tell you yesterday that I'd be there today?

> Yes.

> Then I'll be there today. At two.

> See you soon, Sailor.

"Sunshine."

Peter stands in my front walk, me in the open doorway. He says the word again, this time more languidly, infusing it with warmth. "Sunshine."

My head tips sideways. He looks good. Too good. His pants are a jean material, but they are navy blue. His heather gray T-shirt hugs his biceps, shoulders pushing back against the fabric.

"Are you reporting the weather?" I give the sunny sky a once-over.

"That"—he points at me with one stiff finger—"is your nickname."

I lean against the doorframe, arms crossed. "Are you sure about that? Because you keep telling me I have fire inside me."

His head tips sideways, one eye blinking closed. "The sun is a humongous ball of fire, so technically..." he trails off.

I smirk. "It fits."

He shrugs. "I happen to think so." He peers around me into my house. "Are you guarding the entrance? Is there a password?"

"Penn," I blurt.

His head rears back like he's been sucker punched. Or, *shocked*.

"The password is Penn," I clarify. Following our text messages this morning, I decided that I would be brave and ask the question I've been too scared to ask. Maybe talking to Hugo tapped into a long hidden thirst, and now there's no going back. I need to know more about Penn.

He swallows. Hard. Runs his palm over the back of his neck. Clears his throat. I almost feel bad about his level of discomfort, but then I remember he's standing between me and learning more about the person who has plagued me for years.

"Hugo told me you know him. I mean, I figured you did, because you were hired to clean out his old house."

His lips press together for a moment, peeling apart as he visibly swallows. Given the preamble, I'm expecting a long response. But what he offers is a simple, "Yes."

I step back and pivot ninety degrees, so my back is pressed up against the open door. Gesturing, I say, "Come in. It's a mess."

Peter gives me a weird look. "Of course it's a mess, Daisy. You're remodeling."

So, here's the thing. I'm surprised I allowed him here at all, given the state of my home. I've been very careful not to tell anybody what I have going on inside my house right now. Including Duke. Most of the time we spend together is for the visual benefit of others, which means we are almost never alone together in one another's homes. We will be soon enough, I suppose. After the wedding. We've worked out most of the finer details, with me planning to move into his home but keep this one. Maybe one day I'll use it as a rental, but for now the plan is to keep it as a secondary place. An escape.

I lead Peter into the living room, the one place that's not an absolute disaster. "Can I get you something to drink?"

He shakes his head. "I'm not here to be entertained. I'm here to help you."

"I was just being polite," I grumble.

He crosses his arms. We stand across from one another, my wooden coffee table between us. "You wanted to talk about Penn?"

Was that a wince? Did he just *wince* when he said Penn's name?

My arms cross too, body posture mirroring his. "I know he's the reason you know Hugo. And you're here in Olive Township because of him."

Penn

He nods. "Correct on both counts. What is it you want to know about him?"

Now that I'm here, asking the questions and looking Peter in his eyes, I'm not sure what I want to say. What I want to ask. Fearing I'll sound stupid and whiny if I ask the one question I really want an answer to, I say, "Hugo said he doesn't think Penn is happy."

One of Peter's eyebrows lift. "Is that right?"

I blow out a hard breath. "I guess what he said was that he doesn't know if Penn is happy. Definitively."

"And you want him to be?"

I nod, one long strand of hair escaping the clip holding back half my hair. "Of course."

Peter is quiet for a long moment, and it hits me this is probably weird for him. It's entirely possible Penn never mentioned me, and honestly, why would he? How many guys sit around and talk about their childhood best friends?

Do you want a beer? Have you seen the new movie about the Roman Empire? Somehow I don't think *Let's sit in a circle and bare our hearts about our childhoods* is something a single one of them says.

Which means Peter has almost certainly never heard of me. I have to ask though. I have to know. The answer might decimate me, but this is my chance to ask, and if I don't take it, I might not get it again.

Heart in my throat, I say, "Has Penn ever mentioned me?"

I see it in the micro movements of his face, the fractioned squinting of his eyes. He feels bad for me.

"Forget it," I say, waving my hand. My cheeks are hot, and the heat spreads up and out, to my forehead and my neck. "We were friends back in the day, but we were kids. Practically babies." It sure didn't feel like it at the time. It felt big, overwhelming and all-encompassing. My friendship with Penn did not exist in its own lane, but rather a thread woven into the fabric of my life. He was there. Always there.

Penn.

Penn.

Penn.

And to know he did not speak of me, even to someone with whom he probably spent long hours with nothing to do. It's soul crushing, except it's not supposed to be. I told myself I wouldn't ask, and then I asked. I told myself a positive answer was good, and a negative answer was neutral.

What a lie.

"Daisy," Peter says, voice pained. He feels bad for me, and that makes me angry. Indignant. Embarrassed.

Impending tears sting my nose. "Help me with the bathroom cabinet, ok?" I ask, voice shaky, volume a little louder than it needs to be. I turn on my heel, heading with purpose toward the master bath. The house is silent for a few seconds, the only sound my footfalls, and then behind me there is movement. The swish of pants, the thud of footfalls heavier than mine.

I enter my room and cross it, stopping just before the open entrance to my bathroom, and the mess that lay

Penn

beyond it. Peter hovers in the bedroom door, looking unsure.

Belatedly, I realize I'm inviting a man into my bedroom. A man who isn't my fiancé.

"Duke won't mind that you're here," I rush to say, in case propriety is what has Peter pausing. "He has meetings all day. All week, really. He can't help me."

Not that I asked him. Duke would have, I'm sure. Or, he would've suggested I hire somebody, or maybe even hired somebody without telling me, and they would've shown up and surprised me.

Something flashes across Peter's face at the mention of Duke. He did that before, the first night we met at Summerhill. At the time I was confused, but now I know he was in the military with Penn. Penn must have said things about Duke, shaping Peter's opinion of him. But if Penn mentioned Duke, how could he have not mentioned me?

"Right, of course. The fiancé," Peter says, stepping into my room. He stops and looks around the space. "This is not what I would've expected from looking at you."

I look down at my sundress, the long cardigan I've paired with it to combat the slight chill in the air. It's typical attire for me. "My best friend Vivi calls my room 'Daisy's dark side.'"

The room is moody, with touches of femininity. The headboard of my bed is made of smoky glass tiles and framed in ornate gold. The wall behind it is papered in a matte black with flora in colors of ivory and bronze. On my nightstand is a Tiffany lamp in shades of green, books stacked four high below it.

"I can see why," Peter says, moving deeper into the room. He stops beside a bookshelf I painted black, pointing at the shelf that is mostly framed photos. "May I?" He gestures at the pictures.

I nod as I come closer to his side, and he skims his gaze over the most important people in my life.

"Mom and Dad," I explain, pointing at my smiling parents. My dad wears a flowered shirt, my mom's in a flowy dress. "On a cruise they took a few years ago, before her diagnosis."

Peter's eyes slice to mine. "Diagnosis?"

A lump blossoms automatically in my throat. "Stage four uterine cancer. We didn't find out until it was too late. She"—I swallow back the emotion that comes with saying the words—"she's chosen not to fight. The odds of winning weren't favorable, and she didn't want to spend what time she has left feeling awful."

Peter looks stricken. "Daisy, I'm sorry you're going through this. That's terrible." His hand lifts as if he's going to reach for me, but halfway into the motion, he thinks better of it and drops his arm. It puts an odd feeling in my chest to see him this distraught. I know he is a nice person, but I didn't take him for somebody with this much empathy. Maybe he had someone in his life who has been through something similar.

"Me and my best friend, Vivi," I say, moving on before the reality of what my mom is going through brings me all the way down. "From high school. It was the homecoming football game, that's why our faces are painted blue and white."

Peter nods, reaching for a framed photo sitting back from the others. He holds it for a moment, bouncing it up and down as if it weighs more than a few ounces.

"Penn," I explain, and his head bounces up, gaze expectant, as if I've called him by name. "That was me and Penn, when we were eleven, at the county fair. My parents took us." We ate cotton candy and funnel cakes, and Penn puked disembarking the Tilt-A-Whirl.

Peter stays silent, replacing the photo on the shelf. He is quiet when I mention Duke, he is quiet when I mention Penn. Why is that? Does he simply have nothing to say, or is it more?

Peter moves away from the shelf, and together we walk to the entrance to the bathroom. He looks over my head, eyes bulging. "Daisy," he says, "this is worse than you let on."

My teeth capture my lower lip. "Yeah. It is."

Old, ugly tile sits in piles around the space. I wasn't lying when I said I had to use the pry bar to pry off the cabinetry, but I didn't say I was also using it and various other tools to remove the tile from the walls.

He steps around me, striding to the shower with the glass door thrown open. "Is this even usable?"

"There's a second bathroom with a shower. I've been using that."

Peter nudges one of the piles of tile, and they make a tinkling sound as they knock together. "I guess the pry bar is your new BFF."

"Ha. Ha," I deadpan. "It's not my fault the last person to live in this house decided to tile the entire bathroom, including the walls."

Peter walks the length of the small room, running his hand over the tile that remains on the wall. "How long have you lived here?"

I can clearly see what he's getting at, but I answer anyway. "Four years."

"And you decided that right now is the best time to rip up your master bathroom?"

I bite my lip, choosing to go ahead and tell him the full extent. In for a penny, in for a pound. "My kitchen looks a lot like this, too."

He gives me an inscrutable look. There's something he's not saying, and I bet I know exactly what it is, because I'm thinking it myself.

My *why*. Why would I choose to rip up my house when I'm planning a fast-track wedding? Who has time for that? Someone who wants to distract themselves from what it is they're really doing in life, that's who.

But I won't be having that come-to-Jesus with myself, or anyone else.

Defend. Deflect.

My fisted hands find my hips. "I did not expect you to come here and pass judgment. You're supposed to help me haul all this"—I bend, swiping up a loose tile from the ground—"away. So, are you in, or are you out, Sailor?"

He huffs a laugh. "I'm in, Sunshine. Anything for you."

The tile clatters to the ground.

Penn

Anything for you.

"Right," I whisper, turning away.

It has been years since anybody has said that to me. It's entirely possible the last person to say that phrase was Penn. *Anything for you.* The very phrase he uttered every time I called him into my house to help me with something that final summer.

"I need to grab another broom, I'll be back in a minute," I say in a rushed voice, hurrying from the room.

I could be thirteen years old again, confessing to Penn that I've never been kissed, and asking him to rectify that. The immense mortification, the glimmer of hope, they could be fresh emotions inside me. *Anything for you.* That was his response, followed by cupping my cheek, leaning forward, eyes locked on mine until the moment our lips touched.

I haven't allowed myself to think about that in so long, but three little words and *boom!* there it is, an avalanche bringing with it not just memories, but a barrage of emotions.

Get it together, I instruct, my inner voice harsh. I'm past all that. It's been a long damn time since everything happened. I'm a woman now, with a college degree, and I'm marrying a man most women in this town would give their right pinky toe to have. I'm not just fine, or great, I am OVER IT.

My resolve renewed, I grab the utility broom and dustpan and head back to my bathroom. Peter leans over my counter, pry bar wedged in place, pulling on the top end. He doesn't know I'm here yet, so I take a moment to study him. The man is dazzling, in the literal sense of the word. Sunlight streams through the clouded glass window beside my tub, highlighting his sandy blond hair, which has given up its fight to stay in place and flops over his forehead in the cutest way. The muscles in his upper back flex with his effort, cinching in the center. I bet his ab muscles are coiled tight, too, and those generous thighs are probably hard as he braces.

Am I in heat? Judging by the slickness accumulating at the apex of my thighs, I'm thinking I might be. How could I not be with the waves of masculinity rolling off this man?

"Sunshine?"

I rip my gaze from his backside, finding his eyes in the builder mirror above the sink. His grin is satisfied, the cat who ate the canary for sure, and I know there's no talking myself out of this one. Still, I have to give it the old college try.

I arch a brow, chin lifted haughtily."Yes, Sailor?"

"I'm not sure your fiancé would approve of you eye-fucking another man."

My jaw drops. I wasn't expecting him to say that. Side note: the term 'eye-fucking' coming from Peter's mouth sets a twinge low in my belly.

I recover. "That is *not* what I was doing."

He ignores me, propping his foot on the wall to brace himself as he lifts up on his other foot, bringing all his weight down and, with a cracking noise, dislocates the cabinet from the wall. He pushes off, standing on two feet again, and looks back at me.

He walks closer, tool dangling lazy at his side. There's a playful tilt to his mouth. "Why don't you tell me exactly what it was you were doing standing there staring at me for a full ten seconds."

"Reconnaissance."

He stops a foot away from me. Why does he have to smell so good? Like his usual cedar and citrus, but this time with a dash of peppermint.

"Are you ascertaining strategic features?"

"What? No." I'm not entirely sure what that means.

"Are you locating an enemy?"

"Also no."

He grins. "Then you weren't engaging in reconnaissance."

I blow out a loud, overly done, annoyed breath. "There was a spider next to your foot, and I was watching it to make sure it didn't crawl onto your leg."

"You're cute when you lie."

Ohh this man. He's stubborn, and tenacious, and low-key infuriating. Why can't he let me ogle without rubbing my face in it?

He steps closer, six inches separating us. He looks down at me. "Admit it, Sunshine."

I glare up at him. "Never, Sailor."

He nods slowly, tongue darting out to wet his upper lip. "You are so fucking stubborn."

"Takes one to know one."

We're quiet. His chest rises, falls, his gaze searching my face. The air between us grows heavy and thick. My heart beats like a hummingbird, a thrum in my chest.

What would it be like to run my hand through his messy hair? Scratch my nails over his scalp? Would his eyes close, expression relaxing with the goodness of it?

As if reading my mind, Peter's hand lifts. Fingers sweep my hair. My head tilts up, arching closer to his touch, seeking him. His thumb grazes my ear, his fingers brushing my forehead, fire burning brightly in his eyes.

He steps back suddenly, ripping his gaze and his proximity away from me, working the pad of his thumb over his fingers like he's attempting to get something off his skin. "There was something in your hair," he says, voice strained. He resumes his work on the cabinet, positioning the pry bar and pulling the cabinet further from the wall with a newfound ferocity. "Is your fiancé's job really keeping him"—heavy exhale as a section comes away from the wall—"from being here helping you?"

I blink against the abrupt atmospheric change. My heart rate is still trying to recalibrate from where it went when his fingers caressed my skin, and now I'm hustling to meet Peter at the next place his mind went.

"Duke is not the kind of guy to get his hands dirty." I sweep tile into the dustpan. "Though he would argue my assertion because he *wants* to be a guy who gets his hands dirty."

"Ah. So he has dirty aspirations?"

I widen my eyes, waiting for Peter to get the connection.

"Yeah," he nods. "I heard it."

I grin. "Duke wants to be a man who's handy around

the house. Changes the oil in his car. Yada yada. But he's not."

Peter nods. His face is a mask of nothingness, so it's impossible for me to tell if he has an opinion about this. "He's a good man, though."

"I hope so. You're marrying him." Peter's voice is roughened by an emotion I can't name. I can't figure out why every time we talk about Duke or my engagement Peter becomes pricklier than the cactus in my front yard.

We're quiet after that, working in a companionable silence. Peter focuses on removing the tile from the walls, and I collect the detritus, filling up two black heavy-duty trash bags.

Together we take the bags of tile to his truck, adding them to what's already back there.

"Is that stuff from the Bellamy house?"

He nods. "One of many trips."

"Is it a mess?"

"Everything but the front yard."

"What do you mean?"

"The inside is a disaster, which is to be expected from an abandoned home. The backyard isn't any better, overgrown and who knows what else. But the front yard—" He pulls off the heavy-duty gloves he'd donned when he started working on the tile. "The front yard looks like somebody's been tending to it. For a long time, from the looks of it."

"Hmm." I'm not sure what else to say.

He smacks the empty gloves against the side of his

truck. "You wouldn't know anything about that, would you?"

"About a tidy front yard?"

"Yes."

Of course I would. I know everything about it. Just call me *Daisy the landscaper*.

"Nope," I lie, popping the 'p.'

Peter side eyes me. "If not you, then who?"

Reaching up and gently poking the end of his nose with one finger, I say, "Some mysteries will never be solved."

Like how Penn left me without an explanation. Sometimes in life you don't get answers, and you have to accept that.

"Daisy," Peter starts, scratching at his eyebrow with his thumb. "I don't mean to show up and start interrogating you, or micromanaging you, but what is it exactly you plan on doing with your bathroom? Your kitchen?"

"I didn't get that far," I admit. It's unlike me to jump into a project, or anything really, without looking. "It's hard to explain."

"Try me."

"I had this feeling come over me, this restlessness. I just...I don't know. I needed to do something." It was the day I had the conversation with Hugo, after I hung up the phone. Frustration filled me to the brim, choking and slapping at me. First it was the guilt over choosing daisies for an inauthentic marriage, followed by facing the reality that Hugo and Penn are in touch but he never bothered to reach out to me. It bit at me as I walked into my bathroom to wash my face, and the tile, which had always been old and ugly but faded into the background of everyday life until I no longer saw it, suddenly displayed its flaws. I went into the garage for the pry bar I'd borrowed from my dad at some point and never returned, and I went to town on the bathroom. Until I cut myself.

Peter crosses his arms, leaning against his truck as if settling in. "You needed to break something? Destroy?"

"You saw that bathroom," I protest, waving a hand toward my house. "I'm doing it a favor."

"Right. It's just that most people don't take on more than one big project at a time."

"It's only the master bath, and kitchen cabinets. It's not like I ripped up the flooring."

Peter's eyes lock in on me without moving any closer. Intensity burns in the squall. "I was referring to planning your wedding."

I do my best not to show the fear streaking through me, that jittery feeling right before getting caught. "Why do you keep bringing this up?" I use sass to cover up my dread. "This is the third time."

"Because," he says through clenched teeth. "I'm hoping you'll understand what I'm getting at without having to hear it said plainly."

My fisted hands find my hips. "Say it plainly."

Without hesitation, he bites out, "I think you're having mixed feelings about getting married."

I scoff, but there's that fear again. Pungent and sharp

and accurate. "How could you say that? You barely know me."

"Fair," he concedes with a dip of his chin. "But don't forget I found you hiding out from your engagement party."

Ok, yes. I admit that wasn't my finest moment. "I was overwhelmed. Have you never been overwhelmed?"

Besides, you know, the time he spent broken and concussed in the ocean.

His eyes narrow. "Obviously I have. But it seems like that should be the last thing that overwhelms you. And it makes me think—"

"Did it hurt?" I narrow my eyes.

"Did what hurt?" He narrows his right back.

"For you to think."

"Very funny."

I motion, like I'm saying *continue*.

"It makes me *ponder* the possibility that you're having feelings that are less than joyous. Magical." He frowns at the word, as if it has a sour taste. "Whatever else a person who is getting married is supposed to feel."

I cross my arms. I do not appreciate how deeply Peter is looking into me right now. I feel exposed, and I don't like it. I also can't understand the way Peter seems to know me, in a way no stranger should.

"You know what I think?" I twirl a finger in the air between us.

"Lay it on me."

"I think you hate love."

Penn

"Wrong."

"Right."

"On what are you basing this?"

"You become perturbed every time I mention Duke, or my engagement, even—" I hold up my hand when Peter opens his mouth to argue, and he pauses whatever it was he was about to say.

"Even on the first night I met you," I finish. "So it must not be Duke or my engagement that bothers you, because there wouldn't be a reason for either. It's love that bothers you. Or the concept of it." My lips curve into a smug smile.

"Now who's acting like they know somebody better than they really do?"

I step closer, lifting my face in challenge. "Tell me I'm wrong."

"You're wrong." The baritone of his voice floats down over me, a conviction I can almost feel. He's either telling the truth, or he's a fantastic liar.

"Then what is it?"

"That"—he winks—"is a story for another time." He walks backward until he's standing beside his truck door. "There's a lot that still needs to be done in your home. Are you planning on handling that by yourself?"

"Sure am." Except I don't know a damn thing about how to fix what I broke. I'm better at demolishing than I am at building, but I won't be admitting that to Peter.

He opens his truck door and pauses in the open space, staring at me with shrewd eyes. "You're lying."

"One hundred percent yes."

He barks a sudden laugh. "That's what I thought." His eyes flicker toward my house. "I can help you, you know."

"I thought you were only here to clean out the Bellamy house and sell it."

"I am."

"So why are you taking a special interest in helping me?" I point harshly, a stern set to my eyebrows. "Don't you dare call me a damsel in distress."

"I would never, Sunshine. Except you are a damsel, and the state of your home is very distressing." He scratches his eyebrow, glaze flickering to my house. "There's still a destroyed kitchen in there."

I roll my eyes. "I'm not going to let you work for free though. How about we exchange services? I will no longer charge you for physical therapy appointments, and in exchange, you will help me remodel."

"You have yourself a deal." He walks halfway across the space separating us, hand extended.

I close the space, placing my hand in his.

A colossal misstep. His rough calluses scrape my sensitive palm, thumb sweeping over the ridge of my knuckles, heat infusing my body. His fingers grip me tighter.

"Oh!" I breathe sharply as he tugs me in close.

In a low murmur that falls over me, he says, "I do not hate love, Sunshine. But I do hate the man you're marrying."

Penn

Then he drops my hand, takes two steps away and hops into his truck.

"What did Penn tell you about Duke?" I half-yell, but it doesn't matter. He closes the door, starts the engine, then drives away with a single wave in my direction.

I trudge back into the house, more confused than ever.

Chapter 16

Daisy

"PETER SAID *WHAT?*" VIVI EXCLAIMS, LICKING THE smoked salt rim from her blood orange margarita.

I look around King's Ransom, the secret speakeasy located behind a false wall of trophy bass fish in Lunker, the bait and tackle shop. Dark and cozy, with velvet textured wallpaper and walnut tables, King's Ransom fits my mood.

Taking a long sip from my second mango margarita, I let the sting soothe my confused soul. It's a drink that isn't on the menu, but the bartender makes it for me because I'm not adventurous enough to try the eclectic drink menu. "Peter said he hates Duke."

"But, how?" Vivi swipes her tongue from one corner of her lip to the other. "He doesn't know the guy."

"That's what I thought, but Penn must've been telling him things when they were serving together. How else could he possibly know anything about Duke?"

Vivi purses her lips and nods. "That must be what it

is." She takes another sip, looking thoughtful. "But why tell you?"

I shrug. "I think I poked him until he gave in."

"Poked him about what?"

"Well," I falter, trying to decide how to word it. "He acts different when I talk about Duke, or my engagement. Like he's upset or frustrated or, I don't know, angry."

"Because he was hurt in the past and thinks love is stupid," Vivi says in a way that also says *duh*. "Takes one to know one."

"That's what I assumed, but it turns out I was very wrong. He does not hate love, but he does hate Duke."

Vivi drums her peach iridescent nails on the lacquered table top, eyebrows tugged in consternation. "Have you asked Duke?"

I shake my head, focusing my gaze on the far wall with its gallery of old-timey Western paintings. "What am I supposed to say? Hey Duke, why does the new guy hate you?"

"Well, umm, yes. Something along those lines."

"I kind of don't want to," I admit, tearing my gaze from a charcoal painting of an old, grizzled cowboy coming from an out house with his pants around his ankles.

"I get that," Vivi nods. "It would probably make things awkward when they don't really need to be. How long is this Peter Bravo guy going to be here? Three more weeks? Four, tops? Why even start something between the two of them, right?"

"Exactly," I nod. But not totally. The other reason is

that I don't want to cause trouble for Peter, but buried under that is the truth of the matter: I don't want to cause trouble for Penn.

It might be nothing. Or it might be something, but if Penn has chosen to stay gone, I doubt he wants his old life reaching into his present one. It's best for everyone if I don't repeat what Peter said.

Vivi takes another sip of her drink. "I am curious about something." She lifts her drink in the air, tongue darting out to swipe over the smoky salt. "Why didn't you defend Duke?"

"What do you mean?" Guilt creeps in around the edges. I hate keeping a secret from Vivi. Duke had stressed it was imperative to keep our agreement between us, and he specifically urged me not to tell Vivi. *The fewer people who know, the fewer opportunities there will be for word to get out.* I'd agreed, but I'm starting to wish I'd insisted Vivi be my exception. Keeping this big of a secret from my best friend is beginning to make me feel ill.

"Well, some guy who is mostly a stranger just said he hates your fiancé. I think that warranted a *fuck you* at the very least."

"And what did it warrant at the very most?"

"Death," Vivi answers immediately, and without thought. "Mwahahaha."

"No more of those for you," I say, pointing to her drink. "They bring out your evil side."

She tips the glass sideways, considering it. "They kind of do. Let's keep talking about Peter."

I groan. "I do not want to keep talking about Peter."

"Not about what he said. Let's talk about what a fine specimen he is."

"Absolutely not," I say, shaking my head. "It's bad enough I have to hose down Isla every time Peter comes in for a session."

Vivi laughs. "That woman needs to get dicked down, stat."

My eyes widen, and Vivi holds her drink aloft. "It's not my fault," she says, drawing out the last word so it sounds like *faulllllt*.

I laugh, the kind of deep belly laugh I need. I love this person. She is my ride or die. My soul sister. She's my multipurpose friend, the kind who's down for anything. Run a 5k? She'll train. Bury a body? She's on the way with a single-use shovel. Midnight Mass? She'll go to confession the day before, because as she puts it, *bitch be sinnin' all the damn time*.

"Subject change," I announce. "How are the kids?"

Vivi sighs. "Everly earned time in the calm down corner at school today for calling her classmate a 'fucking idiot', and I got a lecture from the principal about how little ears are always listening."

"How did the principal know Everly didn't learn this language from her father?"

"She ratted me out."

I laugh. "Tell me about my favorite three-year-old."

"And also the only three-year-old you know."

"Very true."

"Knox melted down at my mom's house last week

when I came to pick him up after work. He didn't want to leave." Her shoulders sag. I know how much this hurts her, how her mom guilt eats at her. Running a restaurant takes a lot of time and energy from a single mom who's already stretched thin. Carter, Vivi's ex, has the kids every other weekend and every Wednesday night, and even though Vivi appreciates the break, shouldering everything by herself the rest of the time weighs heavy on her.

"Hey," I say softly, pressing a hand to Vivi's shoulder as she stares down into her drink. "He only did that because your mom slips him extra cookies."

She offers me a half-hearted, perfunctory smile. "Right." She leans back on her stool, getting the attention of the bartender and signaling for another drink. "In other news, an unsolved crimes podcaster emailed my brother."

"What?" I blink twice, mouth hanging open. "You really should have led with that."

"It was equally or slightly less important than your news about Peter hating Duke for no apparent reason."

"I disagree. Tell me more."

"Well," Vivi blows out a breath, thanking the bartender with a nod of her head as he sets down her drink. "It's sort of the same old, same old. She wants to interview Hugo, or me, or my mom. But nothing has changed. We still don't know what happened, or who did it."

We were kids, and my own memory of the time is fuzzy in some parts, but I distinctly remember my parents sitting me down on the yellow living room couch with the oversized rose print, telling me in grave tones that one of my classmate's parents had been found dead, and that it appeared to be a murder. Until that day, I thought of Vivi as my classmate with the long and pretty name, who had the best pencils. She also had pierced ears, something I was desperate to have. But now Vivienne had something I absolutely never wanted. A dead father.

My mother instructed me to be extra nice to her and her brother. I did as I was told, inviting Vivi to Spot for a real tea party. A few weeks later, Vivi's mother brought her over, and stayed for afternoon tea. I noticed the uncapping of the metal canteen, but not until I was older did I understand it was whiskey my mother was adding to her tea, and Vivi's mom's also. My mother, with her superhuman ability to be a good listener, opened her ear for Vivi's mom. Vivi and I spent most of our time in the front room of Spot, trying on fancy hats, until I put on one that had a bird's nest glued to the side, complete with three Robin's eggs, and Vivi cracked her first smile since she arrived.

"That hat is so ugly," she said, taking it off my head and putting it on her own head. "I think I'll wear it."

A friendship was born that day, and cultivated over the years, bringing us to now. A single mom of two young children, and a woman who is marrying for everything but love.

"What are you going to do?" I ask Vivi, watching various emotions play out across her face.

"Hugo deleted her email. We've all worked so hard for so long to move past everything that comes with what happened to my dad. We're not going to reopen an old wound just so some true crime podcaster can satisfy their curiosity."

Vivi speaks with conviction, but I know there's a part of her that is desperate to know what happened to her father on that road.

"It's kind of like you, you know," Vivi says, gesturing to me with her drink. "You don't want to look any deeper into why Peter despises Duke, and I don't want to rehash my father's murder. Let sleeping dogs lie, or whatever."

I lift my drink in the air. "To sanity preservation."

"Amen," Vivi says, clinking her glass against mine. Then she looks past my head, her eyebrows raising. "I thought you said Duke had a dinner he had to go to with his dad tonight."

"He did," I answer, swiveling on my seat. I look across the room, to the space where the wall has swung open. Duke stands in the entrance, blinking as his eyes adjust to the dim light of the place. I wave, though the place is small enough that he would have seen us on his own. He starts for us. "I guess the dinner wrapped up and he decided to come. I told him I'd be here with you."

I'm too busy watching Duke cross the room to notice when the wall swings open again, but Vivi's low murmur of *oh shit* drags my eyes back to the speakeasy opening.

Hugo steps through, Peter by his side.

Chapter 17

Penn

You have got to be fucking kidding me.

There Hugo and I are, minding our own business in Lunker as we choose a few new baits to try out at Canyon Lake tomorrow morning, when Paper Towel Duke walks in the shop. He strolls through the place without a look left or right, heading straight for the back wall. I watch him press down on a bright orange silver-dollar-sized button on the wall, then press his palm to the surface.

The wall begins to move, swinging slowly open to reveal a dimly lit space and ambient noise. I hit Hugo on the shoulder. "What the hell is that?"

Hugo glances over his shoulder. "King's Ransom, also known as a speakeasy."

Duke steps through, pausing in the open space, and I capitalize on his hesitation, rounding the end of the aisle and hustling toward the wall of trophy bass, which it turns out is a front for a speakeasy.

"Penn," Hugo forcefully whispers behind me. "*Peter*, whatever the fuck it is. What are you doing?"

I extend a stiff arm at the closing wall. "I want to go in there."

"We aren't dressed for it."

I look down at the two of us in our sweats, long sleeve T-shirts, and running shoes. "Is there a dress code?"

He sighs like he knows whatever it was he'd been about to say was going to put him on the losing end of this argument. "It's implicit."

"I'll follow the rules when they're explicitly stated. Until then," I push at the wall, and it slowly begins to swing open again, "we go into King's Ransom. And I don't want to hear another excuse from you about why we shouldn't, because you're on my shit list right now."

Hugo rolls his eyes. "It's not like you were keeping tabs on Daisy for the last fifteen years. How was I supposed to know I should've told you about her mom?"

"Sometimes you have to make choices when all you have is imprecise information."

Hugo lightly shoves my back, pushing me closer through the ever-widening entrance. "Don't use military thinking on me."

We spill out on the other side of what I thought was only a fishing store, but is actually a secret hipster spot with bad lighting and drinks with ironic names.

And Daisy.

Someway or another, it seems I can't go anywhere or do anything in this town without ending up around her.

Penn

It's almost as if fate has planted its flag in the idea of us being together.

But this time, she's with Duke. The situation is already less than ideal, and made even worse by the fact that I slipped earlier today and told her I hate the guy. I don't know what came over me, and I definitely shouldn't have done that. She was challenging me about believing in the concept of being in love. Reality, or rather the current reality I've created for myself here, stepped in and took over my ability to form and speak words. There I was, blurting out the truth about how I feel about her fiancé. Might as well have blurted out the truth about my identity while I was at it.

"Way to go, asshole," Hugo mutters. "Looks like you're finally going to have to come face-to-face with a human paper towel."

I eye the group across the room. *Duke, Daisy, and Vivi.*

"Where does that rank on the list of sentences you never thought you would say?"

"Somewhere above *Do you want to watch me press olives* but far below *I'm not a fan of deep throating.*"

I cough on a laugh, patting his shoulder. "I don't know where the hell you get that sense of humor, but it's quick and unexpected."

Hugo stiffens under my hand. We both know his sense of humor came from his father.

"You know we have to go over there, right?" Hugo nods in the direction of the table at the back of the room. Vivi stares Hugo down, giving him a wide-eyed look paired with cinched eyebrows, like *what the fuck are you still doing across the room?*

"You'd better play nice," Hugo warns, starting over. I fall into step beside him, my hands going into my pockets.

"I'm always nice."

Hugo eyes me. "I know Duke was shitty to you before, but his dad was an asshole back then, and he's still a piece of work." He tips his head toward me, quietly saying, "It's not an excuse, just a reason."

I happen to remember far more about Duke's dad than I care to.

My eyes meet Daisy's. Now that I know about her mom, I can't stop seeing the heaviness Daisy carries. It makes me even more determined to insist she be herself around me. She's devastated, living with a broken heart, and trying like hell to be everybody's golden girl. To meet their expectations.

Her lips curl into a smile, and I feel mine unconsciously doing the same in response. She looks so damn pretty in the sage green shirt. It's overlaid in lace, and I don't know what the top with all the rigid lining is called, but it's pushing her breasts up, accentuating how round they are. I want to bury my face there, biting and licking and sucking, and possibly suffocating but dying with a smile. I want to know every part of her now, who she is, what she likes, her regrets, her triumphs, the foods she hates and the ones she cannot get enough of. I want to immerse myself in her.

But, no. I'm in a prison of my own making, shackled by manacles I designed.

Penn

Duke's dumb head with his perfect hair weaves into my line of sight. Of all the places we could have gone tonight, we wound up here (my fault, I'll admit), preparing to make chitchat with someone I would most definitely piss on if he were on fire, but then I'd walk away immediately after.

He stands as we approach, straightening his shoulders and bringing himself to full height, while also making sure we know this is his territory. *Daisy* is his.

I hate this guy. I hate him so fucking much. He is nearly the same height as me and Hugo, but he is dressed for the occasion in navy blue slacks, and a white button-up collared shirt. The fabric of the shirt looks expensive, some kind of thick weave. I have the oddest and most intrusive memory of his asshole father telling him one of the most important pieces in a man's wardrobe is a good, white shirt. His dad threw away a handful of Duke's favorite shirts after that, and me, as the *cleaning boy* as Duke liked to call me, found them in the trash. I already hated Duke by then, but that didn't keep me from feeling bad for him, especially because I heard him crying from behind his closed bedroom door. Shirts in hand, I opened up his door, tossed them inside without looking, and slammed it closed. The next week when I was cleaning Duke's room, the shirts were in his trash.

Why the fuck did my brain decide to serve me that useless and unnecessary memory? The last thing I want to remember is standing in Duke's monstrous house, doing my mother's job because she was unable to get off our couch and go to work.

"Hugo," Duke booms, a wide, white-toothed smile breaking across his face. He leans in for a bro hug back slap, wrapping up my best friend. "Missed ya, man." He pulls aways, but keeps an arm on Hugo's shoulder. "Sorry I had to skip our last meeting. I won't miss the next one. I blocked it off on the work calendar."

Um. What?

"No worries," Hugo replies. "It was mostly more discussion around The Iliad, and what motivated the heroes to fight."

Duke grins, pleasant and good-natured. "Let me guess, Ambrose went into detail about Hector versus Achilles?"

What in the actual fuck is happening here?

Hugo does a head shake half eye roll thing that leaves me even more perplexed. "Of course he did. He's obsessed with how they presented themselves as warriors."

Vivi interrupts by smacking her brother on the arm. "You didn't tell me Ambrose was in town."

"He joined on FaceTime." Hugo shifts his focus back to Duke. "Duke, I don't think you've met Peter yet. He's"—Hugo glances at me—"a friend of a friend." I wonder if anybody else picks up on the hardness in his tone, the irritation simmering below the surface.

I welcome Hugo's irritation right now, because I have some of my own to direct his way. Is he really friends with Duke?

"Peter," Duke extends a hand. "Good to meet you."

I have to shake his hand or else I'll look like an

asshole. So I do what is expected of me, shaking his outstretched hand and telling him *likewise* when what I really mean is *fuck you very much.*

"Have you already met the ladies?" Duke asks, gesturing to the two women sitting across from him.

"Peter is one of my physical therapy clients," Daisy says, and I drag my gaze to her for the first time since we arrived at their table. Not only was I trying to keep from having a meltdown over how fucking beautiful she looks tonight, but I was thrown sideways by my best friend cheating on me with a human paper towel.

"That's right," I nod, tucking away observations about Daisy's appearance as fast as I can before I reach the point of staring, and it becomes awkward.

Her lips, already so plump and perfect, are outlined and shaded in a pink that gives her a deeper pout. Her eyelashes are thick, and darker than usual. And though the lighting in here is shit, her cheeks are flushed. Is that from makeup, or our current situation?

"I haven't formally met you, Peter, but I have heard *a lot* about you." Vivi puts emphasis on the words *a lot*, making it plain she has information on me. Knowledge. What has Hugo told her? He made it clear to me before I came back that although he didn't approve of my decision not to reveal who I really am, he would keep his trap shut for me. I can't imagine Hugo going back on his promise, so that leaves... *Daisy.* And my slip today. Already coming back to bite me in the ass.

"That sounds ominous," I joke. The reactions from the people around me are varied. Vivi grins wickedly.

Duke laughs because he's clueless. Hugo forces a laugh. Daisy blinks nervously.

"Anyway," Hugo says, delivering a small smack on the table. "We'd better get going. Early morning fishing."

"You should stay for a drink," Duke says, eyebrows raised and looking genuinely hopeful.

I don't know what this guy's game is, but he's good. Acting nice? What the fuck is that? I dare a look at Daisy, and damn if I don't see hope twinkling in her brown eyes.

"Nah, we—"

I interrupt Hugo. "One drink."

Reluctance colors his face when he looks sideways at me. "We were buying bait. And we didn't even manage to do that."

"Go buy bait, and I'll grab our drinks. We'll be out of here in forty-five minutes, tops."

The questions rage in his eyes, but I pretend like I can't see them. I have some questions of my own for him, starting with *why are you friends with a paper towel?*

He lopes off, annoyed that I've bogarted our great big plans to do nothing for the rest of the night.

"I'll be right back," I say, pushing back from the table.

"I'll go with you," Daisy's voice melodically rings out, and I turn my body toward the bar, trying to push away the wave of excitement this sets off inside me.

So stupid. It's a walk across a small room, not a trip down the wedding aisle. Plus, the man who's actually meeting her at the end of the aisle will undoubtedly have his eyes on her while she stands at the bar with me. I know I would, if the roles were reversed.

Penn

We walk side by side, saying nothing, and before I can think of what to say to the beautiful woman beside me, we arrive at the bar.

"A beer, please," Daisy says to the bartender. "Whatever you have that's dark."

"Make that three," I add.

He steps away to fill the order, and now it's just the two of us. Daisy drums her fingers on the bar top. "So," she says, not looking up. "You hate my fiancé."

I sigh, low and slow and gravelly. "I shouldn't have said that."

Now she turns to me, propping an elbow on the bar. Her breasts tilt slightly sideways with the sway of her body. Her hair falls, too, revealing an earlobe with an earring in the shape of an ivory bow.

"But you meant it."

I look into her eyes, which is a feat, because every inch of her is a sight to behold. My eyes are not done feasting on her slender ankles, her shapely calves, the slope of her hips, the cute little straps tied at her shoulders, the curve of her collarbone, the hollow of her throat.

I'll have to remain hungry, because Daisy wants eye contact. And an answer. "Yes," I admit. "I meant it."

She's quiet for a beat, then asks, "What did Penn tell you?"

This is tricky territory. I want to tell her the truth, because despite what I'm doing here in Olive Township, I don't actually care for lying. So I opt for skating around the truth, taking a morsel here and leaving a chunk there.

"Penn said Duke was arrogant. Mean. A typical rich bully."

"Is that it?"

"You don't think that's enough?" She must not, if she's marrying the guy.

"It's not enough for him to dislike Duke this much all these years later." She fingers the bow earring. "Truthfully, Duke was a jerk when we were young. But he had his reasons." She shrugs a delicate shoulder. "Penn didn't stick around long enough to learn them." She glares at me, daring me to tell her otherwise. To defend *Penn*, because to her, I represent him. I am his proxy.

It's me, Penn.

Damn, I want to tell her. I want to spill my secret, gather her in my arms, and kiss her again. Not the way I did back when it was our first kiss, but better this time. As a man. My palm warm on her neck, guiding her into my mouth. Gentle, and then urgent, a tangle of tongues. The nip of a lip, hot breath on her pulse, soft kisses strewn over her throat. I want her on me, under me. I want inside her.

Body and heart, I'm needy for her.

But she's someone else's, and the thought rips me apart. It shreds every thought and feeling I have, leaving me desolate.

"I'm sure he regrets leaving," I say, my voice hoarse, raw.

The space between her eyebrows pleats. "And you would know that how?"

Penn

We hold one another's gaze for a long second, and then I shrug. "It's just a feeling I have."

"A feeling?" She steps in closer, her jaw taut. "Well, well, if that doesn't smell like utter bullshit, I don't know what does."

I tear myself away from her hypnotizing gaze. This woman is going to dismantle me, and fuck if I'm not ready to hand myself over to be shredded. My heart didn't stand a chance against her when I was a kid, what was I doing thinking I could come back here and stay strong a second time?

"Hey, you two," Hugo cuts in. I didn't notice him approach, but suddenly he's right there, elbowing his way between us. "Those beers won't stay cold forever. Can we wrap this up and get back to the table?"

Beers? I glance at the bar top. When did those get there?

Daisy grabs one beer and scurries away as fast as a person can while holding a full drink.

"You dumbass motherfucker," Hugo hisses under his breath.

I lay down enough cash to cover the beers and a tip, leaning my elbows on the edge of the bar and stopping just short of hanging my head in my hands. "Whatever you're about to say, Hugo, I don't want to hear it right now."

Hugo ignores me, plowing right through my plea for his silence. "You had your chance to tell her the truth that first night. You didn't. And now here you are, *Peter*, standing in public with Daisy staring at her mouth like you're going to come unglued if you don't kiss her." He gives me a hard look. "Are you trying to make everything you came back to accomplish even harder for yourself? Her fiancé is twenty feet away from you."

It's a hell of a lot easier to point out his transgressions than my own, so I say, "Speaking of Duke, I guess you're cheating on me." I pick up a beer and take a deep drink. "I turned the other cheek when it was Ambrose, but this? Hugo, I don't know. This might be unforgivable."

Hugo reaches for his beer. "It's a men's group. We get together once a month and shoot the shit."

"About The Iliad? That's called a book club."

"Books are one of the topics we cover." He sighs, gathers a deep breath, and slowly lets it go. "It's important for men to have other men to talk to."

I happen to know exactly how imperative it is to have other men to talk to. Some of the deepest friendships formed are that of men in combat together. We literally hold one another's lives in our hands.

I don't say that, though, because I'm feeling about as prickly as the teddy bear cholla we passed walking into what I thought was a fishing shop. "Aww. How cute." My lower lip forms a pout. "Do you sit in a circle and sing Kumbaya? Play that game where you slap your neighbor's hand and sing about a bullfrog?"

"Very funny," he deadpans.

I snap my fingers and point at him in an *I've got it!* way. "It's a circle jerk. That's why you like it so much."

Hugo rubs a hand over his forehead. "You're unbelievable."

Penn

"Hey, I get it." I point back at myself. "I like a good hand job as much as the next guy. I just don't like it from the guy next to me. But," I slap his back once, "you do you, buddy."

"Fuck you," Hugo mutters, grabbing his beer. "Let's go make small talk, finish your stupid beer, and go. I'm done watching you eye fuck Daisy in front of her fiancé."

That is not what I'm doing. I would never put her in that position. But, just in case Hugo's right, and I don't realize I have hearts popping out of my eyes when I look at her, I make it a point to take the empty space beside her, not across from her. And then, even better, I turn to my left to talk, making it so I couldn't look at Daisy if I wanted to.

On my left is Duke, unfortunately.

"So, Peter," he starts, appraising me with cool eyes. "Tell me about your background."

I shrug, appearing nonchalant, but on the inside I'm racing to figure out what this asshole's game is. "Not much to tell. I was in the military for ten years, and I was sent home for an injury."

"A *bad* injury," Daisy adds, lightly elbowing me in the side.

"Pretty bad," I concede, still keeping my gaze trained away from her. "Some surgery. A lot of physical therapy."

"Which is where Daisy comes in," Vivi says, sandwiched between her brother and Duke. I look at her, nodding politely. Vivi's eyes are hard, aimed at me with speculation and suspicion.

"I'm very grateful to be able to continue my physical

therapy while away from home." It sounds canned, a politician's response.

"I'll bet," Vivi says smoothly, shrewd eyes squinting with a mostly fake smile.

Duke brings us back to the topic of the military when he asks, "Which branch of the military were you in?"

"The Navy." I never brag about being a SEAL, even though I know it's pretty fuckin' cool.

"What was your job?"

"SEAL."

He nods and whistles. "Damn. I bet you have some stories."

Sure do. None of which I'll be sharing with this guy.

Vivi leans across Hugo, her forearm against his chest like she's pushing him out of the way. She asks Daisy a question I can't hear, but as Daisy leans closer to answer her, it causes the outer edge of her leg to move the opposite direction, seeking balance. And that means it's pressed up against my leg. I'd really like some Plexiglass right about now to wedge between me and the woman beside me I'm trying desperately not to see, touch, or feel.

Duke follows up with another question about the SEALs, followed by several more. His thoughtfulness and knowledge takes me by surprise.

"I watch a lot of documentaries," he explains, when I ask him how he knows so much.

He comes off as earnest. Even, dare I say it, *likable*. I would really appreciate it if he could be a giant dick so I can continue assuming everything I used to think about him still holds true. People change, evolve, adapt, but that wasn't supposed to apply to Duke. He's supposed to remain that arrogant son of a bitch who called me *cleaning boy*.

Everyone finishes their drinks at roughly the same time, and since Hugo made it clear we had an early morning by brandishing the small bag holding his purchase from Lunker, they all decide to call it a night, too.

Daisy has been quiet since walking away from me at the bar. The conversation was mostly me answering Duke's questions, or Vivi peppering Hugo with questions about the podcaster who emailed him.

We walk out as a group, waving goodbye to the bartender who tells us to have a good night. Vivi teases Daisy about something in a friendly way while we wait for the wall to swing open, and Duke tells Hugo about a new boutique hotel concept his family's company is thinking of acquiring. I listen to the thrum of their voices, the baritone and soprano, the clink of glasses, the smell of sugar and alcohol. Is this what it would've been like if I'd stayed? Would I have grown up with this group of friends? Cheered for Hugo in-person as he won matches, instead of raising a fist in the air from afar? Watched Ambrose on the Olive Township High School football field, sat on the couch beside him at the draft party I'm sure they had?

Every time I think of this place, I think of Daisy first. How I left, thereby taking myself away from her. Ultimately, it was my mother who made the final decision, but I saw the wisdom in the offer, and encouraged her to agree. This is the first time I've stopped to consider what I took away from myself when I left.

It's an uncomfortable thought, one I need to spend more time on later, when I'm alone.

Hugo swings a friendly arm around my shoulders. "I like that you're the same height as me. There's no putting an arm around Ambrose's shoulder. The guy is a giant."

"A *gentle* giant," Vivi adds.

The wall swings open, and we step through. Lunker is quiet and mostly dark, except for a light near the back where an employee sits on his phone.

"King's Ransom gives Lunker ten percent of its Friday and Saturday night earnings to stay open late and let people through," Duke says, like he's reading the question in my mind.

Daisy walks in front of me, hair cascading over her back. Duke reaches over her head, palm flattening against the exit door and pushing it open for her. Jealousy has me grating my teeth. I want to do that for her. I want to be the gallant, chivalrous man who gets her doors, washes her car, places blankets over her when she falls asleep on the couch.

The group pauses outside the store to say goodbye. Duke shakes hands with me first, then Hugo. Vivi wraps Daisy in a hug, her dark hair in extreme contrast with Daisy's burnished tresses. Daisy peeks at me over Vivi's shoulder, and my heart leaps of its own volition. She looks away quickly, but that brief glance has me floating. In an effort not to give away my thoughts, I look away from Daisy and find my gaze aimed at Duke. A perplexed expression has his eyes squinting as he takes me in. He lays a hand on Daisy's back, a territorial move if there ever was one. Has he picked up on my thoughts? Have I been that transparent?

"See you at your next appointment, Peter," Daisy says, flicking a final glance my way. I dip my chin, and she floats away with Duke.

I force my gaze to focus on anything but the golden couple walking down the street. We reach Hugo's car, and I climb into the vehicle that is so low to the ground I feel like I'm crouching. "This car is fit for toddlers," I complain into the plush leather and rarified air.

"Quit bitching," is Hugo's response. He's still standing outside the car, but I can't tell what he's doing. Looking at his phone, I think.

Down the street, Vivi splits off from Duke and Daisy.

Bile rises in my throat. Just because Duke might not be the worst person ever like I thought, doesn't mean I can stomach the sight of him kissing Daisy goodnight. But, like every rubbernecker passing a car accident, I look anyway.

He walks her to her car. Pauses at the trunk. She walks on to the driver's side, never breaking her stride. She tosses him a smile. It's genuine. She looks happy. Her wave is perfectly warm.

My memory rewinds the last ten seconds, playing it over in my mind.

Their body language as they walked was friendly.

Her grin was friendly.

So was that wave.

Duke walks to the luxury SUV with custom rims and drives off. Daisy follows a few moments later.

But me? I'm stuck right here, breathing leather-scented air in Hugo's expensive car that we most definitely cannot drive to the lake in the morning, trying to understand the dynamic I witnessed between Daisy and Duke.

If Daisy were mine, I'd arch her back against the side of her car, kissing her senseless. I'd open her car door and wait for her to get herself situated. I'd stand back and make sure she drove away safely, then I'd get in my truck.

But all those scenarios wouldn't have to happen, because it's a Saturday night, so I'd have Daisy out at dinner, and then drinks, and whatever else her heart desired. I'd take her home, strip her clothes from her body, worship every inch of her, then tuck her into my chest and fall asleep beside her.

Duke didn't appear to desire any of that. Neither did Daisy.

This is none of my business. I know that.

But I made the wrong choice before when it came to Daisy, and I won't make that mistake a second time.

Chapter 18

Penn

Three knocks, in perfect cadence.

Slim Jim pops up from where he was laying on place, ears at attention as he trots with purpose to the front door.

I'm two seconds behind him, pulling my shirt over my head as I go. Checking the peephole nearly makes me laugh.

It's a man with impossibly perfect hair, wearing an olive green dress shirt, and black slacks. What the hell is Duke doing here?

Slim Jim sits by the door, gazing up at me expectantly for his next command. "Good," I tell him, and in his limited lexicon this means *hold current position*.

"Duke," I say, the door swinging open. "To what do I owe the pleasure?"

"Invite me in," Duke demands, crossing his arms and leaning forward. Gone is his friendly demeanor at King's Ransom.

"Why?" I ask, making a show of looking over his shoulder at the houses lined up across the street. "Keeping up appearances?"

"Trying to avoid small town gossip. It will benefit me as much as it benefits you."

I'm perfectly happy keeping Duke on the front porch and making the two of us a hot topic around Olive Township, but I have to think of Daisy and the repercussions it may have on her. She would undoubtedly be dragged into the churning of the rumor mill. So I step back, sweeping my arm open to reluctantly allow Duke inside.

He strides in, but his steps falter when he sees Slim Jim's imposing figure. Slim Jim stares at him, watchful, absorbing my body language.

"What can I do for you?"

Voice hard, Duke asks, "Why are you back, Penn?"

I do everything I can not to reveal the surprise coursing through me. The last thing I want to do is give him that satisfaction.

"You're doing a great job holding back your shock," Duke says, acidic tone prodding me. "I'll admit, I wasn't expecting to find you were hiding your identity. I looked into you after King's Ransom, thinking I would check out *Peter Bravo* the same way I would anybody who showed up in town and made themselves Daisy's new client." He chuckles, an empty, arrogant sound. "You don't look anything like you did back then, but now that I know"—he squints—"I see it. So, tell me *Penn*, why are you back?"

"To offload my old property," I answer, my voice even as if this is a regular conversation, one I'd been expecting.

Penn

"That's all?"

I make a show out of a slow shrug. "What else would there be?"

"A certain brown eyed, long-haired blonde woman named after a flower."

My hands tuck into my pockets as I rock back on my heels. "I do believe I've heard of her. Buttercup, is it? Or, Rose?"

"Cut the shit, *Penn*."

We stare each other down, two men trying to ascertain how much trouble the other is going to be. Is Duke going to out me? Will I reveal who I really am and attempt to steal Duke's fiancée? Perhaps I am assuming that's what has the guy in a frenzy, but am I that far off?

"I'm not here to cause you trouble, Duke."

"Your presence in this town is troubling."

I duck my head like I'm thanking him. "Very kind of you to say so."

A muscle along his jaw tics. "You fucked Daisy up the first time you left. She loves deep, and she loves hard. You were lucky enough to be loved by her then, and you won't be given a second opportunity."

Regret slams through me, closely followed by shame. If I were alone, I'd let myself feel these feelings. But now, with Duke as my audience, I let the emotions channel into something else, something that makes me abrasive.

"Controlling motherfucker, aren't you?" I taunt.

"You don't get to waltz back into town after fifteen years and start fucking shit up."

Duke's not saying anything I don't already know.

This line of thinking is precisely how I decided to keep my identity from Daisy. But that was a choice I made on my own, not because someone told me that's what I had to do. There's no way I'll be outwardly acquiescing, even if I happen to agree with Duke.

"She's marrying me," Duke says, lips twitching like they want to form a snarl, but he's too polished to allow it. "You'd do well to remember that."

There's the haughty, arrogant prick I remember. "How could I forget with that ice skating rink of a diamond you put on her hand? Are you afraid if we can't see her ring from space, somebody will steal her from you? Why don't you tattoo your name on her forehead?"

Duke starts to take a step toward me, but thinks better of it with Slim Jim at my side.

"Are you finished?" I ask, eyebrows raised. "Did you accomplish what you came here to accomplish?"

Duke pinches his lower lip, his other hand slipping into the black coat he wears. He's gazing at me like he's trying to gather his thoughts, and that's about the same time my patience dries up.

"Spit it the fuck out, pretty boy." I'm snarling. No need to be polished, or pretend I am.

Duke releases his lip. "Don't even think about telling Daisy who you really are."

"Aww," I cluck my tongue, just to piss him off. It works. "Afraid if she finds out who I am, she'll drop your sorry ass?" Not that I'm planning to tell Daisy anything, but fucking with Duke is the most fun I've had in a while.

Penn

He exhales an arrogant breath. "Pirate, you're not even my competition."

"You ever seen a big man fight a smaller guy, and the big guy puts his hand on the little guy's head, and the shrimp punches nothing but air?" I laugh once, every bit as arrogant as the fucker standing before me. "Guess who you are in that scenario."

"You've always been a mouthy little asshole, Penn. Ever since you were in my house when your mom—"

Like a snake I strike, forearm against his chest, his back to the wall. "Say it," I goad. "Say a word about my mother, and give me a reason to make sure you're still unrecognizable by the time your wedding day rolls around."

Duke's face tips up, eyes hard, daring me to follow through. He knows I won't, because of Daisy. I'm sure there's nothing Duke would love more than to tell her I beat the shit out of him, probably make up something about me having anger issues, and that would be that. She'd drop me as a client, and a friend.

Letting him go, I step back. Duke shrugs his shoulders, straightening his precious clothes. He reaches for the door handle, pausing. "I want you gone." He turns back to me. "Wouldn't want Daisy finding out the real reason you left."

He opens the door, glides through, and closes it behind him, leaving me standing with my mouth open.

How the hell does Duke know about what went down between me and Daisy's dad?

Chapter 19

Daisy

"You're doing great," I say to Noelle, the town librarian. "Remember to keep up the exercises at home. I really think you'll see an improvement in your shoulder pain."

"Thanks, Daisy," Noelle says, smiling as she situates her sweatshirt over her head. "I swear, it's like I turned forty and my body began to protest."

Noelle's twelve-year-old daughter, Scarlett, rolls her eyes from where she sits waiting for her mom. "That's not how it works, Mom."

"You wait," Noelle wags a finger in Scarlett's direction. "There will come a time when you'll learn the hard way not to stretch out in bed after you wake up in the morning because you might pull something."

Scarlett frowns disbelievingly. She's still young enough that she doesn't truly believe getting older is a real thing that will happen to her someday.

Isla joins the conversation, delivering a pointed look

to Scarlett. "Just tuck away this little nugget of truth for when you're forty. Always walk around for a few minutes after you wake up before stretching."

Scarlett finally catches on, nodding her head and agreeing to remember that for the day she turns as old as dirt aka *forty*.

Noelle lifts her eyes to the ceiling in an exasperated, but joking, way. "I do not have murder on my to-do list for today, Lord, but I appreciate you presenting me with the opportunity."

I laugh. Noelle is snappy, pretty, and intelligent, and I know from a previous conversation she wishes she were in a relationship. Maybe she and Isla should go into the valley and cast their hooks.

"Who's that?" Noelle says, tipping her chin behind me.

I already know who it is, based solely off the clock and the fact Peter is never late for his appointments.

"Peter Bravo," Isla answers, and I catch sight of him walking the sidewalk parallel to my office. He's wearing sweats again, and a plain T-shirt. Clothing conducive to our appointment. It's basic attire, but on him it looks elevated. Maybe it's the arms corded with muscle, the filled out back that looks like he could throw a girl over it and ride her into the sunset.

Whoa, Daisy. Take several chill pills.

"He is not too bad to look at," Noelle says, grinning.

"Gross, Mom." Scarlett's lip curls in disgust.

Isla smirks. "He's the reason Daisy's wearing mascara today."

"And lip gloss?" Noelle's eyebrows are raised.

I send Isla a harsh glare. "He is not."

She shrugs. "Sorry boss, but you didn't start wearing mascara until he started making appointments."

"That is a lie and a half and you know it."

Noelle titters. Isla smiles smugly. Scarlett's gaze flies between the three of us, cataloguing the exchange.

Peter strolls unsuspectingly through the door, and right into a den of women foaming at the mouth. But not me, obviously.

He stops short when he sees us standing in what I admit is a suspicious looking trio. "Hel-lo?" His gaze slices to the young lady sitting in a chair to his right, then back to us.

"Hi," I say, stepping forward. Not staking a claim or anything, but he is my client, and this is my business. Plus, it wouldn't be very nice of me to let him get mauled by the ravenous hyenas in this small but mighty pack of women.

Isla waves, and I introduce Peter to Noelle and Scarlett.

"Nice to meet you," he says, to which Noelle replies, "Do you have any theatre experience?"

We all turn to look at her, trying to understand what it is she's really asking.

"I'm desperately in need of someone to play the part of the hero in the town play." An impish grin dances over her lips. "I asked Hugo, but he said he's too busy running the olive mill. Too bad, considering he'd know how to wield a sword."

"There's a joke in there somewhere," Isla murmurs.

Peter looks like he wouldn't mind if there were an earthquake causing a chasm under his feet at this very moment. "I don't act," he says, gaze meeting mine briefly before darting away.

"Not a requirement," Noelle says cheerfully. "You have to be able to read, and speak. The bar is low."

"I have terrible stage fright," Peter argues, sounding like he is, in fact, horrified by the idea of being on stage.

But Noelle has morphed into a pit bull, and she won't be letting this go. She wags a finger at him. "Nice try. You'll be great." She lightly taps his shoulder on her way past him. "The kids will love you. And so will the town."

Noelle floats out into the warm midday sun, petulant Scarlett in tow. When the door is fully closed, Peter pins me with a murderous glare.

I lift my hands in protest. "Whoa there, Sailor. Don't be mad at me."

"You could have stopped that from happening," Peter glowers.

Isla retreats to her desk, using the excuse that she needs to confirm appointments for the next week.

I tuck back a smile. "Perhaps." My head tips side to side. "But if I did that I would've missed out on sitting amongst the entirety of Olive Township, taking in your debut performance at the *thea-tah*."

He side-eyes my fancy pronunciation, and I see the precise moment my statement sinks in. His eyes bulge, his head rearing back an inch. "The entirety of Olive Township?"

I nod vigorously, enjoying this too much. "Oh yes. Everyone. And then your photo will be hung on the wall in the town hall."

His lips flatten. He smelled my bullshit. I went too far.

"I take back that last part. But," I insist, "the whole town shows up. It's held in Desert Oasis Theatre, and it's a whole thing."

"What if I chase down Noelle and tell her it's not happening?"

"You could, but then you'd be leaving her in the lurch."

Peter frowns. "I think I was fleeced."

"Noelle is awfully good at telling people what to do. You were a victim."

"Wrong person, wrong time."

I shrug. "Maybe it was a case of right person, right time. Think of it," I say, leading him to the table to start his stretches. "Maybe, buried down deep under that tough exterior, you've got Brando level acting chops. You've never had the avenue to explore it. Until now." I wave flattened palms in the air, swooping them back and forth as if I'm in a musical. "A star is born."

"Absolutely not. No. Nope." The vehemency in his tone comes through like it's been shouted into a bullhorn.

He lays back to begin his stretches, and I say, "Good luck telling Noelle you're backing out. She might be a sweet little librarian, but she's also a menace. There's a reason why she's put in charge of all the town events."

"And that would be?"

"She doesn't take no for an answer."

"Former SEAL, remember?" Peter points at his chest. "I get shit done. I was once knocked out of a Zodiac by a flying fish. At night," he stresses.

He moves into his next stretch, not needing me to guide him because he's already memorized the sequence. "I don't speak SEAL," I say, a smile playing on my lips. "What is a Zodiac?"

"A rubber boat."

"So, you were out—"

"On the ocean at night, going almost twenty knots," he interjects.

"And a fish flew out of the water?"

"A *flying* fish."

"Flew out of the water?"

"As flying fish are wont to do."

I press my lips together to keep from laughing. "I'm sure it wasn't funny at the time, but how does this relate back to Noelle and her on the spot casting you as the town play hero?"

"That's one of a hundred scenarios, some of which I'm not at liberty to talk about, and right now, I'm not sure why I chose that one. But what I'm saying is, I was in freezing cold water with blood running down my face, waiting for the Zodiac to circle back and find me. It wasn't pleasant, and neither was a lot of what I've done over the last ten years. All that to say"—he smiles smugly—"I can handle a small town librarian."

"Ohh you can?" I walk over to the spring wall, adjusting the height to accommodate him. He follows.

"Please let me know approximately what time you plan on delivering this news to Noelle. I would like to be there to watch your smug arrogance get squashed by a *small town librarian*."

He threads his hands into the straps. "What do you have going on this afternoon? We need to get materials to start fixing your drywall. I'll swing by the library after I pick you up, deliver the news, and then be on my merry way."

"I have my wedding dress fitting until two-thirty. Creative Sewing is down the street from the library, so I'll meet you there."

A shadow passes over Peter's eyes, turning the everyday storm into a typhoon. He blinks it away, leaving me to wonder if I imagined it. "Perfect. I'll give you a lesson in playing hardball with someone, no matter who it is."

I snort. "Please remind me to thank you later for the show you're about to put on telling Noelle you're out. And also the show you'll put on in about one month when you perform in the town play."

"Speaking of shows," Peter says, pressing away from his body with the handles, "isn't your wedding in about one month?"

"A week before the play," I answer, trying not to liken it to a show in my head, though it is.

Peter continues with the exercise. "Have you been running?" he asks. "I go every morning with Slim Jim, but I don't see you."

"I've been using the treadmill here," I answer,

motioning over to the machine in the back corner of the space. "Somebody creeped me out about running by myself."

"I'd run with you, if you wanted to run around town."

He looks so earnest, so kind, so *willing*.

I could spin it as part of his physical therapy, but that's a stretch. He doesn't need his physical therapist to run.

Yes balances on the tip of my tongue, but I fold it back.

Peter changes the subject to the progress of the Bellamy house, seeming to sense the answer I should give, and not forcing me to do so.

Chapter 20

Daisy

"Daisy," my mother breathes my name. Her fingers press at her lips, her eyes wide and filling with tears. "Oh my word." Emotion wobbles her voice.

I spin in a circle, just for her. The seamstress, Colleen, stands back, wearing a proud grin from ear to ear. My mother's caregiver, Bonnie, sits in one of the chairs Colleen brought out. She, too, is smiling.

My mom dabs at her eyes. "Darling girl, that dress was made for you."

"Thank you, Mom." Colleen worked a miracle, taking the outdated puffy sleeves and lengthening them, cutting off the excess and slimming them into something sleek and long-sleeved. She added beading to the bodice, and a train where there wasn't one.

I look beautiful. I feel beautiful.

But it isn't until this moment, wearing my mother's wedding dress, that I also feel like a fraud. It's not like I haven't known this whole time what I was getting myself into, but seeing myself in a finished dress makes it more tangible.

The door to Creative Sewing swings open and Vivi flies in. She's wearing her chef's jacket, *Dama Oliva* embroidered above her left breast. Her long, thick hair is wound in a braid lying haphazardly over her shoulder.

As if she has been here the whole time, she strides to my mother's side, wrapping an arm around her shoulders. "Our girl is stunning, right?"

"Almost too beautiful for words," my mother croons.

"Ok, ok." I wave my hand, stepping down from the platform. That's enough attention being paid to me.

"Can you believe she's wearing my dress?" my mom says, turning to Bonnie. And Vivi. And Colleen. Anybody and everybody who will listen. "I wore that dress when I married Daisy's father thirty-five years ago, and the luck it brought me!" Her eyes shine, as does her complexion typically dull from illness. It's like somebody has dusted her with shimmery powder, but really it's how she feels on the inside showing on the outside. My mother is glowing. "Life has been good to me." She pauses, remembering her late-stage diagnosis. "Mostly," she amends. "Daisy, I hope you are as happy with Duke as I have been with your father all these years. And you, my sweet girl, have made me the happiest mother. I can't wait to watch you walk down the aisle."

I hug her, and try not to cry, but I fail.

Mostly my tears are for her, for what we will both lose. But if I'm being honest with myself, a small portion of these tears are for me.

Chapter 21

Penn

"But what about the children?" Noelle sets down a stack of books, turning wide eyes on me. She looks like one of those vicious animals that draw a person in by making themselves look innocent and sweet, and then they bite your face off when you get close. Like a honey badger.

"So here's the thing," I say, trying to be delicate. "I'm not planning on being in Olive Township for much longer. I mean, I came here to see what was going on with the Bellamy house, understand what it needs, and then decide if I was going to try and fix it up before I sell it or sell it as is, but at the end of the day, I'm here to sell that house and then go back to where I live in San Diego."

"And you're planning on accomplishing all that within the next month?"

"And help me, too?" Daisy asks, getting in on it. "How are you going to help me with my place, make big decisions about the Bellamy house, and get out of here before the one month mark?"

I cross my arms, staring down at Daisy. Why is she on Noelle's side about this? She should be neutral. "I could leave your home in a state of distress, damsel."

Daisy narrows her eyes at me. I grin in return.

"The annual town play is really for the children." Noelle's tone turns serious. Heavy. She's injecting emotion into her words. Essentially, she's hitting me with the big guns. "For some of those children, the annual play is something they look forward to all year long. They come together, working to put on a show for the town. They even build the set, with some help from adults." A bright smile takes over Noelle's face like she's just remembered something. "I forgot to tell you the best part! We got a famous actress to play the female lead role." Her lips press together as her gaze flits between the two of us.

"Who?" Daisy asks, giving Noelle the question she's seeking.

"Tenley Roberts!"

Daisy's jaw drops. "What?" she screeches. "How?"

"Who?" I ask.

Daisy and Noelle turn astonished gazes on me. Daisy says, "Tenley Roberts. She was America's sweetheart for *forever*. She came to Arizona to film a movie and fell in love with a cowboy. How can you live on planet Earth and not know who she is?"

"I don't watch movies. Or TV."

Daisy throws up her hands. "You're hopeless. Useless.

If you weren't providing the world with something pretty to look at, I'd say we should throw you in a pit of despair."

"Is that a real place? Is there a physical location? An address?" I cock an eyebrow. "Or is it a metaphor?"

Daisy crosses her arms. To my credit, Noelle looks amused. I keep going, because there's one more point I need to make. "Feel free to let me know if I got this wrong, but Sunshine, did you just say I'm pretty to look at?"

"I misspoke," Daisy says through clenched teeth.

An arm slices the air between me and Daisy, swift like a guillotine's blade. "Don't mind me cutting in here," Noelle says, "but let's stay on topic. Peter"—she turns to me—"if you're going to pull a dick move and back out on the kids, I need to know this second, because I was out of time on casting the role about a week ago. What I'm saying is, I'm desperate."

Her eyebrows are lifted, asking for my decision, but also daring me to put my foot down. *Shit.*

"Fine," I bite out. "But I have no acting ability." Guilt rushes in. Apparently, I have some ability to act.

Noelle claps her hands in excitement, and so does Daisy, but I can't make eye contact with her. I'm too much of a shithead, a fucking fraud.

Noelle programs my number into her phone and tells me she will text me the schedule and a PDF of the script.

"Rehearsals start Monday," she hollers after me and Daisy on our way out the revolving front door.

"Cool," I mutter. "That's four days from now."

"I almost feel bad for you," Daisy says, hopping up

Penn

into the passenger seat of my truck while I hold open the door for her. Slim Jim pops up from the back seat, and she lets out a startled cry, palm pressing to her chest.

"Warn a girl," she says, looking out at me from her elevated perch. We're nearly eye to eye, and she looks so pretty in my truck, sitting there in her pink floral print skirt falling to mid-calf, the ivory sweater buttoned halfway with the silky looking top underneath.

What would it be like to gather the hem of her skirt in my grasp, run my hands over the smooth expanse of skin below? I don't need to go higher than her knee. I'll settle for her calf.

Torture has never really been my thing though, so I force myself to stop thinking of her this way.

Leaning slightly left, I look over the back seat and give Slim Jim his *lie down* command. He obeys immediately, and Daisy says, "His commands are in German?"

"Some, but not all." I close her door and round the back of my truck, jumping into the cab. Wisps of plum hit my nose, followed by notes of something smoky, and maybe amber? Whatever it is, my salivary glands are exploding. How am I supposed to spend time in this enclosed space and survive? Daisy smells too good. Mouthwatering.

"So," I say a bit on the loud side, too forcefully, like that one word can push away the intoxicating scent of the women three feet away from me. I start up the truck, backing out of the space, and ask, "How is wedding planning going?"

I've been waiting around to see if there would be any

kind of fallout from my interaction with Duke at my house a couple days ago, but it's been radio silence.

Duke and Daisy's wedding is almost the very last subject I want to talk about, but she was at a wedding dress fitting before the library, and not asking about it seems odd, like it's being left out on purpose.

When she doesn't immediately answer, I glance over. Her hands are on her lap, her right hand twirling her engagement ring.

"Sunshine?" I prompt, shifting into drive and starting forward on one of the side streets.

Daisy looks over, something in her eyes that's impossible to decipher. "Wedding planning is going fine," she answers.

"Sounds like it," I answer, a little more gruffly than I intended.

"It is," she insists, but she sounds tired. It makes me think of the way she and Duke parted on Saturday night, the lack of warmth and care, giving no indication they are anything special to one another.

"Aren't you excited to be getting married? You've found your true love, right?" Honestly, I hope she has. I'd rather she be sublimely happy. "Not many people can say that."

"True love," she echoes, laughing softly, a disbelief in the notes. "The stuff of fairy tales."

My face scrunches. A whole-hearted believer in love of the truest kind, Daisy was always staunch in her position. Downright stubborn. Who is this woman beside me, dismissing the notion? Without thinking, I blurt, "You don't believe in true love any—" I cut off, shaking my head. "Sorry. I misspoke. Too many thoughts in my head at once." I clear my throat, trying again. "You don't believe in true love?"

Daisy doesn't catch my slip of the tongue, thankfully. "There is no such thing as true love. No knight in shining armor."

Of everything Daisy has said to me since I've been back, this might be the most concerning. The Daisy I remember loved love. She hosted weddings for her stuffed animals. The question was never 'what are you dressing up as for Halloween', but 'which princess will you be?' Whomever she chose, her dad dressed up as the prince. Without fail.

"Come on," I urge, side-eyeing her. "What about Sir Galahad? Charlemagne? Hector of Troy? All fabled men considered bastions of chivalry."

She scoffs. "Their mothers probably wrote their bios."

"We should all be so lucky," I respond. In my head, I hear the old Outback steakhouse tune that played on radio commercials around Mother's Day. *No one ever loves you like your mum, mum.*

I keep that little ditty to myself, even though I know Daisy will remember it, the way it would get stuck in our heads as we tromped around her farm, singing it. Instead, I push her a little harder on the topic of true love. I can't let it go, not without digging deeper. There's a lot more to this story, I know it.

"Is there a specific reason you hold this position?"

"I believed in true love once, when I was a child." I

spare her a glance as I drive. She gazes out the windshield, eyes glossy. "Turns out, it was a product, sold to me by books and movies. All those fairy tales, you know? And watching my parents. So stupid. Naïve."

I open my mouth to interject, to defend her against herself, but she continues and I decide to be quiet.

"I didn't only believe in true love, I assumed it was there, waiting for me, distant but on my horizon. It wasn't a hope, but an eventuality. A *certainty*." She sighs. "But then I learned a few lessons the hard way."

My fists curl around the steering wheel. Something about the way she says this tells me I was right, there is more to this story, and it has to do with someone hurting her. Someone who is not me.

"Did someone hurt you, Sunshine?" We've lived a good portion of our lives without one another. It's not only possible, but probable, somebody hurt her along the way. But the question is, how much? In what way?

"Why do you say it like that?"

"Like what?"

"Growly."

Because I want to find creative ways to off anybody who hurts you.

"I'm morally opposed to people hurting other people." Wow. I really pulled that right out of my ass.

"Sure. Right." She crosses her arms, brow raised. "Because you've never hurt someone?"

She has a point. Especially considering the person I hurt is her. "We're not talking about me, we're talking about you."

Penn

"Anyway," she says, the word hard and pointed. "Liam hurt me. My college boyfriend. Four years at Arizona State University, and three of them were spent with him. We were very in love, or so I thought. It turned out he had many other girlfriends. It was this sick and twisted online thing he was doing, meeting up with women and sleeping with them." The corner of her lip curls up. "This might be TMI, but I never hated him more than when I sat in an exam room, waiting to hear whether his unfaithfulness had left me with not only a broken heart but also a sexually transmitted infection."

I have a lot of thoughts racing through my mind right now, but the main one is how to slyly learn good old Liam's last name. Pay him a visit. Maybe permanently alter his smile.

Daisy continues. "It didn't, thankfully. But I learned the hard way that you can love people, and they can love you, and they will still leave you. You can love someone, they can *claim* they love you, and they will screw you over. Then you can love someone who loves you back, and life can take them away from you."

That first one in her list is about me, but there's something about the way she says the third one that prompts me to place my focus there. "Like your mom?"

She nods in this tiny, heartbreaking way, and dammit if it doesn't tear me apart. Make me want to haul her to my chest, keep anything from causing her pain. I hate that life has disappointed Daisy. I hate that my actions so long ago have made it onto her list.

Reaching across the console, I find her hand and give it a squeeze. "I recently lost my mom."

Daisy's head swivels, waiting for me to say more. It's one of the last things I want to talk about, ranking up there with Daisy's upcoming wedding. But Daisy needs me in this moment, needs me to provide her with some sort of comfort, and a platitude doesn't feel like nearly enough.

"Liver failure, a few months ago." Now it's my turn to stare through the windshield, trying like hell not to see my mother's face, the regret she felt for the mother she became for a portion of my childhood.

"I'm so sorry, Peter. That's awful."

I nod, thinking back to my mother's final few months. "You know," I say slowly, a new thought turning over in my mind. "It might've been a blessing in disguise that I was injured. I mean, I don't love the scars," I say, palming the left side of my face. "But it gave me time with her I wouldn't have otherwise had. If not for the injury, I would've stayed a SEAL. And she wouldn't have told me about her health."

"She wasn't going to tell you she was sick?" Daisy asks, aghast.

"No," I answer, shaking my head. "She, uh," I falter, fearing I'm saying too much. That Daisy will hear Penn in my words, see the skinny boy who never had enough to eat, and start putting it all together. "There were times when she wasn't a great mom when I was young. She didn't want to make her problem my problem again. Those were her words." In my mind I see her in those

Penn

final months, the yellow skin and the bruises that seemed to come from nowhere.

"You weren't close, then?"

"That's a tough question to answer. I don't know how grown sons are supposed to be with their mothers, but our relationship was heavy. She wore her guilt about my childhood like a shroud. Being around her was difficult sometimes because she couldn't forgive herself for the past. Our present was being affected by our past, but I didn't have it in me to tell her that, so I stayed away more than I should have. And now I don't have a chance to make that right. Or at least attempt to." The backs of my eyes burn.

What is it Plato once said? *You deal with the emotion now before it festers and explodes and puts your brothers in danger, or bury that fucker so deep it never sees the light of day.*

Maybe, no matter how deep they're buried, all emotions fester and explode given the right circumstances. Like sitting in my truck with my childhood best friend, grappling with the way my heart feels when I look at the woman she's grown into. With the way I want to pour my heart out about every single thing, my mother's death and the reason I left Olive Township, the places I've been and the missions I went on.

It's me, Penn.

Fuck what Duke said. Fuck the fall out from Daisy learning the truth. I'll weather that storm. Fuck it ALL.

"Daisy, I—"

"Peter, look out!" Daisy smacks my arm, pointing with her other hand at the road.

The alarm in Daisy's voice sends my foot straight to the brake, but I hesitate. Daisy doesn't know, but we've been here before, me and her. I've been the driver of a vehicle I couldn't control, one that jumped the curb, Daisy's scream reverberating, and then the teeth-chattering collision. Daisy slumped over the dash, blood pouring from her head. Thirteen-year-old me, staring in horror, knowing that was it for me. Knowing everyone would come to their senses, stop ignoring the way my mother wasn't taking care of me. Would it be juvie for me? Or foster care? And my mom? What would become of her?

I blink back against the awful memory. There was no juvie, or foster care. Just a payout, and a one-way ticket to San Diego.

"Look how cute they are," Daisy squeals, as Gambel's quail, at least a dozen of them, mosey across. The male leads with his comma-shaped topknot of feathers, and the female brings up the rear, herding ten fuzzy golf ball sized babies running zig zags over the asphalt.

My heart rate decreases, not all the way to normal, but better than the galloping pace it soared to when Daisy first cried out.

Nobody's driving behind me, so I come to a full stop. We watch the quail attempt to get all their babies safely across the street.

Daisy coos and *awws*. I open my mouth, about to ask her if she remembers that time we saw a cactus wren swoop in and nab a baby quail, the way she sobbed and I patted her back and reminded her about the circle of life and how quail have a large brood because many don't survive. My mouth snaps shut, and a feeling of frustration shoots through me.

I want to share that memory with her. I want to listen to the way her voice goes higher in pitch as she remembers, a twinge of that sadness she felt back then resurrecting.

Daisy's looking at me now, smiling. "Aren't they adorable? Quail mate for life."

"Very romantic," I agree, and she senses the way I'm placating her, so she thwacks me again. I pretend to rub the spot, putting on a show like it hurt. Right now, I'll do just about anything to avoid the swirling mass of emotion in my chest.

The quail make it across the street, darting into the brittlebush on the side of the road. I let off the brake and keep driving.

"What were you going to say to me? Before the quail? You said *Daisy, I* but then I interrupted you."

I wave a hand back-and-forth in the air between us, like I'm saying *it was nothing*. Spilling my truth on a whim is a recipe for disaster. The last thing I want to do is add more grief and pain to her life. And yeah, maybe it is chicken shit for me to just let her believe a lie for the time being, but it's looking more and more like I'm going to go back on what I said before I came here. I can't have Duke's thinly veiled threat hanging over my head.

I am going to tell Daisy the truth. I have to. Every

minute I spend around her, it becomes more and more difficult to keep this going. I think, over time, I had convinced myself that we were just kids, and Daisy probably didn't look back on our friendship the way I did. Was that me protecting myself from the guilt I felt over leaving her? Or was it me doing what I do best, pushing people away because I don't believe that they could possibly love me, or that I could be worthy of their love?

We're getting closer to our destination, and Daisy has rolled her window down a few inches. I do the same, so the air can flow through the truck. Daisy's hair is picked up by the breeze, moving gently around her face. She seems content to be quiet, to sit in the silence.

A smile begins to tug up the corners of my lips, but I keep it under wraps so that Daisy does not get suspicious. I feel lighter, almost buoyant, knowing there won't be much time until I tell her the truth.

It is no longer a question of if, but when.

Chapter 22

Penn

"Please *pretty please* can we stop in that store?" Daisy parks her hands in front of her chest, prayer style, blinking up at me with big lashes and a hopeful expression.

I finish loading up the back of my truck with all the things Daisy will need to clean up the walls in her bathroom and get them ready to re-tile. Daisy's pointing at one of those fancy home décor stores, the kind where the room is artfully decorated with coffee table books nobody will read, and big glass bowls holding decorative balls.

I look down at Daisy's hopeful face. "I would've said yes without the theatrics."

She smirks, dropping her hands. "I would've gone no matter what you said." She spins on her heel and stomps across the pavement, hopping up onto the sidewalk. She pivots, taking me by surprise, and I have to wipe the look of adoration off my face. I'm not successful though. Daisy catches it, I know she does.

She pops her hip, hand resting on the curve. "Are you coming, or what?"

I trudge after her, not at all excited about this store. But for Daisy? Anything.

We step into the space and I'm immediately hit with a sugary smell, something tropical and fruity. I don't like it. I want Daisy's spicy plum. I will most definitely be turning on the child lock on the windows for the drive home. I want to be high on Daisy's scent.

Daisy steps further into the store, examining something that looks like an oversized cast iron Jacks game piece.

"Add that to the list of things in this store that are unnecessary to own." I spy the price tag hanging off it. "And overpriced."

"Can I help you?" A woman pops out from what feels like nowhere, but is actually from behind a fiddle leaf fig. She's frowning. Come to think of it, her offer to help us wasn't all that friendly either.

"No, thank you," Daisy answers, using her sweet voice. "Just browsing."

"Let me know if you change your mind," she says, not sounding any friendlier. "I know everything there is to know about this store. Because it's mine. I chose every overpriced and unnecessary item in here." Then she turns on her heel and walks away, nose tipped up slightly.

I lean down to Daisy. "Correct me if I'm wrong, but I think she might have heard me."

"You think?" Daisy asks sarcastically. She sends me a look, but I see the way her cheeks shake with the effort to contain her laughter. Probably for the shop owner's sake, because Daisy is a genuinely nice person.

I follow along dutifully behind Daisy, keeping my mouth shut about all the knickknacks. At one point, we come upon a candle burning in a dark blue jar, and Daisy shoots me a warning glare, as if she can read my thoughts.

"I promise not to blow it out," I say, "but can we agree that it smells awful?"

Daisy sighs. "It's not my favorite," she says diplomatically.

Three quarters of the way through the store, Daisy discovers a vase. "I have to own this," she says, picking it up.

The woman appears once more, and at this point I'm fairly certain she's an apparition.

"Let me take that for you," she says in a forceful tone, reaching for the vase.

"I'd really like to look at it a little more, please," Daisy says, nice because she wouldn't be anything else.

The woman stops, hands retracting, but she gives us both a dirty look. "I'll be at the register when you're ready to pay for it." She stomps away. Again.

"She's going to have knee problems later in life if she keeps stomping everywhere."

"Peter," Daisy admonishes.

I look at her lips and the way they formed the name I've adopted that does not belong to me, and decide I'm ready to erase it from her vocabulary. I want to watch those pretty lips form my real name, and I want her to mean it for me.

Think of all the ways I could make her say my name.

Fuck fuck fuckity fuck. I will not go there. *Thou shalt not lust after another man's fiancée, even if you hate said man.*

Commandment number one, for me and by me. I don't have any other Commandments yet, but that seems like a good one to start with, given the circumstance.

"I'm going to buy it," Daisy says, rotating the vase as she completes a leisurely perusal.

"Cool," I respond, taking a step to follow her to the register. But then something unforeseen happens. The rug under Daisy's foot bunches, creating a lip that catches the toe of her shoe. Daisy wobbles, the vase sways, and the rug slides. Daisy's arms shoot out to steady herself, losing grip on the vase. It hits the ground, a harsh shattering sound filling the air. I rush forward, catching Daisy before she can suffer the same fate as the vase. She wraps her arms around my neck, pressing her face to my chest, body rigid, as if bracing for impact.

"Oh," she breathes, in this shocked but somehow tender voice. She's in my arms, and I'm bent on one knee to keep her upright. Brown eyes blink up at me as she peels off me, rosebud mouth in the perfect surprised 'o', a blush spreading over her cheeks. Everything I've been missing for years comes crashing down on me. This is how I always should have been holding Daisy. She never should have had the chance to be someone else's girl. Anybody else's wife.

If a heart can break, can it also cry?

Penn

A few seconds pass as she recalibrates, then her arms untangle from around my neck.

"Thank you," she says, breathless. "I don't know what happened."

"You dropped the vase," the owner says, sneering at Daisy.

I've already given this woman more leeway than I would normally give a person acting this rude, simply because she's a lady, but I'm done. She's fucking with Daisy, and that's unacceptable.

"What happened"—I kick at the bunched up rug—"Is that you chose this rug *all by yourself* but you didn't think to put something under it to make it non-slip."

She gapes at me. A sticker on a large broken piece of the vase declares the cost, so I pull out my wallet and count out what's necessary to cover it, plus a rough calculation of tax.

"Here," I say, striding over and tossing the money on the counter. "Just to let you know, my friend picked the only pretty thing in this whole store." I hold out a hand for Daisy, and she takes it. "You should be more careful how you treat customers." A gentle tug and Daisy and I are backtracking through the store, clearing the front door and making our way to my truck. Slim Jim's face is at the window, nose pressed to the glass as he watches us.

Daisy waits until we're both in the truck before she turns to me, but she's beaming, the kind of smile where rays of sun might actually be streaming from her lips.

"I don't know if anybody has ever stood up for me like that." She shakes her head, astonished. "Only this one time in 5th grade, when Matty French snapped my bra strap and..."

She doesn't have to say it. I remember it like it was yesterday. The way that little asshole snuck up behind Daisy, tugging on her bra strap in front of everyone at lunch, just because he wanted them to know she had started wearing a bra. Daisy, red-faced and on the verge of tears, got up from her seat prepared to run from the lunchroom. I knew she would never stand up for herself, she had a lot more to lose in terms of privileges at home and disappointing her parents. But me? I had nothing to lose. I walked straight up to that smug little shit, reared back, and punched him in the nose. Blood flowed like a fountain, and I got a one week suspension. *Anything for you* I mouthed at Daisy as the teacher on lunch duty pushed me from the lunchroom with his hand on my neck.

"Can you believe he did that?" Daisy smiles fondly at the memory. "Penn wouldn't stand for anybody mistreating me."

And I still won't.

"Doesn't surprise me," I say, clearing my throat into the shoulder of my shirt.

Daisy exhales audibly. "What a bitch," she says, looking at me to gauge my reaction.

"You can call her whatever you want to call her. It's just me and you in this truck, Sunshine. No upkeep of images here."

Daisy relaxes against the seat. "I love to hear that. It gets exhausting."

Penn

Why do I get the feeling there's something she's not telling me? Something more to her sentence, a deeper meaning?

I start to drive as Daisy reaches out, pushing down on the button to lower the window. She does it again, and when it doesn't work, she presses it a third time before turning to me. Outrage tugs at her eyes, mouth agape.

"Did you turn on child lock on the window?"

Dammit. I was really hoping she wasn't going to try and roll down the window, and then my surreptitious use of the child-lock function would go unnoticed. But, no.

"Yes, but—" I check to see if she's mad. Her arms are crossed, and her body is facing me, her knee bent and propped on the seat at a ninety degree angle. She looks less than happy to have been thwarted, but there's a playful curiosity in the lift of her cheekbones. "I like the way you smell," I admit.

She blinks in surprise. "You like the way I smell?"

We roll to a stop at a red light, and I'm able to turn my full attention to her. Her pulse flutters in her neck, and I bet I could feel the thrumming under my tongue, her scent invading my senses.

"I don't know what it is, Daisy. Plum, I think, but I know there's vanilla in there and something spicy." Only a fool would make this known. It's me. I'm the fool.

Daisy's eyes glimmer with satisfaction, and my body exhales. "It's my perfume," she says, a coy smile playing on her lips.

"It's...intoxicating."

She stills, her eyes remain fixed on mine. Attraction

races through the cab of my truck, thick and hot and heady.

She's engaged.

In my peripheral vision I see the car in front of me start to move for the light that has turned green. A self-deprecating laugh wrenches from my throat. "It probably wasn't my most brilliant idea."

"For you to hotbox yourself with my scent?"

"Hotbox?"

"Hotboxing is when you—"

"I know what hotboxing is," I interrupt, laughing. "I guess I didn't think of it that way. But it's accurate."

The light turns green, and I start to drive. "So," Daisy says after a minute. "Are you high?"

I should say no. Or at least say *not yet*.

But I don't.

My knuckles scrape my jawline, and I say, "Sunshine, I might as well be a kite."

Chapter 23

Daisy

"Do you mind if we stop at my house to drop off Slim Jim before I take you back to your car? He needs food and a bathroom break." Peter leans a forearm on the center console, eyebrows lifted as he asks me the question.

"Sure, no problem." A flurry of excitement starts in my belly at the prospect of our time together not yet coming to a close. "You've seen where I live. It's only fair if I see where you're living."

Peter makes a right instead of a left, taking him in the direction of the house where he's staying. My hands press together between my knees, my quiet attempt to keep my thrill at spending more time with him to myself.

"Whatcha doing over there?" Peter asks, throwing a curious glance my way.

I withdraw my hands. "Nothing."

"That was not *nothing*. You were pushing your hands

together like you were crushing something between them. A clear sign of suppression."

"Hmph." I turn up my nose playfully, despite the butterflies racing around inside me. These butterflies aren't from nerves; these are varied emotion creatures, trepidation and unease and concern and, strongest of all, delight. Before today, I would've called Peter a friend and a client, but that was before he held me in his arms in that store, so safe and secure. Before he defended me to the store owner. Before he admitted he likes the way I smell. *Intoxicating.* That was the word he used. What I didn't tell him was that I remember the night I met him, how I catalogued his scent. Cedar and citrus.

I didn't mention it because it seemed inappropriate to say, and maybe that's what has these frenetic butterflies flapping their wings. It's becoming increasingly difficult to deny the chemistry between me and Peter. I'm not sure how much of a problem that is. Is it something I should address with Duke? Or is it only a passing fancy, an attraction that will disappear when he leaves town?

Peter takes the final turn that will lead him to the development.

"It's Hugo's rental property," he reminds me, turning the steering wheel in that way that's been driving me crazy since I got in this truck with him a couple hours ago. He flattens his hand on the wheel, pressing harder with the heel of his palm, to where his fingers aren't touching the wheel.

It's unbelievably sexy. And, leaving the disaster of a trip to the home décor store, his backup camera was blocked by dust, so he hooked an arm over the back of the seat, gripping my head rest, and reversed the old-fashioned way. The sun shone off his blond hair, highlighting the gray flecks in his blue eyes, and all I could think was *well, this is how I die*.

Do not get me started on the rippling of the tattooed forearm. I will surely perish if I spend one more moment envisioning his arms wrapped around me like they were in that snooty store. And then the way he came to my defense. Like some kind of hero, riding in to rescue his lady and banish the awful witch. Or, you know, tell her to fuck right off.

All this to say, the day has been a humdinger. I need a drink. Maybe an orgasm, or three. All delivered by yours truly, because Duke and I don't get down like that.

I take a moment to study Peter's profile. Thick thighs, a shirt that falls just right from developed pec muscles. And those forearms. Sweet mother, those might demolish me.

"Home sweet home," Peter says as we pull up to Hugo's rental house.

I pretend to study the house through the windshield, then say, "All seems to be in order," and throw him a wink.

"Are you a home inspector? Because I don't need anybody else nagging me."

"Who is nag number one?"

"Bobbie from the HOA. Do you know her?"

"No."

"Perfect. Now I can talk shit about her, and it won't bother you."

"Talk all the shit," I say dramatically, adding a grand sweep of my hand before climbing from the parked truck. "What'd she do?"

"Harassed me for allowing the neighborhood kids to draw on my driveway in chalk."

"Seriously?"

He nods. "Yeah. But I used my artistic abilities to deliver her a message." He reverses the truck back down the driveway into the street. Indicating with his chin toward his driveway, he says, "The most recent rain washed it away, but you can still make out a little bit of the outline if you look closely."

I lean forward, squinting. It comes to life, a large white circle, red tufts on the top third. "Are those eyes? And a... red nose?"

Peter nods enthusiastically. "Bobbie the clown."

A cupped hand covers my mouth. "Did you draw that?"

"I can neither confirm nor deny how that clown drawing appeared on my driveway."

My lips press together as I shake my head. "You're a troublemaker."

"Rebel," he corrects, shifting back into drive and parking on the driveway. "Bobbie deserves it. I bet she knows the rude shop owner."

"Those swamp hags are probably best friends," I declare, getting in on it. "Maybe they attend group meetings."

Penn

Peter nods decisively. "Hags 'R' Us."

I hop out, laughing at our antics. "I'll pull the trash can up from the curb," I yell over the vehicle. Trash is about the least sexy thing I can think of right now, and after Peter admitted he likes the way I smell and proceeded to drive in a manner fit for a romantic hero, I need a dose of something unpleasant to quell the thirsty ho living inside me.

My fingers are wrapped around the handle of the trash can when I notice a piece of paper taped to the top. I opt for reading the paper, peeling it off and bringing it up to my face. My eyes bulge. *Oh shit.*

Peter's reaction is going to be epic.

"Ohh, Peter," I singsong.

He rounds the front of the truck. "Yes?" he asks reluctantly.

I hold the top of the paper as it flaps in the breeze. "Bobbie from the HOA sent you a love note."

Peter strides over, and I hand it to him. He scans the paper, face scrunching in indignation. "Over my dead body."

"I feel like she can arrange that."

"Do you have ten minutes to spare so I can write her an email?"

"Depends. Are you gonna fold the way you did with Noelle?" I puff out my chest and pretend to flex my arms. "Come, watch me as I give you a lesson in playing hardball," I say in the deepest voice I can manage. "Never mind, my backbone is a cooked spaghetti noodle. Here,

Bobbie, I'll pay the fifty dollar fine for leaving my trash can out for an extra day."

Peter stands tall, legs spread a little further than hip distance apart, watching me with an amused expression. "You think you're funny, Sunshine?"

I step closer, poking his chest. "No, Sailor. I *know* I'm funny."

He looks down at my finger, eyes dragging back up to mine. We're standing too close to be in his driveway within eyeshot of any of his neighbors. I'm an engaged woman, even if only for show, but still I take a step back. A very big step back.

Peter whistles for Slim Jim, who hustles in from relieving himself against a bush in the front yard.

We walk into the house and I'm pleased to find it's actually pretty clean. I don't know what I've been expecting, but it's a single guy living alone with his dog. Some amount of mess would be expected. But this is pristine, countertops that shine and a floor that doesn't show a trace of dog hair.

"Did you murder someone in here recently?"

"Not recently," Peter says, coming away from the fridge with two beers. He pops the tops, throws the bottle caps in the trash, and hands one to me. I take a deep drink, almost as long as Peter's.

"I forget how quickly you can become dehydrated in this climate," he says.

"How could you possibly know? It's not like you've been here before." I'm running my thumb over the condensation on the outside of the glass, but I see it. The panic that flips across his eyes. And it's not the first time. He did it at my house when he showed up to help haul away the cabinets and tile, and then in the truck today when I told him I no longer believe in true love. Why does he do that?

"Right," he says, sidestepping me. "Would you like a tour of the house?"

"I've been here before, after Hugo closed on the property. Vivi and I helped him set it up to be a rental. She and I stayed the weekend here, trying to live a normal life the way potential renters would, looking for gaps in things a typical house would have."

"Very nice of you." Peter moves to a drawer and opens it. "You're the reason I have"—he looks down at what he's grabbed—"a whisk?"

I step up beside him, peering into the utensils and choosing one. "I'm responsible for this ladle. Vivi and I made soup that weekend, but we had no way to serve it." I tap the bottom of my bottle against his. "I thought you had an email to write."

Before Peter sits down to write his email response to Bobbie, he shows me how to engage with Slim Jim, giving him commands and leading him through exercises. "He has a very sharp and busy mind. He loves to be engaged in activity, but he'll pretty much do whatever you tell him to do."

Peter takes a seat at the four-person dining room table nearby. I do what he's taught me with Slim Jim, leading him through a walking exercise where he's supposed to stick to my leg like Velcro. Then I pay him with a treat, and a scratch under the chin.

"Oh my Lord," I say when I get a solid look at what's between his legs. "He's intact."

Peter looks up from his computer. "I couldn't bear to have him snipped."

Slim Jim sits, waiting for my next command. I take a peek at where his private part is connected to the ground. "You do realize that every time he sits down, he's teabagging."

"Geez. Fuck," Peter groans, pinching the top of his nose.

"Good thing you keep your floors spotless. I don't recommend eating off them though, no matter how clean."

"I would have never ever assumed that sentence would come out of your mouth."

"You'd be surprised the things I'm capable of saying." I regret the sentence as soon as I say it. It sounds so sexual, so flirtatious. And maybe under some circumstances that would be fine, but in Peter's eyes, I'm in love with another man. Whether or not that's true isn't the point. The point is, I probably shouldn't be here. Shouldn't be alone in this house with Peter. Shouldn't be driving in his truck and going into stores together. And then, as if I've summoned him, Duke sends me a text.

Penn

> Don't take this as me stalking you, or tailing you, or anything else that involves me keeping tabs on you, because I'm definitely not, but somebody said they saw you go into Hugo's rental house with Peter??

Damn small town. Damn gossips.

> He helped me buy items I need to fix some stuff around my house. We drove to the store together, but he had to stop at his house and take care of his dog.

> Optics, Daisy.

Eesh. He's using my name. He only does that when he's exasperated.

> I know, and I'm sorry.

> The best thing right now would be for me to show up there, come inside, and then leave with you hand-in-hand.

What? How in the world am I supposed to explain that to Peter?

I lift my phone to type, but there's nothing for me to say. Duke is right. I messed this up, and now I'm going to have to fix it.

> Head over to Hugo's rental house. That's where he's staying. I'll figure out what to say to Peter.

I tuck my phone in my back pocket. I hate this. I really, really hate it.

"Hey, Peter?"

Peter gives me a one second signal, his eyes scanning his email. "Send," he declares, making a big show out of clicking the button. He grins proudly. "Do you want me to read it to you?"

"Yes, I do but first, I just wanted to let you know that Duke's coming to pick me up."

Peter's brow furrows. "Why? Is everything okay?"

"Yes, yes. Everything is fine. I forgot we had something planned."

Peter is not buying it. His eyes tighten. "Daisy." He says my name cautiously. "You can tell me anything."

I bite the side of my lip, unsure how to proceed. I can't tell him the whole truth, but I can offer partial honesty.

"One of your neighbors saw me walk in here with you and got the wrong idea. I don't know how the game of telephone went, but apparently they told somebody who told Duke that I'm here." Peter opens his mouth like he's going to say something, but I stop him with an upraised hand. "Duke knows nothing is going on. He trusts me. But in an effort to avoid further chatter, he's going to come here and pick me up."

Peter closes his laptop, bracing his palms on the table as he pushes to stand. "What about all the stuff in my truck? Do you want me to put it in his car, or bring it over later, when it's dark? I can park around the corner from your house." He grins crookedly. "Maybe send a carrier pigeon."

Relief fills me. If he's being playful, it means he's not upset about this. Something tells me he wants no part of the Olive Township rumor mill.

Duke knocks on the front door a few minutes later. Peter answers right away, a fake smile plastered on his face as he steps back and welcomes Duke inside. It's awkward once the door closes, the three of us standing in the foyer, staring at each other.

"Hey, Peter," Duke says, extending a hand in greeting. "Thanks for taking Daisy to buy whatever it was she needed for her house." There's a manufactured friendliness to his tone that immediately makes me suspicious.

"Sure, no problem," Peter responds with the same tone. "I'm out there fixing up the Bellamy house and I needed a few items, and then it turned out Daisy did too, so we went together."

Slim Jim trots over, sitting down beside Peter.

"He looks like an assassin," Duke says, eyes cast down on the dog.

Peter grunts. "Given the circumstance, he could be."

What the hell is going on? Peter made it clear he hated Duke, but I thought some of that was tempered after their pleasant interaction at King's Ransom. Most concerning of all is Duke's low-key hostility toward Peter. Peter came to Olive Township with dislike locked and loaded, but where did Duke get his?

I put a hand on Duke's upper arm. "Do you think it's safe to go out there now? We'll make a show of it."

"We'd better," he grumbles. I don't think he's mad at me, just the situation. "It was my dad who called me."

I grimace. "Oh, that's bad."

"Exactly," Duke says.

Peter doesn't know Duke's dad, so I explain. "Duke's dad is a hard-ass. Cares a lot about image. The face his family presents."

"That's too bad," Peter says. "I hope he didn't pass it on to his son."

My mouth drops open, but Peter's mouth turns up in a grin. "You'd better be on your way," he says, motioning at the door.

Duke offers me his hand. "You ready, Daze?"

He nicknamed me Daze a long time ago, and for years I've liked the friendly name. But being called Sunshine? It puts a warmth in my limbs, a feeling that it's more than simply a nickname.

I nod at Duke, tucking my hand in his and stepping into his side. To Peter, I say, "Thank you for today." It's not nearly enough to cover the way he helped me, how he showed me the tools and products I'd need. He wasn't doing it for me, he was teaching me.

Peter opens the front door and steps back to allow us through. "Always happy to share my home repair knowledge."

Duke leads me from the home, and in a little twist I wasn't expecting, Peter follows us outside. He stands on the front porch, watching us walk to Duke's SUV. Duke opens my door and I climb inside, then Duke turns and

Penn

looks up at the house. Peter's waving, smiling a little too broadly. Duke returns the wave, a little too emphatically.

I understand they're giving the neighbors a show, making certain they know there wasn't any funny business going on. But is that all it is? Because it feels a little like overkill.

Duke closes my door, and Peter retreats into the house. I pull out my phone and send him a short text.

> What did your email say?

> Dear Bobbie, No court of law in the United States would convict a person of a crime without evidence, and since you don't have photographic proof of the alleged infraction, a guilty verdict cannot be rendered. Have a nice day.

> What do you think she'll do next?

> That remains to be seen.

> I am invested, Sailor.

> I promise to report in, Sunshine.

Chapter 24

Daisy

"What is it you're fixing around your house?" Duke asks, taking his time on the way out of the neighborhood. Probably to make sure everybody gets an eye full of us in his car, looking happy and in love like two people who are close to their wedding would look.

"Um, well..." My hands, folded in my lap, squeeze together. It's not that it's a secret per se, but I wasn't planning on telling people I sort of went batshit and pulled out my cabinets. And peeled the tile off my wall. Telling Duke the truth will lead to questions, questions I don't want to answer. Questions I don't want to ask myself, because I don't want to give light to my response.

"Just some stuff that needs to be fixed around my house." It's the truth, but not totally.

Duke isn't buying it. We've made it to the stop sign that will empty us out onto a main road, so Duke looks over and says, "I've never known you to be a liar, Daze. Current situation notwithstanding."

Penn

"There were some things in my house I wanted to change, and I got a little too...froggy," I finish, borrowing a term from Peter's vocabulary.

Duke's eyebrows raise. "Froggy?"

I nod. He takes a right, and I watch as his hand turns the wheel. No turning with the heel of his palm, fingers suspended in the air. Just a typical grip, and a typical turn.

"I'm guessing that's a term you learned from the SEAL?" He thumbs behind himself toward Peter/Hugo's house.

"I do believe that's where I heard it."

Duke grows quiet. We've been friends for such a long time now that I can read his silences, and this one is saying that he is mulling something over, working a problem in his mind.

"Daze," he starts, "why didn't you ask me to help you fix what's broken in your house?"

He's on to something, and he knows it. He's a bloodhound who has picked up a scent, and there will be no relenting.

"I assumed you would send over a handyman if I told you."

"Fair. I would have. If you wanted to do it yourself, why didn't you consult the Internet? You would've had it figured out in no time."

I resist the urge to slink down in my seat. I sit tall, shoulders back, and ask, "Is there any chance you'll drop this?"

"None," he answers. "We've been close for a very long

time. Tell me the truth."

"I ripped out my cabinets in the kitchen and in my master bathroom. And I pried the bathroom tile off the wall."

Duke winds through town toward my car, quiet. Instead of pulling into a nearby open parking space, he pulls into an empty parking lot behind Rowdy Mermaid. All the hairdressers have gone home for the day, leaving a dimly lit space with sparkling clean stations.

Duke cuts the engine and turns to me. "You're planning a wedding that is less than a month away and remodeling your house by yourself at the same time?"

"You sound like Peter," I grumble.

Duke nods slowly, scratching his chin thoughtfully. "Peter knows about your remodel? Has he seen it?"

"He hauled off the old cabinets for me. Obviously I don't have a car the right size to do it myself, and it saved me from having to hire a truck or a company."

"Daisy, I see two issues here." Duke holds up one finger. "The first is that you've done something impulsive like ripping out your own cabinets, and that's very unlike the Daisy I have known my whole life. The second is that you confided in a near stranger, instead of me." He points back at himself. "The guy you're preparing to marry."

I open my mouth to object, but he keeps talking. "I understand we're not in love. This marriage is something we're doing quid pro quo. But I'm still your friend, and you didn't tell me about the damage you did inside your house. You didn't want me to know, because...?" His voice trails off, and now I know it's my turn to speak.

"I didn't want you to know, because I didn't want you to ask me why I did it."

"Did Peter ask you?"

It's not the follow-up question I expected, and it unsettles me. "I told him to mind his own business. But not in those exact words."

Duke nods. "You don't seem to mind being feisty Daisy around Peter. Interesting, considering you keep it so concealed for everyone else."

"I feel comfortable around him."

"Is there anything else you feel when you're around him, Daisy?"

Well then. Just get right to it.

"I'm attracted to him," I admit, worry rising. It's the first time I've said the words aloud, so close to the first time I allowed myself to see the truth. It's a development Duke nor I saw coming, though it was short-sighted not to consider the eventualities of our agreement.

Duke's fingers drum the steering wheel. "I thought so."

A portion of my worry recedes. "What gave you the idea?"

"Your body language when you were standing beside him at the bar at King's Ransom. You looked..." Duke drags a hand through his hair while he ponders. "You looked like softening butter."

"I cannot begin to picture what you mean by that."

One side of his mouth turns up in a smile. "Sort of like..." He relaxes his body against the black leather seat.

"All your muscles were loose. Languid. I don't know the right word."

"And Peter's posture? What did that look like? Compare it to a food."

He huffs a laugh. "Hmm. I'd say it was one of those fine dining dishes that a famous chef would call *restrained*."

"What a cop-out."

Duke chuckles, a real laugh this time. "I don't know how to compare it to a food, but he looked like he was holding himself back."

"What does a person look like when they're holding themselves back?"

"It's hard to explain, because there's not really a physical tell. It's more"—he motions to his eyes—"emotional. Something in the eyes."

"How would you know this?"

Duke's gaze lands on me, something fluttering in eyes as brown as mine. As quickly as it appears, it is gone. But I saw it. I recognized it. Duke is keeping a secret, too.

"Is there somebody you hold yourself back from?"

Duke looks out the window to the lit neon sign with the mermaid balanced on her tail, arms thrown in the air. "Maybe."

Something suddenly occurs to me, and I can't believe we've never broached the subject before. "Duke, have you thought about how we're going to satisfy our, uh, *baser* desires once we're married?"

This gets his attention back on me. "No. Somehow

that managed to slip my mind. I was mostly focused on getting my dad off my back."

"I haven't thought about it either, not until recently."

"Until the pirate, you mean?"

"Pirate?"

"Peter, sailing the high seas?"

"I don't believe he pillaged and plundered." Though I'll admit to having imagined him doing both to me.

"Are you asking for a..." His eyes roam the interior of the vehicle as he searches for a word. "Dalliance?"

"A...*dalliance?*" I try on a word I don't think I've used before. The offer takes shape in my mind, the logistics lining up for consideration. Would it be one and done? Would once be enough? I doubt that, if the way I felt in Peter's arms today is any indication.

How would Peter feel about it? He thinks my engagement is for real. He doesn't seem like the kind of person who would be ok being the other man. I'd have to tell him the truth about me and Duke, or at least partially. But... it could work. I mean, maybe. Could it?

I close my eyes and shake my head back and forth in a tiny motion. What am I really considering? This is ludicrous. A hall pass from my fiancé I'm not in love with? What world am I living in?

"It doesn't have to be with Peter," Duke adds. "I mean, in general. It's ok."

I'm still reeling from our conversation, but I'm trying to keep up. "And you? Can you have a dalliance with whoever you're holding yourself back from?"

Duke is shaking his head no before I've finished the sentence. "It's not like that with her. She lives here."

I gasp. "It's Vivi!"

Duke makes a putrid face. "Absolutely not."

"Hey," I say, affronted. "What's wrong with my best friend? She's a babe."

"For starters, I'm not attracted to her. But also, she's in love with Ambrose and doesn't know it."

"I know everything there is to know about Vivi," I inform him, proud and sassy. It's a best friend thing. "She is not in love with Ambrose. She would have told me."

Duke gives me a playful, exasperated look. "Hence why I said she doesn't know it yet."

"Duke Cartwright Hampton, are you really Cupid under those perfectly tailored clothes and obnoxiously swoopy hair?"

I reach out to flick one of his locks, but he bats my hand away. "Swoopy is not a word."

"It is when it comes to you."

Duke rolls his eyes, and when he lowers them, he notices a group of people nearby. They're just about to walk in front of his car, so he reaches over, cupping the back of my head and moving me in closer to him. My hair falls forward, providing us coverage. We've done this so many times that at this point we've shed the awkwardness of that first time.

"You can have an affair with someone who doesn't live in town," Duke says against my cheek.

"You can find somebody on your next work trip," I say against his.

"My interest lies elsewhere." His voice is strained. Dare I say *agonized*.

"If you tell me who it is, I'll print out her picture and stick it to the sexiest blowup doll I can find."

Air from his terse laugh streams warm against my face. "You're ridiculous."

"Just fulfilling my wifely duty of making sure my husband is satisfied."

Catcalls sound from outside the car.

We look out the windshield and find Margaret from Sammich, and two of her friends. They shimmy their shoulders, shuffling side to side, and three sets of gravity-afflicted breasts undulate.

"Well, that's a sight I won't soon forget," Duke says, nodding and ducking his head like he's bashful.

I smile sweetly, and wave at the old women. They giggle with hearts in their eyes, because everyone loves love, and one of them pushes the other along until they're all three shuffling away.

When the women have gone, Duke drives me back around the building, dropping me off at my car. Before I climb out, he says, "You might want to think about taking a cold shower when you get home."

I laugh. "Send me some links for blowup dolls who tickle your fancy. It'll be my wedding gift to you." And then, because we're in the middle of town, I place a kiss on his cheek.

Chapter 25

Daisy

"Daisy," my dad booms when I answer my phone. "It's your dad."

I chuckle softly, sitting back on my bed to pull my knee-high boots on over a pair of tall socks. "I know, Dad. Your name comes up when you call me."

"Whoops," he responds, warmth in his tone. "I always forget that."

"What's up?" I ask, pushing myself to stand. "Everything ok at home?" Worry parks itself in my core. We'd been told my mother has another six months for sure, and a year at most, but every time my phone rings and I see my dad's name, I can't help but assume the worst. Because one day, it will be.

"We're doing alright," he assures me. "I was hoping you'd be free to come by the house for lunch today."

"Umm," I hesitate, only because I'm supposed to buy yellow ribbon and labels from the craft store today, before stopping at the liquor store for a bottle of rosé. The ribbon and labels are for the assemblage of my wedding favors. The beverage is for me.

Spending the day assembling wedding favors for a sham wedding requires pink wine.

"I can come over," I say, because there's a ticking clock in the back of my head, counting down the seconds until I can no longer stop for lunch at my parents' house and have both parents present.

"Twelve ok?" my dad asks.

"See you then," I reply, hanging up.

My gaze finds the stack of boxes in the corner of my room, holding all the small jars of local honey I ordered. The biggest box on the top of the stack contains two hundred honey dippers. There aren't that many people coming to my wedding, but I couldn't order a smaller amount in bulk. Maybe Spot can use the leftovers, or Dama Oliva.

I finish the last of my coffee, taking the cup with me down the hallway into the second bathroom. I rinse out the cup, turning it upside down and placing it on the towel I've been using to dry my dishes. Though I'm grateful to have an alternative, it's obvious I made a terrible choice the day I pressed pause on my impulse control and ruined my cabinets.

Then again, if I hadn't done that, I wouldn't have needed Peter's help. Without that, I would've only seen him in a professional setting. There wouldn't have been a trip to a hardware store, a home décor store, a bitchy sales lady and a fall into his arms.

I guess it all happens for a reason, as they say.

With my plans for today delayed, I decide to head over to my parents' house early. I doubt my mom is the one making us lunch, and since my dad should almost never be allowed in the kitchen (two small fires, one blistered grease burn, and a situation with a blender), he would probably appreciate my help.

The air changes on the way to the St. James farm, going from dusty desert to something rockier, more earthen. I don't know if that's real, or imagined by me, but it sets a comfort to my bones. A creek runs parallel to the drive, cottonwood trees standing tall in the creek bed. This time of year they boast leaves a shade brighter than dandelion yellow, a stunning opposition to the red and brown rocky mountains beyond. The rise in elevation is the same as it is if I were to head due east, to the olive grove.

The farm comes into view first, followed by the farmhouse. The driveway is long, dust billowing around my car until I *bump, bump* onto the paved section. I pull my car around the circular drive, coming to a stop and putting it in park.

Outside my car, I hop up the stairs like I always have. In the distance, the whinny of a horse. A blue sky as far as the eye can see.

"Dad?" I say, letting myself in the house.

"In here, hon," he yells from the kitchen.

Great. I should probably check to make sure the fire extinguisher is ready to be used, if needed.

"Hi," I say, walking in. My dad stands at the counter, wearing his customary work-roughened jeans, and a

Carhartt flannel shirt. On his feet are bright white socks, because my mother is a stickler about shoes in the house. I toe mine off, shucking them in a corner and pushing them under the lower lip of the cabinet.

He looks at me with a ready smile. "Hello, Daisy Mae."

Nobody uses my middle name except him, and he always has. Excluding when he's stern with me, or apologetic. Most of the time he's happy, and fun-loving, and I'm Daisy Mae.

I stop for a hug from him, then keep going to the counter-height kitchen stools and wind my purse over the back of one seat. "Where's Mom?"

"On her way down," he answers, stirring something in a bowl. I can't see what it is, because the bowl isn't one of my mom's glass Pyrex. "Good day today, though."

It's his way of preparing me for how she'll look. How she'll act, in accordance with how she's feeling. I appreciate the heads-up, though it doesn't make any of this better. The fact she's dying, and soon, is inescapable.

"How can I help?" I ask, joining my dad at the counter. Peering into the bowl, I determine it is some kind of potato salad. "Did you make that?"

"Uhh, no." He laughs self-deprecatingly. "I bought a basic potato salad, then added bacon and green onion, and a little bit of Dijon mustard. It's one of your mom's oldest tricks."

Swiping a chunk of potato, I pop it in my mouth and am pleasantly surprised. "This is actually good."

"Your mother calls it *upcycling*." He frowns. "I think. Or maybe she calls it a hack."

"Either way, you nailed it."

"Is that my darling girl I hear talking?" My mother's voice reaches us before her, and when she does, it's like a punch to the gut. I don't know why it knocks me out emotionally to see her hollow cheekbones, her sunken skin clinging to her chest bones in the scoop neck T-shirt she wears. She looked the same the past few times I've seen her, and she'll continue to be this way. I have to be able to see past it, to not let it decimate me, so I can savor our time together.

"Mama," I trill, floating away from my dad so I can hug her fragile form. "Dad is taking a page out of your personal cookbook."

"Taught him everything I know," she sasses. "Good thing, too, cause I'm dying."

Dad's head drops. His shoulders slump.

Neither of us are willing to ask her why she makes those jokes, or tell her how they make us feel. Her maudlin sense of humor is a recent development, probably a coping mechanism. How can I ask her to stop something that may bring her a brief respite from facing down the end of her life?

"Oh, Mom." A gentle chide is all I manage. "You're getting saucy."

She laughs, walking slowly but with determination to my dad. Like me, she samples a bite from the bowl and declares it right on the money.

Penn

A timer dings. Dad grabs a pair of tongs, clacking them together in the air and announcing, "That would be the chicken."

Dad informs me we're eating outside in the screened-in porch. I set the table, coming back to help carry food, when I hear my parents' low voices.

"You should have seen her in my dress, Charles. She was a vision."

"I know, honey. You've said so many times."

"I can't help repeating myself." She sighs. "Do we have to talk to her today?" It's almost a whine.

That's odd. I slow down, lingering.

"We're talking to her now," my dad says gently.

"I don't want to upset her," my mom responds, less than gently.

"Neither do I, but we owe it to her to tell her."

"Tell me what?" I ask, stepping in and leaning a shoulder against the wall.

Dad sighs. He gestures out to the porch, saying, "Let's talk about it out there."

I settle in at the table, watching as my dad helps my mom sit back. He fetches two more pillows, placing them between her back and the wicker chair. "Good?" he asks.

She nods and murmurs, "Thank you."

The second he's seated, I say, "We're here. Tell me, please."

He and my mother exchange a look. He picks up the white serving dish laden with juicy barbecue chicken, using the same tongs to place a portion on each plate.

"Da-ad," I pester, worry mounting. This must have something to do with my mom. Did she get more bad news? Did the doctor say she has less time than he initially thought? What about—

"We need to talk about the new friend you've made."

I stare at my dad's forehead because he refuses to look at me, busying himself with dishing out potato salad like it's the most important thing he will accomplish today. "What?"

He sets the bowl down and is forced to meet my eyes. "Peter, I believe?"

"Yes," I say slowly. "He's my patient."

Mom covers my hand with her own. "Are you sure that's all he is?"

Dalliance. Dammit Duke, you and your fancy word.

"Yes, Mom. Well, no." Mom's eyes bulge. "I mean, he's also a friend. He already knows Hugo, it's not like I brought him in from a ravine somewhere and made him my new project." No more projects here, aside from tearing out my cabinets myself, and now I have piles of stuff everywhere and no cabinets.

Mom laughs harder than is necessary, looking to bring peace to this conversation as soon as possible.

"Daisy," my dad says, quiet but determined. "People are talking about how much time you're spending with your new friend."

I arch an eyebrow. "People? Or Glenn Hampton?"

Dad looks surprised I know. "Glenn called me, because someone else called Glenn when they saw you at Hugo's rental property."

"You can rest easy, Dad. I already know all this, and Duke and I have already dealt with it."

Mom claps her hands, eyes lighting up. "Perfect. We have nothing to worry about. You and Duke are still headed down the aisle. No trouble in paradise after all."

"None whatsoever," I confirm, though my father isn't so quick to let my response be enough. He's watching me closely, turning it all over in his mind.

"Remember, Daisy, how you act reflects on everybody."

My molars grind. "I know, Dad. I have *always* known that." I don't need the reminder. At all. Ever.

"I'm sure, Daisy, but do you really understand that what you do also now reflects on Duke? On the Hamptons?"

Under the table, my thighs tighten. Jaw clenches. My heart races, a thoroughbred stomping its hooves in my breastbone.

"Yes," I grit out. "I do."

Stress claws at me. Thickening my throat, a boulder forming. It's everything I can do to chew and swallow, to force the food past the lump.

The conversation moves on. My parents make small talk, and I listen without contribution. My dad is telling my mom about a couple who had a marital spat during a recent tour of the thoroughbred facility. The wife ended up getting in their car and locking herself in. The husband ignored her tantrum, went for lunch at Spot, and hit on the young lady working.

I laugh and smile in the right places, doing an excellent job covering up a mini panic attack, but my mother knows me too well.

"Are you ok, Daisy?"

I press a hand to my stomach. "I think maybe I ate too much, too fast. I'm not feeling great."

"You could sleep in the guest room? I'll make it up for you."

She starts to push back her chair, but I stop her with an extended hand. "I think I'll go home. Sleep in my own bed. But I appreciate the offer." I stand up, gathering my napkin and cutlery and plate, bending to brush a swift kiss on my mom's cheek. "I love you, Mom. I'll see you soon."

I stop in the kitchen to load my plate and silverware into the dishwasher. My dad comes up behind me, footfalls padded from his socks.

"Daisy?"

I close the dishwasher and stand up. "Yes, Dad?"

"I don't mean to upset you, but you need to be careful."

"Right. So I don't sully the St. James name. My shiny reputation."

"Well, yes. But also because you're preparing to marry someone we've known for ages. Whose family is almost our family, whether we've always liked it or not. And, hon..." He reaches for my hand, looking at me with so much care it would bring tears to my eyes on a normal day, if I weren't already emotionally wrung out. "If you were to mess up and make a mistake, Duke might forgive it, but Glenn Hampton would never let you forget it."

"Peter is only a friend, Dad. I promise. And he's going back to San Diego as soon as he sells the Bellamy house."

My dad flinches. "Bellamy house?"

"That's why he's here. To clean it up and sell it off."

Something comes over his eyes, an emotion I cannot ascertain. "Daisy..."

"Dad, I love you. I'm going home now."

He watches me go, murmuring *I love you, too* just before I walk out.

I drive home, box breathing the whole way. In for four, hold, out for four, hold.

I understand where my dad's coming from. He's trying to protect me, but it's having the opposite effect. I'm feeling choked by expectations, held down by what everyone else wants. The pressure is too much, too great. I want to scream. Cry. Punch something. Do more than impetuously rip out cabinets.

So badly I want a break from all this, from my reality. I want to step outside this world I've set up for myself. I want to say what I want, and do what I want. I want to feel without fear of being judged.

I pass the turn off for my house, but my foot never leaves the gas pedal. I drive down Olive Avenue, passing all the stores. Straight to the other side of town. Two rights, and one left, entering a tidy little subdivision filled with matching houses. Down one street I go, and then the next. A slow crawl past his house.

No truck in the driveway.

Maybe it's for the best.

What would I have done if I saw Peter in this condition? Ripped off my clothes, begged him to separate my body from my mind for a while?

I don't know what to do.

I don't know what not to do.

One thing I know for certain is that eventually, pressure wins.

Chapter 26

Penn

> Noelle said the play is based on the movie The Princess Bride. Have you ever heard of it?

Is that a real question?

> Yes, Sunshine. I'm really asking you a real question.

I've watched it twenty-seven times. Give or take.

> Maybe you should play the role of the prince.

Hold up. We need to be clear on this. Are you playing Humperdinck, or Westley?

> Um. I don't know.

It is imperative that you clarify.

> Hold, please.

> Noelle says Westley.

> Dodged a bullet.

> ???

> Read the script and figure it out for yourself. Or, even better, watch the movie.

> I am not watching a movie titled The Princess Bride by myself.

> Why? You're an actor. It's part of your process.

> Not happening.

> You have to watch it. I command it.

> I'm not watching it alone.

> Do you need a friend to watch it with you? I'll hold your hand during the scary parts.

> A movie with a sweet title has scary parts?

> The R.O.U.S part is gross.

> Should I know what that stands for?

> Rodents Of Unusual Size

> Seriously?? What am I getting myself into?

> Prepare to be amazed.

> Or I could read the IMDB.

INCONCEIVABLE.

Chapter 27

Daisy

Just because Duke has approved my *dalliance*, doesn't mean I'm going to rush out and have one.

It might be true that it's been a very long time since I felt the touch of a man in a way that isn't perfunctory or parental.

And it also might be true that living inside me is a woman who is very hard up, and very thirsty.

But, none of these things mean watching a movie with Peter tonight will lead to anything. Am I attracted to the guy? Absolutely. Would he be my choice if this was some other town and I was there for a weekend away? Indubitably.

But there are reasons why Peter is the wrong choice.

Exhibit A: He doesn't like my fiancé, and it's looking more and more like the feeling is mutual.

Exhibit B: He knows Penn, and that might be weird.

Exhibit C-Z: I haven't come up with them yet, but I know they exist.

Penn

So. There you have it. Our two-person The Princess Bride watch party is going to be very tame. I'll arrive armed with microwave popcorn, the butteriest kind, and copious amounts of candy. Peter said he'd grab drinks for us, but didn't ask me what I wanted. I'm curious to see what he'll choose. As an afterthought, I stopped by the natural pet food store and grabbed peanut butter and pumpkin treats for Slim Jim.

In an effort to throw Peter's nosy neighbors off our scent, we waited until later in the evening to hold our watch party.

Peter waits for me in the doorway, taking the bags from me as soon as I'm close enough. "What are you wearing?" he asks, looking me up and down.

He closes the front door behind me, and I turn in a circle. "You don't like it?"

He scratches his head. "That feels like a trick question."

"It's not. It's just a regular question."

"I can't figure out what article of clothing it is."

"It's like a poncho, but it's called a wearable blanket." I turn in a circle one more time, holding my arms out.

Peter's head tilts sideways as he considers me. "You look like a flying squirrel," he concludes, leading the way into the kitchen.

Exactly. That was by design. I also came with my hair tied on top of my head in a messy bun, and a face free of makeup. I'm wearing my ugly bra, and the most boring pair of underwear on the face of the planet.

Tonight, I'm anti-sex.

Not that Peter is interested in me like that. To him, my relationship with my fiancé is very real. There's no reason to assume he'd take part in me cheating (in his mind) on Duke, even if he doesn't like him.

And the bonus of dressing down is that it's comfortable as hell. Why am I running around town in cute little sundresses and wedges? Wearable blankets are where it's at.

"Ok," I say as Peter places the bags on the counter. I lean over and skim my hand along Slim Jim, telling him, "I got something special for you, buddy."

Peter opens the fridge. "Trying to get back into his good graces after the teabagging comment?"

"Yes," I say, nodding my head. "I could tell it hurt his feelings."

Peter laughs, coming away from the fridge with a bottle of champagne. He holds it up for me to see. "Is this ok? This is the same brand you were drinking the night of your engagement party."

My eyes go big. "It's my favorite, but it's expensive."

"You're worth it," he says simply. A beautiful sentiment delivered without fanfare.

I want to grab him and hug him, but I hold back. The gesture disarms me, makes my heart mushy and my muscles malleable. *Softened butter*.

"I don't know if there are champagne flutes," he says, wearing a lopsided frown of apology.

"There are," I respond confidently, "in the back of the top shelf to the right of the sink. I remember putting them there when we helped Hugo set up the place."

Penn

Peter locates the glasses. While he's pouring my champagne, I pop popcorn in the microwave. He fishes a bottle of beer from the fridge, popping the top.

I lift my flute in the air, offering a cheers. "Here's to popping your Princess Bride cherry."

His lips flatten as he shakes his head and taps his drink against mine. "I'm guessing at some point I will stop feeling surprised by some of the things that come out of your mouth."

Maybe at some point you can feel surprised by something going in my mouth.

Ok, yeah. Maybe don't say that out loud. Duke was right. I need a cold shower.

The popcorn heats up, popping sounds starting. Peter pinches my wearable blanket between two fingers, holding it out to the side. "It's soft. I'm jealous."

"Bet you wish you had one."

"This looks pretty big," he says, tugging until it's all the way out from my body. "There is definitely room for me in there."

His eyes go wide after he says it. "I mean, not that I'm suggesting I get inside"—he gestures frantically—"*that*. I'm just saying, two average-sized humans could fit in it."

"This is fun," I say, my pointed finger turning circles in the air. "Watching you reverse out of an awkward spot is prime television."

"Ha. Ha," he deadpans. The popping sound coming from the microwave reaches fever pitch, continues on a few more seconds, then trails off. I go to open the microwave door, but Peter stops me with his hand on mine. "You have to let it keep popping. All the kernels at the bottom haven't popped yet."

He's right behind me. The heat of his chest somehow manages to radiate through the thick fabric, searing my skin. I close my eyes, take a deep breath, and say, "But you risk burning the already popped corn."

He's still behind me, and I don't dare turn around. "And possibly breaking a tooth on an unpopped kernel."

The popping slows to a trickle. "Was it your plan to delay me enough that you knew you would get your way?"

He takes his hand off mine and steps back. "With you, Sunshine, I have to be crafty in order to get my way."

I throw him a dirty look over my shoulder. "I'll be storing that inside information away for next time."

We get the popcorn separated into two bowls, settling onto the couch with our candy and drinks.

"Get ready to be swept away by a tale of high adventure and true love," I say dramatically.

"True love?" He gives me a look like he's reminding me of our conversation from before.

I roll my eyes. "Of course these characters believe in true love. Somebody wrote a happily ever after for them."

"Somebody's writing your happily ever after, Sunshine, I'm sure of it." He glances back at the kitchen lights, then springs up from the couch. "Do you mind if I turn those off? They're going to cause a glare on the TV."

"Please," I say, tearing into the Sour Patch Kids. "I'll just be over here, stuffing my mouth with sugar and drinking champagne in my wearable blanket."

Peter throws me a grin as he walks past. "And somehow you make it look good."

There goes that softened butter feeling again. I may end up a soupy mess by the time this night is over.

Peter settles on the couch. Slim Jim lies nearby on his bed. The champagne tickles my throat, and I'm more comfortable than I've been in a long time. It's not only the clothing. It's the company.

The movie starts.

"If I hate it," Peter says, taking a handful of my popcorn instead of his own, "it's your fault. And you'll have to choose something else for us to do to make it up to me, because I can never get this time back."

The way he says it, almost morose, has me laughing. "Please don't tell me you're one of those people who talk through movies."

"I am not one of those people who talk through movies."

His assurance holds true. He is quiet, breaking his silence only to laugh, and pausing the movie once to refresh our drinks.

When the movie's over, he picks his head up from the couch cushion and says, "The script definitely does not follow the movie."

"They rarely do," I say, tipping up my champagne flute and finishing the last drop. I glance toward the fridge.

"Do you want another glass?"

"I won't feel comfortable driving home if I have a third drink." The fridge pulls my gaze one more time.

"But it would be a damn shame to waste the rest of that bottle."

"It would," Peter agrees. "Think of all that effervescence never getting to fulfill its destiny."

I narrow my eyes at him. "You are a very bad influence."

"You could have it, wait a few hours, and then drive home. Drink lots of water. All the water."

I wiggle my eyebrows.

He pretends to hit the couch with a gavel. "Sold to the prettiest flying squirrel there ever was."

"You flatter me," I say, getting up from the couch to follow him into the kitchen.

He pours the champagne to the brim, enough to empty the bottle, and retrieves a third beer for himself.

Something overtakes me by the time I'm halfway done, a combination of the champagne and the late hour, but my limbs are loose, and apparently so are my lips.

"Dance with me, Sailor." I hold out my arms. "Put on something slow."

Peter eyes me. He's been drinking dark beers, the kind with a higher alcohol content, so I know he's not sober either. Still, he has his mind about him.

"How do you think your fiancé would feel about that?"

"I absolutely, totally, unequivocally believe he would not care."

Peter leans closer, looking me dead in the eyes. "And why is that? Hmm?"

"You and I, we're...friends." Is my voice breathy?

Penn

Maybe it's the champagne making me sound like I'm panting.

"If you were mine, I wouldn't let another man spend an evening like this with you." He gestures from me to him. "Curled up on a couch watching a movie."

"While wearing a muumuu's older, uglier sister?" I stuff my hands into my pockets, because whoever made this loves me and knew I'd want pockets.

"Interesting how much effort you put into making sure you looked like you made zero effort."

"Someone thinks highly of himself," I say, pushing at his chest. It's a mistake, mostly because I push at his chest and then...my touch stays.

He looks down at my hand. Back to me. "Sunshine." He says my nickname like a warning. "I'd be very, very careful if I were you."

"Oh yeah?" This is bad. So bad.

My flat palm glides up, smoothing over him, traveling over his collarbone, climbing his throat. My fingers find his hair, my fingernails scraping over him. His low, guttural groan seeps into me.

I meet his gaze, and then I see his hunger. This man is famished. My fingers curl, guiding his head closer to mine. For the shortest second he allows it, but something passes through his eyes and his muscles become rigid.

"We can't," he rasps. He looks pained. Regretful. But he hasn't moved.

"It's ok," I whisper, smiling softly. "Duke and I have an agreement."

Confusion crosses his face. "What?"

"Mm-hmm. And I'll tell you everything...Later. Right now"—I bite my lower lip and look up at him through my lashes—"I'd like to do other things."

Stunned, Peter says nothing. But his eyes track me. He watches raptly as I step back. Tug the oversized garment over my head and toss it aside. I'm in black leggings, and *damn it*, my ugly bra.

Peter comes to life. He steps in, wrapping an arm around my waist, hauling me into his chest. My breasts press against him, pushing up, but he's not looking at them. He's staring into my eyes.

"Fuck, Daisy. You're more beautiful than anybody has a right to be." His gaze drops, lowering to my chest. "The things I want to do to you."

I arch into him. "Do them, Peter."

Everything shuts off. His hunger disappears. His hand leaves my waist, the ghost of his touch lingering. He steps away, bumping into the table in his haste. "We can't do this." He swipes my dumb, stupid, idiotic wearable blanket from the floor and thrusts it at me.

My face flames as I shove my head and arms through. "I'm sorry," I say, because I don't know what else to say and I'm dangerously close to tears. The last thing I want is to cry in front of him right now.

"There is nobody sorrier than I, I promise you that."

I want to ask *why?* but I'm not sure I want to hear the answer. My purse is on the counter, and I go for it.

Peter's arm shoots out to stop me. "You can't drive."

He's right. I need to sober up.

Penn

Has there been another time I've been this mortified? If there has, I've blessedly forgotten.

"Here," he says, grabbing four bottles of water from the fridge. "Let's drink some water and watch something on TV."

I nod, still too embarrassed to speak. Too afraid if I open my mouth, tears will pour from my eyes instead.

We sit down in our previous seats, and Peter puts something on TV. I'm not sure what it is, I'm not really seeing it. My mind plays those brief moments in the kitchen over and over in my mind, trying to pinpoint what went wrong. He was into it, and then he wasn't. It was as if somebody poured a bucket of ice water over him.

It must be about my engagement. Worry over feeling guilty tomorrow. Maybe worried that I'd have a crisis of conscience after, and he was trying to save me from that.

Peter shifts beside me, and my eyes grow heavy.

The last thought I have before I close my eyes is far worse than the previous.

It's me.

Chapter 28

Penn

"Daisy?" My whisper tumbles down over her prone form.

It's 3:36 a.m., and Daisy is fast asleep on my couch. I was asleep until two minutes ago, until I woke from the dream I have often, where I'm lying in dark water, the stars above me melting, until it's water all around me. Sometimes I feel like I'm drowning, other times I wake myself up before that happens. This time, I knew where I was the second I opened my eyes. Daisy's spiced plum smell was solace from the dream, a comfort I wish I could always have.

That only lasted about half a second because I saw Daisy and immediately understood that we had both fallen asleep. On the heels of that panicked feeling was the memory of Daisy standing in my kitchen, wearing only her leggings and a bra, looking beautiful and vulnerable, sexier than anything I've ever seen, blowing my mind in the very best way.

Penn

Duke and I have an agreement.

What did that mean? An agreement? What kind of a man would allow another man to feast on Daisy, to memorize her curves, enjoy her body?

The memory of me stopping us, and the hurt in her eyes that followed, taints what should otherwise be a blissful remembrance.

"Daisy?" I say again, gently smoothing her messy hair back from her face. She looks like an angel, deep and even breath streaming through slightly parted lips. Daisy blinks a few times in rapid succession, dragging in a deep breath and letting it out. She sits up suddenly, realizing where she is.

"Peter," she half-shouts, gaze swinging around wildly. "What time is it?"

"Middle of the night," I say, attempting to soothe her panic with a soft voice.

Her eyes slice to mine. "Did you fall asleep, too?"

I nod, raking a hand over my face. I know what I have to do. What I have to say. Because I saw what Daisy was thinking when I stopped her last night, and it wasn't good. The last thing I want her thinking is that me not wanting to sleep with her has anything to do with her. I'm a decent guy under most circumstances, but my reason has nothing to do with her fiancé, either.

If I am lucky enough to get to experience Daisy's heart, and her body, it won't be as Peter. And after seeing Daisy interact with Duke, and given what she told me last night about some kind of *agreement*, it solidified what I already knew.

Daisy belongs with Penn. And she deserves to know that's who she's making love with. Selfishly, I don't want Peter to have her. She's mine, and she always was. I may have left her, but she never left me. True love. Daisy might not believe it anymore, but the more time I spend around her, the more I understand very, very clearly that true love does exist.

The first step in restoring her belief in it, is for me to tell her who I really am.

So I take her hand, tugging lightly to make sure I have her attention. Gazes locked, I say, "Sunshine, there's something I need to tell you."

A blush blooms over Daisy's cheeks. "If it has anything to do with last night, I don't want to hear about it."

My heart pinches. "I've done a lot of hard things, but none of them compare to the strength it took to let you go last night."

Daisy blinks up at me, eyes searching mine. "Then, why? Is it Duke?"

"No, but at some point I'm going to need to hear more about this *agreement*." I can't help the way I say it, the disdain that accompanies the word.

"Then, *why?*" She stresses the word.

I take a deep breath. This is it. Looking back, I should have done this that first night at Summerhill, been honest from day one. Once the lie was established, hooks set, it grew, became a living, breathing thing.

Taking her hand, skin so soft in mine, I press it to my chest and clutch it with both hands. "It's me, Penn."

Penn

The muscles in Daisy's face go slack. She blinks four times in rapid succession. "Penn?" A disbelieving whisper. Immediately followed by a wobbling of her chin. Her eyes find my tattoo. *Daisies for Daisy.*

I nod, watching every emotion in her eyes, every micro movement of her face. She's grappling with what I've said, reversing back into her memory and looking for missed clues.

"Penn," she whispers again, her free hand reaching out for my face, faltering. I gaze in earnest back at her, and her shaky touch lands tentatively on my cheek. Her fingertips graze my cheek, sweep over my jaw. Her lower lip quivers.

Devastation forms in her eyes. Tears gather, breaking free and tumbling down her face. It rips me in half to see her crying, and the compulsion to hold her overwhelms me, but I want her to have this moment. Need her to feel what comes naturally to her.

Her hand drops away from my face, and I feel the loss like a torn limb. Her touch belongs on me.

Teary eyes dart over my face. "H-how?"

"I'm sorry, so sorry." My thumb rubs over the top of her hand I still have pressed to my chest. "I want you to know that."

"For what?" she asks, her tone hardening, growing claws. "Tricking me this time, or tricking me last time?"

"For everything," I answer, "but I didn't trick you when we were kids, Daisy."

"You had to have, because friends don't abandon each other the way you abandoned me." Hurt rises in her eyes, a tide, a swell that could drown me. This woman has no idea what she does to me. To my heart.

A heavy sigh heaves my chest. "You don't know what was going on at the time."

"Right," she nods, yanking her hand away. "Because you didn't confide in me."

She's right. I didn't. Because I couldn't. How do you tell someone their father paid you to leave town, even arranged a place for you to live? How do you tell them that despite it being something you're ashamed of, it's also probably what saved your life?

The day is burned into my memory. Daisy's dad showing up unannounced, my embarrassment at the state of our home. The way he stood across from my mom, helping her understand how much trouble I was in. Revealing a path to health for her, and a better way for me. *It's best for everyone*, he'd said, shoulders hunched as if he carried a heavy weight.

I can't tell Daisy the truth about her dad, not when she's preparing to lose her mom. He's all she'll have left.

"Daisy, I—"

"No," she shouts, standing up. The blanket thing she wears swallows her frame. "You let me ask questions about you. You let me wonder how *Penn* was doing. You danced around questions of him." Her eyes are ablaze, and I'm pretty happy there isn't a door stop anywhere near by, because I'm certain it would be sailing at my head right now. "You told me"—her voice breaks, words dying off into a whisper—"he never mentioned me." Her arms wrap around herself, like

Penn

she's seeking comfort. It fucking kills me to know I'm the reason for her pain.

"Why are you really here?" she asks, voice hoarse.

"I came back to deal with my house."

"Because of your mom?" she asks, momentarily softening. "Or was that a lie, too?"

"That was the truth. Daisy, I have told you the truth as many times as I could. I promise."

"Why lie to me at all?"

"It's complicated."

She crosses her arms. "Make it make sense."

I don't want to make it make sense. I want to grab her, hold her, kiss her until our lips bruise. Because even with her looking at me like she'd take a machete to me if one were available, I feel the biggest sense of relief at having this weight lifted from my chest. I was so fucking sick of carrying that lie around, but I didn't realize just how much until I put it down.

"I didn't want to bring chaos into your life. I wanted to slip into town, deal with my house, and be on my way. I thought it would be easier for you if I left you alone."

"Oh, so you were being altruistic."

"Not so much. I've been in excruciating pain since the moment I showed up and saw you teetering across the grass at Summerhill."

"So much for leaving me alone."

"Have you noticed how often we're thrust together? I had ideas to avoid you. Plans! Hugo told me you—"

"Hugo." His name is a snarl. "I'll be having a conversation with him."

Did I sign my best friend's death warrant just now? It's looking like *yes*.

"For what it's worth, he advised against it. Told me I was a dumbass."

"All this time," Daisy murmurs, shaking her head. "Hugo knew it was you, but I was walking around like an idiot, trying to understand why you felt familiar. Why I was drawn to you. The way I immediately felt comfortable around you confused me, but I brushed it off because some people click in that inexplicable way."

I get up from the couch and start for her, but she sticks her hands out, stopping me. "Don't touch me."

I stay put, and say, "I was drawn to you, too, from that first night. I was on my way to Summerhill because I arrived in town ahead of schedule and I wanted a place to hide out until it was dark and I'd be less likely to run into you. Little did I know I was heading straight for you."

Daisy shakes her head, and her messy topknot tips precariously one way, then the other. "I don't know what to say Pet—" She sends me a death glare. "*Penn*. I need space." She fans her face. "I'm hot. I need air."

"We can go sit out on the back porch."

"No." She shakes her head. "I want to be alone. I'm going to go."

"Let me walk you to your car."

"Optics."

"If anybody sees you leave at this time in the early morning, optics are the least of your problems." Which reminds me. "You and Duke have an agreement?"

"Now is not the time. We"—she motions between us

—"are not chatting, I'm not confiding. You did a bad thing, and you're spinning it like you did it for a good reason, and I'm really fucking confused right now. I need time to process this. And I'm also going to figure out something creative to get Hugo back for being your accomplice."

"He was unwilling."

"And yet."

I walk her as far as I can, which turns out to be the front door. "Daisy, you have every right to be furious with me. But please know I've been struggling with keeping this from you. And—" I hesitate, looking for signs she'll be receptive to what I'm about to say. There's a fifty/fifty chance she'll haul off and kick me in the balls. "The plan has been for me to be here long enough to figure out my house, and admittedly, my time back in town has been lengthened by this play I was coerced into participating in."

"You barely protested."

"I was basically held at gunpoint."

"Pshh."

"Agree to disagree. The point is, I don't know how much longer I'll be in Olive Township." Internally, I wince at the words. Now that she knows who I am, I want to stay here forever. Except that would mean I'd see Daisy become Mrs. Hampton, and that's not something I can subject myself to. Not after getting to know Daisy as a woman, the fantastic person she is now. If I can't have her, I won't stay and watch her be somebody else's. "I propose we hash it out, you let me have it at a volume that doesn't wake the neighbors, and we figure out how to move forward as friends."

"Does 'hashing it out' include you telling me why you really left in the first place?"

If it wouldn't destroy her to know, I'd tell her everything as fast as I could make my lips move. The truth is acidic and sour, setting a burn to my chest. She takes my silence for what it is. My answer.

"That's what I thought." She turns the doorknob and looks over her shoulder. "You made a bed of lies, and now you get to lie in it."

Chapter 29

Daisy

Peter is Penn.

And I'm a fool.

When he told me, I felt devastation, anger, turmoil. Relief. But more than that, I wanted to throw myself in his arms. Hug him fiercely. Ask him how he truly is, what he's been doing for the past fifteen years. Does he still love heirloom tomatoes, thickly cut and sprinkled with flaky sea salt? What did he think of the new Top Gun movie? Was it as good as the original? He'd loved the first so much. I wanted to wrap my arms around him and tell him I was sorry, so sorry, to hear about his mother. He'd loved her the way a boy loves his mama, with utter devotion. Even through her dark times, he'd protected her with ferocity.

I lie here in this soft bed, staring up at the ceiling, letting the events of last night roll through my mind. The whole night was convoluted. Confusing. Fun, embarrassing, then shocking.

Anything for you.

I roll to my side, my eyes finding the picture of Penn I keep on my shelf. That day he was here helping me, he saw that photo. Picked it up. I told him about my old friend.

The whole time...

He doesn't look like the man I'd envisioned him growing into. My imagination did a poor job, taking thirteen-year-old Penn and making him taller and a little more filled out. The broad shoulders, the height, the strong jaw, my imagination provided none of that. The Penn of my memory had been scrawny, a late bloomer.

I feel like an idiot for not knowing, but maybe on some level I did. Because wasn't he so familiar to me from the very first moment? That was my soul recognizing his.

And Hugo knew.

I reach for my phone, bringing up my last conversation with Hugo, and fire off a text.

> You are a dirty liar.

> Considering I'm working in the olive grove today, then yes, I will be filthy before the day is out. But how exactly am I a liar?

> Here, meet my friend Penn. I mean, uhhh, Peter.

> Lie. What a great big pile of LIE.

> You would have done the same for my sister.

Penn

> But I am sorry for lying.

> I feel like an idiot.

> I know. If it helps, he didn't do it to hurt you.

> Right. He was trying not to interrupt my life.

> Does it interrupt your life?

> Of course not.

> Now who's lying?

> I'm getting married, HUGO. I don't have time for it to interrupt my life.

> I don't think that's how interruptions work, DAISY.

I toss my phone face down on the empty space in my bed. I don't want to talk to Hugo anymore, or think about the truth in his words. Penn is a massive interruption in my life. An interruption I am very angry with, while remaining very much attracted to. The emotions are opposing, and confusing, and I cannot wrap my mind around them.

There's a knock at my front door.

Penn.

I throw off the comforter and pop up from bed. Not a single care about my bedhead or the mismatched pajamas I threw on when I got home so very early this morning, when the sky was at its darkest and the birds were silent.

Emotions tumble through me, but the greatest is relief. My Penn is home.

I throw open the door, not bothering to check to see who it is first.

The man standing on my welcome mat brings me up short.

Duke.

"Hi," I greet, stepping back so he can come in. My neighbors from down the street are on their morning pilgrimage, and now they're peering at us with well-meaning nosiness. When Duke steps inside, I wrap my arms around him. He hugs me back, shutting the door with his foot.

"What's up?" I ask, letting him go.

He shrugs, looking around. "I had some time in my schedule this morning. I thought I would come over and see how much damage you've inflicted on this place without anybody knowing." He throws me a wink.

Spying all my kitchenware stacked up in one corner of my living room, he says, "I take it you don't have cabinets yet? Bathroom or kitchen?"

"That would be correct," I answer, walking with him to the kitchen. Internally, I'm cringing because I know what he's going to see.

"Dai-sy," he admonishes, whistling in surprise when we walk in.

"I know it looks bad," I say, taking in the scene. My kitchen is practically a skeleton except for the large appliances.

Penn

He turns to me. His eyes are soft, but worried. "Why don't you get dressed, and we'll go get some breakfast."

At his mention of food, my stomach growls. He grins at my hunger, telling me he'll wait for me in the living room.

I dress quickly in boyfriend jeans and an oversized sweatshirt. I don't have the energy for one of my cute dresses today, and I'm feeling raw. I want the softness of these worn fabrics, a plate of comfort food, and the biggest coffee they can pour.

Duke's standing in my living room like he said he'd be, back to me and on the phone. "I'll leave her front door unlocked. Thanks again, Scott."

"Who was that?" I ask, rolling up the sleeves on my sweatshirt.

"A contractor friend. He's coming over now to measure for new cabinets."

I snap my fingers. "Just like that, huh?"

He frowns at me. "Tell me it's wrong for me to use my connections. Tell me it's wrong to want you to have a functioning home."

"It's not wrong." I bite the inside of my lower lip as I try to parse through my feelings. "I feel stupid. It was dumb of me to rush forward with a remodel without doing any planning."

Duke wraps an arm around my shoulders, giving me a friendly squeeze. "I'd say it's true you've made better decisions on other occasions."

We exit the house, leaving the front door unlocked, and Duke drives to Good Thyme Café. The hostess seats us at our normal table, and the server grins as she approaches, taking our order and asking how much longer until our wedding.

"Three and a half weeks," Duke says, hand snaking across the table to affectionately squeeze mine. "Can't wait to watch my bride walk down the aisle."

I smile my Daisy St. James smile, the one that is expected of me. "I'm the luckiest girl in the world," I tell our server, handing her my menu.

When she's gone, Duke leans forward, gaze earnest and intent. "Things have seemed off with you lately, and I want to check on you. Despite the deal we've structured, you're one of my closest friends, and I want to make sure you're ok."

My hand is still in his, our heads bent toward each other. To an observer, we look like we're having an intimate conversation. And I suppose we are, but it's more secretive than intimate.

"I actually learned something shocking, and I'm still reeling from it." I drop my volume even lower, and Duke leans in further to hear me. "Peter Bravo is Penn Bellamy."

Duke is well trained in how to school his reactions, a talent needed when he is in meetings and boardrooms. But his total nonchalance, the flicker of *nothing* in his eyes, tells me something I wouldn't have guessed.

He already knows.

"I figured it out after the night at King's Ransom," he says, his volume matching mine now. "I'm wary of anybody new showing up. Due diligence is important in my work, and it bleeds into my life."

"So you looked into him?"

He nods. "It was incredibly easy, which tells me he didn't go to many lengths to truly hide his identity." Duke sits back, giving our server space to deliver our coffees.

"With a side of real whipped cream for the bride," she says, smiling jauntily at me. I thank her and spoon a dollop on my creamy coffee.

"You're injured," Duke says, bringing his black coffee to his lips.

"Healthy as a horse," I respond.

"Emotionally," he amends, placing his cup on the table. "You're most indulgent when you feel injured. You ordered your normal egg and bacon breakfast, but you added a side of cinnamon swirl pancakes. That's a dead giveaway."

"I guess I am injured," I say, stirring my spoon in my coffee, watching the whipped cream melt into the hot liquid. "Not only was Peter, er, Penn lying to me, but so were you." I sip the sweetened caffeine, nearly groaning as it hits my tongue. I needed this, and Duke knew it. "Why didn't you tell me as soon as you knew?"

His fingers, still wrapped around his mug, tighten. He hesitates, and now I'm seeing Penn in the middle of the night, refusing to tell me why he left. There's something here, a piece integral to forming the puzzle so it makes sense to me, but neither Penn nor Duke will speak it. And it means they share the same secret, or at least facets of it.

"I wasn't sure what him being back would mean for you. For us."

"Duke, that's not right. I deserve to know."

"Of course you do." Duke slides out from his side of the booth, and I scoot over to make room for him beside me.

He loops an arm over my shoulder, and I lean into him. He smells the same as he has for years, something clean and citrusy with a hint of pine. He smells like my friend. Into my hair, he murmurs, "I need to know, Daisy, if him being back changes things."

I think of Penn, of what he said in the middle of the night. *I don't know how much longer I'll be in Olive Township, but it won't be forever.*

Then I think of my mother, of the last time I saw her, the way she gasped at the sight of me in her dress at my fitting.

"No, Duke. Nothing has changed."

My head dips with his strong exhale, as if he'd been holding his breath while he waited for my answer.

Duke has skin in the game, too. It's not only my mom we're supplying with a manufactured happily ever after for her daughter. It's Duke's parents, too.

Our server delivers our food, placing both plates on one side of the table. "Look at you two," she coos. "Can't bear to be apart, even when it's only a table's distance."

"Very true," Duke says, pressing a kiss to my hair.

There's a twinge of something in my chest, something *not good*.

Until now I've been apathetic towards Duke's kiss. It

Penn

was a non-event. It went part and parcel with what we're doing. But the feeling inside me now? It's a real problem.

At the press of Duke's lips was the inclination to recoil.

Because it's Penn I want, even if I am furious and hurt.

My heart refuses to line up with my mind.

Stubborn bitch.

Chapter 30

Penn

INCONCEIVABLE!

Cute name for a store that sells random knickknacks, and bonus points to me for understanding the movie reference behind the store's name.

I haven't tried calling Daisy since she left my place under the cover of darkness yesterday. A phone call, or a text, isn't enough. I need action, something that speaks for itself.

I don't know exactly what it is I'm trying to say, but I can't allow time to pass without attempting something. Plus, I still need to help her with that drywall. Unless Paper Towel Duke decides to man up and help her himself.

I'm waiting for the other shoe to drop where Duke is concerned. He made it abundantly clear he didn't want me telling Daisy who I really am, not that I cared. There was no way I was going to be intimate with her under the guise of another person.

Penn

According to Daisy, my lies have made me a bed and now I'll have to lie in it. But the thing about me is that I don't stay down long. Apologies won't be made if I'm sitting around feeling sorry for myself. I need her to know that I never intended to make her feel like a fool. I want her to know that she's beautiful and smart and loyal to the core. And I'm deeply regretful of the hurt I caused her.

I have an idea, and I'm not sure it will work, but if it makes her smile even once, it will be worth it.

Walking into this kitschy store is like hitting pay dirt. Funny keychains, handmade wooden bookmarks, bottles of local olive oil (no offense Hugo, but I'll pass), mini-puzzles, a deep freeze loaded with ice cream bars, a take-one leave-one library and DVD selection (do people still have DVD players?). The list goes on and on.

I select a bookmark with a bouquet of daisies carved into the wood, a lavender leather-bound journal, a keychain that says *Fresh Outta Fucks,* and a mini-puzzle of a pygmy hippo family. I don't know if they're still Daisy's favorite animal, but she'll know that's where my mind was. I add to my basket until I've reached fifteen items. A gift for every birthday I've missed.

I consider a pink apron outlined in a delicate ivory lace. It looks so much like Daisy, feminine and soft and beautiful, and it's way better than the only other choice of apron, a burgundy color fabric printed with white dinner plates and wineglasses that reads *Wine me, dine me, get your mind out of the gutter*.

In the end, I decide against the apron because I don't know if Daisy cooks, and it's probably not an appropriate gift for a woman I'd call a friend. It isn't until I reach the small counter with my haul that I realize there isn't a store clerk, and there hasn't been one the entire time I've been in here.

"Hello," I call out. I'm met with silence.

And then I spy in the corner a small folding table with an old-timey cash register, and a notebook lying open beside it, pen nestled in the crevice between pages. Paper-clipped to the top of the register is a small hand-written sign that reads

> Inconceivable! is an honor system store.
> Tally up the cost of your items, add 8% for tax
> and place the money into the register. If you're
> paying with plastic, use the card reader.
>
> P.S. if you take advantage of the honor system,
> we wish you a sudden onset case of
> tummy troubles on your next date.
> With love,
> Olive Township

Well, damn. If that isn't the quaintest, cutest small-town quirk I've ever seen.

It feels odd now, knowing I'm the only person in here, but I do as I'm instructed, rounding up on the tax because *who carries coins anymore?* and place the cash in the appropriate spaces in the register.

My next stop is a gift wrap store, where the store employee helps me find little boxes for each item. Rolls of wrapping paper line the wall, hundreds, at least, and I choose a pink pearlescent paper, with an ivory ribbon. Like the apron in Inconceivable!, the color combo feels like Daisy. I go home, Slim Jim lying by my side, and pull up my internet browser, watching video after video on how to wrap gifts. It's not like I've never wrapped a gift before, but when I finish, it always looks like something not much better than what a four-year-old could accomplish.

And wouldn't you know, I have been missing out on the rules of perfectly wrapping a gift this whole time. The cutting, the corners, the folding, it's practically geometry. When I sit back, gifts wrapped and bows perfectly tied (another shout out to the Internet for helping me learn that) I feel very proud of myself.

I'm not trying to earn Daisy's forgiveness with these gifts, I only want her to know I'm sorry.

Early tomorrow morning, when the sky is at its darkest, I'll place one package on her front door mat. My hope is that she'll discover it on her way to start her day, and I'll be on her mind all day. Selfish, perhaps, but I want her to think of me. To know I'm sorry, and that it's she who fills my mind, invades my thoughts, owns my heart.

Until then, I head to my mother's house to continue the removal and clean up project, Slim Jim by my side. I work until two blisters form under my thick work gloves, and sweat streams down my back despite the quickly declining air temperature.

On the way home, I grab takeout from a café that wasn't in business when I lived here before, then I grab an overpriced sweatshirt from a boutique next door. I forgot how quickly a warm day turns into a cold night in the desert.

I pass Sal on his way out of the bakery, Adela on his arm. He sends me a wave, and I return the gesture.

Olive Township is coming to life as the sun sets, restaurants filling up and the music from bars spilling out into the main street. This place is special, no doubt, an eclectic blend of gritty, desert charm mixed with high-end details.

It's unbelievable, but as I drive through town, it becomes clear to me that Daisy and Hugo were not all I missed of Olive Township.

The town itself is lodged in my heart.

Home.

Chapter 31

Daisy

THE SUN BEAMS OFF A BEAUTIFULLY WRAPPED GIFT on my welcome mat, sending colors an inch into the air around it. A quick glance around my neighborhood confirms there is nobody out there, waiting for me to receive this present.

A tag dangles, string tied into the ribbon, but I don't want to look at it. Somehow I know in my heart who it's from, so I save the tag for last.

A journal, bound in lavender leather. The smell of new paper floats from the book as I flip through. The pages are lined, save for the first page, where a single line in the center reads *This journal belongs to* and the name is filled in.

Sunshine

A faint smile ghosts my lips, my fingertip tracing the letters written by his hand. The gift tag reads:

To hold your thoughts.
Happy birthday.

My birthday isn't for eight more months. Why has Penn left me this?

With one last glance down the street, I retreat into my home, gift in hand. Depositing it in my nightstand drawer, I stare down at the lavender leather, knuckles brushing over my lower lip.

This is Penn's way of apologizing. It doesn't work instantaneously, like flipping over a coin, but there's something to it. A nudge. An in-road.

I shouldn't indulge my heart this way, but I can't help it.

Not when it comes to Penn.

Chapter 32

Penn

On Monday I show up to Desert Oasis Theatre, where Noelle told me to be for rehearsal.

It's a large space with stadium-style seating for a couple hundred people. There's a scuffed stage, bracketed by thick curtains. It's hard to describe what the place smells like, only that it's not terrible, but also not good. Musty, I guess.

Noelle waves me over when I walk in. "This is Peter Bravo," she says, introducing me to the woman she's standing with.

"Actually," I clear my throat. "My name is Penn Bellamy." It feels good to say my name.

Noelle makes a face. "Does Daisy know that?"

"Yeah," I nod. "It's a long story, though, and I'm not telling it."

"That's...weird," Noelle says.

"Tenley Roberts," the woman beside Noelle cuts in. "Nice to meet you, Penn."

"You as well," I respond. "I hear you're famous."

She laughs. "I'm famous in people's memories." She goes on to tell me she's not officially retired, but she has backed out of the limelight.

"We're lucky Tenley agreed to take this on," Noelle says. "Otherwise I'd be playing the princess, and that would be a bit of a stretch." Tenley starts to say something, but Noelle steamrolls on. "Tenley's been bringing her nephew to story hour for a couple years now. Her brother-in-law comes and signs for a couple kids who need ASL."

"Including my nephew," Tenley adds.

"That is..." I struggle to find the words, coming up with, "unbelievably wholesome."

Tenley cackles. "It really is."

Noelle drifts away to round up the other actors, and Tenley and I spend a few minutes introducing ourselves. She says she has two step-kids, and one toddler, and as she put it *the family I married into is a whole thing*. But there isn't a trace of exasperation in her tone, and she smiles when she says it, and a flash of envy pinches my heart. I will never have that. A great big family, complaining about them but loving them far more. I have my brothers-in-arms, but they are deployed now, off on another mission. I have Hugo, but eventually, Hugo will meet the right woman, and he will form his own family. I have Slim Jim, and I can't begin to think about a day when we're not together or I'll break down.

Noelle introduces the cast, and all the kids who will be running the show. I was expecting something small and poorly organized, but I was off-base. Way, *way* off-base. The director, a frizzy-haired redheaded twelve-year-old wearing a plain black ball cap, is akin to a tyrant. Her name is Lincoln, and she doesn't crack a smile, not even once during the entire rehearsal. She is all business, directing us to our spots, rolling her eyes at me when I forget a line. I'm inclined to tell her I've engaged in hand-to-hand combat in crumbling buildings in the middle of nowhere with men who wanted to see me dead, but decide against it. I don't think she'd have the response I'd want her to have.

Tenley rescues me by having her lines memorized, and mine too. She whispers them to me when I pause a beat too long.

I yawned more than I meant to, a product of waking up at four a.m. to take that first gift to Daisy, and Noelle kept shooting me annoyed looks. I wanted to remind her that I was neither willing, nor am I being paid to be here, but decided against that, too. These theatre people are intense.

"That's a wrap for today," Lincoln says, still seated in her director chair that swallows her small frame. "Penn, please work on memorizing your lines. It's not Tenley's job to whisper them to you."

Beside me, Tenley stifles a laugh.

"Yes, chef," I answer, and earn a dirty look from the pre-teen.

"Don't worry about her," Tenley assures me as we walk out to the parking lot. "Girls of that age come preloaded with cutting remarks."

"So it's not me?"

"Oh, it's definitely you. But it's her, too." Tenley veers off toward her vehicle, a vintage Bronco that has me whistling low.

"She's a babe, right?" Tenley affectionately pats the car. "Her name is Pearl."

"Pearl is a babe," I confirm. "I'll see you on Wednesday."

Tenley waves and drives off. I hop in my truck, checking my phone for what feels like the seventy-second time today. I'm not expecting Daisy to say anything, but I'm hoping for it. There is a message, but my burst of excitement is short-lived when I see it's from Hugo and not Daisy.

> You sent the HOA a nasty-gram?

> Not nasty. Just strongly worded.

> You told them you refused to pay the fine for leaving out the trash can I told you not to leave on the street longer than twenty-four hours.

> Correct.

> Well, congratulations buddy, Bobbie agreed to waive the fine, but stated she wouldn't be so lenient next time.

> LFG!!!

> Is this what your life has come to? Arguing with HOA presidents?

Penn

> I think the kids call it 'adulting.'

> Next you'll be feeling immeasurably pleased by the cleanliness of your fridge drawers.

> Ok but I already do that.

※ ❀ ※ ❀ ※

ANOTHER FOUR A.M. WAKEUP.

A second gift left at Daisy's front door.

Chapter 33

Daisy

There, in the same place as yesterday, is another gift. A bookmark.

To keep your place.
Happy birthday.

I'm smiling to myself when I go into my house. Another birthday gift? I'm not yet sure where he's going with this, but I'm sensing a pattern.

And a thawing in my heart.

Chapter 34

Daisy

Six more days of birthday gifts.

I'm up early today, hoping to catch Penn. I want to see him as himself, not as Peter. I want to see the boy I loved, who grew into a man.

The sun is only slightly above the mountains in the east when I open my front door.

Too late.

A present, wrapped in that same paper, waits for me on my mat.

I unwrap it on my way into my bedroom to get changed for the day. Duke's contractor friend, Scott, will be here soon to double-check his measurements before he orders cabinets. I have a day full of clients and wedding favors to assemble.

I laugh softly to myself as I tear away the paper, revealing the prickly pear flavored rock candy sugar sticks. A vestige of my childhood, a treat I haven't had in years.

To satisfy your sweet tooth.
Happy birthday.

Once I'm dressed, I make a cup of chamomile tea, using the rock candy to stir and sweeten. The second sugar stick I'll save for Vivi, who loved them also.

The sweetness hits my tongue, the flavor nostalgic. As a kid I nibbled on the pure sugar, but I like it this way now, stirred into tea.

One thing is for certain, Penn is good at gifting. And remembering. And apologizing.

Warmth trickles through me, and it's not only the hot tea. It's Penn's gesture, working its way into my heart.

I leave a key under a rock in the front yard for Scott, and on my way to work I stop at Dama Oliva. Vivi has her staff gathered near the walk-in freezer for a morning meeting.

"Just wanted to drop this with you," I say, pressing the cellophane-wrapped candy into her hand. "Sorry for interrupting."

Vivi glances at the candy. "I haven't had this in forever."

"Me, too. That's why I wanted to share it with you." I back out of the kitchen, waving at the group wearing curious gazes. "Have a good day."

I spend the day seeing patients and surreptitiously glancing out the front window, hoping for a glimpse of Penn, or Slim Jim, or even Penn's truck. Isla told me he rescheduled his appointments, probably to give me the

Penn

space I asked for. That warmth in my heart is pushing at me to consider hearing what Penn has to say.

Duke takes me to dinner at Dama Oliva, and comes home with me to help put together the favors.

"Scott was here today," I say as we tie ribbons around the honey stirrers. "I gave him the go-ahead to order the cabinets."

Duke nods. "I asked him to make sure the drawers are slow-close. They're kinder on the fingers than what you used to have."

"Thank you for everything," I tell him when he's leaving. "I appreciate the way you care so much about your friends."

He gives me the same friendly hug he's been giving me for years. "I know sometimes this is all awkward, and certainly unconventional, but we're friends first, no matter what."

"Agreed," I say, squeezing him a little extra.

He leaves, that loud engine growling its way down my street. I make another cup of tea, swirling the rock candy, tasting the sweetness of the prickly pear, and think of the man who left it at my door.

Chapter 35

Daisy

I set my alarm for thirty minutes before the sun rose.

I didn't linger in bed like I wanted to.

Still, I missed Penn.

It's been nearly two weeks of gift-giving, and I've yet to see him. I could text him, or call, or show up at his mom's house, or even the house where he's staying, but I don't want to. I want to see him on my doorstep, gift in hand. There's something about the gesture that's romantic, and calling or texting is too modern. Too impersonal.

It's safe to say I have thawed all the way, and I'm ready to see Penn. Talk to him. Find out who he is now. I'm ready to absorb everything that makes him who he is today.

Tearing into the package, I find a plastic keychain, the words *Fresh Outta Fucks* written in hot pink on a white background.

Penn

To make you laugh.
Happy birthday.

It does. But it also makes me determined.

I have a foolproof idea, one that will not fail me.

After all, it's not the early bird who catches the worm, it's the one who hangs around from the night before.

Chapter 36

Daisy

Bundled in my wearable blanket, plus leggings and a long sleeve T-shirt, fuzzy socks, and slippers, I sit in my front porch chair, legs tucked up to my chest. The cool of the night air swirls around my face, a cold that feels colder because of the lack of humidity in the air.

My neighborhood is older, and quieter, a stretch of homes on a street without lights or sidewalks. I bought it four years ago when I came back to town after graduating from physical therapy school. The world outside my idyllic small town had taught me a few lessons, one of which was that there was no way I could return to living on the St. James farm. My parents would've welcomed me with open arms, but I knew that wasn't the right way for me. I think about that sometimes, how I would've had more time with my mother had I moved back in with them. It's a useless regret, but I wonder if it's played a role in this plan I've made with Duke.

It's an errant thought, one that makes me restless and

uncomfortable, so I push it aside and hit 'play' on my phone. I'm listening to a podcast interview with an author who wrote a fiction book based on her marriage to a firefighter who developed a drinking problem, and the roller coaster they went on because of it. She says a lot of things that make me think, but none so much as the moment she mentions *true love*.

A few weeks ago I would've said that notion was utter bullshit, but now I'm not so sure. Can the path to true love consist of broken roads? According to this woman, *yes*.

Huh. I've always thought of the path to true love as shiny and pristine, white marble lined with waxy yellow tulips.

It's nearing midnight, the full moon providing me with light, and I've been out here for an hour. It doesn't matter how much longer I need to sit out here, because I'm on a mission. Besides, I'm kind of loving the thrill of lying in wait. At any moment he could pull up, creep up my driveway, and here I am in the shadows, waiting to say some form of *boo*. I'm actually not sure what I'm going to say when I see him, I figured I'd do it off-the-cuff so it's organic.

He's going to laugh, I know that. What else will he do? Maybe take me in his arms? Give me a bone-crushing hug as his real self? No more *Peter* being careful around me. He can be Penn now.

The night grows darker, a stretch of clouds blocking the moon, and a hearty yawn momentarily transfigures my face. Popping my AirPods out, I nestle them in their case and toss it on the seat beside me. I take the pillow I brought out here with me and prop it up behind my head, like I'm settling in for a long winter's nap.

I'll rest my eyes for a few minutes while I wait.

"Sunshine?"

The word is a whisper in my mind. There's a gentle shake of my shoulder.

"Sunshine?" The word is closer now, breaking through my sleep.

My eyes fly open. I was on a mission. How dare I fall asleep!

Penn is nearly at eye-level with me, bent on a knee with his hand on my shoulder. His hair flops on his forehead in that exact way I adore, and his eyes are crinkly and cute.

"Why are you out here?" he asks.

"Trying to catch my gift giver," I say, stifling a yawn as I sit up taller. The pillow I'd propped behind my head tumbles to the ground.

"It was me," Penn says, grabbing the pillow and tossing it on the other empty chair.

"I know." I look up at him, backlit by the glow of the full moon. I've known him as Peter, but now *oh my gosh it's Penn!* Look how tall he is! How big! He's a man now. He has muscles for days and veined forearms and his jaw is chiseled and he grows facial hair and his voice is deep and curls into me and he has tattoos.

Tattoos.

Daisies. For me.

My childhood best friend grew up and never forgot

Penn

me. He cared so much he inked me on his skin, added me to a place with near-constant visibility.

Penn motions to the empty seat with my pillow lying on it. "Can I sit?"

"That depends," I answer. "Are you going to tell me why you left?" The question has plagued me for years, I can't help but give my truth-seeking mission another attempt.

Penn shakes his head, his gaze genuinely sad. "Sometimes, knowing things makes life worse, Daisy."

I nod, the last of my sleepiness slipping away as I tuck my knees into my chest, wrapping my arms around my legs. I'm insatiably curious still, but I understand what he's saying. Maybe whatever it was that made him leave that he won't share with me, maybe it hurt him as much as it did me.

I motion to the chair and he settles in, sitting back and crossing one ankle over the opposite knee. A very manly posture, one he never did when I knew him before.

It's new to me. All of it. All of him. Some of it's familiar because I knew him as Peter, but it mostly feels like I'm discovering Penn. Honestly, I like what I see. All of it. Every mannerism, every coy smile, every crooked grin, every dubious eyebrow lift. I like it all.

Penn gazes at me, the air thick with possibility. Anticipation. The question of *What's next?* hangs between us.

I slice through the heaviness by saying, "Hi, Penn."

He grins impishly. "Hi, Daisy."

Thrill sweeps through me. Jubilation. "It's good to see you again."

A smile breaks onto his face. Relief. "You have no idea how it feels to see you and know you're seeing *me*."

"I wish you would've told me from the beginning."

"Me, too, now that I'm looking back on it." He shakes his head slowly back and forth, rubbing the pad of his thumb over his lower lip. "I almost did, that first night at Summerhill. But once I found out you were engaged, it solidified my plan to keep my identity hidden. I figured it was easier for everyone."

"It was a bonehead move."

"Hah!" He palms the back of his neck. "I haven't been called a bonehead in a long time. Probably not since you."

"I don't think I've called anybody a bonehead since you, either."

"I'm...honored."

We share a friendly smile in the muted white swath of moonlight, happiness flickering in our eyes. Old friends delighted to be reunited.

Penn reaches down beside him. "I have another gift for you."

My legs straighten out from under the blanket I'm wearing, meeting the cool night air. I reach out, fingers fluttering. "Ooh, gimme. This has been fun."

Penn presses the gift into my hand with a flourish. "It's the last one. A gift for every birthday I missed." The pearlescent paper shimmers in the light from the moon.

"Did you wrap these yourself?"

He nods, looking proud. "I watched some how-to videos."

Penn

"That is unbelievably cute." I tap the top of the box. "May I?"

"Go for it," Penn says, scooting his chair closer.

Cedar and citrus swirls around me. His knee presses against mine, body heat moving through his gray sweats and surrounding my leg. His Adam's apple bobs with a hard swallow. Desire unfurls in my belly, slow and hot. It takes me back to our movie night, to the fire in his gaze.

I pause with my finger under a flap of wrapping paper. I'm nervous to bring up last weekend and the way I basically threw myself at him, but if not now, when? "Penn, when we were at your place last weekend after we watched the movie, and...you know. Did you stop it because of Duke? Or was it something else?"

Penn leans forward, elbows resting on his knees, chin propped on his hand. He's so close, I could stroke his cheek. Fire ignites in his gaze, hot desire plain on his face. "Sunshine, there's no part of me that doesn't want to ravage you. Please understand that."

The things I want to do to you. That's what he'd said, and it's been tormenting me relentlessly since.

He continues. "I know you and Duke have some kind of agreement, which I still need you to explain." He's looking at me, chin still in his hand, his head tilted. I can't believe we're having this conversation, so calm and matter-of-fact. "Daisy, I've never stopped thinking about you. Caring for you. I thought I could come back here and make it out in one piece, but that was foolish, because a piece of me was always with you. I haven't been whole since I was thirteen. Since I was last with you."

Oh, my heart. It's twisting and turning, flipping and cartwheeling.

"Please believe me when I say it has been a unique form of torture to be around you and know you're engaged. In my mind, I have done all manner of delicious and dirty things to you. Touching you, making you see stars, would be a privilege, but I won't do it while another man's ring is on your finger."

I squirm as heat pools low in my belly. I want to take Penn in my house and see what I can do to get him to change his mind.

But I also need to be honest with him, just like he was honest with me.

"It's not real," I whisper in my quietest voice, one that makes Penn scoot his closer, until our knees are touching. "Duke needs to get his dad and the board of Hampton & Co. off his back. And my mom, she's..." My voice trails off. I hate thinking about the eventuality. "She wants to see me walk down the aisle in her wedding dress. It's been her dream since I was a little girl."

Penn reaches for my hand, his fingers threading through mine. "Do you really think she'd want you to marry someone you don't love?"

I've turned the same question over in my mind hundreds of times. And the answer is no, she would not want me to marry somebody I don't love. But she thinks I love Duke. She thinks she's going to leave this world behind, and her little girl will be happily married. It

Penn

brings her peace to think I found the person I want by my side for the rest of my life, and how can I take that from her?

"It's complicated," I murmur.

"Sounds like it," is all that Penn says in response.

"Thank you for not judging me."

"I would never." He flips my hand over, tracing the lines in my palm. His touch creates a spark that goes flying through my limbs. "It all makes more sense now," he says, catching my gaze. "You and Duke have zero chemistry."

"Not like me and you, Pete." I can't help but tease him.

"Very funny," Penn says, a smile tugging at his mouth. "Open your present."

He drops my hand, and I reach for the box perched in my lap, turning it over to read the tag.

To make you smile.
Happy birthday.

Carefully, I unwrap the gift, revealing a mini-puzzle of a pygmy hippo family.

"Oh," I whisper, my hand pressing to my mouth. "They are my favorite."

"I was hoping they still were."

This gesture does something to my heart, but it's twofold. The more I feel for Penn, the more I question what Duke and I are doing. And that line of questioning is a dangerous little game to play, a slope that could easily become slippery.

"Thank you," I say, holding the box to my chest. "This is so thoughtful. Every gift was."

In the distance, the sky is turning a muted baby blue over the mountain range to the east. Soon the sun will peek over, making Penn's presence more visible to anybody out early.

"I should go," he says, his thoughts in the same place as mine.

"I wish you would come inside."

I hear it. The double entendre. Penn gives me a meaningful look, and I press my lips together.

And you know what? I've heard what he said about this ring on my finger, and I respect it, but that doesn't mean I can't have a little fun with it.

In a voice as thick and golden as local honey, I say, "You can do that, too. Inside. Outside. Consider me your canvas."

Penn sits back in his seat. Closes his eyes. Pinches the bridge of his nose. "Fuck, Sunshine. *Fuck*. Go into your house. Go into your house *right fucking now*."

But I don't really feel like listening. "Or what?" My eyebrows are raised, my chin lifted.

"Or I will fuck that ring off your finger."

I stand up, bending slightly, placing my lips near the shell of his ear, and whisper, "Don't threaten me with a good time, Sailor."

Then I walk into the house, puzzle in hand.

Chapter 37

Penn

It's official. Daisy St. James was created to ruin me. I was made to burn for her.

Chapter 38

Penn

> There is a massive spider in my kitchen.
>
> PLEASE PLEASE PLEASE.
>
> You have to come over.

I'll be there in ten. Keep an eye on it in case it moves.

> What do I do if it moves?

Track it, so you can tell me where it goes.

> It has fangs. One giant eyeball. Spiked legs. I think it knows my name.

Is this spider real?

Hello?

Sunshine?

See you soon.

Penn

Daisy answers the door while I'm knocking.

Her eyes twinkle, her cheek muscles flexing with the effort to keep a smile from her face. I narrow my eyes. "Little liar."

She ignores me, pivoting. I step inside, closing the front door behind me. And then I die. Once, twice, three times. A rip in the seat of Daisy's jeans is enough to send me six feet under.

"Daisy, where are the rest of your jeans?"

She's walking in front of me through her house, heading for the kitchen. I'm trailing along behind, staring at the curve of her ass. Correction, one ass cheek, bare. It's beautiful, like the curve of a Cheshire Cat smile. I want to sink my teeth into it, trace it with my tongue.

She wears a nondescript white T-shirt, but on her, it's elevated. I definitely made the right choice wearing jeans today. Sweats would not have hidden the ever-lengthening erection in the front of my pants.

Daisy pauses halfway through her living room, one hip popping out as she gazes over her shoulder, eyes cast down. "Are you talking about the rip in my jeans? These are my house pants, Pete."

"Stop calling me Pete."

"Old habits," she says, continuing on into the kitchen.

"You never called me Pete," I argue, following her. "Where's the Dracula cyclops spider?"

She points two fingers down, miming a break-neck run. "Scurried away."

"I thought I told you to keep an eye on it?"

She shrugs. "Too fast for me."

Obviously I knew there wasn't a spider, but I'm on pins and needles now waiting for whatever it is Daisy really called me over here for.

I stop and lean against the kitchen wall, watching her head disappear into the fridge. She's bending over, ass stuck out, a deep curve in her lower back. My hips practically thrust her direction, the second brain in my pants dying to rub against her. But I said I wouldn't touch her, and I mean it.

I cross my arms. "You are downright devious."

She pulls away from the fridge, a pitcher of water in her hand. "And so good at blow jobs, too. I consider myself the whole package."

My hands sink to my sides.

Do not picture Daisy on her knees. Do not picture Daisy on her knees.

Attempts to block the image are futile. All I see are Daisy's brown eyes watery as she takes me to the back of her throat.

She grins broadly, knowing she has gotten to me.

"So I tell you I won't touch you while you wear that ring"—I point at the frozen pond on her left hand—"and all you heard was *he needs to be properly convinced.*"

"Well, Sailor," Daisy says, sauntering forward. She

Penn

stops just out of arm's reach from me, lips pouty. "I do love a challenge."

"Daisy, you have no idea how stubborn I can be."

"Is that supposed to dissuade me?"

Alarm races through me. As much as it's going to kill me to deny this woman, I'm going to enjoy the ride. She can tease me all she wants. I have to die someday, might as well be at the hands, hips, and ass of Daisy.

"No, Sunshine. Just making sure you know to bring your A game, because I play to win."

"Funny you should say that," she says, lifting the pitcher of water. "Because I do, too." Then she overturns the pitcher, soaking her chest.

Two things become instantly clear. The water is cold, and she isn't wearing a bra.

I have vastly underestimated my opponent.

I spin around. Stomp out.

"Thanks for coming over, Penn," Daisy shouts, her voice light and airy and pleased.

I pause at the front door. "Anything for you, Sunshine."

Chapter 39

Daisy

> Hey, Sailor. Are you planning to help me drywall and re-tile the bathroom? My new cabinets will be installed soon. No worries if not. I'm sure I can figure it out on my own.

Am I allowed to park my truck on your curb during the day? Tongues will be wagging.

> I grabbed dinner at Sammich last night and told Margaret the same guy who's working on the Bellamy house is helping me with repairs at my house. My guess is that most of the town will know by now.

Now I understand why Sal tried to hire me for handyman services this morning when I stopped by Sweet Nothings for a bagel.

> Did you take the job?

Penn

It was a light bulb change out and a bathroom fan replacement. It took me less than half an hour.

I am so sorry!!!

It's fine. Sal is funny. He and Adela bicker constantly.

I know. I think it's their love language.

I'm meeting an appraiser at my old house at 10. I can come over after that to see what it is we're going to need to do and buy. I have rehearsal for the play at four (we have to wait for the tyrannical director to be let out of her sixth grade class).

<crying laughing emoji> See you soon.

Chapter 40

Daisy

"Good news," Penn says, when I answer my front door. His faded blue jeans fit him snugly, and his gray T-shirt, printed with NAVY across the front, has a worn-out neck. A handful of paint droplets dot the hem, and there's something about this I love.

"What's that?" I ask, stepping back to allow him inside.

He reaches into his pocket, pulling something out with a flourish. "I got these cool new glasses." He slides them on. The lenses are dark brown, the frames a cheap looking plastic tan. "They are magic."

"How so?"

"When I have them on, I can't see you, but I can still see everything else. This means I can tile your bathroom, and be impervious to your feminine wiles."

I laugh so hard, I'm dangerously close to snorting. Reaching over, I pluck them from his face and break them in half. They snap in a way only the cheapest of sunglasses can.

His mouth drops open and I hold them up for his inspection. Then I tuck each half into the pockets of my lemon yellow maxi skirt.

"Wicked," Penn comments.

To which I say, "I really hope that's not your A game."

"Invisible force fields were my backup plan," he responds, and it makes me laugh.

"You are so bad at this."

He runs a hand through his perpetually unruly hair. "I've never had to fend off a woman I'm desperate for."

Pleasure ripples through me at the word *desperate*. "I've never had to work this hard to make a man want me."

"Daisy," Penn says through clenched teeth. "You donned a wearable blanket the other night, and all I wanted to do was duck my head under it. Please believe me when I say your very existence makes me want you."

That stops me short. Sends desire racing through me, but not the physical kind. Desire for an emotional connection. Something I won't have with Duke. We'll have friendship, sure, something good and solid and time-tested, but we won't lie in bed at night and recount our day. The realization is distressing.

And then I look at Penn, and the secondary realization I have is far more of a bombshell.

I would have that with Penn. With someone I loved.

Dammit. What am I thinking?

I'm marrying Duke in less than two weeks. My mother's dress has already been altered to fit me. The cake is chosen, the venue is booked, Vivi has picked her dress. I can't go back now. And my mother...

Pushing those crazy thoughts aside, I tap Penn's chest, right above the NAVY lettering. "Sailor, you don't have to talk your way into my thong. I'm a sure thing."

But Penn knows, doesn't he? He sees deep down into me, and he knows I'm deflecting, using sex to keep us from tumbling down the rabbit hole, to keep me from throwing away everything Duke and I have worked for, the deal we designed to satisfy familial responsibilities.

Penn lets me slide, yielding to my cover-up, knowing I cannot yet face what I'm really doing with my life. That maybe, I never will.

"Let's get that bathroom re-tiled." Penn inclines his head toward my room. "Did you get everything from that list I sent you?"

"It's all back there." I thumb behind myself.

We work, and we work. From what I've read, tiling a wall doesn't take a great deal of knowledge or special talent, but it does require precision and patience. I am low on both, but luckily, Penn has it in spades.

Following instructions from a video, we use a trowel to apply a coat of thin set. Penn pushes a tile into place, and I hand over spacers. He applies them to the four corners of the tile, and we keep on like that, placing tile and spacers until we're done.

Penn works hard, barely stopping for the water I bring him. His eyes flash to the front of my shirt as I hand him the cup, but I put my hands up and promise no more

Penn

wet T-shirts until he tells me he wants one. "The ball is in your court, Sailor."

He frowns at this, but gets back to work applying the grout. Taunting and teasing Penn is fun, but I want him to be a part of it, too. I understand where he's coming from about not wanting to touch me while I'm engaged, and I respect that, so if he wants me to make it hard for him to say no, he's going to have to tell me.

Penn and I finish up the grout, and he applies a waterproof protecting agent to the tile while I start cleanup.

"Whoa," I say, waving a hand in front of my nose. "The smell of that stuff is not pleasant. And it's really strong."

Penn's making a face too, increasing his pace so he can finish faster. "Wait for me in the living room, Daisy. You don't need to be in here smelling this." He looks down at the debris I'm sweeping. "None of that is going anywhere."

He's right. I hustle from the room, and Penn follows five minutes later.

"I turned on the ceiling fan in your bedroom," he says, heading for the fridge. He grabs the pitcher of filtered water and refills his cup. "I was starting to get a headache from that stuff. Do you have anywhere you can go for a few hours? I don't think it's toxic, but it probably won't be fun to sit around and smell it."

"Duke is working, and so is Vivi. I have quarterly taxes to work on, so I can go into the office for a little while."

Penn's lips twist like he's considering something. "Or, you could go for a drive with me."

"A drive? Like we're eighty and it's a Sunday afternoon?"

He laughs. "More like we're almost thirty and I have to be back in two hours for a play rehearsal I am still vehemently opposed to."

I grab my purse. "When you can't change your circumstances, change how you feel about your circumstances."

"Is that one of those bland inspirational quotes you have up in your office?"

I gasp and punch him in the arm. "How dare you?"

He keeps going. "When life hands you lemons—"

"Add vodka," I interject, pushing him out the front door.

"That is definitely not what the sign in your conference room says."

"This is beautiful," I say, looking around in wonder.

The scenic vista provides an unadulterated view of the Sonoran Desert, nearly all the way south to Tucson. Mountain after mountain juts up in the distance, majestic peaks and orange and red hued valley walls. To

Penn

the west is the olive mill, to the east, nothing but desert, on and on until New Mexico.

"I would've brought you here," Penn says, smiling from where he sits beside me on the hood of his truck. The air temperature is a perfect seventy-two degrees, the breeze just enough to lift my hair from my shoulders every so often. "If I lived in Olive Township when I was sixteen," he amends. "And if I had a vehicle. I would've asked you on a date, and I would've brought you here."

"I would've said yes," I tell him. "I would've spent hours picking out my outfit, and making Vivi curl my hair."

"In another life," he murmurs, and I know what he's thinking.

If I weren't marrying Duke. If my mom weren't dying. If I didn't feel like it was my responsibility to make sure she sees her daughter get married.

"How did you find out about this place?" I ask, looking out. It's stunning, the way the bright mid afternoon sun pierces the mountains. Sunset is probably even more beautiful.

"My mom used to bring me out here. Before she got bad."

I remember a time when Penn's mom was simply Ms. Bellamy with the kind eyes and infectious laugh. Penn loved watching baseball games, but she didn't have the money to take him to Phoenix to catch a game. When it came time to watch the World Series, she drew us both tickets to the game, plus a handful of fake money, and sent us to stand in their front yard. She opened the front door like a seating attendant, hollering "Peanuts, popcorn, CrackerJacks!" We filed in, handing her our tickets, and 'paying' for a soda and snacks.

I never forgot that day. Never forgot the love she showed Penn, how she made a way for him to get the feel of a ballpark when there wasn't money to attend a game.

If she'd always been a bad mom, it would've been easier to write off her behavior when she fell so deeply in a dark depression. Penn's dad had returned for a year, and when he left again, Ms. Bellamy was never the same. She stopped smiling. Stopped shopping for groceries. Penn went to the grocery store, but with Ms. Bellamy rarely getting off the couch to go to her house cleaning jobs, the money eventually ran out. Penn never told me, but I knew he was trying to make it to her biggest job, the house where she earned the most money.

The Hampton home.

It's another piece to a puzzle that still won't fit together. Penn admitted he hates Duke. Duke showed animosity toward Penn, and I still don't know why. Something lies in their history, something Penn doesn't want to talk about. I'm torn between demanding answers, and letting sleeping dogs lie. If I'm being honest with myself, I'm scared of the answer. Scared that whatever it is may have the power to alter the present. And even, the near future.

"She was a really good mom, Penn." I reach over, give his shoulder a squeeze.

"She was," he agrees. "And she got better, too. After we moved. She found a place where she could heal. She got on the right dose of meds. Learned ways of coping. And it helped that my dad didn't know where we'd went. I think it would've always been impossible for her to get away from him. He was toxic, you know? She was incapable of escaping his web."

"So you leaving was good for you? For her?" My voice wobbles. I'd always wished for Penn to be happy, wherever he was, but I hadn't thought about what it would take for him to reach that point. The healing that would be required of both him, and his mother.

"Yeah, it was. She needed a fresh start, and an awakening. She called it a 'Come to Jesus.'" He rubs a hand over his face. "Our relationship was never quite the same after the bad years, but we tried. Some things are just"—he shrugs—"not fixable. It's hard to come back from what her illness put me through."

"Do you think you've grieved her?"

He sighs. "Probably not. Have you already begun grieving your mom?"

I look at my hands, folded in my lap. My nails are painted carnation pink. My mother's favorite color. "I think that's why I'm doing something so crazy. Marrying Duke, when I'm not in love with him. I keep telling myself it's about making her dream come true, and in some sense it is, but it's also about making sure I was the best daughter I could be for her. She wanted a big family, and they were only able to have me. In a way, I guess it's really about control. This is my attempt to control how sad I'm going to feel." My voice cracks. Did I know I felt this way? I didn't. These thoughts, these emotions, they've been buried so deep. "If I go out of my way to make her happy, if I marry somebody I don't love just so she can see me walk down the aisle in her dress, then I'll know I did my best to make her happy. I won't have to feel guilt, or resentment, or other emotions I'm really fucking scared of feeling." A plump tear rolls down my cheek.

Penn leans over, reaches for me. He pulls me in close, until we're almost nose to nose. I look into those blue eyes flecked with gray, fringed in dark blond lashes, and see how torn he is. For all my salacious teasing of him the past few days, I'm not usually forward. And because he said he wouldn't touch me while I wear the ring that is still very much on my finger, I will not be the one who makes a move right now.

"Ball's in your court, Sailor," I remind him on a whisper. The very last thing I want is for him to regret our first kiss as adults. If he's going to kiss me right now, I want him to know what it is he's going back on.

He's quiet. Still. Sucks his lower lip in between his teeth, where he bites down gently. I moan at the sight of it, a sound I did not mean to make.

This is what breaks him.

His hands extend, gripping my hips, turning me to face him. I push up on my knees, gathering the fabric of my skirt to mid-thigh, and swing one leg on the other side of him. I'm straddling him now, and his thumbs dig into the skin around my hip bones.

"So beautiful," he says, his eyes an angry storm roaming my face.

Penn

My legs open wider, knees sliding on the hood, until I'm fully seated on his lap. A lusty exhale steals up my throat.

He groans, and I move over him. Grinding.

"Sunshine," he groans, fingers flexing over my hip bones because he still hasn't moved his hands.

"Is that apology I hear in your tone?" I should go still, but I don't. My hips no longer belong to me. My vagina is in charge now, and that bitch is bossy.

"I said"—he groans again, sounding pained—"I wouldn't touch you."

"Congratulations. Your superhuman strength is self-control. But mine is not."

He gazes up at me, eyes feverish. Famished. "The sun is lighting up your face. Your hair. You look so pretty."

"You don't look so bad yourself, Sailor." I give my hips a little shimmy, and he grips my hip bones harder, his fingers ass-adjacent. I wouldn't mind if his hands drifted a little lower and dug into that round flesh.

"You're making this hard, Daisy."

I lean back, bracing myself on his legs, rubbing back and forth. "I can feel exactly how hard I'm making it."

He hisses. An honest to goodness, rush of breath between his teeth.

I'm dying to reach out, run my hands over his ridiculously muscled shoulders. Let my touch fall down, climb back up inside his shirt, fingernails tracing his abs.

My tongue darts out, tip pressing against the center of my upper lip as I wait for him to guide whatever happens next.

His eyes on my mouth, he says, "I said I wouldn't touch you, but maybe you could touch yourself. For me."

My core tightens, from nerves or excitement I can't tell, but I'm feeling them both. "I've never done that in front of anyone."

"You don't have to do anything you're not comfortable with. And—"

"I want to." The words rush out of me. My pulse, already quickened, races now. My heart thunders in my chest.

I lift myself upright, freeing my hands, sliding back so I'm straddling him lower, almost mid-thigh. My right hand slides up my chest, slipping under the strap on my left shoulder. Smile shy, I push until the fabric lies against my arm. I do it again to the strap on my right shoulder.

"I'd kiss your collarbone," he says, strained. "Bite it. Gently, I promise."

"I'd like that," I respond, getting into it a little more. I'm feeling more and more comfortable with every passing second. I run my fingers over the top swell of my breasts, watching as his breathing turns shallow. "Should I pull down my shirt?"

"Please," he coughs out.

Satisfaction rises up inside me. The power I feel at having this effect over him is akin to being buzzed.

Gripping the fabric in my hands, I slowly pull it down, dragging it out. Lucky for him, this top has a built-in bra. My breasts spill out, the balmy air instantly hardening my nipples.

"When I tell you..." he trails off, looking like he's about to propel himself off the hood of the truck with an animalistic roar.

"Tell me what?" I ask innocently. My fingertips lightly trace over my skin.

"What I would do to those," he answers, teeth clenched. "Lick, suck, fuck."

I close my eyes, and pinch my nipples. "I want you to do all of that," I groan, opening my eyes. The front of his jeans is swollen, like he's dying to get out from the straining fabric. "You can do it, too, you know."

He shakes his head slowly back-and-forth. "My self-control is good, but it's not that good."

"Shame," I say, pouting.

I let go of my nipples, my hands drifting lower. Collecting the fabric of my skirt, I lift it and gather it behind me. Today, I wore my pretty underwear, an emerald green lace.

"Sexy, right?" I ask, running my fingers horizontally across my lower stomach.

"I might die, Sunshine. I'm not even sure how much I'm joking right now."

I chuckle lightly, rubbing my hand over myself. My head lolls back, enjoying not only my own ministrations, but his blatant appreciation.

Dipping lower, I hook a finger on the side of my panties, pretending to tug. Teasing him. "Would you like to see me, Sailor?"

"Fuck," he whispers, breathing harder.

"What do you say we test that self-control?" The fabric slides away smoothly.

"Perfect," Penn grunts, jaw tight, eyes feasting on the most private part of me. "Pretty and pink and perfect."

"For you," I answer, and I don't know where that came from, but it doesn't feel wrong. I feel made for him.

"For me," he echoes possessively. And I love it. I really, really do.

I slip a finger inside myself. He reaches for his zipper. "If I don't, I'm going to finish in my pants like a teenager," he admits.

"Take it out," I instruct.

He does, and it's long and thick, something I desperately want to feel inside me.

He fists himself, and I moan. "You look like a feral fucking caveman, and I love it."

"You look like my dream, legs wide and hand working yourself. Hair blowing in the breeze." He pants, breathing labored. "Lips parted, eyes hooded. You're the most beautiful thing I've ever seen, and I want to get between your thighs and never come up for air."

"Ohhh." The idea of reaching down, scratching my nails over Penn's scalp while he drives me wild, is otherworldly. Pleasure builds low in my belly. "I want you to do that."

"I know," he says, arrogant now, pumping harder. Stormy eyes locked on my center. "Puffy lips. Pouty and wet. I would make you scream."

Penn's hand works in a relentless and punishing rhythm, eyes hot and steady, focused on me. The sight of him spurs me on, taking me there, pushing me to the edge. And I fall.

"Yes," I whisper, knees shaking, head tipping back. My eyes close as fireworks detonate, body trembling as I shatter.

Penn moans, a sound deep and delicious, and something warm and wet hits my breasts.

I look down, then at him. He still has a hold of himself, and my hand is in place as I recover from my high. The faintest blush creeps onto his cheeks.

"No blushing, Sailor. I do believe I volunteered to be your canvas."

I take my hand from between my legs, swipe a finger through the mess on my chest, then place it on my tongue. The taste is absolutely disgusting, but his wide eyes, his slack jaw?

So worth it.

And me? I feel good. Confident. Sexy. And happy. Deliriously happy to have done something, *anything*, intimate with Penn.

I blow him a kiss.

He laughs softly, almost disbelievingly. "I don't know what to say right now. My brain isn't working yet."

He puts himself back in his jeans, and I situate my skirt before returning back to the seated position I'd been in prior to our shenanigans.

"Don't move," he tells me, glancing at my breasts that are still free, bearing the evidence of his climax.

"Not going anywhere," I quip, gathering my breasts

and holding them together to keep Penn's release from getting on my top.

He slides off the hood, opening his passenger door and digging in the glove compartment. He returns with a handful of napkins, printed with the name of a restaurant unfamiliar to me. Bracing his foot on the front tire, he settles in front of me. "May I?" he asks.

I smirk. "Sure, but remember, no touching."

He huffs a laugh. "Right. No touching."

Gently, dare I say *lovingly,* he wipes his release from my skin. I affix my top, and he tosses the napkins on the other side of the hood, but he doesn't go anywhere. He sits back, gazing at me.

"Daisy, that was—"

"Hot."

"That too, but I was going to say special. The way you were comfortable enough with me to do that, to let me see you that way, that's not lost on me." He takes my hand, traces the tip of one finger over my fingernail. "I wish things were different."

"Me, too." The regret, the longing, is strident in my tone.

"I wish I'd come back earlier."

"Me, too."

We stare at each other, a chasm between us. We know we care for each other, but at the end of the day, that can only take us so far.

Hard truths:

I'm marrying Duke.

Penn isn't here to stay.

Penn

I don't know why he left, and he still refuses to tell me.

Penn climbs down, turning back and offering his hand to help me. I take it, and when I get settled on my feet, he reaches out. Tucks a lock of hair behind my ear, one finger straying to trace the shell. "Are you ready to go?" he asks.

"No."

"Me neither."

He opens the passenger door for me, watching me climb inside. Instead of closing the door right away, he leans against the frame, regarding me with a warmth in his eyes.

"Hi," I say softly.

"Hey," he responds, his voice a low rumble.

"What we just did," I pause, trying to gather my thoughts, but it's nearly impossible.

"Just say it, Sunshine," he urges. "Say whatever it is you're thinking."

"I loved doing that with you."

"So did I."

"Then why do I feel"—I search for the best fitting word to describe the odd emotion tumbling through me—"bereft?"

"Because you're realizing we are not one and done. This won't be enough for us." His hand reaches out, fixing the twisted strap of my top. "And, maybe, you're starting to see what you got yourself into." Regret blooms in his eyes. "What I set into motion a long time ago."

"You couldn't have known. Besides, the choice was mine."

He nods. "I'm feeling all that too, you know. I'm starting to realize how messy this is."

He closes the door, and I watch him walk around the front of the truck.

We're quiet on the drive back, and at some point, Penn reaches for my hand. His fingers weave through mine, and they don't leave.

The emotions inside me swirl, cresting high like a rogue wave.

I want the physical connection.

I want the emotional connection.

I sneak a peek at Penn's profile as he drives.

This is dangerous.

We are dangerous.

He's making me rethink everything. The consequence, the fallout, I'm considering it all.

More than anything, I'm rethinking my stance on true love.

Does it exist, after all?

Penn drops me at my house, squeezing my hand in a silent farewell before heading out to the play rehearsal.

I go inside, and call Vivi. It's time to be honest with my best friend.

Chapter 41

Daisy

"This explains a lot," Vivi says, dipping a chip into a glass jar of homemade queso.

She showed up at my door thirty minutes ago, telling me she had less than an hour before she had to get back to her kids because her mom needs to go to her book club meeting. Then she held up a bag of chips in one hand, the dip in the other, saying *besties need snacks*.

She's unhinged, and I wouldn't have her any other way.

Now we're in my living room. I'm seated on the couch, she's sitting on the ground below me, her back against a cushion.

"Say more," I instruct, reaching out to the coffee table where the food sits. I load an obscene amount of queso onto a single chip.

She shrugs. "The announcement of your engagement came out of nowhere. I mean, obviously he's been your friend for a really long time and so it wasn't completely out of left field that you would fall in love one day. Friends to lovers, I believe that's called. That's a pretty common trope in romance novels."

I gave her a look, because as far as I know, Vivi's not much of a reader.

She waves a hand dismissively. "You know my mom and my aunt, they can yap endlessly about books."

I nod and eat another chip.

"So you two dating felt kind of expected, I guess. But you were never very hands-on, if you know what I mean. Not that you needed to be draped all over one another, but you were just sort of"—her shoulders pull up to her earlobes and she drops them as she says—"asexual."

"Asexual?" I ask. "I thought we did a better job than that."

She points up at her face. "Not to these trained eyes."

We crunch through a handful of chips, and she says, "Peter is Penn, huh? The man, the myth, the legend."

"I am definitely not telling him you said that."

She laughs. "And my brother knew? I will absolutely be kicking his ass."

"Don't be mad at him. He was just trying to be a good friend." I elbow her lightly in the side. "You would do the same for me."

"For you, I would cut a bitch."

I grin broadly. "Same."

"So, what do you do now? Where do you go from here?"

I groan, dramatically flopping over onto the couch. "I don't know."

Penn

"Do you want to hear what I think?"

"I invited you over here for queso, not to hear your opinion."

Vivi reaches up over the couch and smacks me hard on the rear. "I think what you're doing for your mom is very kind, and also very stupid."

I wheeze. "Rude."

"We don't have time to tap dance around your feelings." She waves a chip in the air. "There will be no circling the maze that is your heart, trying to get to the center. We're gonna have to parachute right in."

I nod. "Proceed."

"Does Penn love you?"

"Love? I don't know about that. It hasn't been enough time. I know he cares for me though."

"Do you love Penn?"

I squirm. Bite my lip. Think about how happy I feel when he smiles. "Maybe? I don't know."

Vivi nods solemnly. "Ok, got it. You're getting dirty on the hood of a truck, but you're pussyfooting around about your feelings." A glint appears in her eyes. "Did you see what I did there?"

"Very funny," I retort.

Vivi grows serious. "Daisy, I remember when you were friends with Penn. I remember what he meant to you, and how devastated you were when he left. You're adults now, and maybe it hasn't been that much time, but I think you owe it to yourself to really consider what it is you're doing with Duke. Don't think about your mom, don't think about yourself in one year, or two years.

Think about yourself in five years, in ten, in twenty. What does that look like for you?"

I don't have to look out that far to know the picture is grim. But how do I give it all up? If I reverse course now, I'll not only be not fulfilling my mom's dream, but taking it away from her also. Two strikes with the same sword. How could I possibly do that?

Vivi pushes herself to stand. She looks down at me, sad and slightly pathetic in the fetal position. "I can see I've given you a lot to think about."

"Vivi, I don't know what to do."

She reaches for me, digging a hand under my shoulder and hauling me upright. "You're in a tough spot, but lucky for you, you're a tough cookie." Hands grasping my shoulders, she bends at the waist so she can look me in the eyes. "I'm not going to let you sit here all night and worry yourself sick. So, you can either come with me and help with the bedtime routine, or you can find Crazy Cliff and ask if he wants to play a game of hopscotch."

"What?" I laugh incredulously. "What kind of an alternative is that?"

"I need help with bedtime, so I gave you an alternative you were unlikely to choose."

"You're incorrigible."

She urges me up. "I don't know what that means, but I'll take it."

The temperature has dropped, so I grab a sweatshirt and lace my arms through. "Duke said the most interesting thing to me the other day," I say, popping my head through the top of the sweatshirt.

Penn

Vivi's eyebrows are raised, waiting.

"He said you're in love with Ambrose."

Vivi rolls her eyes. "It's a good thing Duke's handsome, because he sure is a dum-dum."

She marches through the front door, but her response is one I note in the back of my mind. So often we are unable to see what is obvious to others.

I follow Vivi back to Summerhill, and spend the evening overseeing slippery small humans in bathtubs. We make words out of rubbery letters that stick to the tub, and shape hats from soap suds, and the kids run barebottomed through the house as we chase them with towels.

It's the perfect evening with my best friend. A great way to take me out of my head, delivering a much needed reminder that although the situation I'm in doesn't have an easy way out, there are far worse places to be.

Chapter 42

Penn

Hugo and I have agreed to meet for dinner after the play rehearsal. He sent me the address for a sports bar called Hen Pecked, which is a damn clever name.

An agro-tourism conference in Denver called Hugo away for a week, and he's been busy at the mill. This is the first time I've seen him since I told Daisy the truth.

He's already here, sitting up at the long bar, a draft beer sweating on a coaster in front of him.

"What's good, buddy?" I say, smacking Hugo lightly on the back. I pull out a leather topped stool and settle in beside him. "Cool place. Great ambiance."

It's a chill place with TVs everywhere, the walls decorated with signed framed jerseys of various sports teams, and pennants on the wall. The bar top is reclaimed wood, bearing scratches and grooves and covered by epoxy.

Hugo eyes me suspiciously. "Why do you sound jovial?"

Penn

I point at my chest. "Me?"

His eyes narrow further. "Yes. You."

I thank the bartender with a lift of my chin when he delivers a bowl of honey mustard pretzels, and the same beer Hugo's drinking. "Hugo, my friend, I am on the other side of my lie. I think that deserves some jovialness." I frown at the word that is most definitely not a word. "Joviality? I don't know. Words aren't my thing. The point is, I get to be around Daisy as myself." The relief has grown exponentially since the moment I told her. I feel like one of those classic movies where a woman sings on a prairie, never losing the smile plastered to her face.

Except for the *teeny tiny* little fact Daisy is marrying Duke. While I'm sublimely happy Daisy knows the truth, there's a katana swiping at my heart no matter how relieved I am.

Hugo side-eyes me as he drinks. "Well," he says, setting his beer down. "You're still alive, so that's saying something. Daisy didn't kill you when you came clean."

I hold my hands out in front of me like *I know, right?*

Hugo laughs. "She called me a dirty liar."

"You are."

Hugo mimes stabbing me with what I assume is a sword. "You're such a dick, Penn."

"Little too much affection in that tone of voice for me to take you seriously, buddy."

"Hugo!" A man's voice carries across the place.

I swivel on my seat, watching three men approach.

"Hugo, you better tell me right fucking now that this is a mirage."

"No can-do. How was I supposed to get you to join guy's night?"

"With Duke The Twat?" I say, doing my best not to stare down Daisy's fiancé.

"I thought he was Duke the Wet Paper Towel?" Hugo says under his breath, standing up to greet the men.

"Guys," Hugo says, shaking hands. "Elijah, Chris, this is my friend, Peter."

"Nice to see you again, Peter," Duke interrupts.

I ignore him, focusing on Elijah and Chris. "My name is actually Penn. Hugo here"—I clap him on the back —"calls me Peter sometimes. Inside joke."

Duke stares me down. Hugo does his best not to gape.

Now that Daisy knows my true identity, there's no reason everybody else shouldn't know also.

"Why don't you guys grab that big booth in the back corner?" Duke says, gesturing out into the place. "Penn and I will bring over a round."

Hugo glances reluctantly between me and Duke, but doesn't put up a fight. He grabs our half-empty beers, leaves our bowl of pretzels, and leads Elijah and Chris to the big booth.

Duke steps up to the bar, and I step up beside him. "If you wanted to get me alone so you could apologize, let me tell you in advance, I accept."

"Shut the fuck up," Duke hisses. "I don't know what the fuck it is you think you're doing, going by your real name, but it doesn't go any further than right here." He points a finger at the floor of Hen Pecked. "You are not

Penn

back, Penn. You have not returned with the intention to stay. Quit telling people the truth when you know you're moving on anyway. It's bad enough you told Daisy, don't go making it worse by telling the rest of the town."

I get the bartender's attention and order another round. "I have to tell you, it feels pretty good coming clean. I don't think lying is for me."

"I'm sure there are some lies you're planning on keeping." Duke's in control of himself now, his voice smooth and practiced. "Can't lay all your shit bare."

He props his forearms on the bar top, not looking at me. Millions of dollars, and the fucker looks like he could grace a magazine cover for women to drool over, but he's so threatened by me he's trying to dictate what I do. The lies I tell, the truths I uncover.

"You know, Duke, it's looking like I might. And that scares you, right?" He is ramrod straight, nothing moving, save for a tic in a muscle near his jaw. "The question is, why?"

He says nothing.

"Why, oh why?" I wax poetic, ready to break into iambic pentameter. Did pissing off Duke just become my favorite pastime? Possibly.

"You could let her out of your agreement," I murmur, discreet.

He flinches. Finally, a break in that stone cold veneer. "That's right, bud. She told me."

He bends his head, turning it my way so I can see his lips when he says under his breath, "You're the dalliance."

"I can honestly say, that's something I've never been called."

"Your fucking one-liners are obnoxious."

"That's a matter of opinion."

"She talked to me recently, wanting to know how we were going to address"—he gives an uncomfortable cough—"our personal needs. I told her we could have a *dalliance*," his eyes meet mine pointedly, like *now are you understanding?*.

I already knew what he meant, but the explanation of it blows my mind. Is this what mega-wealthy people do? Make marriage a means to an end? And consider sex a *dalliance,* a task completed?

"Gives new meaning to *get in, get off, get out*."

I wait for him to take the bait, to give me more shit for my one-liner, but he ignores it. "I'm guessing Daisy has chosen you?"

Is this smooth faced fucker actually asking me this question? I swipe a hand down my face. I can't decide if this conversation is real, or if it's the worst dream I've ever had. But here's what I know for damn sure: I won't be talking about Daisy in this way. Anything Daisy and I do in the future, or have already done, is not up for discussion with anybody else.

I'm about to tell him just that, but he opens his mouth and says, "It might be hard for you to believe, but I genuinely care about Daisy. If it were only about me, or Daisy, I would back out. But this isn't just about us."

The bartender sets down two of our five beers. I grab one and chug half. "Mrs. St. James."

Penn

He nods.

"I don't know her nearly as well as you, but something tells me she wouldn't want her daughter marrying somebody she doesn't love."

Duke takes the other beer, drinking deeply like me. "She most definitely would not. But who's going to be the one to tell her? You? You're going to drive onto the St. James farm in that big, loud truck? Dog trotting by your side? You're gonna tell them that even though you've been passing yourself off as Peter Bravo, you're really Penn Bellamy and now you're all grown up and here for their daughter?"

"Fuck you," I say under my breath, but his words hit where he intends them. He's not wrong, and he knows it. Who am I to show up at the St. James house and tell them I'm back? What is it I bring to the table?

The bartender delivers the remaining three beers, and Duke offers his credit card to keep the tab open. When the bartender turns away, Duke says, "You should have stayed Peter."

I tap the bottom of my glass against the bottom of his. "You should do a better job hiding how much I intimidate you."

I spend the next ninety minutes getting to know Elijah and Chris. Duke retreats into himself, becoming a sullen motherfucker, and when he excuses himself to go to the bathroom, he returns with two shots of whiskey, both of which he takes.

"Is this your fault?" Hugo asks quietly when Elijah and Chris are in conversation about the financial markets.

His gaze slices over to Duke, who sits between Elijah and Chris in the booth, in the middle of their conversation, but not taking part in it.

"You mean the petulant millionaire pouting in the corner?"

"Yep." Hugo stands, motioning me up with a lift of his chin. "We're grabbing refills," he announces to the table.

When our backs are turned, I say, "If anything, I'm the one who should be sad-eyeing my beer. He said some mean shit to me while we were getting drinks."

"You threaten him."

"I did not threaten him."

"No," Hugo shakes his head. "You *threaten* him. Your presence." He orders another round, but I decline. When the bartender leaves to fill the order, he turns to me and says, "Imagine you're Duke. You're about to marry Daisy, it's a big deal wedding. The whole town is excited about it. The St. James and the Hamptons have a long history, one that will finally be shared. And now here you come, a guy who Duke remembers his fiancée loving. He remembers the way you and Daisy ran around together. We all do. So here he is, watching and waiting for Daisy to change her mind about him. How do you think he feels?"

Like he doesn't actually love Daisy, and she needs to have one night with me to get me out of her system.

I can't say any of that of course, because that's a Great Big Secret, to go along with my own.

So I say, "I'm guessing Duke feels like he'd prefer if I left town and never came back."

"Something like that." The bartender sets down the

Penn

next round, and I help Hugo carry it. "For the record," Hugo says, "I don't want you to leave. If I could write down my perfect outcome, it would be that you and Daisy and Duke could find a way to coexist."

I chew on that for a moment, then say, "What if Daisy loves me, Hugo? What happens then?"

Hugo's worried gaze slides over to me as we walk around tables that are now full. "Then I'd say you better act fast. Their wedding is fast-approaching."

We get to the table, and Hugo slides a beer in front of Duke. "I was drinking whiskey," Duke says irritably, a slight slur thickening his words.

"They were out," Hugo lies smoothly.

Duke drinks his beer in silence, then announces it's time to leave. Hugo, Elijah, and Chris have just joined a pool game, so Hugo points at me and says with a wicked gleam in his eye, "Penn, you're on Duke duty."

I flip him the bird as he walks away laughing.

"Let's go, asshole," I say to Duke, watching him stand up unsteadily from the booth.

We get outside, the quiet and cool night air a welcome reprieve from the sounds of sports games, and the intermingling smells of cologne, aftershave, and beer.

Duke steps toward the parking lot, swaying.

"Order an Uber," I bite out. I have almost no tolerance for this person right now.

Duke picks the closest car to lean on. "Want to know what I've been thinking about?"

I make a face. "Changing the part in your hair from the left to the right?"

He gives me a blank look.

"I don't fucking know, and I don't fucking care. Order a ride home." I'm two seconds away from leaving him in this parking lot, but then I realize I can't. Or, that I shouldn't. Because Duke is connected to Daisy. And if Duke does something stupid, and hurts himself or somebody else, it will reflect on her. Unleashing the town gossip will make life harder for Daisy.

"Nope," Duke says, pushing off from the car. He scans the parking lot, his face lighting up in recognition when he spots his huge, ultra-luxury SUV. He bumbles that way, and I follow. I'm not going to let him drive, but he can at least wait there for a ride home.

When he reaches the vehicle, he opens up the back left passenger and climbs inside. Door wide open, he gives me a contemptuous look and says, "I was thinking about how instead of going to the St. James farm and telling Daisy's family your intentions, you could do one even better."

He waits for me to say something and when I don't, he continues. "You could tell the whole town you love Daisy and you're going to win her from me. The sad boy who hurt the town princess in a car accident has returned to steal her heart from the man whose ancestors founded the town. The man who subsidizes the library program. Who founded an outreach program for low-income kids to receive bikes at Christmas. The man who—"

My fist lands squarely on his cheek. He topples over, yelling unintelligibly one time, and then he's quiet.

I walk around the backside of the car, open up the

other passenger door, and check for a pulse. Not because I'm worried there isn't one, but because I feel like it's the right thing to do. And, just like I thought, he's passed out cold.

I close the car door, return to the other side and make sure his feet are tucked in, then close that door too.

He'll wake up with a headache, and a sore jaw courtesy of yours truly, but he'll be fine.

I don't need someone else telling me I'm not good enough for Daisy. That I never was in the first place.

I know that already.

Chapter 43

Daisy

Good morning, Sunshine.

Hey, Sailor.

I miss you. Is it ok to say that?

Only if there's nothing wrong with me saying it back. I miss you, too.

What are you doing today?

I have clients all day, including a certain someone who is my last client of the day.

Planning to torture me more today?

That depends. Am I speaking as your physical therapist, or...

Speaking as my sunshine.

Your sunshine?

Penn

> Mine. My own personal sunshine.

> Torturing you also means torturing myself.

"Aww, look how cute you are, smiling down at your phone like a lovesick bride-to-be. What did Duke say?" Isla cranes her neck to my phone screen, but I lean away, tucking the device to my chest. "Ohh," Isla wiggles her eyebrows. "It's a dick pic, isn't it?"

"Ew, no."

"Why is that an *ew*?"

"Receiving pictures of private appendages is not my cup of tea."

"Ohh-kay," Isla says, in this nasally and affected voice.

I ignore her and tuck my phone into my purse.

"Well, whatever it was, your smile started here"—she points at the top of one cheek, swinging her fingertip across her face and ending at the top of her opposite cheek—"and ended here."

I feel the warmth of a blush steal over my cheeks, and I turn away to keep Isla from seeing.

"Would you mind printing out the list of clients for the day?" I ask over my shoulder as I head back to my office to stow my purse.

I sneak one more peek at my phone as I'm hanging the straps on the hook affixed under my desk.

> I'll take torture if it's at your hands. See you this afternoon, Sunshine.

I read the message to myself three times, grinning like a loon.

Chapter 44

Penn

"Help me understand why I found Duke passed out cold in his car last night," Hugo says, joining me in the line to order lunch at Sammich.

I pluck a bag of barbecue potato chips from the wire rack near the cash register. "He fucked around and found out."

I'm expecting Hugo to lecture me, but he laughs. "I miss having you around here. I miss you being"—he shrugs—"you."

"Stop," I say, peeling apart the top of the chip bag. "You're going to make me cry." I say it like I'm joking, but is there a heat pressing at the back of my eyes? There sure is.

"Well, hey there, fellas," Margaret says as we step up to order our lunch. "Are you here for a Monte Cristo, Peter?"

Hugo glances at me, waiting to see if I'm going to

correct her. And I do. "Margaret, I've been *fibbing* since I came to town."

Beside me, Hugo mutters the word 'fibbing.'

"I gave you a different name because I wasn't sure how the people of Olive Township would take me being back. But I've decided that it's better to be honest. My name is Penn Bellamy—"

"Bellamy," she breathes. She leans over the counter to get a better look. "Dear Lord, you look nothing like the boy who disappeared. Where the hell did you go?"

"My mom and I moved to San Diego. That's where I've been since."

"I always liked your mom. How is she doing?"

Someone talking about my mom with affection in their tone is making my heart do weird things. Namely, swell.

"She passed away a few months ago, actually."

Margaret's face falls. "That's why you came back. That first day you were in here, you said..." Her voice trails off as she recalls our conversation. "You said you were in town to deal with a house that had been abandoned a long time ago."

Pinching my pointer finger and my thumb, I wince and say, "It was a little bit of truth."

She guffaws. "I've been known to spin some yarns myself a time or two." Winking at me and Hugo, she rings us up for two Monte Cristo's and hands over a plastic number to place on our table. "I'd pick a spot inside," she advises. "Looks like we're going to be getting some moisture pretty soon."

Penn

The sky, a muted gray when I walked in here, has already darkened. Hugo and I take her advice and grab a table next to the window.

"Only people from the desert want to watch the rain," I say, giving my best friend a little shit.

"I've been in plenty of places when it's been raining," Hugo reminds me. "Something about a storm in the desert hits different."

"I didn't notice when I was a kid, but I'll pay more attention in the future."

Hugo lifts a brow. "Does that mean you're sticking around? Longer than selling off your house?"

Duke's words from last night nestled their way into my mind, and I hear them again. Am I supposed to stay here and fight for Daisy? When I'm with her, it's a resounding yes. But then there's Duke, and his words that were unkind yet true. Would Daisy really choose me, when she has so much riding on her impending wedding? Who am I to ask that of her, to put her in that position?

"I don't know, Hugo."

"Time is not on your side, my friend. You better figure it out."

A Sammich employee, a young kid with shiny braces and floppy hair, delivers our food. We tuck in just as the first raindrops fall.

Across the street, an old white-haired couple exits a store. He wears a plaid golf hat, she carries a purse on her forearm. She frowns up at the sky, but the husband reaches for her arm, tugging. She looks back at him, and he takes his hand away, only to offer it to her once more, gallantly this time. She shakes her head, but smiles at him affectionately, like she knows what he's doing. And then she places her hand in his and tucks her shopping bag up over her shoulder. He pulls her in and she spins into his chest, a slow revolution, all their motions at half speed. When he has her positioned against him, he puts his cheek to her cheek, and they sway slowly. Raindrops tap dance around them, but the couple doesn't seem to mind.

"Think of everything it took for them to get to this moment," Hugo says, ripping my attention away from the couple. "You look at something like that, and you have to wonder if maybe they were just lucky to have found each other."

"It's true love."

Hugo stares at me in surprise. "You believe in true love?"

"Yeah, I do, even though it probably seems like I shouldn't. I didn't watch two parents in love. Mostly all I saw was my dad's back when he was leaving, and my mom trying to hold herself together every time he left, until one day he stopped coming back and she stopped getting up off the couch. But why did they keep doing that, time after time? It was the search for true love, propelling them to give it chance after chance."

Hugo scratches his head. "I guess when you think of it like that, you could see it as them teaching you everything not to do."

"That's the spirit," I say, biting into my sandwich. We watch the old man spin the old woman out from the safety of his chest. She does a sweet and borderline sassy shake with her hips, and the old man laughs. They step in together, sharing a chaste peck. The rain picks up, and the old couple walks hand-in-hand down the sidewalk.

"Do you want that some day?" I ask Hugo. He doesn't talk much about dating. I think a lot of it has to do with his dad's death. Hugo once told me it's difficult to date with that in his past. If he says it on the first date, women either get spooked, or weirdly into it. If he saves it for a later date, women feel like it's something he should have revealed sooner. *How do you tell somebody your dad was murdered, and the case is still unsolved?* he'd asked. I understood, to a much lesser degree. I wasn't particularly jazzed about telling dates at any point in the dating stage about my childhood.

Hugo looks at the spot where the old couple danced. "I want that," he confirms. "My fencing career is behind me. I'm back home for good. I'm helping run the mill. And..." he sighs. "I want that. How about you?"

"More than anything." Funny how, just one month ago, that would not have been my answer.

"With Daisy?" Hugo asks, pushing the last of his sandwich into his mouth.

"How can you ask that when you're friends with Duke, too? Don't get me wrong, I prefer you on my side."

Hugo shrugs. "Duke's my friend, but so is Daisy. And she doesn't look at him the way she looks at you." He lifts his flattened palms in front of his chest. "I'm just calling it like I see it."

Chapter 45

Penn

By the time I get back to my house to feed Slim Jim, the soft rain has turned into a downpour. It's raining so hard that at first I don't notice the sedan parked on the street, but it would be impossible to miss the man standing under the front porch overhang at my house.

He's put together, wearing dress slacks, a collared button-up shirt, and tan trench coat. Not a single silver hair is out of place, and it serves to sharpen an already shrewd gaze.

"Hello?" I say, stepping out of the rain. I don't immediately recognize this person, but he knows me.

"Penn Bellamy," he says evenly, and it's frustrating I don't remember him. I don't like being at a disadvantage.

"I'm Glenn Hampton. Duke's dad."

Of course. The icy blue eyes, sharp and calculating, are exactly like his son's. The last time I saw this man, he was standing over a crouching thirteen-year-old Duke, raging at him.

Penn

"What do you want?"

"I saw my son this morning at the office. His cheek was..." He pauses, like he's searching for the word, but it feels too practiced. Too on purpose. A boardroom tactic. "Colorful."

"That's nice," I say dispassionately. "What do you want?"

"He told me how he got it."

"And?"

"Have you ever been charged with battery?"

"Can't say I have."

"Hmm. That might be something you'll have first-hand knowledge of soon. I'm encouraging my son to press charges."

Fuck. This isn't good.

"I know you didn't come here just to say that to me, so spit it out. What else do you want?"

"I want you gone. You pose a threat to my son's relationship with his fiancée."

"That's between me, Daisy, and Duke. Nowhere in there were the words *Glenn Hampton*."

"You better watch it, boy. I will make your life hell. That payout you took to leave town when you were thirteen? Did you really think Daisy's dad had the money? That money came from me." He points back at himself. "I set your mother up in San Diego. I bought that condo near the beach, and put it in her name."

What. The. Fuck?

My mind races, trying to understand his words, his

revelation, the reason behind it. But I can't. I'm coming up with nothing.

"Why would you do all that?" I ask.

My floundering has no impact on Glenn. He remains stony-faced as he says, "Daisy's dad and I go way back. We've had disagreements and agreements, we've been enemies and we've been friends. It was in our mutual best interest for you and your mother to go away."

My jaw tightens at the idea of someone, *anyone*, needing my mother to go away. "How could that have benefited you?"

"That will be my little secret." He tucks aside his fancy camel-colored pea coat so he can smoothly glide his hand in his pants pocket. A power move. "I'm here with a proposal. I will buy that old piece of shit house of yours outright, plus twenty percent."

"And do what with it?"

"None of your fucking business. It'll be mine to do whatever I want with it. I can piss on it, tear it down, or hang up ugly Christmas lights and keep them there all year."

"No. Fucking. Way." The plan was always to sell it, but to this guy?

He is unruffled by my response. "Are you planning on stealing my son's fiancée, and then going to jail? Do you think Daisy's going to come visit you? She's not. She's going to marry Duke next Saturday afternoon, and you're going to wise up and accept my offer." He walks out into the pouring rain, unfazed. His car slowly pulls away from the curb, then disappears.

Penn

I let myself inside. Slim Jim trots over, sitting back on his haunches to stare at me. He takes in my face, reading my expression, then moves his body until he is putting his weight against the front of my legs.

My hands run the length of his silky, reddish coat. The shock of defeat rolls through me, my body aching with it. Anger arrives next, heating up my limbs. All these years later, something, *someone,* wants to keep me from Daisy.

All I ever wanted was to be with her. As a friend when we were young. However she'll have me now, as adults.

The more I think about it, the angrier I feel. Daisy and I aren't kids anymore. The adults aren't running the show like they used to. We have voices now.

But what is it they're saying?

Chapter 46

Daisy

Penn doesn't show up for his afternoon physical therapy appointment.

"This is unlike him," Isla says. "He's always five minutes early, and he's never a no-call no-show."

I glance out the window to the driving rain, then back to the cuticle I've been picking. A dot of blood blooms beside my nail bed. "You can go home, Isla. Drive carefully," I say, before retreating back to my office. Grabbing my phone from my purse, I check it. It's only been one minute since the last time I checked, and not shockingly, there is no communication from Penn.

What if something happened? Fear knots my heart, panic sweeping through me. I place my tenth call to him, and when it goes unanswered, I've made my decision. I'm going to find him.

Penn

❀🐜❀🐜❀

"Penn," I yell, banging on his door. This is the third time I've knocked. I know he's here. His truck is in the driveway.

My hand is poised to knock when the door swings open. Penn, hair wet, has a towel wrapped around his waist. "Daisy," he reaches for me, pulling me inside. "How long have you been out there?" His eyes rake over my body. "You are soaking wet."

My clothing sticks to me, and I'm betting my ponytail closely resembles a rat tail at this point, but none of that matters, for two reasons. One, Penn is ok. Two, Penn is wearing a towel. *Only* a towel.

I drag my eyes up from the view of his hips, the *bump bump bump* of his ab muscles. There were six. I counted.

"I was worried about you. You didn't show up for your PT appointment."

His face clouds. "I know, and I'm sorry. I just got out of the shower, and before that," he hesitates, rubbing a hand over the back of his neck. "I was struggling a little bit. But I should have at least texted you and let you know. I'm sorry for worrying you."

I take a step toward him to hug him hello, but my sneakers squeak on the floor. "I'll just get out of your hair," I say, pointing back to my car. "I'm not trying to make a mess of your floor."

"No," he rushes to say. "Stay. Let me grab you shorts and a T-shirt." He looks down. "And maybe some for myself."

I manage a relieved chuckle. "Sounds good." I watch him walk up the stairs, the way the thin towel drapes over his ass. I desperately want to reach out, pluck the fold in the front that's keeping it tied, and watch the towel fall to the floor. I already know what he looks like, how he's thick and veined.

The worry that inundated me on my way over here has melted, turning into something else that has my blood rushing in all directions. Desire.

Penn returns, wearing soft, gray shorts, and a plain black T-shirt. He hands me a towel. "I laid some clothes out on the bed for you."

I toe off my shoes, doing my best to dry a little of my legs and my arms and my hair before going up the stairs. I head for the main bedroom, where I find shorts similar to the ones Penn is wearing, plus a button-up collared shirt.

"I'm sorry it's not a T-shirt," Penn yells up the stairs. "I need to do laundry. That's all I had, and I figured it would look better on you than on me."

That makes me smile. It also gives me an idea.

I change quickly, skipping over the shorts and buttoning the shirt halfway up. I use the small comb in my purse the best I can on my hair. Gently I tousle it, and lightly pinch my cheeks to give them a little color.

"Where is Slim Jim?" I yell down from the top of the landing.

From somewhere out of sight, Penn says, "I put him in

his kennel when I saw you were out front. Rain tends to get him excited, and I didn't want him to jump on you or knock you down."

Following the sound of Penn's voice, I find him in the kitchen. Rain pelts the window, the sky outside deep gray. Penn's back is to me as he says, "I bought champagne after the last time you were over, just in case you came back. Are you interested in a glass? Or are you trying to make me do physical therapy here? You did say you were going to torture me."

"I'd love a glass, but maybe later." He spins around at the sound of my voice this close to him, eyes widening as he takes me in. "I don't know if this is the form of torture you were thinking of," I say, toying with the button between my breasts, "but it's most definitely what I had on the menu for today."

"Daisy." Penn says my name like it's agony.

"Penn," I respond, pulling the button through the eye.

A flash of lightning streaks through the window, closely followed by a clap of thunder.

"Keep going," he instructs, eyes locked on my fingers.

I do as he says, and when the buttons are undone, I grip each side of the shirt, slowly pulling it away until I'm holding it out to the side.

The rule has been no touching, so I expected relentless teasing, ending in something similar to last time.

But that's not what happens. Penn charges across the kitchen, wrapping an arm around my lower back, cupping the back of my head. He hauls me in, flush with him.

His eyes search my face. "Please tell me every inch of you is on the menu."

His words go straight to my center, making it ache. "What happened to your rule? Your self-control?"

His hand leaves the back of my head, finding my cheek. "I changed my mind. I don't want to live another day without knowing how good you taste. How perfect you feel."

"Me neither," I whisper.

"I'm going to kiss you, Sunshine." His fingers flex in their grip on my waist.

My hands travel into his hair, pulling him a half inch from my waiting lips. "I've waited so long for this, Sailor."

I'm not sure if his lips dip, or if mine lift, but they find each other, and *damn*. In an instant, I'm lost. Lost to him. Lost to this kiss, lost to this moment. His thumb runs over my cheek sweetly before his hand moves to grab my hair, tilting my head back, angling me so he can come down over me. His tongue dances over mine, tasting me, and I respond.

He groans into my mouth and it releases something feral inside me. The front of me is naked, so I press against him, wiggling my hips, rubbing.

"Yes," he growls into my mouth. His hands leave me, only to slide up to my shoulders and find the opening of the shirt. In one swift motion, the shirt is over my shoulders and hitting the floor with a soft thud.

My heartbeat skitters. He takes a half-step back, eyes leisurely perusing my body. He looks hungry, and wolfish, and I love it.

"I thought of you so many times," he murmurs. "All these years, I pictured the woman you'd become." My skin heats as his eyes rake over me. "Nothing I came up with compared to reality. I couldn't have dreamed up perfection."

"I'm not perfect." His gaze, on my legs now, climbs upward.

"For me," he clarifies. "Perfect for me."

Oh.

I want him. Desperately. I have to have him. Now. He must be thinking the same thing, because he cups one of my breasts, and instead of being slow or gentle, he pushes me back against the wall and sucks one nipple into his mouth. My back arches, wanting more, more, more, wanting everything.

Reaching for his shirt, I slide my hands under the hem, finding the magnificence that was on display when he answered the door in a towel.

Hard muscle. Rigid bumps. Warm skin.

Not enough. I want more. All of him.

My fingers find the waist of his soft shorts, and in one deft motion, I push them down. They fall to the ground, pooling at his feet, and he kicks them away. He releases his hold on my nipple to reach behind himself, pulling off his shirt in one movement.

He groans when I take him in my hand, pumping, dew leaking over my fingers. Dropping his forehead to mine, his hands press to the wall on either side of my head, caging me in.

"You're going to have to stop that soon," he grits out. "But fuck, I love it."

"I can tell," I say on a grin, tilting up my chin, capturing his lower lip with my teeth. Biting down gently as I work him, gathering his moisture and using it.

Penn's firm grip comes over mine, forcing me to still. I release him, and let out a surprised *oof* as he reaches under my backside, lifting me onto his midsection.

"Bed," he grunts in explanation, heading for the stairs.

"Ok," I respond, too lost in my sensitive core pressed against his many, many abs. I shift. Wiggle. Squirm, until I find a rhythm. "Ohhh," I moan into his neck.

"That's it, Sunshine. Use me."

I love it. I love this. I love this man.

Fuck. Oh no.

Penn climbs the stairs quickly, arms holding me securely while I work myself. In seconds we're at the bed, the shorts I never donned lying on the other side. I push until I'm lying in the middle, and Penn comes up over me.

My legs drift open, expecting him to push his way inside me, but he shakes his head. "If you don't come on my tongue, my life won't be complete."

I laugh, but I feel shy, so I make a joke. "So dramatic."

He doesn't respond, sliding down my body, hooking my knees over his shoulders. He breathes deeply once he's there, pressing a long, full kiss to me. Then he says, "Hang on tight, Sunshine."

He ravages me.

Devours.

My limbs turn to rubber as he uses his tongue relentlessly, pairing soft and languid with frenzied circles.

"I think I might be dying," I choke out, and I feel his smile, his muted laughter. Then he goes in for the death blow. Suctioning to me, pulling me into his mouth, his tongue lapping until I grab the pillow and press it to my face.

I *shatter*.

Disintegrate.

My hips buck and he holds me in place, my toes gripping the sheet. His face stays between my thighs.

I throw off the pillow, looking down at his blond hair. "You can come up here now," I say, embarrassed at my absolutely over-the-top orgasm.

"You're still coming," he answers. He's right. I feel myself convulsing.

"Need to feel it," he says, and I startle as his tongue slides into me.

Is this the hottest thing I've ever done? It's ranking right up there with what happened on the hood of his truck. But I like this with him, handing myself over to what I feel.

I reach for his hair, drag my nails over his scalp. "Can you feel it?"

He nods, just the tiniest bit.

I squeeze my muscles. "Do you feel that?"

A rush of air from his laugh streams over me. He pulls out of my body, dragging his nose up through my center, placing a kiss at the top of me, drawing an involuntary buck of my hips.

"I'll be right back," he says, standing up from the bed and disappearing into the bathroom. His ass is a sight, solid and muscled like the rest of him.

"You don't have any other tattoos," I say when he returns, climbing back onto the bed and splitting my legs so he can fit between them.

My bent knees bracket him as he opens a condom, sliding it over his length. Rising up on his knees, he winds his hands around my thighs and tugs me closer to him. "I only mark myself with things that own my heart. The SEALs." He directs himself to me, pressing in. He stops there, looks down at me. I see it in his gaze, this warmth. A softness. "And a woman named Daisy."

Oh, my heart.

He notches another inch, going slow. Then one more. Torturing us both. I pop up on my elbows, extending my touch to his ribs. To his scars. Gently I trace them. Wanting him to know it's all ok. He looks down at my touch, then back to me. He never stops his rhythm, but I see what it does to him. To his heart.

When he's all the way inside, he comes down over me. My legs wrap around his lower back. He moves in unhurried, luxurious thrusts.

He sighs deeply, a sound of relief and contentment. Eyes locked on mine, he says, "There's no part of me that doesn't love you, Daisy St. James."

My hands roam his back, finding his neck, fingers weaving into his hair. I press my lips to his, letting them hover against his, and say the truest words I've spoken in a very long time. "I love you, Penn. I always have."

Penn

The very last thing I want to do right now is cry. So I take the heat burning the backs of my eyes, the despair tearing at my heart, and place it inside a box deep inside, to be dealt with another day.

I've never seen life as being cruel, the way others do. But what other justification is there for finding true love one week before I'm supposed to marry another man?

Penn keeps a steady, leisurely rhythm. Is he drawing it out, savoring the connection between our bodies? I am.

I kiss him everywhere I can reach. Touch every inch of skin I can, my fingertips committing him to memory.

Pleasure builds, gathering steam, and my breathing becomes labored. "I...I..."

"Me too, Sunshine," he whispers.

"Cover my mouth," I tell him. I want to be loud. I want all control gone, handed over to Penn. I have so little to give him, but there's this, though it's not nearly enough.

Penn increases his pace, and when my whimpers grow louder, he covers my mouth with his left hand. My hand grips the tattoos. Eyes on mine, fingers over my lips, the center of our bodies slice the air, jerking together in the rawest way. So intimate. Beautiful, even.

Eyes screwed shut, he opens his mouth, his roar soundless. But I feel him. Heaving, twitching, spilling.

Penn drapes over me, his weight welcome. Lightly I scratch my nails over his back.

"Let's run away together," I say to the ceiling.

"If only that would solve all our problems," he answers, cheek pressed against my breast.

We lie like that for a while, catching our breath. Finally, he pulls out of me, pressing a kiss to the inside of my knee as he backs up on the bed.

"I'll be right back," he says, returning a minute later. He has disposed of the condom, and brought a warm washcloth. "I didn't make a mess of you, but I thought you might appreciate it."

"It sounds amazing, actually." I reach a hand out for the cloth, but he shakes his head, leaning one knee on the bed. "May I?"

"Um, sure." Am I really going to feel shy about this, given where his face was pressed only a handful of minutes ago?

Penn leans forward, brushing a kiss over my forehead, and his hand goes between my legs. The warmth of the washcloth is welcome, a slight ache already beginning. My muscles down there aren't accustomed to being used this way.

It's probably only a few seconds he spends cleaning me, but it takes my heart that is already his, and places a sealant over it. Penn is a good man. Someone who deserves true love.

Can I give that to him? Is there a way out of the terrible mess I've created for myself?

Penn walks to the entrance to the bathroom, tossing the wet cloth across the room, where it lands with a *thwap* in the bathtub.

He returns, pulling back the covers, asking with his eyes for me to slide in beside him. I shimmy in, pressing

Penn

my body into him. And then he says the very last thing I expected.

"Duke's dad came to see me."

Chapter 47

Penn

Daisy presses a hand to my chest, using me as leverage to prop herself up. "Duke's dad? When?"

"Earlier today. When I said I was struggling with something." I lie back, look up at the blade of the ceiling fan.

She's leaning over me, golden hair spilling out around her like a halo. She's an angel, a sassy, funny, feisty, sweet to her core angel. She's everything I could ever need in life. Was it unfair of me to tell her I love her? I can't figure it out. Maybe it would've been kinder to keep it to myself. Let her carry out her convoluted plan, and have the chips fall where they may.

"Hey," Daisy says softly, palming my cheek, urging me to drag my gaze back to hers. "Old man Hampton is the definition of a narcissistic asshole. He should be studied."

Apprehension courses through me. I have to tell her

Penn

everything he said. Everything he offered. With one exception.

She reaches up, fingers smoothing over the pinch between my eyebrows. "You can't say anything to me about that man that will surprise me."

If only that were true.

"I'll have to give you the background, first."

"Uh-oh," she teases. "There's background?"

My answering smile is lopsided. "I thought I was meeting Hugo at Hen Pecked last night, but—"

"He ambushed you," Daisy interjects, laughing. "It was guys' night."

"Exactly. So that means you know who else was there."

Daisy nods, her nails dragging over my chest in circles. "Correct."

"Duke got drunk, and mouthy. I walked him out to his car, and he said something shitty. I lost my temper, and—"

Daisy's eyes are wide. "That's why he has a bruise? He told me he had too much to drink and tripped on the stairs when he came home."

"That's not even a good lie," I say, earning me an open-palmed *thwack* across my chest.

"Fast forward to Duke's dad," she says impatiently. "What did he say to you?"

"He's encouraging Duke to press charges against me."

"What? No. Absolutely not." Daisy's head shakes vehemently. "I will put a stop to that."

I smile at her tenacity. Her willingness to go to bat for

me. "I appreciate that. You." I stroke her face, running my hand over her bare shoulder. Her breasts, pushed against my ribs, are plump and pressing together. I want to lift her over me, let their softness fall over my face, take one in my mouth.

She taps my chin. "Focus," she grins. "You can have my tits after you tell me about this."

"Busted." I manage a smile, though I'm not feeling exactly happy about what I'm preparing to tell her. "He said he'll buy my old place outright, plus twenty percent."

She sputters an incredulous laugh. "What?"

"Yep."

Daisy's gaze narrows. "And the catch is?"

She knows this family, the way they throw money around to get their way. And now, I'm included in that. It makes me sick.

"I leave town." I say it simply, but there's anger hiding behind my tone.

Laughter spills from between her pretty lips. It disappears when I don't join in.

"Penn," she says, fear shrinking her voice. "Please tell me you didn't say yes."

"I didn't say yes."

"But you're thinking about it?"

A cold knot forms in my stomach. "It's not the money. I promise you, it's not that."

"Then what is it?"

"You, Sunshine." I toy with a lock of her hair, twirling it around my finger.

"What about me?" Her voice is small again. I hate that I'm the one who made it that way.

"Glenn Hampton seems to think my presence in town is causing you grief."

"It is."

Her honesty is a sucker punch. My twirling freezes, and Daisy's hair unwinds itself from my finger. "The last thing I wanted when I came back was to be a problem in your life. To make anything hard for you. I even thought I could *avoid* you."

Daisy rolls her eyes, hand trailing over my stomach. "You're doing a great job avoiding me." She sits up, reaching over the side of the bed to gather the comforter that found its way to the floor during the past hour.

"Spectacular view from behind," I tell her, and she shakes her ass.

"Don't tempt me," I warn.

"'Tits and ass after we talk," she chides, wrapping the comforter around herself like it's a towel. She gets herself situated, then begins. "It's true your presence is causing me grief, but only in a *good* way. You're a problem I needed to have. I'm so sick of playing the role of perfect Daisy St. James. With you, I can be myself. I like saying what I'm thinking, and feeling how I'm feeling. I like being intimate with you, just simply existing and giving myself over. There's no role to play when I'm with you. I'm me, and that's it."

I'm about to add how special that is, but she continues.

"I was jaded, and I needed to be reminded love exists. True love." A blush steals over her face, but I'm quick to sit up, running my hands over her cheeks.

"Don't blush," I instruct, and when she opens her mouth to speak, I'm quick to say, "And don't even think of taking it back."

"I won't," she promises.

"Daisy, you already knew true love existed before I came back. You only needed reminding." I tuck her hair behind her ear. "Think about what you're doing for your mom. What do you call that?"

"Insanity."

I breathe a laugh. "It's true love."

"Oh." She looks genuinely surprised. "I didn't think of it that way."

"True love doesn't have to be romantic."

She drums her fingers on her mouth, letting that sink in. "Where does that leave us?" she finally asks, so soft. So vulnerable.

I wish we could run away together, like she suggested. It's a fantasy, maybe even a delusion, and entertaining it is pure agony.

"Unless you're planning on canceling your wedding—"

"And you're planning on telling me why you really left—"

"—we're right where we've always been," I finish.

Daisy's eyes fill with tears, but she holds them at bay.

I refuse to let her hide. Push away her emotions. Not my girl. Not my Daisy. She can feel whatever she wants to feel, and I'll take it all. I'll welcome it. "Cry if you want to, Daisy. Whatever emotion you want to have, have it. I don't mind."

Penn

"That's what you told me that first night, at Summerhill. You told me I could take that low moment I was having and sink into it a little deeper." She smiles fondly at the memory. "It was so freeing to hear that. To know I could be myself, feel my feelings, and everything would be ok."

I take her hand, winding my fingers through hers. "How do you feel right now?"

"I feel...rage," she admits. "My mom is dying, and I'm stuck in this awful web I spun. It feels like I can't get out."

I wish I could tell her how deeply I empathize.

Instead, I reach for the comforter, and she lets me slide it down.

"Penn," she says, but my name is shaky. "I don't know how all this will end up, and losing you again, I..." She shakes her head, says nothing more.

"I know, Sunshine." I try not to feel the desolation, but it's there. Sour and pungent and *there*, in the pit of my stomach.

Leaning forward, I claim her mouth. I kiss her like I didn't recently have her.

I kiss her like I might not ever have her again.

Chapter 48

Penn

EACH DAY PASSES, AND I WAIT FOR A KNOCK ON MY door, for a uniformed policeman to tell me I need to come down to the station.

If Duke plans to press charges, he's taking his sweet time. Maybe Daisy was successful in putting a stop to it.

My realtor called to tell me he received a cash offer twenty percent above asking price. I told him I'd think about it. I'm not sure if I'm considering it, or if I like envisioning that grade A asshole squirming in his plush office chair, waiting to see if the big, bad wolf is going to steal his son's fiancée.

My realtor said if I don't take it, I'm a fucking lunatic. Verbatim.

I've seen Daisy twice since last weekend, both times for physical therapy. My evening schedule is packed with final preparations for the play, including dress rehearsals (mandatory, Noelle said. Doesn't matter if your grandma died, or you broke your leg.). What the

Penn

kids have managed to put together in this short of a time is nothing short of incredible. I am still very opposed to the fact I am acting in the play, and when I'm not fantasizing about Daisy, I'm envisioning different scenarios in which I tell Noelle *I quit*. But I have to admit, I like helping the kids, and the youth theatre program. (Take that, Duke The Twat, with your library subsidy.)

Daisy has been different at our appointments this week, and I know it has nothing to do with what happened between us. She's jittery, like she's on the edge of something in her mind. I wait until Isla's busy booking a new client over the phone to confront Daisy, but all she says is, "My brain is an unpleasant place to be right now." I offer to help, and she looks at me so long without speaking I think maybe my offer has fallen on deaf ears. Then she says, very simply, "No, thank you."

What I hear is *You've done enough*.

I want to wrap her up, ferry her away from Olive Township. I want to give her the space to be Daisy from last weekend, the woman who muffled her pleasured cries by pressing a pillow to her face. The woman who laid her head on my chest, smiled down at me, kissed my cheek. Joking, laughing, sassy Daisy. I wish we could go back to that evening, stretch out the moment, live in it forever.

She's so far inside her head, keyed up and consumed, and I don't know what to do. Should I show up at her house, insist she open up to me? Would that really be what's best for her? I know the Daisy of yesteryear, but

I'm still learning Daisy as an adult, and I don't know if she'd appreciate me doing that.

If only she would talk to me about what's going on in her mind. If not me, then I hope she's talking to Vivi. She needs somebody. I'm up against an asshole with far too much money, but Daisy has her mother's happiness riding on her shoulders. And the town, too.

Is it fair for Daisy to shoulder all that pressure? All these people, looking forward to her wedding, building it up to be an event bigger than what it really is.

It's not only her mother, but the people of Olive Township counting on her to marry Duke.

Collectively, the whole town will shutter to attend the St. James/Hampton wedding this weekend. Store windows bear signs announcing modified store hours. It's all anybody will talk about. As for me, dull dread and sharp panic alternates for top emotion.

The girl I love is getting married, and I can't see a way out of it. The stories, the lies, the good intentions, they're twisted and tangled into a snarl. How does one break free from it?

A bomb.

The only way to be free from it all, is to blow it up.

I refuse to be the bomb, to force the explosion on Daisy.

But there is one person I want to see.

And a visit to him is long overdue.

Chapter 49

Daisy

"Sweet mother of petunia's," Vivi grumbles, hauling a sack of groceries into my house. "It's cold outside. Like, really freaking cold. Have you made sure Hugo has heaters set up for the reception?"

"Um, yeah," I nod absentmindedly, helping her unpack the groceries. Vivi and I always split *buy one, get one* deals from the grocery store. "He texted yesterday and asked if I'd looked at the weather forecast for the weekend. I said I hadn't, and he told me not to worry, that he had it all covered."

When Hugo asked if I'd checked the weather for my own wedding, I didn't feel bad admitting I hadn't. Ever since last weekend when I spent the evening with Penn, I've been turning over uncomfortable thoughts in my head. A man as controlling as Glenn Hampton would certainly be upset by something possibly threatening his son's impending nuptials, and paying to make the problem go away is undoubtedly in his wheelhouse, but it still feels like I'm missing something. There are obviously things I don't know, and I haven't pressed because I'm haven't been certain I wanted to know. There are some situations in which Pandora's box is better left with the lid intact. That's the way I felt when I first found out Peter was Penn, but as my wedding day creeps closer, I'm not so sure that's how I feel anymore. Maybe that's why checking the weather for this weekend was the last thing on my mind.

Vivi flicks her ponytail over her shoulder, saying, "You're the first wedding being held at Summerhill. I think Hugo's freaking out a little bit."

"It's good it's only me and Duke. Trial run."

"Ri-ight." Vivi closes the fridge, examining me with her mom eyes. "What's wrong with you? Besides the fact you're marrying one of our closest friends for fakesies."

I know she's being funny, but her words hit with the swiftness of an arrow.

I bite my lip. Look away. Try like hell to keep from feeling the tsunami of emotions rising up inside me, over and over. But the truth is, I can't. Everything is too big. Too much.

"I'm in love with him, Viv."

She grabs me, wraps me in her arms. For all her tough, brash talk, she is a nurturer at heart. My tears spill over, dammed up for too long. She lets me cry, and when the tears subside, she stands back, looks me directly in the eyes, and says, "Timing has not been kind to you."

I sniff, pulling two tissues from the box on my coffee

table and loudly blowing my nose. "I don't know what to do."

"Is there an alternative?"

"Sure." I shrug like the answer is too easy. "Upend my life."

"I know that, but I mean, *is there an alternative you would actually choose?*"

Confusion knits my brows. Vivi blows out a heavy breath. "I mean, is there something between upending your life and getting what you want?"

Her phone rings as soon as she's done with her question. "It's my mom," she says, answering with a, "Hey, Mama."

Does Vivi know she smiles when she talks to her mom? Pain slices across my heart. It's premature grief from expected future loss, because my next thought is *How many more phone calls will I have with my mom?*

While Vivi is answering her mother's question (something about how to cut a peanut butter and jelly sandwich for the kids the way Vivi does it), I go down the hall, sit on my bed, and call my mother.

Bonnie answers. "Hello, dear."

Disappointment flashes through me. I'd wanted my mother to pick up, to hear the familiar way she says my name when she answers my call.

"Hi, Bonnie. Can my mom talk?"

"She's napping right now, but I bet she'll be up soon. She's so excited for this weekend, it's been interrupting her sleep."

Nails from the hand I'm not using to hold a phone

curl into my palm, pressing deeply until the pain of a physical sting distracts from the emotional.

"I think I'll come by for a visit, unless you have an appointment you need to get to."

"We'll be here," she responds. "Busy day around the farm. The feed store made its delivery, your dad has been running tours all day, and now he has a visitor waiting for him in his study. Handsome young man showed up about ten minutes ago, but he didn't seem very happy."

This has me straightening. "Did his visitor drive up in a truck?"

"Let me see," she says, and I picture her walking across the wood floor of her room next to my mother's, pulling over the lace curtain to peek. "Yep. And there's a dog sitting in the front seat. At least I think it's a dog. It could be a statue. The thing isn't moving at all."

Surprise steals through me, holding onto my breath for a few seconds. *Why would Penn go to see my dad?* "Thank you, Bonnie," I choke out, miserably failing at my attempt to sound normal. "I'll see you soon."

I rush out to the kitchen just as Vivi is hanging up with her mom. "What?" she demands, eyebrows drawn when she sees the frenzied look on my face.

"Penn is at my parents' house." The sentence rushes from my mouth, sounding like one long word.

She grabs my forearms, steadying me. Had I been swaying?

"Do you think he's telling your parents the truth about you and Duke?"

I shake my head. "He wouldn't do that."

Penn

"Then what else does he have to say to them? *Sorry I nearly bashed your daughter's head in fifteen years ago.*" She rolls her eyes, like it's absurd.

Vivi's words tumble around my brain. Sink in. Spread out.

My heartbeats pick up pace. "Vivi, that might actually not be far off."

"But, Daisy," Vivi gazes at me with concern. "He did that already. After the accident. We were all there. Penn was beside himself. He was sobbing, and apologizing to your parents. Don't you remember?"

"Yes," I whisper. I try not to think of that day, the horror in my best friend's voice. *I'm sorry, I didn't mean to. I love her.*

"I need to go to my parents' house. Now."

"Well, duh. Of course. I'd drive you there, but I have to get to the restaurant." Vivi winds her purse strap over her shoulder. "I'm catering a wedding this weekend, but I'm not one hundred percent sure it's going to happen. I could tell you the whole situation, but you might not believe me." She winks at me. "If you hear word the wedding is off, tell me, ok? That's a lot of food prep for nothing."

"I promise," I tell her, gathering my purse.

"Are you still staying the night with me tonight?"

We'd decided on the plan weeks ago. I try for a smile, but it feels off. "Wouldn't miss a night with my best babe."

"I'm making almond cake petit fours with strawberry rhubarb jam in a lemon curd buttercream."

I nearly laugh. That's the wedding cake flavor I didn't choose.

"And a bottle of crisp bubbles to go with bedtime stories and songs."

"Everything I dreamed of for the night before my wedding." I really can't think of a better way to spend my time.

"Girls gone mild," Vivi confirms.

I'm right behind her out the door, waving to her as we climb in our cars. She blows me a kiss, saying, "Let me know if I need to crack any skulls."

Chapter 50

Daisy

Penn's black truck sits in front of my parents' house, shiny and sleek and stark against the farmhouse with the white clapboard siding. I pull up on his passenger side, shutting off the engine. Climbing out, I glance into the truck. Slim Jim stares back at me.

In an instant, my brain understands what my heart refuses. Penn would only keep his reason for leaving from me if he believed it would hurt me. And what would hurt me? Knowing my beloved parents had something to do with it.

I start for the house, and in the distance, a horse whinnies.

Instead of walking in the front door, I quietly let myself in the side door off the kitchen. The large room smells of dough, and through the oven light I see biscuits rising inside. Butter sits on the counter, softening. Duke's remarks from that day we hid behind Rowdy Mermaid in his SUV bubble to the surface. He'd said I looked like *softening butter* when Penn was close to me at the speakeasy. I found it funny at the time, but now it makes more sense.

My corners round. My color changes. I soften.

Penn. Why are you here?

Walking on soft feet through the house, I drift to my father's study in the back corner. Voices filter out into the hall, muted by the closed door.

When I arrive at the door, I don't linger. I don't take a deep breath, or prepare myself. No need for eavesdropping. I want the truth, and I want it right now. I crash in, like a rhino. Or a pygmy hippo.

My father sits at his desk, horror on his face as his gaze falls on me in his open door. Penn whips his head around, and he doesn't wear the surprised look of someone who has been caught. He looks relieved.

"Why is he here?" I ask my father. Blood pounds in my ears, because *I know*. The details are blank spaces, but the events are taking shape. Penn crying over me, my blood on his hands. My father on phone calls behind a closed door in this same room. The way I overheard him say *I won't wait for this to happen a second time.*

And now, my father, the man who spent his entire life caring for me, loving me, sacrificing for me, looks me in the eyes and prepares to lie.

"Hey, Daisy Mae," he greets, almost covering up the tremble in his voice. Almost, but not quite. "Penn had some questions about that property he's selling. His old house."

Penn

Penn's shoulder blades bunch, agitation in his muscles and the flex of his jaw.

"Is that right?" I ask my dad, crossing my arms. "You're a real estate lawyer now?"

He chuckles uncomfortably. "Well, no."

"Real estate agent?"

A second chuckle, tighter this time. "Also no."

"What specific knowledge do you have that would lead Penn"—I glance at the utterly silent man across from my father. His head dips fractionally, as if urging me on—"to come see you?"

"Oh, you know, this and that." It's heartbreaking to watch my dad hustle, like he has a broom and he's cleaning up the detritus of the past.

"Enough," Penn speaks, a quiet strength in his voice. "Stop lying to her, Mr. St. James. Just *stop*."

My dad has the absolute gall to look surprised. "Daisy," he licks his lips, a flush creeping over his neck. "I'm not sure what Penn is talking about right now, but—"

Penn pushes back his chair, the legs protesting with the swiftness of his movement. In two strides he reaches me. I'm starved for his touch, but he keeps his hands to himself. "He paid me, Daisy." Penn's voice is urgent, like he needs me to know this old truth. "He offered my mom and I money to leave, and we accepted it. A new home for us in California. An opportunity for her to get better."

The words are a physical blow, as if they've grown hands and reached for me, pushing me back until my shoulder blades hit the wall behind me. My mind spins. Nothing that happened at the end of that summer made sense to me, and all those times I've looked back on it, I saw it through the eyes of a child. Muddy memories, blurred by time.

With two hands on Penn's upper arm, I push him aside as though I'm merely opening a closed curtain. My father, still seated, has prayer hands propped under his chin. He looks desolate. Exhausted. But not sorry.

"You paid him, Dad?" When he doesn't answer, I say, "How could you?"

"Dammit," my father cries, smacking his hand on the top of his desk. "It's been fifteen years. You don't get to come in here now and act like this breaks your heart."

I can't believe what I'm hearing. *All this time.* "There is no statute of limitations on bad behavior. And you *did* break my heart back then. And this? Right now? This *does* hurt my heart." My lower lip trembles. "Dad, I loved him, and you paid him to go away."

"My job as your dad is to do what's best for you, and back then that meant keeping you away from this boy." He points at Penn, the boy who is now a man, and bigger than my father. "Penn, one day you will understand that. You will have a little girl, and she will become the center of your universe, and you'll watch her develop an impossible love for a boy who doesn't stand a chance at living a normal life. And then, when he hurts her, *even when it's an accident*, you will make a difficult choice in her best interest. That is the painful side of parenting. Making decisions that will be hard on them, knowing it will benefit them in the future."

"Daisy?"

Penn

Three pairs of eyes swing to the door. To my mother.

She grips the handle, the other hand braced on the frame. She looks tired and frail, with dark circles under her eyes. Bonnie stands unobtrusively behind her, her face a practiced blank mask.

"Mom," I say, glancing at Penn as I pass him on my way to her. He steps aside, his hand brushing mine. His face is stricken. This is his first time seeing my mother in this state.

"How was your nap?" I ask, reaching her. I lean in, folding her into a careful hug.

"Fine, until we came downstairs to check on the biscuits Bonnie made while I was sleeping, and heard raised voices." Her gaze starts with me, then darts to my father, and lands on Penn.

Penn offers his hand to my mom. "Mrs. St. James, it's me. Penn Bellamy."

"Penn Bellamy," she says, a smile blooming on her face. She glances at me, worried confusion in her gaze. I smile intentionally, letting her know it's ok. I'm ok. Content with my response, she turns back to Penn. "Welcome home. You grew up to be handsome."

"Thank you, Mrs. St. James."

"Now," she says, remaining in position in the door. My heart breaks a little, knowing she's standing there only because she needs the assistance. "What's this all about?"

"Oh, it's nothing," my dad answers before I can. "Penn is selling his old house and wanted to run a few things by an old friend."

She doesn't know? The relief consumes me. Already I feel this is all too much to carry. I couldn't possibly hold the weight of being upset with my dying mother.

My dad's eyes plead with me. Two different thoughts war within me. *She should know!* competes with *Why put that on her?*

I look at Penn, and suddenly I want to cry. Scream, sob, fucking lose it. This dance we do to keep my mother happy, to facilitate the least painful end of life for her, is draining me.

Does Penn sense this? Read my mind? He must, because he steps up. Smiles his winningest smile, and I think if he'd given me that wide-mouth grin the first day at Summerhill, I would have recognized him in an instant. "I haven't given you a proper greeting, Mrs. St. James." He folds my fragile mom into a gentle embrace, saying, "It's been so long, and it's nice to see you again."

Her gaze sweeps to me, and she smiles. "He always was a good hugger," she remarks.

"The best," I confirm, and damn if there isn't a tear rolling down my cheek.

Penn pulls back, but stays close. "Selling an old house brings a unique set of problems, and I wanted to bend your husband's ear."

"Ahh," she nods, eager to accept the words. The last thing she needs are old transgressions paraded around. I understand my dad choosing not to tell her. I'm not any better.

"Pardon the interruption, folks," Bonnie says apologetically, peeking around my mom. "Ms. Brenda, it's time for your medication."

"It certainly is," my mother responds, sighing heavily. "I'm aching from head to toe."

My gaze collides with my dad's, a conversation passing between us. *She will be gone, and it will be just us. We're not ready.*

"Daisy," my mom says, like she's only just thought of something. "I can't wait to see you in my dress, baby girl. You're going to be a dream."

"You've already seen me in it, Mom," I remind her gently. "At the fitting."

"Ahh, yes, but the aisle and the flowers and your hair and makeup done makes all the difference. Tomorrow's not so long to go." She smiles, but her lips quiver. She's in pain.

Bonnie seems to understand. She loops an arm around my mom's, saying, "You just wait until you all see how I'm doing Ms. Brenda's hair for the wedding."

Penn twists a pinkie finger around mine, support I need. A reminder that he is here. "You can't be prettier than the bride, Mom," I tease, like there isn't a knife ribboning my heart.

Mom makes a *pshhh* sound with her lips. "Such things are not possible."

I tell her I love her, and I kiss her sunken cheek.

Bonnie walks Mom away, making it look like they are going the same pace, when in reality she's leading. I look to my dad. In her absence, he's sobbing silently. I rush to him. I am so, so mad at him, furious. But this terrible pain he's in supersedes my anger.

"Dad." I wrap my arms around him.

"Just when I think I've come to terms with her dying, it hits me all over again." He dabs at his eyes with a tissue from the box on his desk.

"Me, too." I wipe at my wet cheeks.

"Daisy, I'm sorry for everything. For the way it all happened. I never wanted to hurt you, and I know you're looking back on it now and thinking I was in the wrong, but—"

"You weren't totally wrong, Mr. St. James." Penn, an observer of the grief in the room, comes closer. "I don't like the way it all happened, and I have a lot of complicated feelings around it, but I don't think you were all the way right, or wrong." His eyes shine, so pure of heart, and I fall a little more in love with him. "If my life had continued on that way, there would've been a lot of mistakes in my future. Mistakes going far beyond taking my mother's car and crashing it with Daisy in it. Living the way I was, becoming a teenager with a mom who had checked out? She needed help, and there was no way I could've gotten her the help she needed."

Penn. Sweet, kind Penn with his good heart and his wry sense of humor and his openness to let me feel what I feel. I love him, from the top of my head to the tips of my toes.

I let go of my father, rounding the desk. My hands slip over Penn's shoulders, wrapping around his neck as I

Penn

bring him to me for a hug. I breathe him in and I hold him close, and my heart feels like it's home.

My dad clears his throat. "Daisy?"

Oh. I step back. Meet Penn's eyes. The corners of his mouth turn up.

"You're marrying Duke. Tomorrow," my dad says slowly, a reminder I don't need.

Regret sweeps through me, the feeling mirrored back to me in Penn's stormy eyes. "Right," I answer on a strangled whisper. It's all set. Every last detail.

"Your mother—"

"I know, Dad. I know."

Realization widens his eyes, slackens his jaw. "Oh, Daisy Mae."

"The apple doesn't fall far," Penn says, bringing a moment of levity to a grim situation. He takes my hand, winding his fingers through it. "I love your daughter, Mr. St. James. I loved her when I was a kid, and I love her today. And in case you're wondering, I'm not going to run into the ceremony tomorrow and cause a scene."

"You're not?" I ask without thinking. A part of me had entertained that fantasy, not only because it's the epitome of romantic, but because if someone outed me, exposing what Duke and I agreed to, it would be over. An ending that wouldn't be my doing.

"I'm not going to put you in that position, Sunshine." He smirks, giving me that playful look I desperately love. "Did you want me to?"

I bite back a smile. "I might have daydreamed about it."

"Me, too," he admits.

We share a smile, a quiet laugh, and everything falls away. For a moment we are Daisy and Penn, best friends running around my parents' house, and we have all the time in the world in front of us.

A quiet heaviness settles over us as reality intrudes. By this time tomorrow, I will be as far removed from Penn as I can possibly be. I will be Duke's wife, and Penn will eventually return home to San Diego.

"Will you walk me out?" I ask him.

He nods eagerly. "Of course."

Nearly unforgotten on the other side of his desk, my dad says, "Daisy, about tomorrow..." He trails off. What is there to say?

"I'll be there, Dad. I'll give Mom her dream. I'll do everything I said I would."

He opens his mouth, hesitates. Blinks hard and shakes his head. "For what it's worth, Penn, I'm happy to see you're back. You bring something out in my little girl, that frankly, nobody else does."

"Thank you, sir."

I glance back at my father on our way out the door. Wrinkles pull at the corners of his eyes. He looks tired. Deflated.

We walk back through the house, then into the kitchen. I'd been hoping to catch my mother, give her one last hug and tell her I love her again. I could say it one hundred times a day and it wouldn't be enough to make up for all the future I love you's we will miss.

Penn

She's already disappeared with Bonnie, so I let us out the side door. Slim Jim's expression changes when he sees Penn, going from stoic to a goofy dog smile.

"So..." Penn turns to me when we're between our cars. We forgot ourselves in my father's office, but we're in public now, and we keep a polite distance just in case. The inverse of me and Duke. This whole situation is the messiest of messes, a snarl that looks impossible to untangle.

"So," I echo.

"I don't know what to say."

"Neither do I."

"This feels a lot like letting go."

My lower lips trembles. "It really does."

"I'm going to get hammered drunk tonight."

"That's probably a bad idea."

"I plan to still be drunk tomorrow."

"That's going to be a painful recovery."

"Nothing will torment me more than knowing you're someone else's wife."

The tears spill over. How could they not?

"Fuck, Daisy." His head hangs, and he grips it with his hands. "I'm sorry. I'm not trying to make this harder on you than it already is."

"Every second that brings me closer to being married I become more confused and sad and scared. It's the eleventh hour. What am I doing?" I swipe under my eyes. Sniff. Penn reaches for me, and I'm yearning to step into him, to feel soothed by him.

He thinks better of it, and drops his hands.

Something in my peripheral vision catches my eye, and I look up at my mother's window. There is nothing there, except perhaps a slight movement of her lace curtain, but maybe I'm imagining it.

Chapter 51

Olive Township

Sometimes I wish I could take physical shape. Arms and legs, a mouth and fingers.

If I could, I'd have stopped Penn from taking his mother's car that day, and Daisy from getting in the passenger seat. A flat tire would have kept the accident from ever occurring.

My abilities start and end with sitting, watching, and loving my inhabitants, and I was relegated to watching it unfold. I had no way to stop what I saw put into motion when Penn took his mother's keys from her purse.

It was hot that day, the kind of heat that soaks into concrete sidewalks and makes everything hotter. Late summer, and my residents were restless. I watched Daisy tell Penn she was dying for a soft serve ice cream cone, dipped in chocolate. *If I don't have one, I'll perish.* Those were her exact words.

Penn, who only ever wanted to make Daisy happy, was positive he could drive her to get ice cream.

Daisy argued, but Penn was insistent. Daisy refused to get in the car, but when Penn got behind the wheel, Daisy screeched and got in, too. She swore at him, but he smirked, and then she laughed and said *if you're going down, I'm going down, too.*

I've seen it time and time again over the years. Young people never consider the consequences of their actions.

I watched Penn hit the curb on Olive Avenue, the car plowing into a store that had already closed for the day. Daisy's head hit the windshield, blood pouring down.

There was screaming, and crying, mostly from Penn.

My inhabitants are helpers, and I'm proud of that. They ran to the car, doing what they could.

Daisy's injury was the only one that day, but the shockwaves were felt long after.

Glenn Hampton, a man with a heart half the size it should be, stepped in. He'd been turning over the idea for awhile, and he knew this was the perfect time. Capitalizing on Charles St. James' fear for his daughter's safety, Glenn presented the perfect plan.

A whole new life for the Bellamy family, away from Olive Township. The money would come from Glenn, but the plan would be executed by Charles.

Glenn insisted he be the silent money, and refused to tell Charles why. Charles, distraught over his daughter's accident and injury, decided the *why* didn't matter.

I know Glenn's *why.*

He has a secret, which means I do, too.

Chapter 52

Penn

I picked up a six-pack of beer and a bottle of tequila, settling in for a night of unhealthy soothing. If I get stupidly drunk, I'll forget the love of my life is marrying a guy I might actually like if I gave him a chance, but hate on principle.

I'm two beers deep, the bottle unopened on my counter, when there's a knock at my door. Slim Jim trots beside me to answer it.

"Hugo?" I step back to let him in. "Were we supposed to meet up, and I forgot?"

"Nope," he answers, finding his way to my kitchen and cracking open a beer. "Just thought you might like some company on the night before the love of your life marries somebody else."

"Wow," I deadpan. "Go right for it. No lube."

"No time for lubrication, my friend." He plunks down on a chair at the kitchen table. "We need to have a talk."

"Well, you see Hugo, the penis enters the vagina, and that's how babies are made."

He snaps and points at me. "That right there is how I know you need an ass whooping."

"Bring it, sword boy."

"A *verbal* ass whooping."

"Ugh." I throw myself into the seat across from him. "Get it over with."

"I'll start by saying you should get your head out of your ass."

My eyebrows lift, as does my beer. "Here, here."

He steamrolls ahead. "You came back to Olive Township using a name that has the same initials as your real name. You returned on a bullshit excuse, like you couldn't have sold that house from San Diego."

"I wanted to see it in person," I argue.

"And why is that?" Hugo challenges.

"To see what it was I was really dealing with."

"I could've sent photos."

I say nothing, taking a pull of my beer.

Hugo smiles smugly. "You wanted to see your old house, Penn. You *wanted* to come back. And, most of all, you *wanted* to see Daisy. And"—he looks so proud of himself—"when you found out she was engaged, you didn't leave. You could have. One might argue that you should have. But you didn't. You went and made her your physical therapist. You helped her with her home remodel. You slipped right back into your old friendship with her, before she knew your real identity. And then you told her who you really are. Why? Because you needed her to know. If she was going to feel something for someone, it had to be you. You were jealous of your own self." He shakes his head at me. "What an asshole! Do you see what I'm getting at, Penn?"

"That I'm unbelievably foolish?"

He points a stiff finger at me yet again. "Even that is an excuse." Fingers curled in air quotes, he mimics, "I'm a fool and that's why all this happened." He drops the act. "No, Penn. You cannot blame this on being a fool. What you can do is get over everything that happened in the past. Yes, you made a mistake when you were thirteen. Yes, you put Daisy in a dangerous situation, and it had a bad outcome. That was a long time ago and honestly, you were pretty fucking dumb back then. We all were." He taps his forehead. "These bad boys don't fully develop until we're almost thirty. Congratulations to us, we're super close to officially making mature decisions."

"What are you saying to me right now?"

He sighs. Gusty, long and loud. "I like Duke. I really do. You would too, if you gave him a chance. But all that is beside the point. What I'm really saying to you, is that I cannot sit by knowing that you love Daisy, and let's be honest, we all know she loves you, too. If things had gone differently, you two would've probably been married five years ago."

"You make it sound simple, Hugo, but it's not. Daisy already knows I love her. I told her."

He's unfazed by this information. "Ok, so you've told her. But have you shown her?"

There's no way for me to make him understand

without telling him Daisy and Duke are a farce, and I won't betray her confidence like that.

"There's no way for me to show her, Hugo."

He shrugs. "Storm the castle."

I blink. "Come again?"

"Summerhill. Tomorrow. Wedding is at eleven."

"I couldn't avoid that information if I tried. Shit's posted all over town."

He shrugs a second time, pushing back from the table. "Do what you want with the information."

I frown at him, at his half-empty bottle. "I already gave my word to Daisy that I wouldn't interrupt her wedding."

"Ok, fine. I get that. But"—those expressive De la Vega eyebrows climb his forehead—"perchance, does Daisy want you to interrupt her wedding?"

I tug my lower lip together in the center, thinking about Daisy, everything I've learned about her, what she's explicitly stated, and all she's left unsaid. "I think Daisy wants someone to give her an out. She's willing to survive the fallout, but not be the reason for it all."

"Be her reason."

"I can't, Hugo." I rap my knuckles twice on the table. Slim Jim perks up, lowering his head when I don't change my body positioning. "Daisy has spent a lot of her life reacting to other people. Being the person Olive Township wants her to be. If her wedding day is going to implode, I want her to be at least a part of it. A decision-maker in it."

Hugo whistles low, and Slim Jim perks up again.

Penn

"Look at you Penn, loving selflessly. You came back to sell your mom's house, but it looks like you learned a lesson or two along the way."

"What are you, a wise old owl? Shut the fuck up."

Hugo stands, smirking down at me. "Hoo," he says, mimicking an owl. "Hoo."

I pluck the bottle from his grasp. "Thanks for coming over here and wasting a beer."

He pats my shoulder, looks me in the eyes. "Storm the castle."

Chapter 53

Penn

I'm headed toward Sweet Nothings for an early morning coffee before they close for the day to attend the wedding I'm trying desperately (and failing) to forget. Distraught would be the most optimistic word to describe me this morning.

I'm almost to the bakery when Margaret steps out of Sammich, arm waving wildly to flag me down.

"Penn," she greets, grinning ear to ear as I approach. "I have been wracking my brain trying to remember your mom's favorite sandwich. But I did it," she says proudly, tapping her temple with one finger. She presses a paper bag into my hands. "Fresh carved turkey, muenster cheese, dijon aïoli, lettuce, tomato, and—here's the special part—house made potato chips. On toasted sourdough." She pats my chest. "Enjoy."

She ambles away, leaving me staring after her, fingers gripping the top of the paper bag. Only when my knuckles turn white do I loosen my grip.

Penn

I knew my mother had a favorite sandwich, but I never would've been able to recite the ingredients. Opening the bag, I allow myself the shortest sniff.

Tears instantly sting my eyes. I'm sitting at a table in Sammich, my mother across from me. Sunlight streams through the glass, lighting up our table, and her. She's wearing her blue silk shirt, the one that matches her eyes. She's smiling happily at me with that look mothers get in their eyes, the one that tells their child they are the center of their world. The most important thing. I remember how I felt that day, the unbridled happiness, the sense of belonging. My dad always went away, but not my mom. I was hers, and she was mine.

I cough into my fist, dashing away my tears. To my truck I go, coffee forgotten.

I know right where I'm headed. The place that brought me back to Olive Township. To Daisy.

Home.

※ ❀ ※ ❀ ※

I STARE AT THE MODEST, ONE-STORY STRUCTURE. Memories, both good and bad, peek at me from broken windows.

Slim Jim sits beside me on the tailgate, and I remove the sandwich from its wrapper. Lifting the sandwich in a salute, I pretend I can see her in the living room, hair tucked back as she wrestles with that awful wallpaper.

I bite into the sandwich, and realize I've had it wrong this whole time. There is something superior to the Monte Cristo.

Slim Jim eyes me with hope. I never feed him people food, but I'll make an exception this one time. We're celebrating. Tearing off a chunk, I toss it over my shoulder into the truck bed. He leaps after it, and I grab my phone.

"Justin," I say, when my realtor answers. "Cancel the listing. My house isn't for sale anymore."

It was safer for me in San Diego, where I could be in my condo without having to face Daisy and the ramifications of how I left her. Just me and Slim Jim, going about our business. But was that really right for me? Was I being the best, or even an *acceptable* version of myself?

I was meant to love Daisy. I've loved her as a friend, and then I loved her in memory, and now I want to love her as a woman.

A ship in the harbor is safe, but that's not what ships are meant for.

Chapter 54

Daisy

The day is bright and sunny, but the cold remains, unyielding in its grip on the town.

Last night's champagne buzz turned into this morning's fogginess, but that has burned off. The room where I'm getting ready at Summerhill has an ornate oval mirror fixed to the wall above a vanity. Strewn atop the vanity are tubes of various makeup and tiny compacts of blush and eye shadow, and every makeup brush I own. My makeup is done, and my hair is day-old to help it stay better in the updo I coaxed it into. My plastic-wrapped dress hangs from a gold hook on the opposite wall.

I look like a bride, and I feel like everything but one. From the moment I woke up today, I ruthlessly banished every emotion skipping through me. But no matter what I do, I cannot get rid of the incessant feeling that what I'm doing is wrong.

Wrong for me. Wrong for my mother. Wrong for Penn. Wrong for Duke.

"Hey, bride-to-be," Vivi says, peeking her head into the room. She's wearing a beautiful ruby red, floor-length dress. And, because it's cold, a gray zip-up hoodie. "Your mom and dad just pulled up."

"They're early," I say, looking at my phone. I have three text messages from Duke, but I haven't looked at them. I'm so keyed up, so distressed, I can't bear to add to the tornado building strength inside me.

I walk out to the main room with Vivi, where there are already chairs set up, a white runner, a makeshift arch. Hugo recently placed an order for a custom built arch, a piece so intricate and detailed, hand carved by a man in a town a couple hours north of here. I'm relieved to not be getting married under something that exquisite, that special.

Through the large picture window I watch Bonnie exit the back seat door, opening my mother's car door. My dad comes around, standing by in case Bonnie needs help. My mother must be having a good day, because she holds up a hand, letting Bonnie know she can get out of the car herself. And then she does, and I feel a flush of thrill at this tiny victory.

Vivi and I meet them on the sidewalk out front. "Mom, you look beautiful." She wears a dusty rose silk shift dress, and a smart little matching bolero. Bonnie has pinned her hair back in a chic chignon.

"I asked Vivi what color she planned to wear," she answers, smiling ear to ear. "That way I didn't clash with her."

I fold her into a hug. She smells like hairspray, and

cucumber lotion, and her favorite Jo Malone perfume. She is tiny in my arms, but she's here and she's vital and the day is bigger for her than it is for me.

I lose it. Right there on the sidewalk, where Summerhill employees pass me and try not to stare as they work on setting up the ceremony.

"Little girl," my mom says, hands on my cheeks, searching my face.

Huge, ugly tears roll down my cheeks, tumble off my jaw, meeting their maker in the fabric of my robe. My mascara streaks down my face, because I wasn't expecting to cry today, so why bother with waterproof?

"I'm sorry," I sniff. "I don't mean to cry."

Vivi steps up, wrapping an arm around my shoulder. "Let's go to Daisy's dressing room." Without waiting for a response, she turns me and leads me away. Once we're safely away from eyes and ears, Vivi and Bonnie leave me with my parents.

"Daisy, what's going on?" My mom guides me to the small couch, urges me to sit down with her. "Why don't you tell me what's going on?"

"It's ok," I lie. "Wedding day jitters, that's all."

"Sweet girl," my mom soothes, brushing away my tears. "This looks nothing like wedding day jitters. Come on. Talk to me."

I hesitate, but my dad settles himself on the chair at the vanity, urging me to come clean with a nod of his head.

Sniffling, I take a deep breath and say, "I made a mistake, Mom. A big one."

"There's nothing you've done that you can't come back from. Tell me what it is, and I'll help you solve the problem."

"It's Penn, Mom."

Mom sighs, this gentle little sound, like maybe she knew it all along. "Of course it's Penn, Daisy. For you, it's always been Penn." She turns tender eyes on my father. "When a heart knows true love, it recognizes it in another." She folds my hand in both of hers. "And for you, my precious daughter, that man is your true love."

"Duke—"

"He'll understand, Daisy." Her voice is rich and certain, soothing me in a way nothing else could. "It was a smart match, but you lacked fire. Maybe you would've been fine with that, but with Penn in the picture?" She shrugs. "What's a heart to do but yearn for its mate?"

I'm *stunned*.

This whole time, I forgot one of my mother's firmest beliefs. *True love.* She dreamed of seeing me walk down the aisle in her wedding dress, but more than anything, she wanted me to find true love. The wedding dress, the ceremony, they were only symbols of the most important thing.

How could I have been so blind?

So foolish?

The answer was right in front of me, but I'd already convinced myself it didn't exist.

A love true enough to marry for the wrong reason. A love so genuine, so pure, it would put me first.

Penn

Outside, there are voices. Cars pulling up, engines turning off, doors opening and closing. Guests arriving.

Duke's messages.

I grab my phone, find there are now four.

> Daisy, we need to talk.
>
> Daisy, I'm rethinking this.
>
> ANSWER ME
>
> I'm coming to your dressing room.

"Oh, thank God," I say, showing my parents my phone. I'm smiling so wide it hurts.

Chapter 55

Duke

My dislike for Penn Bellamy began sometime around the sixth grade.

For years, his mother came to our home once a week and cleaned. She was kind, and quiet, and brought me portions of homemade baked goods. She was far better to spend time with than my own mother, who is still cold and standoffish, a woman who regularly looks at me and my siblings like she's surprised we exist.

Ms. Bellamy was the only good thing about living in my house. One day a week, I actually wanted to come home from school, because I knew she'd be there.

Until she wasn't. Penn arrived in her place on a Saturday. My mom either didn't notice, or didn't care. As long as she wasn't breaking a nail or a sweat on the upkeep of her ostentatious home, what did it matter to her?

With Ms. Bellamy coming on a weekday, she never had to run into my dad. That meant she never had to see

Penn

how he acted. How he treated me, his first born. The child he expected everything of. Nothing I did was good enough, no matter how hard I tried. Every A+ grade left him unimpressed, anything lower left him furious.

Penn saw it all. Every Saturday, Penn kept to the shadows of my home, staying invisible. But me? I was in the spotlight. Every cruelty my dad threw my way, Penn was privy to. And then came the day my dad decided I should know how to throw a fastball. Me, the boy who'd never picked up a baseball, suddenly needed this skill. According to my dad, it was *imperative*.

Throwing a baseball was not something I took to with a natural aptitude, and I'd never seen my father so angry. What he said that day is etched into my heart, my brain, my soul. *How is it possible I have a son who can't throw a fucking baseball?* Then, he threw it at me. It hit me in the side, just left of my stomach, and I dropped to the ground. He stood over me, telling me to get up, but how could I when dragging a single breath through my body felt impossible?

I gasped for air while his face contorted into a mask of disgust. He walked away, leaving me there in the hot sunshine, and then I saw *him*. Penn. Standing in an upstairs window.

Rage like I'd never felt filled me. Somebody with a loving mother, my own classmate, had witnessed the most embarrassing moment of my life. After that, he tried to be nice to me, but it only made me angrier. Meaner. I didn't know what to do with the overpowering emotions I felt, and so many of them were directed at Penn. I belittled him for cleaning our house, I made messes on purpose, and one day, after my dad yelled at me for forgetting to close the garage door, I made a comment to Penn about his mother. *You must hate your life, Penn, trying not to let people see that your mom can't get off the couch.*

The second the words left my mouth, I hated myself. What I really wanted to do was ask Penn if his mom was ok, but I was too jealous. Too sad that he got one good mom, and I got two bad parents.

It was only a handful of months later that Penn and Daisy got in that car accident, and soon after, Penn and his mom left town.

If it weren't for a few too many celebratory whiskeys after a particularly lucrative acquisition a few years ago, my dad would've never admitted what he'd done. The money he gave to Daisy's dad to get Penn and his mother out of the picture. To this day, I don't know why he did it. His lips might've been loosened enough to tell me about it, but he zipped them up after that.

My dad may be harboring a secret, but I know my motivations behind what I'm about to do.

There are two exits from the room where Daisy is getting ready, one that leads inside the building, and another that opens to the outside. In an effort not to gain the attention of the wedding guests, I am approaching from the outside.

"Daisy?" I knock on the door.

She opens it one second later, as if she'd been waiting for me.

"I just read your text messages," she says, breathless.

Penn

Her eyes are red-rimmed, her makeup smeared around the edges. She wears a knee-length white silk robe. On her feet are fuzzy pink slippers.

Daisy has been my friend since before I can remember. We've always been solid, and we thought this plan we concocted was solid, too. But Daisy was hurting when she agreed to all this, and she was anticipating future pain. I was thinking about one thing only: get my overbearing, intrusive family off my back. From my father I've only seen stoicism and displeasure, but the day I told him I was going to marry Daisy, he almost smiled.

No matter what this is going to mean for me, and admittedly, the end results will be substantial, I can't go through with it. I care for Daisy too much to put her in this position, relegating her to a life of pretense and lies, and giving her a husband who doesn't love her as she should be loved. Penn's return has shaken me, displacing all that had sunk to the bottom. Daisy has somebody who will love her the way she deserves. She loves him back, I see it in her eyes, in the way her body goes slack when he's around. It's her soul settling into his. They were made for each other. How can I stand in the way of that?

"Daisy, I think we should talk."

She steps back, allowing me in. I freeze mid-step when I see her parents in the room. Coughing, I say, "Hello, Mr. and Mrs. St. James."

Daisy's mom leans over, kissing my cheek and patting it affectionately. "I really wish you would call us by our first names."

"You know I'm not allowed to," I smile sadly at her, because I can't muster up anything happier.

"Pfft," she sasses. "Your dad and his stupid rules." Her gaze swings between me and Daisy. "We'll leave you two alone now. You have a lot to discuss. But, Duke?"

"Yes?"

Mrs. St. James looks at me fondly, the way my mother never has. How terrible for her to be the one on her way out of the physical world, when she still has so much love to give. "Daisy told us about your arrangement. It was," she falters, "half-witted, but well meaning. And partly my fault, I've been filling Daisy's head with the importance of true love since she was a little girl." She shakes her head. "Here I thought I'd learned all the lessons I needed to in this lifetime."

Mr. St. James takes her by the hand, and she leans on him. "I wish you the very best, Duke. I wish you love, and happiness, and maybe someday you'll get the chance to tell your dad and your grandfather and the board at Hampton & Co. that they can fuck right off."

Daisy gasps. I chuckle. Mr. St. James rubs his thumb lovingly on his wife's chin. "That's my girl," he says to her.

She winks at him. "Still got it."

They leave the room. Daisy's scared eyes find mine. "Duke," she whispers.

"We aren't getting married today, Daisy."

Her head moves slowly back-and-forth. "No, we aren't."

I open my arms, and she sails in. "What are you going to do about your dad? The company?"

Penn

"Take your mom's advice."

She quakes with quiet laughter. "Seriously, though. What will you do?"

I shrug. I haven't figured that part out yet.

We're quiet, and then Daisy asks, "Are you going to press charges on Penn for punching you?"

I frown at the top of her head. "What? No."

"Your dad told him you were going to."

This is news to me. The only reason I told him the truth about what happened is because he was in my office and relentless, like a dog with a raw steak held just out of its reach.

"I guess my old man paid Penn a visit. I don't know why I'm surprised."

Daisy steps back, turning her attention to her reflection in the mirror. "He offered to buy Penn's house, plus twenty percent." She wipes under eyes with a tissue, cleaning the smeared makeup.

"Of course he did. To him, all you have to do is throw money at a problem, and that solves it." I rub my fingers over my temples, at the dull ache that's starting. "It's almost poetic, in a sick way. He fronted the cash to get Penn out of town fifteen years ago, and here he is, trying to do it again."

"That's it," Daisy breathes, motioning wildly with her hands in front of her chest. "That was the connection between you and Penn. I could not figure it out." A few strands of hair have come loose from the pins holding up her hair, framing her face. "Between our current lies, and their old lies, I have been so confused trying to piece it all together."

"I think the picture is now complete. And I apologize for not telling you, but to be honest, I don't understand why he did it." The noise outside the door has increased as we've been talking. The guests are in the main area, chatting animatedly. "What do you think we should—"

Above the low hum from beyond the door, a loud voice rings out. It's followed by a second voice, shouting.

"There is no backing out!"

"There will be if I say there is!"

"My son is getting married today!"

"Not to my daughter!"

Daisy and I look at each other, and we do the only thing we can do in this moment. We laugh.

"I guess we don't have to make an announcement now," Daisy says, wiping under her eyes. She removes her engagement ring and hands it to me.

I place it in my pocket. "As much as I would like to escape out the other door and hightail it out of here, I'll go out there and deal with them." My gaze flickers to the exit that leads outside. "Take this as your chance to get away."

Daisy tips her head, listening to the voices of our fathers who are still yelling at each other. "Normally, I'd say we should present a united front, but I might take you up on your offer."

I reach for the door handle, but Daisy stops me. "Duke, you know how much you mean to me. How much you've always meant to me. It's not lost on me what you're doing for me right now, and for Penn. I hope you know

Penn

that I will return the favor for you, whenever you decide to man up and go after the woman you love."

"I appreciate that, Daze." I open the door, and what I hear next has me hustling down the small hallway, careening around the corner into the large room set up for a wedding ceremony. Though I'm here for a reason, I allow myself the briefest glance in the direction of the woman I can't have, but that's all I get. The tiniest morsel before I turn my attention to the irate man at the top of the aisle.

"You," my father growls in Penn's face. "I told you to leave town."

Penn glances at my dad like he's nothing more than an annoying fly. Daisy's dad steps between Penn and my dad. "Go somewhere else with your red-faced blustering."

My dad reaches for Penn, but Penn shakes him off. His eyes are on me, hurrying across the room. I don't know what's going to happen next, but I need to diffuse it.

"She loves me," Penn shouts, coming to life as I get closer. His gaze is fierce, his lips a hard line. I stop in front of him, and his chest puffs out. He's ready to take me on, fight his way to Daisy, slay any dragon.

Just like she deserves.

Chapter 56

Penn

STORM THE CASTLE.

I told Daisy I wouldn't, but here I am. Staring Duke in the face, and his dumb ass father, and the rest of the town who are all standing up from their chairs, watching the scene unfold.

I don't give Duke the chance to say a word. Pushing a stiff finger into his chest, I say, "She's not marrying you."

Duke opens his mouth to respond, but then from behind him comes the sweetest voice. Literal music to my ears.

"Penn?" Daisy steps around Duke. Behind me, there is shuffling, but I pay it no mind. Daisy's dad won't let that son of a bitch Hampton near me. He told me as much when I saw him outside the entrance. I was frenzied when I parked my truck, running so fast across the lot that I almost missed him. He said my name and got my attention, and when I told him I was here for Daisy, he asked for five minutes to break the news to Duke's dad. I paced out front, waiting, until I could take it no more.

Daisy tucks an escaped lock of hair behind her ear. My heart swells at the sight of her, her white silk robe draped over her creamy skin. She's wearing her bow earrings, the ones that are made up of tiny diamonds. "I thought you said you weren't going to interrupt the ceremony."

"I was wrong." I grab Daisy's hands, hold them in my own. "You can't marry him." Murmurs from the crowd, gasps and *ohhs*.

"You have got to be fucking kidding me," Glenn yells. Duke says something to his dad that I don't hear before walking away quickly. Glenn follows, but because he's a massive asshole with an ego to match, he turns back to Charles and sneers, "I won't forget this, St. James."

I ignore it all, blocking out the familiar faces and focusing only on the woman I love with my whole heart. "I'm not great with words, and I don't know how to say beautiful things. But I love you, Daisy. I loved you when I was a kid, and I love you now as a man. I know things have been messed up, and life hasn't been very kind, and if we're a fairy tale, we are fractured. And maybe that's ok. Maybe some people need broken roads. If all this struggle and strife means I get to have you at the end of the day I would do it over and over again and again and again. You might be the princess of this town, but you are my queen, Daisy." Big round tears roll down her face. I let go of one of her hands, only so I can dash away her tears with my thumb. "If you loved him, I would leave you alone. But you don't, and I know you're trying to do something nice for your mom, but Sunshine, if all you're wanting to do is show your mom the vision of you walking down an aisle in her dress, I'll put myself into that picture. I will marry you right now."

Collectively, the gathered guests draw in a breath.

"Penn, I love you," Daisy says, throwing her arms around my neck. "You definitely know how to say beautiful things." She pulls back, holds my face in her hands. "I'm not marrying Duke. We talked about it. We worked it out. I told my mom the truth." The short sentences trip from her mouth in her haste. "I was going to change and come to find you when I heard your voice."

"I came for you. I couldn't let it happen. No matter the repercussions, I had to lay it all out there."

She beams. Her eyes glimmer. "You crashed my wedding."

"Anything for you."

I kiss her. Long, devouring her softness, her touch singing through my veins. One hand wrapped around her lower back, the other cradling her head, and when our kiss is finished, I brush my lips over her forehead. "I will love you for the rest of my life, Daisy St. James," I murmur against her skin.

"I look forward to it," she whispers. "And when we get married, it's going to be our own wedding, under that special arch Hugo ordered."

"Nothing will stop me from meeting you at the end of the aisle, Sunshine."

"I might beat you there, Sailor."

Penn

A throat clears beside us. Daisy's mom. "You two sure know how to clear a room."

We look around, realizing the place is empty. From beyond the windows, I spot Hugo and Vivi directing people to the reception hall.

"All the food," Daisy groans, covering her mouth. "Vivi put so much work into this day."

Brenda pats her back. "Don't worry. I'm sure there will come a day when you make it up to her."

"We're going to be the talk of the town for, well, forever." Daisy rolls her eyes.

"Most definitely. You're probably already trending on the YouTube."

"Just YouTube, Mom." Daisy laughs, but cuts off when she realizes something. "That was all recorded, wasn't it?"

"I think I counted ten phones capturing it."

Daisy groans. I lift her hand, kissing her fingers. "If it bothers you, I'll go one by one to every guest who was here today and make sure they don't post it."

"I love that about you," Daisy says, smiling at me with so much love it makes my own heartbeats stutter. What a relief it is to say these things to each other openly, without reserve.

"Hey," Vivi says from the entrance. She's gripping the door jamb with two hands, the upper half of her body in the room. "We're turning this day into a party. Might as well." She eyes me and Daisy. "It's not like we don't have something to celebrate. Maybe we'll call this day *'two fools finally figure their shit out.'*"

Daisy laughs. "I don't think that will fit on the town calendar."

Vivi blows her a kiss. "Get changed, then meet us in the reception hall. I have to take the bride and groom off the cake, and smooth out the top."

"Kathleen already did it," Brenda says. "She said it was the first thing she was going to do."

"Well, then." Vivi straightens. "Let's go get a drink, Brenda. There's a margarita calling my name." She cups a hand around her ear, pretending to listen. "There it was again. Come on." She motions for Daisy's mom.

"She is certainly not subtle about giving you two alone time," Brenda whispers loudly so Vivi can hear her. She takes a step away from us, but Daisy's arms fly out, stopping her.

"I'm sorry I made such a mess of things," Daisy says, wrapping her mother up in a hug.

"I'm sorry I made you feel such pressure, sweet girl. I loved you wholly and completely from the moment I laid eyes on you. Nothing you do could make me love you more, or less." She pulls back, lightly pinching Daisy's chin between her fingers as she gazes into her daughter's eyes. "That's true love."

Brenda joins Vivi, and they walk away. Daisy looks up at me, eyes watery. "It's just like you said. True love doesn't have to be romantic."

I surprise Daisy by picking her up, spinning her around. She holds onto my shoulders. When I set her down, I say, "But it can be that, too."

I follow Daisy into the dressing area, watching her

change. She slips the robe from her shoulders, standing only in a strapless bra and a thong. Every cell in my body is at attention.

"Do we have to go to the reception?" I complain, my eyes performing a leisurely and greedy perusal of her curves. "I want you in my bed."

"Like this?" she asks, bending over and grabbing the back of the couch, the perfect globe of her ass stuck in the air.

Without giving it much thought I'm next to her, biting down. She yelps, and I step back.

"Did you just bite my ass?"

"Yes," I answer, without shame or hesitation. "And I'll bite it again, if you serve it up to me like that."

"Oh, Sailor," she says, pulling one of her floral dresses over her head. It skims the floor, and she adds an oversized sweater that opens in the front. "We are going to have so much fun together."

She slips her feet into her shoes, and I pull her close. "I'm yours, Daisy. Body and soul. I meant what I said to you. This is the truest of true love, the kind that will walk through fire if called upon to do so."

"You are far better with words than you give yourself credit for." She rises on tiptoe to press a kiss to the corner of my mouth. "I always hoped you would return, Penn. I dreamed it, and I prayed for it, and I imagined what it would be like to see you again. But all of this? I couldn't have dreamed it this way." Her tongue traces my lower lip, changing course and returning, this time with a tug of her teeth. "I love you, Penn."

"I love you too, Daisy." It takes everything I have not to throw her over my shoulder, march her out to my truck in full view of everybody in the reception hall, and drive her the hell out of here. The only thing stopping me is how much work Hugo and Vivi put into this day.

Hand in hand, we leave the building. The midday sun shines bright, doing its best to break through the cold front that has moved in.

Beside me, Daisy smiles, the sun glinting off the diamonds in her earrings. "You broke up my wedding."

"Ehh..." My head tips back-and-forth. "Sounds to me like it was already broken up."

"You know what I mean," she says, shouldering into me. "You arrived prepared to object."

"That I did."

"You restored my faith in true love. Your words, and your actions."

"I had some help."

"From?"

"Hugo."

Her eyebrows raise. "So he was here this morning, working with his event planner on the first wedding hosted at Summerhill, all the while knowing you were going to show up?"

"I didn't tell him I was coming here. He came to my house last night and gave me a very parental talking-to." Daisy laughs. "And this morning, Margaret brought me my mother's favorite sandwich." Daisy's jaw drops. "Something about that got to me. Drilled right through the layers of bullshit, and made me see everything clearly.

Penn

It almost felt like it was my mom, reaching out. Giving me a push in the direction I needed to go."

"I miss your mom," Daisy says, smiling at me sadly.

"I miss her, too."

"We'll make her a part of our day, ok? Whenever that day comes, we'll make sure she's represented."

I pause outside of the reception hall, pull Daisy in close. "We were made for each other, Daisy. I knew it when we were kids, but I could never articulate it. And then I saw you again, here, and it was like everything inside me sighed in relief. My heart had finally come home. Not just to Olive Township, but to you."

"You woke me up, Penn. I was living this muted existence, but it was no life."

I kiss her again, a kiss we could both sink into and stay for a while, but Vivi interrupts us. "Hey, lovebirds. You know you're standing in front of a window, right?" Hugo, quiet beside her, rolls his eyes. "Come in. Enjoy yourselves. Don't worry, Mr. Hampton is not in here."

Daisy winces. "What about Duke?"

Hugo shakes his head. "I don't know where he went, but he's not here."

Vivi pulls Daisy out of my arms, dragging her through the open door. "Happy Rectified Fools' day," she announces.

"No way." Daisy shakes her head. "That is not going on the town calendar."

"We'll see about that," Vivi says cheekily, handing Daisy a margarita.

For the next half hour, people approach Daisy,

unsure of what to say, but trying their best. She is gracious, explaining that things got a little messy, but they're back on track now. She promises that Duke is fine, they're still great friends, and she is right where she wants to be.

Margaret pulls me aside. "It was the sandwich, wasn't it?"

"Maybe," I say, chuckling.

"Knew it," she says confidently. "Thanks for providing us with one hell of a show today."

"You're not horrified your town princess is ending up with me instead of the golden boy?"

Margaret sends me a disapproving look, but her eyes are soft. "I wonder what it will take for you to realize you are one of our own. You were born here, and this was your home for the first thirteen years of your life. You might have lived your teenage years somewhere else, and gone on to be a big, tough man doing big, tough things, but Olive Township is in your blood. The same way you are an integral part of the makings of Olive Township."

I don't know what to say, because it's everything I needed to hear and never would have asked for. To cover up my discomfort (and underlying jubilation), I make a joke. "You are only saying that because I'm supposed to act in the town play, and you don't want me to get cold feet."

Margaret guffaws. "I wish you the very best if that's the course you take. Noelle would happily knee you in the balls."

I make a face at the mention of that tender area being

Penn

on the receiving end of violence. "Never mind. I'll see you at the play."

"I'll be in the front row," Margaret assures me. "My granddaughter, Lincoln, is the director."

That makes perfect sense.

Margaret ambles away, and Daisy replaces her. "You ready to take me home, Sailor?"

I look around the room. The party is in full swing, everybody eating and drinking. There are furtive glances being sent our way, and plenty of gossip shared around tables. I wouldn't have expected anything less, nor do I anticipate it dying down anytime soon.

"Follow my lead, Sunshine." I head for the kitchen, where I know there is a back entrance, because Hugo mentioned it on one of our phone calls when he was telling me about the design of the new buildings.

Unfortunately, Vivi the Shark is in the kitchen, helping her staff. She glances at the clock on the wall. "You lasted longer than I thought you would."

Daisy laughs, and Vivi pulls her close. "I am so happy for you."

They hug for a few extra seconds, and I say, "That is exactly how I hug Hugo."

Vivi pulls back, leveling me with her serious gaze. "This is the part where I tell you that if you hurt her, I hurt you."

"I think you'd have to get in line," I reply. "Daisy is kind of a big deal around here."

Daisy rolls her eyes, and Vivi is quick to respond.

"Believe me when I tell you, I'd be first in line. And you would never see me coming."

I look at Daisy, thumbing at her best friend. "Does Vivi not know I was a SEAL? I've done things I will never be allowed to talk about."

Laughter tugs at Daisy's cheekbones. "Flying fish," she says.

"Never mind. Vivi, your warning has been noted. Bye." I tug Daisy through the stainless steel labyrinth, past the walk-in fridge, and out into the fresh air.

I lean her up against my truck, rake my fingers through her hair until the pins fall and her golden hair tumbles down. She breathes out once, heavy and hard, her hands holding onto my ribs, finding their way to my back. "Take me home, Penn."

Chapter 57

Penn

Home is Daisy's house.

I pull into the driveway and cut the engine. "Your car was left at Summerhill," I say, not remembering it until this moment.

Daisy's shaking her head, telling me she doesn't care. "I'll get it later. Tomorrow. Next week, next year."

She's crawling over the center console, plunking herself in my lap. "Someone is eager."

"So eager," she murmurs, dragging her lips over my mouth. My head tips up, changing the angle so she can come down over me. She holds my face in her hands, her favorite thing to do it seems, and plants kisses at either corner of my mouth.

My hand searches for the hem of her shirt, but when I can't discover one, I remember she's wearing a dress. I growl, and she hums a contented sound. "You have to start at the bottom."

I reach lower, finding the bottom of her dress and dragging it up over her knees. "Like this?"

"Mm-hmm," she sighs, grinding small circles on my lap.

My touch drags up and down her thighs, and she goes from pleased to pouty in a nanosecond. "Tease me another time, Sailor. Right now, I'm dying for you to touch me."

I capture her mouth. "Touch you where?"

Her fingers come over mine on her thigh, stopping me from making yet another pass. She pushes down, sliding my palm over the inside of her thigh. "Here," she whispers, gliding my fingers up until they meet the silk of that white thong I saw her in earlier. "Remember when you threatened to fuck the ring off my finger?" She grins fiendishly, holding up her bare left hand. "You managed it."

The sight of it sends me into some other realm, one where Vikings sail the seas and wear clothing made of fur. Swiftly, I haul her thong aside and plunge two fingers inside her. She gasps, tightening around me. "You're fucking right I did. You're mine, Daisy. My lady. And the next time you wear a ring, it's going to be from me." I curl my fingers and she leans forward, panting in my ear. "Yes," she breathes.

"Now, let's go inside before your neighbors take one of their nosy-ass strolls."

"They're all at my wedding reception," she huffs, hips moving with the motion of my fingers.

"Still," I say, moving my touch from her. She sulks,

and it makes me smile. "Nobody gets to see you lose your mind except me. And I'm not taking chances."

Daisy returns to her seat, rights her dress, and leaves the truck. I hurry after her, placing my hands in my pockets and pushing out on the fabric, giving my throbbing erection room to breathe. Daisy looks down as she is putting the key in the lock, and discovers what I'm doing. "I'm going to take care of that," she says, turning the key.

We make it inside in a civilized manner, but after that, all bets are off. She pushes me against the door, fumbling with my belt. It resists, but Daisy is persistent. She smiles up at me when it gives way, followed by the button of my jeans, and finally the zipper. "My prize for all that work," she rasps, sinking to her knees.

She drags warm breath across me, teeth skating. An anticipatory hum sings from my lips as I watch her. She is *everything*. Everything that is good, and beautiful. My fingers run into her hair, cradle her head, stroke her jaw.

Too soon, I'm telling her to stop, offering her a hand. She takes it, wipes at her eyes. "Someday soon, that will be something I do when you least expect it. And it will be to completion."

"And I will love it," I promise, trying not to think of that nebulous moment in the future. "But now, I want you in a bed." Then I bend and scoop her up, tossing her over my shoulder and smacking her ass on the way to her bedroom.

We make it to her bed, and I tug her dress over her shoulders. "You," I point an accusatory finger at her. "Turn over."

She already knows what I'm after. "Like this?" she asks, flipping around, sticking her thonged ass in the air.

I slip a finger under the tight fabric, running it across her skin. "You knew what you were doing to me."

"Played you like a fiddle," she boasts.

I grunt a laugh. "Not for the first time."

Those ripped jeans...that wet T-shirt...the hood of my truck.

I bend down, pull the fabric aside, and press a kiss to her. She arches, my name rolling through her like the tide. "Shh," I murmur, wrapping my hands around her thighs to keep her locked in place. "The name chanting can begin in approximately two minutes."

And it does. I hold her tight while she falls apart. Safe in my arms. Always.

"My muscles are useless," she says, sinking into the bed. Still, she manages to roll over. I drag the thong down her legs, ridding myself of my clothes in the time it takes her to pop up on her elbows and shed the strapless bra. Her knees fall open, and she reaches up, trailing her fingers over my scars. I've never told her what that does to me, how it makes me feel.

"I like when you do that."

"I love everything that made you the person you are today. Scars and all."

I grip myself in my left arm. My Daisy arm. "Sunshine," I groan, dragging myself up her, circling at the top, gliding back down. Daisy's chest moves faster, her stomach tightening.

"Bare," she says. "Need to feel you."

Penn

"Birth control?"

She nods.

I notch in. She exhales. "All of it," she encourages.

When I'm fully seated, I lie down over her. I kiss the valley between her breasts, her collarbone, her neck. Her legs wrap around my waist, heels digging into my ass. Her fingernails scrape my back, drag up through my hair.

She feels so good. So perfect.

"Mine," I groan into the hollow of her throat.

"Yours," she agrees.

"Forever."

"Forever," she echoes.

My mouth presses to the soft skin of her neck, her pulse thrumming under my tongue. I thrust deeper, harder, and Daisy rises up to meet me. My heart feels like it might break through my breast bone, beating with an intensity not from exertion, but because it memorized Daisy a long time ago. She owns me. I want to share all of our holidays, and coffee every morning. I want to be her sounding board, her shoulder.

Daisy's head moves on the pillow, and I place my hand between her head and the headboard, just in case. She grins in a lazy way, reaching up to run her fingers through my hair. "You look like you love me, Sailor."

"Only for most of my life." I drop a kiss to her lips, nibbling at the corner. "And the rest of it, too."

Leaning my weight on my right forearm, my Daisy arm disappears between us, sliding down to my destination.

"Oh," Daisy says on a long blink. Sensitized from my

earlier work, it's not thirty seconds before Daisy is tipping her head back, crying out.

"So beautiful when you come," I grunt, picking up the pace. Daisy bends her legs, draws her knees up beside her body. I bottom out, heat curling up my spine, and at the last second I palm Daisy's cheek, my thumb pressing over her lips. She opens her mouth, biting down on my finger, and I finish on a roar.

I look down at Daisy. She grins up at me, her teeth still biting my thumb.

I nearly laugh at the playful look in her eyes, but I'm too exhausted to manage it. I roll over onto my side, and she does the same, backing up into me.

"I love you, Sunshine."

"I love you, Sailor."

My nose presses into her hair. "I love you, Daisy."

I feel the release of her slow laughter. "I love you, Penn."

Daisy rises to take a shower, and I join her. Daisy wants to wash the heavy makeup from her face, and I want to be wherever she is. I wash her back, the scent of plum fills the air, and I'm hungry for her again. Palms pressed to the new tile, I take her one more time. Her wet hair covers her back, and I bite down on her shoulder.

Sated and exhausted, we find our way to the kitchen. Daisy whips up two grilled cheeses, and I cut strawberries.

"Cabinets are going in on Tuesday," she says, pointing at the empty space.

"Nice of Duke to handle that for you," I respond. I

can be pleasant about the guy now, since he's no longer in my way.

After we eat, we get dressed, and I drive us into the next town so we can avoid running into anybody we know. We are in a bubble now, our own cocoon, and tonight, nobody else is welcome. We pick up ingredients to make spaghetti, and two bottles of champagne, and make it back to her house.

The rest of the night is like being in a fairy tale, but one that involves great sex. Tomorrow I'll work out how I should approach my old house, and Daisy will begin returning wedding gifts, and we will bear the brunt of chatter.

Tonight, we are us. Drunk in love. High on each other.

Chapter 58

Daisy

"Sailor, it's not that I don't love helping, it's just that maybe I'm better suited for other activities."

Today is day one of the Bellamy house renovation, and though I volunteered to be Penn's right-hand, I am deeply regretting my choice.

Penn may have spent the last month since he returned cleaning out the house and donating old furniture that was left behind, but the real work has only just begun.

We need to bring in professionals. The pipes are crusted with mineral deposits from hard water. Calcium is built up on all the faucets and shower heads. The floor is rotted, and when Penn poked at a crack in the drywall, it crumbled and revealed mold.

This is far beyond what Penn is capable of, and light-years away from my abilities.

"You sure?" Penn asks, raising an eyebrow, but pairing

Penn

it with a flirtatious look. "You are quite talented with a pry bar."

I look through the front window, to the tidy front yard. "Actually, I think my talents lie elsewhere." I bat my eyelashes. "In landscaping, perhaps."

The half-full heavy-duty trash bag Penn holds falls to the ground with a thud. "It was you. You were keeping up my front yard."

"Guilty." I shrug. "I learned a lot about desert landscape, and how to care for it. I guess I should say thank you for giving me the opportunity to cultivate a lifelong skill."

Penn wraps his hand around my wrist, pulling me into his chest. "Sunshine, you are something else."

He smells delicious. Citrus and cedar, with the salty sting of sweat. I love this man so deeply, it feels as though my heart could beat right out of my chest. "This was your home, Penn. I wanted to preserve it, as much as I could."

"That means a lot to me, Daisy," he says, emotion trickling into his voice. "I couldn't believe it when I showed up that first day with Hugo and saw that the yard was in good shape. I almost thought it was a joke, or I don't know, something other than someone preserving it for me."

My heart settles instantly. This man has no idea how loved he is. How much the town missed him and his mom when they left. I may have grieved for them the hardest, missed them the most, but the town was lined up right behind me, feeling the same feelings.

Except for Glenn Hampton, of course. I hope that for the rest of Glenn's life, he has the day he deserves.

The sound of tires crunching out front pulls me out of Penn's embrace. Slim Jim streaks past, bumping my leg as he goes.

"Oof," I breathe, bobbling for a moment before regaining my balance. "I need to remember how fast that guy is."

"You'll get used to it," Penn promises, going to the window. "It's your dad's car." He pauses, then says, "And your mom's with him."

I hurry to the front door. I've talked to my mom once on the phone to ask how she's feeling, but I haven't seen them since everything went down at the wedding a few days ago.

"Mom, Dad," I shout, coming from the door. Slim Jim tries to move in front of me, but Penn gives him a command and he snaps back in a seated position.

Mom waves from the car as Dad helps her climb out. I stand on the top stop of the front porch, waiting for them.

"We thought we'd stop by and see how you're doing, Daisy Mae," Dad says as they come closer. "We tried your house first, and when you weren't there, your mother suggested we try here next."

"Mother's intuition," she says, winking at me. "You look good standing there, darling girl. Like the woman of the house."

The tears are instant. They weren't there, and

suddenly they're overtaking me. It's the words, it's the way she said it, and the way I feel it.

One day, Penn and I will share this house. We'll make it a home again. A place where we hang Christmas lights and wrap the Saguaros in strings of red, dodging the sharp needles sticking out. We'll raise a family here. We'll love, and we'll fight, and we'll live.

And now I'm crying more.

Dad asks, "Honey, what's wrong?" My mom and dad converge on me, wrapping me in their arms.

"I actually don't know," I say, wiping at my eyes and laughing. "Feeling overwhelmed, I guess."

"I get that way, too," Mom says, brushing her hand over my hair.

"Me, too," Penn jokes, stepping from the home carefully so that Slim Jim stays inside.

Mom and Dad release me, and Penn steps up, wrapping an arm around my shoulders. With his free hand, he shakes hands with my dad.

"Mr. and Mrs. St. James, how are you today?"

Mom clucks her tongue. "Brenda and Charles."

Penn nods. "Yes, ma'am."

"Show me what you have planned, Penn," my dad says, and Penn steps away from me. He turns for the house, and my dad loops an arm over his shoulders. Penn startles, recovering quickly.

He opens the door, introducing Slim Jim, and then begins to tell my dad about the first phase of the renovation.

The door closes behind them, and when I look at my mom, I find she's already staring at me.

Tears well in her eyes. "Darling girl, I'm thrilled for you. You're glowing, from the inside out. Happiness, contentment, they'll do that to you." She takes a tissue from her purse, dabs at her lower lash line. A smear of concealer comes off on the tissue, revealing a swath of dark color under her eyes.

I take her hand. I wish I had a chair for her. "How are you feeling today?"

She chuckles. "I'll be honest with you. I'm high right now."

I choke on a mixture of shock and laughter. I really wasn't expecting her to say that. "Adela's special brownie?"

She nods, eyes mischievous. "I only had a couple bites. Just enough to take the edge off."

"Good, Mom. You should. There's no reason for you to walk around in pain." She'll take the heavy painkillers later, when she's home.

"Let's go inside," she says, vining her arm through mine. Her open palm finds my hand, and she intertwines our fingers. "I want to hear all about how you're going to make this house a home."

Chapter 59

Penn

THE WHOLE FUCKING TOWN IS HERE, AND I WISH I were exaggerating. There's Margaret, front and center like she said she'd be. I look out into the crowd and spot Vivi with her two children, Hugo beside her. Daisy sits with her mom and dad, and Bonnie. Even Sal and Adela from Sweet Nothings are here, selling cupcakes and brownies and promising fifty percent of the proceeds go to the youth theatre.

I catch Daisy's eye, and she offers me a thumbs up. She's been reading the script with me all week, helping to make sure I've memorized my lines. Despite this, I am one hundred percent certain I'm going to flub my lines multiple times.

Tenley appears beside me, pulling back the curtain to peek with me. "There's my husband," she says, a smile in her voice as she points to a man in the front row. He wears Wranglers, ostrich boots, and a sage green collared button-up.

"Who's that beside him?" I ask, my attention on a cowboy in nearly the same outfit, except he wears a frown like it's part of his ensemble.

Tenley waves her hand. "That's my brother-in-law, Wes. He always looks like that. His wife is sitting beside him, she's my best friend."

All three are now looking our way, waving at Tenley. The husband looks friendly, but his brother has his eyes narrowed at me. Right now I'm feeling pretty happy the twelve-year-old tyrant did not include a kiss in her play. Not that I would have anyway, now that I'm with Daisy. There isn't a chance in hell I'll be locking lips with anybody but her, acting or not.

As I watch, the frowning brother clocks my arm, and the tattoo there. He must recognize it for what it is, because his frown turns a little less frown-y.

"Aww," Tenley says, "look at that. Wes is almost smiling at you. Must be a military thing."

"Must be," I echo, but now I'm more nervous than I was before.

Ten minutes to showtime, Noelle corners me. "Don't forget your lines," she warns me.

"Tenley knows all of them, so even if I forget them, we'll be good."

Noelle has no time or patience for my backtalk. "This entire night is for the children. The only way the youth theatre exists is if people come to the play, enjoy it, and enroll their children or grandchildren in the program. Do you get that?"

"Yes, Noelle."

Penn

"I'm perfectly aware you can act, *Peter*, so go out there and act."

There's a pretty big difference between acting and performing, but I would really like to keep all my baby-making parts intact, so I keep that comment to myself.

"Noelle," I say dramatically, clutching at my chest. "Nobody is a bigger supporter of the *thea-tah* than I."

She stares at me for a long minute, then walks away grumbling something that sounds like *I don't know how Daisy puts up with you.*

Tenley and I take our places. The stagehands, the techies, the producer, they are all children. Only the actors are the adults, and it's actually really cool to be a part of something put together by younger minds. One of the props breaks before the scene in which it needs to be used, and the kids work together to fix it. The youngest on the crew stumbles, making his way into a sword fighting scene. Instead of getting flustered and running off stage, he leans into it and pretends it's a schtick. The audience laughs, and when he lops off, Lincoln scolds him with a cutthroat coldness I admire (but only because it's not directed at me).

I forget my lines no fewer than seven times, but Tenley is there, whispering them to me, sometimes even preemptively knowing when I will go blank. In the end, it all works out.

Afterward, people line up to take pictures with Tenley. Her husband is the dutiful photographer, a road it looks like he travels often.

Daisy throws herself in my arms, kissing me square

on the mouth in front of everybody. Not that it matters. We've been engaging in some heavy public displays of affection all week.

"You were great," she says animatedly. "But don't quit your day job." Her head tips sideways, thinking. "Which is...what?"

"For now, it's remodeling my old house."

She pumps an enthusiastic fist in the air. "Yay remodeling."

"Not your kind of remodeling," I remind her, wrapping my arms around her waist. "Thoughtful. Planned."

She grins. "I'll handle the landscaping."

I brush a kiss across her lips. "Have at it, Sunshine."

Chapter 60

Olive Township

With bated breath, I waited for Penn Bellamy and Daisy St. James to be free of the mess of their own creation.

Penn's return brought trouble, but the necessary kind. Like an earthquake revealing ancient artifacts. A little more digging through the rubble, and they will make discoveries that will shake their world.

I can't guess when this will happen. Some individuals need to look closer, some need to relinquish control. Others need to shed the cloak of the past, to go back so they can go forward.

One, in particular.

Chapter 61

Epilogue

Penn

Brenda passes away six months later, with her true loves by her side. Daisy holds one of her mother's hands, head bent as she cries softly. I do my best to console her, resting my head on her upper back so she can feel me there, saving my tears for later, so I can be strong for my wife.

Daisy and I married three months after the fiasco at Summerhill. We talked about waiting, about not rushing into anything, but when the man who built the arch came to deliver it, and Daisy realized it was his wife who wrote her favorite book, she insisted that we be the first to use the arch, and soon. I was more than happy to oblige. I would've married her three months prior. I would've married her standing on my head wearing scuba gear. All that mattered to me was having Daisy as my wife.

Brenda surprised us by making a request. She asked that, instead of Daisy wearing her wedding dress, she cut a piece off and pin it below a dress of her choosing. The

Penn

ceremony was simple, but beautiful. Daisy was radiant, a vision I could not look away from. I never expected this much happiness in my life. Never thought I would be the recipient of Daisy's love. I'm not sure how I got so lucky, but I don't spend time questioning it. I revel in it, thank God every day for broken roads and crooked paths.

Duke is well. His father was furious, threatening to have me charged with battery since his son refused. In the end, local law-enforcement declined to charge me themselves, and without evidence, and Duke's refusal, Glenn Hampton went home empty-handed. I see Duke once a month for guy's night. It was awkward at first, and we earned plenty of stares from people around the room of whatever establishment we chose to meet up, but it has worked itself out. At one point, Duke apologized for how he treated me when we were kids. I accepted the apology, and once he explained that he genuinely cared for my mom, I felt an odd kinship with him.

"How is Daisy?" Hugo asks, the week after Brenda's heavily-attended funeral.

"Struggling," I reply, swinging my leg under the open tailgate of my truck. Hugo had some free time in his schedule, and when he called me and heard I was waiting at my old house for a contractor to arrive, he stopped by. "I don't know if you can ever really prepare for a loved one's passing."

"Expected or not," Hugo says.

It takes me by surprise. He rarely brings up his father's murder.

I wait to see if he'll say more, and he does. "That podcaster emailed me again."

"Tell him to fuck off."

"Her."

"The true crime podcaster is a woman?"

He nods. "Yep."

This woman is Daisy's opposite. She won't even watch the news because it frightens her. Forget any scary movies.

"What have you said to her?"

"Not a damn thing."

"Maybe if you ignore her, she'll go away."

"Here's what I know," Hugo says, pushing off the tailgate as the contractor's truck pulls in. "I want nothing to do with reopening my father's case. I don't want to talk about it. I don't want to think about it. It's in the past, and there is nothing back there except emotions I don't want to be a part of."

My easy-going friend has never sounded so emphatic.

The contractor gets out of his truck, and we move forward to greet him, our conversation forgotten.

That night when Daisy gets home from work, I have a warm dinner ready for her. Her remodeled kitchen looks nice, though I still need to update the backsplash. When we're finished eating, I prepare a bath for her. She smiles at me gratefully, and I can tell she's doing her best to come out from under the cloud of grief hanging over her head.

"It gets better," I promise her. I would know.

Penn

"Get in with me," she says, working my shirt over my head.

"I was trying to do something nice for you. Let you have a little alone time," I protest, but not with much fervor.

"I'll have alone time with you," Daisy insists.

I strip her of her clothes, then remove my own, following her into the warm water. She leans her back to my front, relaxing against me.

"Thank you for being here for me," she says, drawing a finger through the surface of the water.

"There's nowhere else I'd rather be."

"Not even on a tropical island somewhere, drinking fruity drinks with umbrellas?"

I drop a kiss to the top of her head. "My place in this world is beside you. Wherever you are, I'm there."

Daisy turns around, gathers my face in her hands, kisses me. We go from gentle kisses, to something searching and hungry, and then she sinks down onto me. A natural progression. This is one of so many ways we communicate.

I touch my wife as she moves, the water displaced and smacking the side of the tub.

"Love you," she murmurs.

"Love you more," I reply, lost in her.

When it's over, we towel off and get in bed. I'll clean up the kitchen in the morning. I hold her as she falls asleep, her wet hair strewn over her pillow. I listen to her deep, even breathing, and think about the past year.

A decade spent with the SEALs, mission after

mission, doing important work, and then one day it's over. That's it for me. I come back from a physical injury, only to lose my mother. I know firsthand, emotional injuries take longer to heal.

Something propelled me to return to Olive Township, something I still don't quite understand. Maybe it was Daisy's heart, calling me home. And I was the fool who came here with so much pride, thinking I could avoid what waited for me here. That I should.

Daisy sighs, a tiny contented sound. It's the sound my heart makes every time I see her.

I fall asleep to the scent of plums, and Daisy in my arms.

The End

Excited to read about Hugo and the true crime podcaster? His story releases May 29th, 2025. Preorder now!

Also By

Olive Township Series
(A contemporary twist on The Princess Bride)

Penn

Hugo (May 29th, 2025)

Ambrose (Fall 2025)

Duke (Early 2026)

Hayden Family Series

The Patriot

The Maverick

The Outlaw

The Calamity

Standalone

What We Keep

Here For The Cake

Better Than Most

The Least Amount Of Awful

Return To You

One Good Thing

Beyond The Pale

Good On Paper

The Day He Went Away

The Time Series

Our Finest Hour (optioned for film/TV)

Magic Minutes

The Lifetime of A Second

Acknowledgments

Readers. The first acknowledgment must go to you for being on this journey with me. I am so very grateful to you for reading my work, for spending your precious time in the worlds I create, for letting my characters have a little of the love in your hearts.

My editor, Nicole Purdy. You always make me look harder at the characters, go deeper into their minds and motivations and thoughts. Thank you for helping me make Penn and Daisy the best they can be.

My beta readers for this book: Crystal, Brittany, Danie, Catherine, Katie, Chelsea, Mindie, Paramita, Lillian, Natalie, Amanda, Erica, Brittany. THANK YOU! The insight of early readers is invaluable, and I'm eternally grateful you helped me make Penn shine.

About the Author

Jennifer Millikin is an Amazon Charts bestselling author of contemporary romance and women's fiction. She is the two-time recipient of the Readers Favorite Gold Star Award, and readers have called her work "emotionally riveting" and "unputdownable". Her third novel, Our Finest Hour, has been optioned for film/tv. Jen lives in the Arizona desert with her husband, children, and two dogs. With eighteen novels published so far, she plans to continue her passion for storytelling. Visit www.jennifermillikinwrites.com to connect.

Made in United States
North Haven, CT
06 February 2025